THE
WAY
AHEAD

THE
WAY
AHEAD

Kaleb England
aka NorskDaedalus

Podium

To my beta readers Roland Hansson, Aelia Aeldyne, Pel-Mel,
Magma, Pastafarian, Heavenly Daoist, and w1k3d

Copyright © 2022 by Kaleb England

Cover design by Podium Publishing

ISBN: 978-1-0394-1023-7

Published in 2022 by Podium Publishing, ULC
www.podiumaudio.com

Podium

THE
WAY
AHEAD

CHAPTER 1

Today's Forecast Includes a Miniscule Chance of Planeswalkers

Confusion.

An eternal void.

An enormous tree, orbs glistening in its branches.

A sea of crystal, shining bright yet filled with darkness.

Falling.

Falling.

FALLING.

Edwin jerked awake as his brain told him he was *definitely* falling this time, and not just experiencing something in his dreams. Annoyed at whatever nightmare had roused him, he reached to grab his pillow ... grab his ... his pill— What?

His eyes shot open as he couldn't feel his pillow, or bed, or anything save air rushing past him; it slowly sank in that, no, he wasn't experiencing a nightmare, but rather genuinely hurtling through the air at heart-dropping speeds. Far below him, what vaguely looked like rolling landscapes swept by, slowly approaching as he fell from the sky. His half-asleep, half-adrenaline-filled, and hyperawake brain struggled for a few futile seconds to comprehend what was happening to him before giving up and releasing him back into blissful unconsciousness.

Edwin jerked awake as his brain told him he was *definitely* falling this time, and not just ...

He sat up suddenly, experiencing déjà vu for a ... nightmare? The question mark could stay. He had no idea what was going on, but he knew for a *fact* that he hadn't fallen asleep in the middle of a clearing in the woods. And he certainly hadn't fallen asleep in an *Edwin-sized crater* in the middle of said woods. Did he even go to bed? He was still fully clothed at least, dressed for being outside, and the last thing he remembered was ... being in the lab?

That didn't make sense. His memory must have been wrong, considering there weren't any forests like this near his college, and the weather certainly wasn't this warm this—or was it yesterday?—morning.

Apparently, he was plucked away from his research and tossed into a forest with no local trees or other plants. Actually, he couldn't recognize *any* of the plants. They were all vaguely familiar, but subtly different from what he was used to. Ferns were larger than he was accustomed to; the bark on nearby trees was a slightly different shade from normal.

Okay, take stock of what he had. Socks, shoes, pants, belt, shirt, jacket ... but nothing in his pockets, missing watch, and annoyingly, missing *glasses*.

Edwin could see all right without them, so long as he didn't need to read anything at long distances, anyway, but he'd need to find them sooner or later. At least what he *did* have was in pristine condition, like it was all brand-new. It wasn't even dirty from his apparent crash landing.

Something *really* strange had clearly happened, and Edwin wasn't sure what. He could feel the edges of his mind want to start panicking, but he crushed that impulse before it could take root. He needed to focus on figuring out what had happened, and how he could get out. Attempting to poke at the fuzzy holes in his memory only prompted a sudden headache to lance through his skull, but after a moment of pain, and a few more of disorientation, the jumbled mess of memories slowly started sorting themselves out.

While it didn't provide much actionable information, he was able to more clearly understand what had happened. He had been falling. Actually falling, that much was certain, and he had definitely passed out in midair, but he seemed ... fine? It didn't *feel* like he had hit the ground at terminal velocity, anyway.

His body felt vaguely fuzzy, perhaps, but not like he was dead or had broken every bone in his body. In fact, he felt fine, other than a distinct sense of tingling across every inch of his body, like his foot had fallen asleep. Looking at his hand, he didn't notice any apparent cause of the sensation, though when trying to touch his arm, there was a definite resistance against his fingers. Frowning, Edwin pushed against the barrier surrounding his skin, trying to figure out what it was, when—

You have unlocked the Basic Mana Sense Skill!
Accept Skill? Y/N
Congratulations! For destroying a tree with no weapons, you have unlocked the Way of the Empty Hand Path!
Congratulations! For felling a tree on your own, you have unlocked the Lumberjack Path!
Congratulations! By surviving a skydive, you have unlocked the Daredevil Path!
Congratulations! By venturing deep into the Verdant with no guide, you have unlocked the Explorer Path!
Congratulations! For visiting a different continent, you have unlocked the World Traveler Path!
Congratulations! For being the first to arrive in Joriah from an unknown world and making a Path for others to follow, you have unlocked the CharLimitCanttalkmuchNocluewhathappenedDidmybesttohelpyouli Path!
Congratulations! For being involved in something that requires Moderator attention, you have unlocked the Path Less Traveled Path!
Congratulations! For bringing a wholly novel language into existence, you have unlocked the Linguist Path!
Congratulations! For coming to Joriah from another world, you have unlocked the Realm Traveler Path!
ERROR RESOLVED.
Apologies for any inconvenience.
Logs are being distributed to the appropriate entities.
Personalized compensation has been provided.
ERROR.

ERROR.
Requesting Moderator Attention.
FATAL ERROR.
Please stand by.
ERR—
ERROR.
ERROR: Debug not—
ERROR: Error loop detected. Attempting to fix.
Congratulations! You have arrived in Joriah from—ERROR: Invalid
Location. Reevaluating.
Congratulations!—ERROR: User not found. Triggering user
integration.
Congratulations! You— ERROR:
Congratulations! You have—ERROR: User logs not found.
Congratulations! You have been—ERROR: Event not found.
Reevaluating.
Congratulations! You have arrived in Joriah from—ERROR: Invalid
Location. Reevaluating.
Congratulations!—ERROR: First log to user. Triggering user
integration.
Tasvalika—ZEZEZE: Tor kollis. Sil vorlamilating new language.
Success.

"What?"

Edwin recoiled, the strange sensation swiftly forgotten, as his vision was suddenly blocked—no, not blocked; he could still ignore the messages and see past them. His vision was *crowded* by the torrential influx of words.

"Hello? What's this?" With no answer forthcoming, he took a second look at the words. "Hallucination?" he wondered aloud and waved his hand through the last message. It vanished as he did so, shrinking away at the touch. "*Interactive* hallucination? I don't *think* hallucinations can respond to touch, but maybe? Hmm. Probably not a hallucination. Too coherent. Then, the barrier and the nightmare … Am I in shock?" He felt his pulse. "No? My heart would be fluttering way more if I were, right? I think that's how it works? Meh.

"So, not in shock, not a hallucination … maybe. Not worth treating this all as a hallucination, though." He glanced back at the messages, reading them and trying to piece together what they said. It took him a moment before he realized they were all displayed in inverse chronological order. Once he'd figured that out, reading from bottom to top made everything make way more sense.

"Different world? Moderators. Mana. Is this a computer sim or a fantasy world? Hmm. I wonder if I should stop talking to myself? Or are the moderators listening? Hey, moderator guy! Can you hear me? Can you understand me? What is this? Can I get a tutorial? I'll accept a really annoying fairy that won't shut up if you're out of everything else." He didn't get a response, to no real surprise. It seemed like they were quite limited in their ability to communicate, and they had an unknown amount of knowledge. That was something he could deal with later. In the meantime …

"Okay, one step at a time. First, whatever this is doesn't seem to have been familiar with English at the start. Point for being in another world. Second, I am apparently *not* the first person to arrive in this world, though apparently I *am* the first from Earth? So then … I'm probably alone, in that regard." Edwin sat in silence for a moment as he processed that. He might have not had *that* many ties back on Earth, but he still … Actually, nope. He was *not* going to deal with that right now. Shove those emotions in a box, set it next to his panic about being in an apparently alien world, open it all later. He could do that. Survive now, have emotional crises later.

"Lots of errors, and lots of Paths, whatever those are. They seem important, even if I have no *clue* how to use them." He dismissed most of his messages with a wave of his hand, leaving the single block of text that actually appeared actionable.

You have unlocked the Basic Mana Sense Skill!
Accept Skill? Y/N

"So … mana. As in magic? Is this how you become a wizard? *Heck yes*, I want to be a wizard." As soon as the thought of accepting the Basic Mana Sense Skill fully manifested in Edwin's mind, the message winked out, replaced with a rapidly scrolling list as it apparently acknowledged his request.

Thought based? he thought to himself—and his notifications, he supposed. *Privacy concerns notwithstanding, that's interesting.*

Level Up! Basic Mana Sense

Level Up! Basic Mana Sense

Level Up! Basic Mana Sense

Level Up! Basic Mana Sense

Level Up! Basic Mana Sense

Basic Mana Sense

If it's glowing and isn't a mushroom in a cave, it's probably magic.

Detect nearby magic.

Increased range per level.

The vague sensation of tingling around Edwin's body solidified as soon as he accepted the Skill. He didn't get much better resolution, but it *did* feel like there was a *lot* of mana right around him. It took a minute to properly orient himself to the new sense, though it wasn't really new ...

This is confusing. Okay, what do I know?

He was on a new world: Joriah, according to his messages. Magic, and mana, were allegedly real things here, and the latter completely surrounded him. Presumably, it was also how he'd not died when falling from the sky. There was some kind of System in place that monitored thoughts and actions and could provide rewards of some kind. According to his Basic Mana Sense, the notifications themselves were *not* magical, but Edwin was rather skeptical of that prospect.

Hypothesis: The System works with a different type of magic compared to what I can sense.

It was soothing to think of it in scientific terms, and if this really was magical? Well, that was just science waiting to be discovered.

He *did* pity whatever poor souls had to maintain the System. His short time on Joriah had already thrown up, what, a dozen errors? Edwin tried to pull up the notifications he'd dismissed, but he didn't even know where to start. He'd have to rely on his memory for now.

Great.

Okay. What did he know about the System? It had errors and moderators, notifications and Skills. Perhaps it was some kind of monitoring system that just kept track of what people did? No, that didn't track with his experience with Basic Mana Sense: when he'd accepted the Skill, his ability to sense mana had improved. That implied it wasn't fully descriptive. In any case, it did make sense that even if it was prescriptive, there should be some way for him to see what he'd earned.

Going by video-game logic … Well, no. Video games didn't have diegetic stats.

"Hey, moderator guy. How do I see my menu?" Edwin felt a little silly talking to the air, but it wasn't like there was anyone around him to see. "Skill list? What 'Paths' I've unlocked? My Status?"

The last one seemed to do the trick, though he didn't get quite what he was expecting.

You have unlocked the Status Skill!
Accept Skill? Y/N

"Uh, thanks? Why the prompt, though? Is there some reason I wouldn't want it?" he mused, and the prompt seemed to treat that as an acceptance, as it resolved into a new series of messages.

Name
Edwin
Age
Very Young
Race
Human?
Class
None
Attributes
None
Skills
Basic Mana Sense
Status

Paths

CharLimitCanttalkmuchNocluewhathappenedDidmybesttohelpyouli

Daredevil

Explorer

Linguist

Lumberjack

Path Less Traveled

Realm Traveler

Way of the Empty Hand

World Traveler

Level Up! Status

Status

Bypass the need for personal introspection entirely.

Call up a summary of your personal achievements.

Increased detail and greater customization per level.

There was a lot of information on hand, and Edwin was momentarily offended by his Status showing him as "very young" before realizing it must have just been based on when he arrived on Joriah. An annoying glitch, but understandable. He wasn't sure about how he should feel about being a "Human?," though it at least implied there *were* humans on Joriah, if nothing else.

He had also been expecting numbers, given the vaguely computer-ish aesthetic of the System, but perhaps that was part of the "increased detail" the Skill description had mentioned. How did he level it, though? He waved his hand through the pop-up, dismissing it. A few seconds of trial and error later showed him he could call it back up again by not exactly *thinking* "Status"—it was closer to flexing a phantom limb—but close enough.

Level Up! Status

There weren't any changes to the Status when he pulled it up this time. Well, he now got a vague sense as to his Basic Mana Sense being twice as "strong" as his Status, but that was about it. In addition, other than a vague sense they were even "weaker" than his Skill, there was no further indication what his Paths were or what to do with them. Whatever. He could deal with that later.

For now, he needed to find some food, water, and shelter. He was still in the middle of the wilderness, after all. Magic didn't change that fact, and it may well have made it even more dangerous. With no real knowledge of where he was or where he should try to go, Edwin picked a random direction and started walking. Sure, you were generally supposed to stay in one spot when lost in the wilderness to make it easier for search and rescue teams to find you, but there was no *way* he'd be found by someone.

As he walked, Edwin decided to keep flickering his Status up and dismissing it. So far as he could tell, there wasn't any reason for him *not* to, and the level-ups were probably a good thing as well as being generally satisfying.

Level Up! Status
Level Up! Status

It quickly hit diminishing returns, though, and after he went ten minutes of playing with his Status without earning a level, he decided it wasn't worth the distraction. He needed to focus on the task that was *actually* at hand: namely, finding shelter. Thanks to the trees, he had no way to tell what time it was, as the thick canopy above diffused the sunlight and bathed the ground in an emerald glow that— Hmm.

Wait, why are they all glowing green? Are they letting light through them? How is that effective? Well, it is green, so they might still be getting their red and blue allotment before just passing on the remainder. How would that work for the leaf structure, though? I've never seen anything that would suggest that sort of thing is possible.

Then again, if we're talking about magic *here, maybe trees are capable of sustaining a leaf structure that doesn't rely on reflecting the unwanted green light, but just filters out all red and blue light from the sun, and allows green light to pass through unimpeded? That could be … very interesting. I wonder if the leaves would look black from above, if they allow all light to pass through them? And then wouldn't that mean there should be a lot of black or purple undergrowth down here, taking advantage of the green light let through? Though that would explain why all the plants here are so dark in coloration, if they're evolving to become black. Actually, what even is the advantage of having transparen—* "Whoa!"

Edwin was snapped out of his musing by something appearing in his peripheral vision. He danced back, but whatever it was, it moved alongside him. Then he realized he was being ridiculous as his eyes properly focused on the notification in front of him.

You have unlocked the Visualization Skill!
Accept Skill? Y/N

"Wait, *Visualization*? Is everything a Skill? I mean, sure, I guess, but what?"

Level Up! Visualization
Visualization
Picture this:
Thoughts are more detailed.
Increased clarity per level.

Okay then. "Thoughts are more detailed." That's singularly unhelpful, he mused. *How does that even work?* Despite his efforts, he was, rather ironically, wholly unable to visualize the Skill's effects.

Level Up! Visualization

Edwin glared at the notification, but when it failed to wither under his stare, he swiped his hand through it, dismissing it with a sigh and continuing his quest. This time, he *would* stay focused on walking and not get distracted!

The entire forest was oddly empty. Other than a few smaller animals, one of which looked *strangely* like a squirrel if he was supposed to be in some distant world, and the background noise of buzzing and chirping insects, there were no larger animals to be found, which was really odd, as a forest like this should be teeming with life.

Then again, he couldn't keep relying on his old instincts for what should or should not be the case. There were demonstrably at least two types of magic in this world, between mana and the System, which meant the creatures here probably also had magic to work with. It was far too valuable a trait to *not* be evolutionarily selected for, and even if there weren't unicorns or the like, what would an *octopus* with a Stealth Skill be like? They could practically turn invisible back on Earth, and that was entirely through good old-fashioned chemistry and biology.

Hypothesis: Animals have Skills and/or magic, and as a result prey animals are way better at hiding.

If *prey* animals had hiding magic, though, that also meant that *predators* would have senses and stealth abilities to keep up with their food. The thought that there might be an invisible mountain lion just behind his back sent a shudder through him, and Edwin picked up the pace to try and get somewhere—anywhere—safe. Pity he didn't have a Skill for—

You have unlocked the Walking Skill!
Accept Skill? Y/N

The notification startled him with its timeliness, but it was perhaps the first time the reality of his situation fully registered. Basic Mana Sense, Status, and Visualization were all cool in an abstract way, but none of them were really tangible. Walking, though? Walking was something he always did, and now he was being offered a way to magically enhance it?

A grin crept across Edwin's face, and he turned around to survey the forest behind him, a wake of trampled plants from his passing already springing back into place. He was alone on an alien world, surrounded by unknown dangers and with no sign of civilization, shelter, or food. By all rights, he was doomed. He very well might *be* doomed. But if he lived? Well …

Back on Earth, Edwin had been all but nobody. He had been smart enough to get by but not enough to *really* stand out. Certainly not smart enough to pioneer any kind of research or to push the bounds of humanity's knowledge. Here, though? Here he had the chance of a lifetime. He was a scientist *with* magic. He knew the rules, he knew the laws. And with magic? Well, with magic, those laws started looking a lot more like guidelines.

Look out, world. I'm coming for you, and I have magic.

Level Up! Walking
Walking
And if you would walk five hundred miles, you'd get pretty tired.
Increased stamina while walking.
Endurance increases with level.

CHAPTER 2

Decidedly Sarcastic Skills

It was a bleary-eyed Edwin who blinked awake the following morning, curled up and shivering in the hollow of a tree. He absently reached for his glasses, wondering why he was so cold and still dressed, before he remembered the events of the day before. It fortunately hadn't gotten too cold overnight, because his thin jacket and jeans would *not* have been adequate if it had. Still, it hadn't rained and was, as a result, far from the most miserable night he'd spent outdoors.

It hadn't been easy to fall asleep, between his highly uncomfortable sleeping spot and the worry that some giant predator lurked just out of sight, but he had tried and gotten a surprise for his efforts.

Level Up! Sleeping
Level Up! Sleeping
Sleeping
A very underrated part of the "not killing people" process.
Sleep to recover and become energized.
Increased restfulness per level.

He was starting to wonder what *wasn't* a Skill, and idly wondered how many Skills other people must have, if he had already picked up five in less than a day of being on Joriah. Hopefully he'd keep up the pace, and maybe even get a Skill that helped him survive longer?

Three days without water, three weeks without food, three hours without shelter in extreme weather. At least the last of those doesn't apply at the moment, but I don't know how long that will last. Come on, wilderness survival books, don't fail me now.

As the sun began to rise, returning light and warmth to the forest, wildlife woke up and began to chatter. Was it just him, or were there suddenly a lot more birds and other wildlife active in the area? Did they get less skittish of him? Was there something else in the area yesterday that was scaring them away? Was he just noticing them more today? Maybe—

No. Bad Edwin. Focus. *Science later. Just keep walking in the direction you were going last night, and oh hey! A shrub with purple leaves! I knew there would have to be a few. Gah!*

"Hey, System moderator guy, I don't suppose I could get a Skill to help me focus?"

...

...

...

"Please?"

...

"... Fine," Edwin grumbled, ducking between a fallen log and a tree, stopping suddenly as he *felt* a spiderweb right in front of his face.

Level Up! Basic Mana Sense

Wait, was that magical? He couldn't see it, possibly thanks to his missing glasses, and he could only really tell it was literally inches in front of his face thanks to his Basic Mana Sense. Great, now he really *didn't* know if an invisible predator was sneaking up behind him. He kind of wanted to grab a long stick and poke the web to see if it was supernaturally strong as well, but not knowing if the spider was also supernaturally *venomous* tempered that desire.

He wouldn't do it. He wasn't that impulsive. He didn't need his curiosity satisfied *that* much.

No. No he did not.

...

So as it turned out, the web *was* incredibly strong and sticky. And while he didn't know if the spider was venomous, he *absolutely* wasn't testing that without some kind of Poison Resistance Skill. Would it be poison resistance, venom resistance, or toxicity resistance? Hmm. Well, maybe—

Nope. Not the time.

While he didn't know if the spider's venom was dangerous to humans, the mere fact that it was *the size of his hand* when it had suddenly popped into visibility at the center of its web and started skittering toward the stick—firmly stuck on the strands, though Edwin hadn't tried *too* terribly hard to dislodge it—meant that he was *absolutely* running as fast as he could away from it, trying to get as much distance as he could from that nightmare fuel.

Level Up! Walking

Wait, Walking? Was there not a Running Skill? Why was it called Walking if it covered running as well? Did it also cover hiking? Swimming? Flying? This would require a lot of testing.

Soon, Edwin was out of breath from his mad dash away from that horrible creature. Spiders were fine, so long as they weren't *bigger than his hand*. He stopped to recover, gasping for air as he leaned against a tree. Fortunately, his magic sense (spider sense?) didn't tingle this time. He did *not* want to tangle with another one of those monsters.

You have unlocked the Breathing Skill!
Accept Skill? Y/N

He tiredly accepted, happy for any kind of reprieve.

Level Up! Breathing
Breathing
You can breathe easy; you've got this.
Breathe deeply.
Increased efficacy per level.

Increased efficacy ... would that mean the Skill extracts more oxygen from the air for each breath? That could be very useful. Edwin considered it for a moment. *I hope I don't have to give CPR anytime soon. If the Skill ever gets me to the point of using 100 percent of the oxygen in any given lungful of air, CPR would just pretty much straight-up fail. Interesting potential consequence. Wait, could it get above 100 percent efficiency? Probably not, but this is magic so who knows? If it transforms air into oxygen, then CPR might be extraeffective.*

"Further testing required," he murmured. Promising himself he would get around to figuring out the intricacies of *magic*—and the thought of that tickled his heart—would probably be the only way he could stay focused long enough to *survive* to the point where he could test out all his Skills.

He still needed to find water, now more than ever.

Level Up! Breathing

With his breathing relatively under control, Edwin set off at a relatively brisk pace. The fact that no predators had bothered him yet meant one of two things: either there genuinely was nothing that saw him as potential prey living in the area, which had its own set of interesting considerations, or he was insanely, absurdly lucky and his crashing through the forests had somehow escaped the attention of *all* predators in the area. Maybe they were nocturnal? But what could keep predators away?

Or maybe fantasy media lied to me and walking through woods isn't likely to result in being attacked by wolves.

Edwin broke himself out of his musing as he came across a fairly steep slope. Given his goal of trying to survey the area, he wasn't convinced he should head down, though it would be possible to do so, and following it along the top would keep him from going in circles. Staying a few feet back from the edge to ensure he didn't fall, he decided to head ... left. Because why not?

Just as he got into a routine, he felt the ground underneath his foot crumble and give way. Time seemed to freeze as the sudden lurch made his stomach drop. He had never been good with falling, and being literally dropped from the sky yesterday had hardly helped. Though Edwin would have loved to say he managed to come up with some ingenious plan in between the two heart-stopping moments, all he was really able to clear his head enough to think about was a single, simple thought:

Oh great.

While he was fortunately sliding down the slope feetfirst at the moment, Edwin desperately hoped he could maintain that status quo. A few frantic handfuls of dirt failed to yield anything save a couple of thin roots, which broke off in his grip, and digging his feet into the ground did nothing save break loose clods of soil. Then— Salvation. His foot connected with a protruding rock, and for a single moment, he thought he might be able to brace against it.

Unfortunately, his momentum couldn't be stopped so easily, and all the rock managed to do was turn his descent from a semicontrolled slide into a chaotic tumble. Edwin's senses blurred together as he tucked himself into a ball and tried to protect his neck and head.

The next thing he knew, he was half buried in a bush, covered in a significant amount of detritus he had knocked loose in his descent, and with his ankle *far* too close to his ear for comfort.

You have unlocked the Flexibility Skill!
Accept Skill? Y/N

Edwin could have sworn the message was mocking him. Groaning, he extricated himself from the bush—ow! Was that a thorn?—and propped himself up to accept the Skill.

Level Up! Flexibility
Flexibility
Useful when in a tight spot.
Enhanced ability to stretch.
Improved range of motion per level.

It felt nice to just lie down for a little bit. His clothes were filthy, he had a hole in his jacket, and he was desperate for a drink, but at the very least, he wasn't dead and wasn't hurt beyond some scrapes and bruises. Even his internal monologue seemed too exhausted by the fall to pipe in and get his mind off just how *sore* his lower back was.

No chance I could get that Focus Skill now, or something like Willpower, is there?

...

Figures.

At least, he reasoned, *I didn't fall the entire way down.*

Edwin was on a bit of a flat stretch maybe a hundred feet below where he started, though without his glasses he couldn't be entirely sure. On the other side, the slope continued beyond what he could see. Really, he should go back to the top or finish going down, but his weakened legs would never allow him to climb back up. Going down of his own volition might have been possible, but would most likely just result in his legs giving out and he'd go for another tumble, which he really wanted to avoid.

You're just trying to justify not climbing back up that thing, Edwin accused himself, continuing a pained walk to the left of the base of the cliff. *But fair enough.*

Level Up! Walking

He trekked onward, legs burning but unwilling to stop his aggressive limp.

Level Up! Walking

Several hours later, Edwin heard the rush and crash of water up ahead, and he redoubled his pace from a sad limp to a pained jog, hopeful that he might soon find a river and something to drink. He turned around a bend on his ledge and came face-to-face with the largest waterfall he'd ever seen.

He *really* should have just bitten the bullet and gone back up the slope when he first fell down it. Now, Edwin was faced with a fifty-foot rocky cliff on one side and a several-hundred-foot drop on the other.

Very, *very* mindful of the drop and how the water had washed away all traces of dirt from the edge and left the stone very slippery, he carefully, *carefully* maneuvered to the edge and peered over, attempting to get an indication of how far up he was. Unfortunately, the residual mist from the crashing flow of water blanketed everything, leaving the distance purely to his imagination.

Level Up! Visualization

It … wasn't a pretty picture, regardless of how much the System continued to sass him with its timing.

I refuse to become afraid of heights alone. Falling is more than enough of a fear, thank you very much.

With shaking hands and weak knees, he crawled away from the edge and collapsed the moment he felt halfway safe. It took a moment, but his limbs eventually regained enough strength to push himself up to standing once more. Even then, his fingers stubbornly refused to stop trembling as he tried to think of what to do.

Okay. At least I found water. Unfortunately, I'm going to have to scale a fifty-foot cliff to get to the top and hope I can get water there or figure out some way to collect the mist from the air.

… Climbing it is. Not where it's this wet, though.

Backing up a ways away from the precipitous drop, Edwin evaluated his options. The rock face was decently craggy, though of debatable strength, and there was the odd tree that clung stubbornly to the narrow strip of soil he found himself on. It could help him clamber up the rock face, and all he would need to do is *not look down*. He would just need to start there … and move over there … and probably try to end up over there. Piece of cake.

Level Up! Visualization

The alternative was backtracking to where he'd fallen down the hill, or thereabouts. Was that the right call? It would take him several hours to walk back there, then he'd have to deal with a very crumbly slope to scramble up, and then take several more hours to return this way, all while not falling again. It might be marginally safer, but did he really have the time to backtrack almost an entire day of walking?

Okay, climbing it was. But was that ever a terrifying proposition. Edwin took a deep breath to calm himself.

Level Up! Breathing

Was the System mocking him? It was probably mocking him. After a short break to let his legs recover, he got to work, firmly wedging himself between a rock and a hard place. Well, the hard place was really just a tree that *did not* feel sturdy enough to be safe, and the rock was a bit of stone jutting out at a convenient height. It wasn't exactly *comfortable*, he noted, but it was better than any of the alternatives.

Oof. He was in nowhere *near* as good of shape as he once had been. Once upon a time, he would have scrambled up this sort of rock face in minutes, but now he was out of breath mere minutes after starting.

Level Up! Breathing

Granted, hiking all day likely hadn't helped his endurance much. His legs were *screaming* at him to stop, but they were still better at lifting him than his arms. He was ... what, ten feet up? It'd only get harder from here, and he vaguely hoped he might get a Skill to help out with—

You have unlocked the Athletics Skill!
Accept Skill? Y/N

Thank you, System timing.

But why Athletics? Why not just "Climbing"? Was whatever he was doing not close enough to true climbing for the System to be happy? Just "Athletics"? Wouldn't that be part of Walking? *Was* there not a more specific Skill for climbing? Were there actually limits about what could—

His foot slipped half an inch, and Edwin froze. No more getting distracted. He accepted the Skill but didn't look at it. In fact, he switched entirely to doing his best to ignore all System notifications so he could just focus entirely on *not dying*.

He reached up. Grabbed a protrusion. Hauled himself up. Braced against the trunk. Panicked as the tree swayed slightly. Looked for the next spot. Set his footing.

He reached up. Grabbed a protrusion …

Repeat. Repeat. Repeat. Repeat.

Make sure my foot is secure. Keep three limbs attached to the wall.

Let go of the tree as it gets too unstable.

Why hasn't the wall ended yet?

Next handhold.

Next handhold.

Repeat. Repeat. Repea—

WHERE'S THE HANDHOLD. Oh.

He had … made it? He made it! Hooray!

He had survived! He was uninjured! Well, other than some minor scrapes that he couldn't clean effectively. He was exhausted! He was so, *so* tired.

Gah, he was tired.

It was kind of amusing. Before today he would have never thought of a forest floor as being "comfortable," but right now? It felt as soft as a feather bed. Edwin glanced back at his notifications, seeing what he'd gotten for his efforts, and the pop-ups swam back into view.

Level Up! Athletics
Level Up! Breathing
Level Up! Athletics
Level Up! Visualization
Level Up! Athletics
Level Up! Flexibility
Level Up! Breathing
Level Up! Athletics
Level Up! Flexibility
Level Up! Athletics
Level Up! Status
Level Up! Athletics
Athletics
Who even needs steroids, anyway?

Improved athleticism.
Increased muscle efficiency per level.

Why had his Status leveled up? Hmm. What was it, increased cus-tomizability per level? Did it level up by him ignoring his notifications somehow? Could he level it up by *not* using it, however that might work?

"Further testing required," he promised himself.

First, he needed water. He so very much needed water. His mouth felt like sandpaper and tasted like dirt—probably because of how much he'd eaten lately.

First, though, he was going to lie here for a minute. Maybe five. Yeah, just five minutes. Just five ... more ... minutes. This was fine. This ... was ... totally ... fine ...

...

Level Up! Sleeping

CHAPTER 3

Revelations of Varying Fortune

Edwin woke up surprised, parched, and starving. Surprised because it was apparently sunset already? No, wait. That was birdsong. *Sunrise?* Sheesh. He didn't mean to fall asleep for even a nap, let alone overnight.

He supposed it continued to be fortunate there weren't predators here. Well, they hadn't found him yet, at least, and he didn't want to press his luck too much. Shelter was a must-find, and soon.

He didn't want to get up quite yet ... If this were Earth, he'd grab his phone and read something or other. Here, though, his options weren't quite so technological. But they were *just* as fun.

Status.

Name

Edwin

Age

Very Young

Race

Human?

Class

None

Attributes

None

Skills
Athletics
Basic Mana Sense
Breathing
Flexibility
Sleeping
Status
Visualization
Walking
Paths
CharLimitCanttalkmuchNocluewhathappenedDidmybesttohelpyouli
Daredevil
Explorer
Linguist
Lumberjack
Path Less Traveled
Realm Traveler
Way of the Empty Hand
World Traveler

He vaguely wondered how he was supposed to level up his Status. Just summoning and dismissing it stopped leveling it relatively quickly, though he half remembered it leveling up yesterday before he fell asleep. Had that been from his effort to *not* see the notifications?

It had only half worked and he needed to fight himself to not check them, even as he hung perilously above certain death, but it was better than them hijacking his visual processes and attention every time. He casually tried to "turn off notifications," but while he supposed there was no way to tell if it worked, it didn't feel like it had latched on to anything. Maybe he needed a higher level in his Status Skill? How could he manage that? Could he edit his Status?

Hmm …

Level Up! Status
Level Up! Status

Level Up! Status
Level Up! Status

About ten minutes later, he had managed to "hide" his Skills, Paths, and Attributes, whatever they were. That left him with four categories, at least three of which were inaccurate.

Without information about how to get a Class—was it level based? He didn't seem to have an overall level, but his Skill levels were also invisible, so maybe he did—his "None" entry was probably accurate, but he was absolutely human, and the question mark was annoying him.

It didn't accept his insistence that he was just a "human," but after another couple minutes of haggling with the System, he had gotten it to display "Extraplanar Human" as his race, and his age was now correctly listed as twenty-two. He got the vague sense of a clock ticking as he studied it, but he couldn't get any concrete measurement of how long he had been on Joriah.

Level Up! Status
Level Up! Status
Level Up! Status

Fixing his name, by contrast, was as simple as fully enunciating the thought, *My name is Edwin Maxlin.*

Level Up! Status

Satisfied enough with his progress for the time being, Edwin finally decided to do something about the stick digging into his back and hauled himself upright. His muscles yelled at him in annoyance, but he ignored them and unsteadily got to his feet.

With a yawn, he rubbed the sleep from his eyes and set off toward the waterfall. Really, it spoke to how utterly *exhausted* he must have been last night to have fallen asleep with its roar and endlessly churned mist constantly in the background.

No matter how close he was, it still felt like an effort to get near enough to the river to get a proper look at it. Literal tons of water rushed by with every moment, swept off the mountainside and into clouds of white, which were in turn pulled from sight after mere moments. Falling in that river would mean Edwin would very quickly either become the greatest swimmer of all time or find out if he had developed general immunity to falling from the sky.

Either way, he wasn't about to risk it. Unfortunately, the side of the river he found himself on had no bank, putting Edwin barely a foot above the rushing waters. There was no *way* he was leaning over the river while on mostly bare rock rendered nigh frictionless from the endless mist of the falls, no matter how much he needed water.

Naturally, the other side of the river had a nice slope and perfect access to the water, protected as it was from the worst of erosion.

Because nothing can be that easy, can it? He mentally sighed, trying to figure out a way across.

Level Up! Visualization

Hmm. He briefly toyed with trying to jump the river but abandoned the idea almost immediately. Even if he could make the twenty-foot jump, the stone was too slick for it to work. Well, other than that one little spot there with the bush.

Focus, Edwin. That's not going to help.

Anyway, there *were* a few trees nearby, not that they'd help without tools to chop them down or otherwise work them.

Other than whatever the Lumberjack Path might do. Not that I know what Paths do, or what sorts of effects they have, or how to progress along one, or anything even close to that. Sheesh, couldn't this thing have come with an instruction manual?

It was maddening, being so close to the water yet so far away. *Then again, there's probably a matching bank on this side if I explore upstream a little ways,* he realized, *certainly easier than trying to weave a rope out of ivy or whatever. Actually, would it even need to be woven?*

Edwin poked at the ivy covering some of the nearby trees and ground leading up to the rock—it didn't look like poison ivy, not that it really meant all that much when pretty much everything looked slightly different from what he was used to—giving it a few experimental yanks.

His brief tests indicated that while it detached from the tree trunk it was attached to with surprising ease, he wasn't able to break it free from the canopy, even when applying his full weight.

… Nope, still not trying it.

Fortunately, Edwin's luck wasn't uniformly terrible, and he was able to find *accessible* water after a short-yet-painful walk. He almost collapsed, quickly falling on his knees to cup water in his hand and drink it, blissfully cold, crisp, and clear water. It was running fast and clear enough to likely be snowmelt and safe to drink, not that he really had any other option.

With water, he could probably manage to survive. Food was still an issue, but he hoped that he could make do until he found proper civilization. Three weeks was *lots* of time, after all, and that didn't include any food he might find or any new Skills he might obtain.

With his thirst satisfied for the time being, Edwin allowed himself to relax with a sigh as he looked at the two notifications that had blinked at him.

You have unlocked the Survival Skill!
Accept Skill? Y/N
Congratulations! For surviving in the outdoors with no assistance and finding water, you have unlocked the Survivor Path!

Interesting. Were those related? It brought up intriguing questions about what it took to unlock a Skill. Was it connected to Paths somehow? None of the other Paths had unlocked a Skill alongside them, but these two seemed pretty clearly connected.

Or they were just both triggered by the same thing. Correlation is not causation, et cetera, et cetera. Maybe demonstrating survival skills is what let me get the Survival Skill? And I hadn't demonstrated it adequately before now? Is that why I didn't get the Climbing Skill or any kind of Focus Skill? I feel like I ought to be offended if that were the case.

I am fully capable of focusing when I want to. Oh hey, is that— No! Bad Edwin.

But climbing is strange. I figured Athletics might just have been as close as it got, but …

"Further testing required," he told himself. "Further …"—standing up was still a struggle, but far more manageable now that he was hydrated—"testing … required. Oh right, Skills. Accept."

Level Up! Survival
Survival
Because some people clearly need the help.
Subsist on your own longer.
Improved self-sufficiency per level.

I swear, this thing is mocking me. Also, I need to see if I can hide the initial level-up messages when I get a Skill.

But that Skill is perfect! It presumably means I'll have to eat and drink less, and that's just what I need right now. I wonder if I'll just no longer need to eat or drink at a certain point?

"So! Food and shelter, then I'm all set." Edwin broke himself out of his thoughts with a clap of his hands and a definite target to work toward. The river served as a useful landmark, one that he would absolutely need as he explored. And what better place to start his exploration than the cliff edge now that he could actually look properly? There was bound to be a *killer* view, and it might let him know if there was any kind of development nearby.

"Whoa." Edwin's comment may have been drowned out by the roar of the absolutely *enormous* waterfall, but the sentiment stood. Whatever mountain he was on—and it was absolutely a mountain, there was a snow-capped, albeit blurry, peak he could clearly see if he turned around—rose miles and miles above the forest below, which was thick and strange. If the top of the mountain was anything like what he saw below, it made sense that he might have gotten lost or gone in circles a few times.

Forest stretched out for miles, blanketing the mountainside as the slope descended thousands of feet before leveling into a sprawling carpet of trees of all kinds. He strained his eyes to look as far as he could—

You have unlocked the Seeing Skill!
Accept Skill? Y/N

—and while he could see that the endless expanse eventually came to an end, it was difficult to tell what lay beyond. It all blended together at the horizon, past the glittering tapestry that lay before him.

The forest shimmered with colors, all he could really distinguish without his glasses. It was predominantly green, yes, but patches of other colors peeked through on occasion, and a sort of rainbow shimmer was overlaid on some patches of trees.

Maybe there was civilization in the forest—it looked *perfect* for an elven enclave—but there wasn't a frat's chance at a scholarship that he could find it on his own, somewhere in the endless forest. The view was spectacular, though, and he must have spent a half hour alternating between marveling at the primal beauty of the sight and hoping he could spot something significantly *less* primal and more developed.

Level Up! Seeing
Level Up! Seeing
Level Up! Seeing
Level Up! Seeing
Level Up! Seeing
Seeing
All the better to see with, my dear.
Enhanced visual senses.
See farther per level.

Very useful, probably. None of Edwin's leveling up had given him any obvious advancement, with the exception of his Status, which made it possible that it would require dozens to hundreds of levels for him to notice any kind of tangible boost from his Skills. He was definitely hopeful about Seeing, though. He probably wasn't getting his glasses back, but if he could get magically enhanced eyesight? Worthy trade.

Assuming, of course, the Skills actually do provide a benefit and aren't just a marker of progress, but then why would they exist at all? he mused and hoped.

Anyway, he was still *starving*, and so needed to find some kind of food. He had yet to see any plants that looked safe to eat, though he had admittedly not been looking all that closely, mainly focused on finding signs of water. Now that he had found water, though, he could probably trek up the riverbank and find some kind of fruit-bearing plant. With renewed determination, he continued his endless hike across the rough ground, tinkering slightly with his Status on the way.

Level Up! Walking
Level Up! Status

Determined or not, though, walking was still incredibly painful, *and trying to stay close to the river to not get lost certainly doesn't make it any easier*, Edwin thought as he scrambled over a larger rock.

Level Up! Athletics
Level Up! Flexibility

This was probably a good rate of leveling? He was absolutely pushing himself, and if fiction had taught him anything, that most likely meant this would be a fast improvement speed. He still wished it were faster, though. At least he had water readily accessible now.

Edwin's exploration bore fruit less than a mile upstream as the river split slightly, the offshoot forming a slow-running pool. Next to the pool, there was an almost picture-perfect wild grove, lush green grass surrounding a handful of what looked to be fruit-bearing trees, framed in by a massive boulder covered in black, stringy moss.

The beauty of the place caught him off guard, but he quickly sharpened his wonder into suspicion. What kind of self-respecting fruit grove in a fantasy world wouldn't be tended to by a dryad or something? Were they poisonous?

Looking at the fruits, which bore resemblance to a pear with the skin of a cherry, he was paradoxically relieved to see a few of them looked like they'd been pecked on by birds. Wait, how could he see that so well at this distance? He should only be seeing colorful blurs without his glasses.

Level Up! Seeing

Ah, that was how. So Skills *did* supernaturally improve your capabilities! That was *amazing*.

Anyway, animal damage made it seem less likely that there was some supernatural force tending to the tree, or other danger inherent to the fruits, and there were still plenty that Edwin would be able to reach from the ground no problem.

Nonetheless, he approached the grove with caution. "Hello?" he asked the clearing. "Is it all right if I take some fruit? I haven't eaten in three days." When there was no response forthcoming, he picked up a couple of rocks from the riverbank and carefully ventured forward, tossing the stones at a tree in case it were a mimic or something. Nothing happened as it clattered off the trunk, nor as it struck and knocked off a leaf.

As his final test, he threw one as hard as he could at one of the fruits … and promptly missed. It took him a good half-dozen stones before one finally connected, causing the pear-thing to explode into a shower of juice, and providing yet another bonus.

You have unlocked the Throwing Weapons Skill!
Accept Skill? Y/N

Well, that seemed to confirm his suspicion about Skills being tied to actually accomplishing something. Also that he had indeed managed to hide the first level-up notification, very nice. Still needed further testing, though. No need to fall into confirmation bias.

He wasn't sure why he had gotten Throwing Weapons specifically, though. Was it like Athletics? Was there no Climbing Skill, or Rock Throwing Skill? Was there an even more generic Ranged Weapons Skill, and if so, why hadn't he gotten that one?

"Further testing required." It was practically a mantra at this point, and Edwin couldn't *wait* to find time to actually test everything. He accepted the Skill as he hesitantly picked one of the lower-hanging fruits from the tree, withdrawing quickly with his prize.

Throwing Weapons
The most basic and most advanced form of human weaponry:
Throw a rock at it.

Throwing weapons are more effective.
Increased proficiency per level.

Interesting Skill, he mused as he bit into the fruit. It tasted *sublime,* though that may just have been a result of how hungry he was. There seemed to be small seeds embedded in the flesh of the fruit, which helped him be just a touch more relieved with the thought that it probably wasn't poisonous.

I wonder if there's a Poison Resistance Skill. Maybe if I get poisoned I'll unlock it?

Edwin's first fruit was gone in seconds. The second and third followed shortly after, but by the time he got to his fourth, he was beginning to slow down. He wondered how nutritious these fruits were, or if they were just tasty. Probably provided lots of fiber, and a frown crossed his face as he hoped the biochemistry of the fruit was close enough to what he was used to for his metabolism to work with it. He was on a foreign planet; did he have any assurance that the chirality of the food would match what he was used to? Did indigestible glucose still taste sweet?

It did taste slightly tangy. Was it citric? He might need a better source of protein in the long run, but this should work for now. He paused as three notifications appeared; the first was an offered Skill, which he quickly accepted.

Nutrition
Because eating all the food in the world can still leave you starving to death.
Food is more nutritious.
Increased health benefits of food per level.

That was unhelpfully vague. Did it affect the food he ate? The food he made? Did it magically make the food he ate healthier, or did it just let him extract more calories and nutrients from it? It was probably the most vague Skill he had gotten, and the next two notifications were even more interesting.

Congratulations! For demonstrating highly advanced knowledge pertaining to the functioning of the body on its most basic level, you have unlocked the Micro-Biomancer Path!

Congratulations! For demonstrating highly advanced knowledge pertaining to the makeup of physical matter, you have unlocked the Physical Alchemist Path!

There were some interesting things Edwin made sure to note. For one, apparently musing about calories, chirality, and vitamins was "demonstrating highly advanced knowledge," which implied unfortunate things about the technology of the world. Not that he really *expected* an advanced magitech society, but it would have been a nice surprise.

Second, *alchemy*. Hopefully, that meant what he thought it did— namely, science without pesky things like physical laws holding him back, and not just chemistry sans the scientific method. He would need a word with whatever ran the magic on this planet if it were the latter, but if it were the former? Oh *man*. Would he ever *love* to be an alchemist. He didn't focus on materials science in college for nothing, and while his recollection of specifics left much to be desired without his textbooks on hand …

Yes please, I'll be an alchemist. Transmutation, potions, bombs, and golems? Sign me up.

Still, with no real knowledge of what Paths were or how to use them, it would have to be put to the side for the time being. In the meantime, he was going to focus on his food.

After his fifth cherry-pear (perry? Chear?), Edwin finally felt full. It might not be sustainable in the long term, depending on what exactly Nutrition and Survival did and how strong those Skills were, but it would keep him alive for the time being.

Food and water? Check.

Next on the list was finding shelter, and while his ideal locale would be a cave or the like, he could settle for a log lean-to or overhang. Just something to keep the rain off, really.

Edwin rose to his feet, cracking his neck as he continued his journey upstream. The boulder near the grove on the riverbank was there and annoying, but he should be able to climb over it easily enough. Surprisingly, the black moss he thought was covering the rock was in fact just small patches of similar moss, stone gray and dense enough that he thought it *was* the stone from a distance.

It also felt really coarse, not soft like most moss would be, and giving a gentle tug on it didn't pull it off whatever stone it was resting on. It wasn't like any moss he had ever seen or heard of before. And was it *moving*? What *was* this stuff?

You have unlocked the Identify Skill!
Accept Skill? Y/N

Perfect.

Identify
Because sometimes you just don't know what you have.
Learn about your target.
Increased range per level.

Oh cool, just what he needed. Did it work on plants? He focused on trying to examine the moss, flexing the same mental "muscle" he used to call up his Status.

Identify.

Level Up! Identify
Mature Giant Stonehide Bear

Oh.

CHAPTER 4

An Unstoppable Force Meets a Movable Object

Bushes tore at Edwin's arms as he sprinted through the underbrush. Behind him, he could hear his pursuer crashing through the fallen log he had vaulted over just moments before. He winced as the sound of a splintering tree resounded through the forest. Edwin was running as fast as he could, and that meant he couldn't get too close to the river-bank or he'd risk falling in, or tripping on some of the loose rocks lining it, or something similarly catastrophic.

Yes, the proper response to encountering a bear was supposed to be making yourself look big and scary and avoid provoking it, but he was pretty sure that didn't apply to bears the size of a *car* that were already mad at you.

He was unsure whether he was lucky or unlucky that he'd only noticed the "boulder" was alive and angry while actively climbing over it. On the one hand, he had eaten enough chears that he had enough energy to run. On the other, if he'd noticed before eating, he would have more of a head start from the massive predator and wouldn't have to deal with the cramp in his side from running before the fruit was fully digested.

Another tree fell and Edwin flinched at the sound, just long enough to miss avoiding a thin twig at head height, and he winced as it whipped him painfully. That would probably draw blood, but he didn't have time to stop and check right now.

On the bright side, it was doing wonders for his Skills. From the moment he took off running, he had been praying his Walking boost also applied to running and that his Athletics would help out there as well. He seemed to be right, at least.

Level Up! Walking
Level Up! Athletics

They were leveling up once every couple of minutes, and with each level he could maybe feel a bit more sure-footed, each step that much easier. Then again, it might be adrenaline and the placebo effect. Not like he had any way to really check.

Edwin dodged a fallen log, bringing him closer to the riverbank. This stretch of the river was fairly muddy, which proved to be his downfall as a slightly exposed root caught his foot, making him stumble just enough for his other foot to get stuck in the mud, sending him sprawling.

With the literal jaws of death bearing down upon him, Edwin turned to face the beast and threw a ball of mud as best as he could at the bear's snarling mouth. He was hoping to blind it and was half successful, most of the mud splattering on its snout. Enough did bounce off or hit true to cover its eyes with the almost claylike dirt, though, and a fair amount went into the beast's open mouth and covered its nostrils, making it pause as Edwin got to his feet and took off again.

Level Up! Throwing Weapons

On an impulse, he picked up another handful of mud in the hopes he could repeat the stunt. It took up a hand, but he could *probably* make do with only one for the time being, especially if he started sticking closer to the riverbank. Though that would have to wait, as there was no way he'd be able to run through this mud. Hopefully he could make his way back to the riverbank in time. From up ahead, he could hear the roar of the waterfall growing steadily louder.

Level Up! Walking
Level Up! Athletics

He was almost there, a half-formed plan in mind as his only vague hope for survival. Then all other thoughts were once again chased out of his mind as he heard the bear resuming its pursuit, slowly closing the gap between them. Risking a momentary glance backward, Edwin swore he could feel anger in its unblinded, glowing orange eye.

He felt terror grip his mind as his imagination flitted to picturing exactly how those enormous teeth could be used to tear his skin and break his bones, ripping muscles from their tendons and …

Level Up! Visualization

I hate you, you know that?

A momentary twinge on his Basic Mana Sense was all the warning he got, and he dropped to the ground in a slide as a nigh-invisible spiderweb was strung up right where his head would have passed had he not reacted.

Level Up! Flexibility
Level Up! Flexibility
Level Up! Athletics
Level Up! Basic Mana Sense
Level Up! Basic Mana Sense

Two levels in two Skills? Was it the stress? It had to be the stress. That, or legitimately life-and-death situations somehow improved his ability leveling-up speed in an unknowable manner. Stress would do as a temporary hypothesis. Was there any way to exercise his Skills without distracting himself, maybe? Something to consider for the next time—he didn't doubt there would be a next time. Right now he was in mortal peril. He regained his footing, scarcely slowing, and continued his mad dash onward.

Behind him, the bear muscled straight through the two trees Edwin had just passed through, the cracking and snapping giving no indication that the supernaturally tough spiderweb had even been noticed by the rampaging carnivore.

Edwin's mind focused, struggling to keep up with his senses and make sense of everything he saw. Avoid the prickly bush, duck under the branch, avoid the loose stone, grab—oh shoot, that was going to need two hands—blindly toss the handful of mud at the bear, hear the additional roar of annoyance that meant it had to have at least hit it—no time to check where—grab the vine and hope it holds ... Yes! Use it to swing over the tiny creek, hit the ground running, avoid tripping over that root, duck left around a tree trunk, dodge right around a stump, bob and weave through the bushes ... It was a breakneck pace, and he was *certain* he was running on pure adrenaline.

Edwin's side no longer hurt in the slightest, and his attention was as narrow as it had ever been. There were more notifications in the corner of his eye, but he wasn't paying attention to them. If he lived, he'd check then.

An incentive for survival, he grimly thought.

Finally, he managed to get to a section of forest that looked more familiar than the rest, and the roar of the nearby waterfall confirmed it. His only hope now was in the vines. They wouldn't hold the bear, that was certain, but they should be strong enough for him. He seriously, seriously wished he had more time testing this, but ...

If this didn't work, he was dead anyway. If the bear didn't cooperate, he was dead; if the vine broke, he was dead. So many ways this could go wrong, but Edwin didn't have any other options. He glanced behind him, not to check if the bear was still following him—that was never in doubt. Rather, it was to see if it still had mud in its eye. All the better. The less it could see, the more likely this would work.

Edwin angled toward the riverbank as he approached the cliff and, just as he broke free of the tree line, grabbed the thickest vine he could see on the thickest tree in the area. Just like before, it detached easily from the trunk but stayed attached to the canopy far, far, *far* above. He'd have to time this just right.

Hopefully the bear wasn't so strong as to fell the massive tree Edwin had selected as his lifeline. It seemed his worries were unfounded, though, as the bear instead muscled its way through a smaller tree nearby, disintegrating the trunk. It was the first time Edwin had actually *seen* the monster just ... overpower a tree, and while it was "only" about a foot across, it was still *utterly terrifying* to witness a two-ton ball of furious muscle and fur just decide to run straight through something that should have stopped it dead in its tracks. It didn't so much as scratch its mud-crusted muzzle or slow it down in the slightest.

There was a moment of even further heart-stopping terror as it looked like the tree knocked over might hit the vine he was holding, something that would absolutely doom his hopes of surviving, but it came up short. Edwin breathed a sigh of relief as he started to put weight on the vine, using it as a support to keep his footing while running over the profoundly slippery rocks. He was very, very close to the waterfall and there were even a few shallow puddles here and there from the amount of mist in the air.

His foot lost traction as he hit a puddle, and he started to fall forward. Edwin bit back a curse. It was sooner than he wanted, but hopefully he'd still manage.

Edwin's grip tightened around the vine and he pulled himself up, taking both feet off the ground like he was on a rope swing. He tried to pull himself up the vine, but after only a single hand-over-hand haul, he couldn't overcome his death grip and the shaking in his muscles. Time seemed to slow down as he looked down, and saw that he had overtaken the cliffside, and was now swinging over the edge.

Below him, the cliff dropped away sixty feet then into a virtual infinity. His mind froze in terror, but the phobia-based side of him was fortunately in agreement with the plan that the only thing to do was to *hold tight and pray the vine doesn't break.*

Edwin traveled in a surprisingly gentle arc over the yawning gap, and he managed to wrest his eyes away from the drop just in time to see the bear frantically try and backpedal on the oh-so-slippery rocks, digging in its claws in a vain attempt to break all the momentum it had built up. Its roars were subsumed by the waterfall's, and the anger on its face was replaced with fear followed by terror, as it sailed over the cliff into the fathomless mists below.

An utterly drained Edwin lay on the ground beneath his gently swaying vine, both emotionally and physically exhausted. He was hungry and thirsty again, though with a preestablished source of food and water, that was much less of a hazard than it might have once been. His arms trembled, and there was no way he'd be pulling a stunt like that again anytime soon.

Still, it was nice to know that hard work really was rewarded.

Level Up! Improvisation
Level Up! Improvisation
Level Up! Improvisation
Improvisation
Don't just think outside the box. Use the box as a weapon.
Make creations with nonstandard materials.
Increased effectiveness of creations per level.
Congratulations! For slaying a foe far stronger than you, you have unlocked the Titan Slayer Path!
Congratulations! For slaying a Mature Giant Stonehide Bear, you have unlocked the Stonehide Vanquisher Path!
Congratulations! For using your surroundings as a trap for your enemies, you have unlocked the Trapper Path!
You have unlocked the Improvisation Skill!
Accept Skill? Y/N
Level Up! Athletics
Level Up! Flexibility
Congratulations! For reaching level 12 in Athletics, you have unlocked the Athlete Path!
Level Up! Athletics
Level Up! Walking
Level Up! Athletics
Level Up! Flexibility
Level Up! Walking
Level Up! Seeing
Level Up! Throwing Weapons

I should get up. And I am not *falling asleep this time. It's, like, noon. But I think lying here sounds nice for right now.*
Very nice.

CHAPTER 5

Identifying Identify

Edwin groaned as he pulled himself up from the ground. He'd stayed awake, though almost wished he hadn't. Well, tonight would just feel all the sweeter when he finally *did* go to bed. For the time being, he carefully approached the edge of the cliff, ever-more mindful of the dangers it presented.

Heh. Caution: Stone slippery when wet.

Crouching down, Edwin ran a finger along one of the new divots in the stone, marking where the Stonehide Bear had dug in its claws in an attempt to slow itself. They had to be an inch deep and stretched for a good ten to fifteen meters before ending suddenly at the cliffside, itself seeming to be missing a few stones compared to its previous shape. He whistled to himself upon realizing the bear's claws were *that* hard and sharp, not to mention just how massive the bear must have been for its struggles to have proven unsuccessful.

Level Up! Visualization

Edwin rose, cautiously keeping his balance, and returned to less treacherous terrain. Following his tracks back was hardly difficult, the wake of destruction left by his former adversary—yeah, he liked thinking about it like that—leaving a trail clear as day.

Level Up! Survival

Interesting. Survival seemed to level up based on general survival and wilderness competence, like tracking. But that only decreased food and water dependence? Or did Skills have other hidden effects they didn't display outright? Now that he had a bit of time, he might be able to poke around a little bit, though without proper tools it could yet prove difficult to adequately measure this stuff. And if the System was subtly providing knowledge on survival tips, how could you accurately measure that anyway? Maybe a test involving a ton of questions on survival tips and tricks, taken after every level-up, so long as that leveling wasn't triggered by learning anything survival based ... Where would the knowledge come from, though? And would it be directly downloaded into the brain or something? Further testing was obviously required, but *how*?

Idly, Edwin ran his hand over the roots of a tree that had been uprooted rather than splintered by the creature. Did the bear leave this kind of a path everywhere it went? It couldn't have. There was no *way* that kind of thing was sustainable for a predator. Actually, how did that big of a creature ever survive? How did something the size of a truck get enough food to live? Maybe it spent most of its time in a hibernation-like state, only waking up when it sensed prey large enough to bother with or it was otherwise disturbed. With magic it was probably possible. Though Edwin had to be careful when just blanketing anything strange with the explanation of "magic," because that way lay superstition.

Arriving back at the chear grove, he grabbed a couple of the fruits and started munching on them. Now that he was no longer famished, he could properly savor the flavors, and it actually was pretty good, especially for a wild fruit. Despite its appearance, the texture of its flesh was closer to that of a watermelon and the flavor was vaguely citrusy, though it also reminded him of a plum. On a whim, he turned one over in his hand, studying it.

Identify.

When there was no response, Edwin frowned, the motion causing a bit of milky fruit juice to dribble down his chin, which he quickly wiped off. Why hadn't that worked? Did he do it wrong? Focusing on himself, he tried triggering the Skill again.

Level Up! Identify
Infant Extraplanar Human

Oh come on. That's so singularly unhelpful, he mentally grumbled, *and I thought I fixed that besides.*

A quick glance at his Status confirmed he was still supposed to be a twenty-two-year-old Extraplanar Human. Unless twenty-two was an infant on this planet? That didn't match up. Still, it did show that Identify wouldn't always be fully accurate per se. That information was worthwhile. Anyway.

Having confirmed that he was using Identify correctly, he tried again targeting the chear. After a notification once more failed to pop up, Edwin ran through the possibilities.

Okay ... Hypothesis: it only works on animals. So I need to try and find something that isn't an animal but that it does work on, or an animal on which it doesn't. In the latter case, I then need to figure out what does count as a valid target.

Attempting to Identify the ground at his feet failed, as did trying to target the insects buzzing around. Even a bird, perched on a branch in a tree at the edge of the grove, didn't register. Same with the tree itself, and a minnow he saw swimming along the bank of the river, and a caterpillar crawling up the trunk of one of the chear trees.

Level Up! Seeing

Okay. I must be doing something wrong. At least one of those should have registered. Hmm ... Are they out of range? Edwin tapped his leg. That seemed particularly likely. The Skill had said something about range increasing with level. He tried to resummon the Identify Skill description, but found he couldn't do so. *One way to test.*

He grabbed a stick off the ground, walked over to where the caterpillar was now crawling along a branch, and maneuvered his stick to pick up the insect. Then, angling it in such a way that the future butterfly was about a foot from his face, he tried again.

Identify.

Scintillating Butterfly Caterpillar

Okay, that worked. He held out his arm, extending it as far as it would go, so the bug was probably about two meters away from him, all told.

Identify.

No result. He pulled his arm closer and tried again. Still no result. He repeated the process a few times, until his arm was about half extended and the Skill worked.

Level Up! Identify

It was, counting the length of the stick … a little over a meter? A bit more testing confirmed that the range had indeed increased, though not by much, just a few centimeters … probably. He'd need to figure out some kind of way to make consistent measurements. There was no *way* he'd be able to figure out proper SI units from first principles, but he might be able to get close, if he was lucky. Maybe he could get a Skill for it?

With a range established, though, he could properly test things.

Level Up! Identify
Level Up! Nutrition
Level Up! Identify

An hour later, Edwin had Identified a ton of insects and a few fish (and eaten more than a few chears), though he hadn't gotten close enough to any birds to target them. So far as he could tell, there weren't any animals he could find that didn't have an Identify result. The one exception to that were some gnats swarming near the stream, though he couldn't tell if that was because they couldn't be targeted or he personally just wasn't able to target an individual gnat due to his failure to focus on one in particular. The time hadn't been completely wasted, though, not by any stretch of the imagination. In addition to slightly satisfying his curiosity (though not to the extent he could make a final call on his hypothesis), there were the notifications that had just appeared a few moments ago.

Congratulations! For engaging in scientific research, you have unlocked the Researcher Path!
You have unlocked the Research Skill!
Accept Skill? Y/N

How do you improve Research? … Accept?

Research
Uncover forgotten truths, discern the unknowable, discover the new.
Learn new things easier.
Improved ability to make connections per level.

I don't think that clarifies anything. Does it help … problem solving? Pattern recognition? Or is it, like, I see how these things are connected? Is this useful for detectives? Students? Heh. Conspiracy theorists? And connections … Does that apply to just mental connections, or does it help with stuff like networking? Probably not that one, but still… I need to have a word with whoever makes these descriptions.

Edwin still didn't know what the Paths did, exactly. Seeing them listed on his Status just gave him an empty feeling, like they were supposed to fill up and do something. All his Paths were equally empty, though. And how were they different from Skills? All good questions that he really should answer, though with the time he'd spent—not wasted, *spent*; that was his story and he was sticking to it—analyzing Identify, he didn't have any to spare at the moment.

Stuffing a handful of chears into his pocket, Edwin set off on his continued exploration along the mountain river. It was midafternoon and a few miles later before he came to the next point of real interest, strange trees and a few shallow spots in the river notwithstanding. Here, the river branch he was following, much smaller than the raging torrent he was used to, was a gentle stream flowing over a small drop, just some ten to fifteen feet tall. While Edwin wasn't about to go rock climbing, he also didn't need to, not when there was a cave practically right next to it.

Well, "cave" was perhaps a bit of a misnomer, in all honesty. It was a large, jagged boulder that had fallen next to the small cliff at some point, creating a natural shelter. While the space wasn't terribly large, perhaps five feet across by ten feet deep, it was more than enough for Edwin to fit inside with some room to spare.

The roof, if you could really call it that, had light seeping through, and there was a thick layer of moss—*actual* moss this time—coating one of the walls; it was even green! Edwin still checked it to be sure, though. The space looked as though, with a bit of work, it would be a secure enough shelter from the weather and any creatures that *weren't* the size of a truck that might try to attack him. Its proximity to water just made it better.

After a quick check to ensure it wasn't hiding too many spiders, Edwin decided to settle in. Moving the smaller rocks was tough but, with the exception of one stone that was mostly buried in the soil, doable. He piled up the removed rocks outside, and breaking off a particularly leafy branch from a nearby tree, managed to sweep/rake out a lot of the twigs that had accumulated inside.

Level Up! Improvisation

Huh. So did it also apply to just *using* objects for nonstandard purposes? Would Improvisation pair with his Throwing Weapons Skill so long as he was just using random clutter? Would it eventually get to the point where he would be better off using the wrong item for a job just to get the bonus? And how did the System figure out if something was "improvise-worthy"? Anyway, he wanted to get this in a decent setup before nightfall. Yes, he had slept the last two nights just out on the open ground, but getting a half-decent bed situation for tonight would surely do wonders for his mood. Fortunately, there were enough dry leaves and very leafy branches around to make a nice semimattress, particularly when combined with most of the moss previously on the wall of his new cave. The next step was trying to patch up the holes in the "roof." That was mercifully simple, as he piled leaves and twigs everywhere he saw a gap, then covered them with some really nice, thick clay from the river, forming a decent seal where the two rocks met.

Level Up! Visualization
Level Up! Improvisation

His immediate goals for the night complete, Edwin rinsed his muddy hands off in the waterfall, bemoaning his inability to properly clean the dirt caked all over himself. Once cleanish, he retrieved his saved chears from his jacket, hanging on a nearby branch. As the light started to fade, the last thing he set out to do was grab a really big fallen branch and drag it so it acted as a bit of a door for his shelter. Better safe than sorry, and his encounter with the Stonehide Bear had somewhat reinvigorated his fear of predators.

It was a cold night for sleeping, especially without the bone-deep exhaustion of the night before, but after tossing and turning for a while, Edwin gave a mental "tug" on his Sleeping Skill, which, while it didn't send him off to the land of Nod immediately, certainly helped.

Tomorrow, he promised himself, he was going to figure out how to get a fire started.

Level Up! Sleeping

CHAPTER 6

Sparks Flying

Edwin's back was sore. Although that may not have been all that noteworthy on its own, especially considering his sleeping conditions, it was the first time he had woken up any less than perfectly rested since he got the Sleeping Skill. It probably wasn't helped by the fact that his "door" had fallen on him in the middle of the night, jolting him awake and causing him to lie sleepless for a while, even using his Skill not enough to pull him back into slumber.

Guess it's not high enough of a level yet, he mused, rubbing his lower back and stretching.

Edwin surveyed his domain. A small waterfall, two giant rocks with mud caked into the gaps between them, a pile of stones, and a bunch of branches and leaves. It certainly wasn't much, but it was all he had at the moment. Today's tasks were relatively simple. Get a fire going, gather some more food, and maybe build up his shelter a bit. All that could be really hard without any tools to speak of, but he believed in himself. There was a chunk of stone that was already somewhat knife-shaped to begin with; maybe he could knap it into a more usable form? Build himself up from the Stone Age.

Level Up! Visualization

His chosen rock in one hand and a complementary stone in the other, Edwin sat down on a conveniently sized rock he mentally dubbed his sitting stone and started hitting the rocks together. While knapping was a new experience for him, he felt a slight tug to hit them at a specific angle instead of head-on or just barely scraping them together. It was a bit odd, as it felt like muscle memory for something he had never learned, but he guessed that was a result of—

Level Up! Improvisation

—Improvisation. Yep. So did the Skill lead him toward doing actions correctly or did it just magically improve the results? Both? Something else entirely? Where was this knowledge coming from?

Level Up! Research
Level Up! Survival

His Skills seemed happy, anyway. Was Research just "learning"? It seemed like it, and if that were the case, it was absolutely amazing. Magically enhanced learning capabilities! Would it help him level up his other Skills, or figure out what they did?

Level Up! Improvisation

About an hour later, Edwin had something that would … probably … pass as a knife. It was pointy and had a sharp edge, at least. It also would probably break really quickly, but it was better than nothing. With a tool finally in hand, he could try to start his fire. There was lots of dry wood and leaves around to serve as kindling, and a bit of hunting turned up a sturdy, dry stick and some rough wood that would serve as excellent material for getting a spark. He tried cutting a few shavings of wood with his new blade, but while it *looked* like a knife, it didn't act like one, and it snapped in half the moment he put too much pressure on it. He threw the pieces off to the side in frustration, burying his head in his hands. Then, he took a deep breath, composed himself, and settled for using what tinder he already had, grabbing his chosen stick and spinning it.

Half an hour later, Edwin was bored and his hands were sore. He'd known this wouldn't be easy, that it would take a while, and that it would be boring. But having not actually *done* it before personally he wasn't prepared for just how tedious making the point of a stick spin on a single spot would be. It was starting to heat up, at least, so he knew he was doing something right, but it was still just so *boring*.

An hour after *that*, there was no improvement and he figured he was doing something wrong. In frustration, he snapped the stick he was spinning and tossed it to the ground. It clearly wasn't working and if he continued too much longer, the blisters he could feel forming on his palms would be full-blown.

He sat with his head in his hands for a few minutes before starting to look around. It was a bit of a long shot, but maybe he could find some flint around here?

It took him a while, but eventually Edwin's gaze fell on his broken knife. He wasn't *sure* if it really was flint, but he didn't have any better options. It did look vaguely flintlike from what he remembered of the mineral, but striking its two halves together didn't yield anything.

Hmm. Did flint not spark against itself? How did flint and steel work, anyway? It wasn't something he had ever really thought about before, so … He wished he had steel, that he could see if this rock really was flint. But his pockets were still empty of all modern conveniences, and he didn't think his jacket's zipper had enough metal in it. What else did he have on hand? He didn't have much, but maybe something he had might work? Shoes, socks, jacket, pants, shirt, belt …

Ah. He had his belt. He wasn't totally sure the belt buckle was steel, but it wouldn't hurt to try?

It took him a minute to get the angle right, but sure enough, his "flint" and belt buckle produced sparks. Neat! He gathered up a few wood shavings and some dry needles and grass, piled them on some dead leaves, and started sparking the pieces together.

It still took a few minutes, but Edwin nearly jumped as a set of notifications broke him out of his distracted, aimless musings.

Level Up! Survival
Level Up! Improvisation
You have unlocked the Firestarting Skill!
Accept Skill? Y/N

The thought of getting something, anything really, to help him not have to go through that entire process again (notwithstanding how much easier using flint made it) brought Edwin to instinctively accept the Skill, before rushing to grab the dry kindling he had nearby and feeding it to the tiny spark before him.

About a minute later, he had enough of a steady fire going, fed by twigs and dried leaves, to take a moment to glance at his notifications.

Level Up! Firestarting
Firestarting
Burn down a house with nothing but a lemon.
Make fire.
Increased ease per level.

At this point, Edwin felt confident enough in the Skill's ambiguity to figure it would only make starting fires easier. His hope, however, was that it only made things he *wanted* to burn more flammable and wasn't a walking fire hazard. Well, at least he had made a bit of a firepit, lining a small area with the rocks he had removed from his cave, so it shouldn't burn down the forest or anything.

He did have to wonder, though, if it made him more fireproof. Probably not, but was there a Fire Resistance Skill? Fire Resistance was a common enough fantasy and game-type effect that it probably had a corresponding Skill here. Maybe he could unlock it?

Firestarting did not, it seemed, improve Edwin's resistance to fire. Even just a second with his hand in the flames hurt, and his brain refused to let him keep bare skin exposed in his tiny campfire any longer than that. And with no corresponding Skill, it was probably safe to assume he wouldn't unlock Fire Resistance in this manner.

... though assumptions were always dangerous.

... and he was hardly *safe* at the moment. He needed to take risks if he wanted to survive.

...

Twenty minutes later, Edwin felt significantly more certain this wasn't the way to unlock Fire Resistance. Or if it *was*, he wasn't willing to keep at it. His hand, currently soaking in the frigid mountain stream, agreed that he should probably stop sticking his extremities into flames. With a sigh, he stood up and inspected his fingers. The skin was still a bit red and what little hair had once been on his wrist had burned off, but his hand seemed otherwise relatively unscathed. Small mercies, he supposed. He only had a first-degree burn from his experiments.

In my defense, he told himself, *it was entirely possible that would work.*

It was almost noon now, and Edwin was getting hungry. He fed the fire in front of his cave a few more sticks, then piled on a few larger branches. Overall, it should keep the flames going until he returned.

Level Up! Walking
Level Up! Survival
Level Up! Nutrition
Level Up! Improvisation

Walking was absolutely getting easier, as this trek to and from his chear grove showed, and while it was still hard to tell if that was just a result of Edwin getting in shape or his Walking Skill leveling up, given his lack of adequate nutrition and the sore muscles that usually accompanied extensive exercise, he was fairly certain it was the latter.

It was a bit of a surprising realization, honestly. Sure, there were magical floating text boxes and bears the size of a truck, but it was another thing to realize that he personally, legitimately had magical gamelike powers that were invisibly helping him survive. It made him wonder what other aspects of this System he was missing out on.

That said, he didn't regret prioritizing his mundane survival needs over "grinding out" Skills. The former was a known quantity, whereas the latter was much more mysterious and unknown. For all he knew, he was doing everything completely wrong and he should already be fighting dragons or shooting lightning from his fingertips.

Why couldn't the stupid System have come with a tutorial or better descriptions or, at the *very* least, actual *numbers*? He mentally resolved he was going to beat that "improved accuracy" in his Status description until it gave him actual, wonderfully concrete *numbers*. The vague impressions he got about the level of his Skills relative to his other Skills, while useful, weren't the pure mathematical digits he knew how to deal with.

He might also be able to figure out what was up with Paths! He still got a similar feeling when looking at them as when he was looking at his lower-leveled Skills, and maybe if he got numbers, he would be able to figure out what exactly they needed to advance. He had a sneaking suspicion it was related to his (lack of) Class and was rather keen on filling in his missing knowledge on that aspect of this world. Would it unlock new Skills? Let him use magic? Do something with the conspicuously empty Attributes? So many possibilities!

Edwin was rudely jolted out of his daydreaming when he hit his head on a low branch he had missed, and as part of his flinch, bit down hard on the chear he was in the process of eating, catching his finger in the process.

"Gah!"

Edwin winced with the pain, and then, reaching to rub his head, he managed to scrape his recently injured finger on the same branch his head had just smacked into. He sighed. *And I had managed to go so long without walking into anything, too. I suppose it would have been too much to hope for that Seeing and Walking both would somehow prevent me from not noticing stuff like that.*

Carefully ducking under the offending branch, Edwin continued rubbing the sore spot on his head with what he realized too late was a juice-covered hand. *I was on such a roll, too. Getting a fire going, finding water and food, and killing that bear,* he bemoaned to himself. *Note to self: magically improved senses still don't protect against general obliviousness. Now, snap out of it before something actually dangerous comes around.*

The rest of the journey back was fortunately uneventful, and he safely arrived back at his little shelter, setting his harvest off to the side, and tended to his fire. It hadn't completely gone out while he was gone, which was nice, though it did take a bit of poking the embers and a few handfuls of dry nettles before it returned to open flames.

Level Up! Firestarting

His survival-related tasks finally complete, Edwin collapsed onto his sitting stone, reveling in the sensation of allowing his increasingly sore legs some measure of relief. Pity this rock was so uncomfortable. Hmm. Nah, he was going to lie down. That would feel *amazing*.

His bed did not, in fact, feel amazing, but it was certainly better than a slightly moss-covered boulder, especially after removing a few of the more uncomfortable sticks in it.

Status.

Once he had his Status up, Edwin started playing around with it. First, he tried reorganizing the categories themselves. Changing what order they appeared in was fairly easy, and breaking out the notification wasn't much harder, either, giving him more of a HUD-like display of his Status. Granted, he didn't have any *need* for this, and it was impractical besides, but it was fun nonetheless. But he was getting distracted.

Unsurprisingly, simply requesting that numbers appear on his Status didn't work. So it was time to get inventive. It was pretty simple for him to organize his Skills by strength with just a twist of mental will.

Where to go from there was a bit trickier, though. He was fairly certain that his Firestarting was only level 3—it had only leveled up twice since he had unlocked it, after all—and he was able to "tag" it as such with only a bit of effort.

Level Up! Status

Oh! Perfect timing. With the notification up as well as his Status, Edwin compared the strength of his Status with Firestarting, the former being ... exactly five times stronger than his level 3 Skill, and with that knowledge in mind, he concentrated on the level-up message until it cooperated.

Level Up! Status Level 16
Level Up! Status Level 15

Excellent! Now he could see exactly what level his Skills grew to when they leveled up! Hmm. Maybe there was some way to consolidate them?

Level Up! Visualization Level 10→11
Level Up! Status Level 14→17

Apparently this was also good for his Visualization Skill. Interesting. It did provide a convenient opportunity for him to try and combine multiple different Skill notifications into the same message, though. Hmm.

A bit of tinkering later and Edwin finally had something he was happy with. It had been surprisingly hard to keep his previous changes intact while combining different Skill notifications into a single message, but he eventually managed.

Level Up!
Status Level 14→19
Visualization Level 10→12

Excellent. Edwin dismissed the level-ups and, with a twist of will he was *pretty* sure worked, made it so he could call them up as a separate entity from his Status, and disable notifications completely if he wanted. Now, to test it …

Leveling.

Level Up!
Status Level 19→20

"Yes!" It worked! Edwin raised his hands in triumph, accidentally dismissing the notification in the process. Eh, no matter. He'd accomplished his goal, and now it was time to turn to the rest of his Skills. He cracked his knuckles in preparation for another round with the interface.

* * *

In the end, it was surprisingly anticlimactic. All it took was him mentally trying to apply numbers to the Skills on his Status page, and then it happened automatically. Apparently leveling really *did* make customizing things easier.

Name

Edwin Maxlin

Age

22

Race

Extraplanar Human

Class

None

Attributes

None

Skills

Status: 20

Athletics: 13

Visualization: 12

Improvisation: 10

Walking: 9

Basic Mana Sense: 8

Flexibility: 8

Seeing: 7

Identify: 6

Breathing: 5

Survival: 5

Sleeping: 4

Nutrition: 3

Firestarting: 3

Throwing Weapons: 3

Research: 2

Paths

Athlete

CharLimitCanttalkmuchNocluewhathappenedDidmybesttohelpyouli

Daredevil

Explorer

Linguist

Lumberjack

Micro-Biomancer

Path Less Traveled

Physical Alchemist

Realm Traveler

Researcher

Stonehide Vanquisher

Survivor

Titan Slayer

Trapper

Way of the Empty Hand

World Traveler

Edwin's Status was looking pretty impressive, if he did say so himself. Well, it was probably impressive. "Realm Traveler" and "Stonehide Vanquisher" were almost *certainly* not common. But okay. Now that he knew how much easier it was to customize, he directed his Status—though not his notification settings, he didn't want to mess with that again at the moment—to reset, and his Skills lost their numbers, returning to alphabetical order. His age also returned to "Very Young." Interestingly, his name and race stayed in their altered forms instead of going back to just "Edwin" and "Human?," which implied the System had updated his classification there. It also confirmed his suspicion that his altered age was indeed just cosmetic. Annoying, but manageable.

He requested that his entire Status display itself in numbers, and while there were some very interesting things happening down below with his Paths, he figured he should take care of his age first. That, at least, should be pretty quick.

Age

223 days

22, 3 days

22 years, 3 days
22+MOD(3 days, 365 days) years
22 years

Eventually, after a few iterations, he managed to get his age to display as 22 years, plus his System age divided by 365. Probably. Assuming it didn't change the formatting of his age once he was here for a week or whatever, it should automatically update on the anniversary of his arrival on Joriah every year, assuming a year was the same length of time it was on Earth …

The idea of possibly being in this new world for a year, away from everyone he had ever known, literally worlds away from his friends and family, hit Edwin all at once. He had been very carefully *not thinking about that*, because he needed to survive first and foremost.

Once he was actually secure in his safety, he could think about the ramifications of his existence here. People had to be missing him, after all. He might not have had more than a couple friends, but he had vanished with literally no explanation, no warning, nothing. It was—

Edwin interrupted himself before he could break down. No. Pitying himself wouldn't get him anywhere. Given the messages he had gotten when he first woke up on Joriah, he came from a world allegedly utterly unknown by whatever entities ran the System, who were presumably quite powerful and knowledgeable.

Odds were good there was no way back to Earth, and he may as well accept that. This was a whole new world besides! There was magic, too! He could do *science* here! It was amazing! There were almost certainly other people here as well; he could find them and befriend them. All he needed was to *survive*, and to do that meant he needed to *focus* and *not let his emotions control him*. He had practiced this, and with a deep breath he blinked away any lingering wetness around his eyes.

It was what it was, and there was no point trying to get the world to change. The sooner he accepted that fact, the sooner he could properly adjust.

Okay. Where was he? Right. Modulo. The Status was pretty similar to a computer program, once he figured out how to more or less hijack the code. It wasn't quite like what he knew of SQL injection, but it felt like a similar idea. He didn't have much experience with programming, but this didn't seem to be too complicated. It might also be totally broken, who knows? He'd find out … in a year.

Checking his notifications, Edwin noticed he had gotten to level 21 in his Status and earned a level in Breathing, of all things. Where had that come from?

Anyway, his Paths were now *very* interesting.

Paths
Skill Points: 122
Athlete 0/60
CharLimitCanttalkmuchNocluewhathappenedDidmybesttohelpyouli 0/120
Daredevil 0/60
Explorer 0/60
Linguist 0/60
Lumberjack 0/60
Micro-Biomancer 0/90
Path Less Traveled 0/90
Physical Alchemist 0/90
Realm Traveler 0/120
Researcher 0/60
Stonehide Vanquisher 0/60
Survivor 0/60
Titan Slayer 0/90
Trapper 0/60
Way of the Empty Hand 0/60
World Traveler 0/60

Skill Points … Were those from his Skills? A bit of addition later, he determined that he had exactly 122 total Skill levels, which probably wasn't a coincidence. Edwin felt a bit of a tug, seemingly directing him to advance along a Path. After a moment of consideration, he focused on his "CharLimitCanttalkmuchNocluewhathappenedDidmybesttohelpyouli" Path. Would Survivor perhaps make more sense if he was trying to sustain himself in the wilderness? Probably. However, he also knew that when it came to surviving in a *fantasy* wilderness, he'd need all the help he could get, and if there was to be any sort of gift from the creators of the System, it would probably be in the closest thing to a direct message he had gotten from them.

Level Up!
Status Level 21→22

Oh right, he still had notifications on. He considered toggling them off but figured that for the moment he liked knowing what made him level up. More satisfying that way. Maybe if they got too annoying, he'd fix it, but that was Future-Edwin's problem, not his.

Anyway, when he increased his Path, he had noticed that his Skill Points had briefly dipped down to 121 before the Status level had come through. So did he increase his progress along a Path by assigning Skill Points to them? It seemed like it.

Paths
Skill Points: 122
CharLimitCanttalkmuchNocluewhathappenedDidmybesttohelpyouli
1/120

Well, no time like the present. While it may not have been the *best* decision, he'd had enough and had made up his mind. So he dumped the rest of his points into the Path all at once.

His System exploded with notifications.

CHAPTER 7

Firmly Outside Normal

Level Up!

Research Level 2→3

Congratulations! For having your first Class be a unique Class, you have unlocked the Pioneer Path!

Congratulations! For gaining your first Class, you have unlocked the Outsider Path!

You may evolve your Status Skill into the Outsider's Almanac Skill!

Accept Evolution? Y/N

Done!

…

Calculating Rewards …

Class Change!

None → Outsider

You have completed the CharLimitCanttalkmuchNocluewhathappenedDidmybesttohelpyouIi Path!

You have made your way to an unfamiliar world. Ahead of you lie possibilities beyond imagining. Your unique perspective will be your greatest tool and greatest hindrance. Taking this Path first has opened many new destinations for you, yet closed off many you would otherwise have been able to reach.

Congratulations! For spending 120 Skill Points, you have unlocked the Trainee Path!

**Congratulations! For spending 60 Skill Points, you have unlocked the
Beginner Path!**
**Congratulations! For spending 12 Skill Points, you have unlocked the
Novice Path!**

Edwin stared blankly at the wall of text. Discounting the slew of errors he'd woken up to on day one and the pile of rewards he'd received after killing the truck-sized Stonehide Bear, it was the most notifications he'd ever gotten.

It did seem as though his assessment of how to get a Class was correct, as well as the purpose of Skill Points. He got a total of five new Paths for completing one, though it didn't look like that would happen every time.

It was also interesting that the System seemed to be base 12. He had somewhat expected as much, what with his Paths being 60, 90, or 120 Skill Points across the board, but it was nice to have it mostly confirmed. Did it just translate to displaying in base 10 because those were the numbers he was used to?

Ewin *was* confused as to why there were apparently achievements for spending 12 and 60 Skill Points, when they would both be completed simply by the first Path one took, but glancing at them on his Status showed they only needed 12 and 30 Skill Points, respectively, to complete. Were most Paths cheaper than what he had?

It does kind of make sense. If people have the System from birth, they probably get a lot more mundane accomplishments, which I skipped by falling into the middle of the wilderness. I also got a lot of Paths, but maybe I didn't qualify for the cheaper ones, for whatever reason? I don't know.

Still, he had an immediate choice to make and an eminently obvious answer to the question.

Outsider's Almanac
Become the guy who "wrote the book."
Record information.
Increased limit per level.

And we're back to supercryptic Skills. Cool.

Edwin called his Status back up, but didn't see any obvious changes to it, beyond a section at the bottom with his Completed Paths. Well, the Skill said he could "record information." So he looked at his hand.

Outsider's Almanac, he thought at the appendage, similar to him trying to Identify it or call up his Status. There was no immediately obvious change, but he got a vague sense that his Skill was asking for an … input of some sort? What?

Edwin looked away, and then reactivated the Skill on his hand. Oddly, there was no response beyond the same mental prompt as before, but this time he also felt a sensation as though the input would replace … something. Weird. Um.

Identify?

Outsider
What?

Wait, what? Did he Identify as an Outsider now? What was going on? He tried using the Almanac again, but this time, when the Skill asked him for an input, he mentally provided, *Testing.*

Identify.

Outsider
Testing

Oh cool! He could leave notes for Future-Edwin that would show up with Identify. Increased limit per level, though—did that mean he could only leave a limited number of notes, or that his notes were limited in size? He sat up in his bed and grabbed a nearby stick.

Outsider's Almanac. TestTestTest—the note was cut off suddenly, a distinct note of being "full" permeating the feedback.

Level Up!
Outsider's Almanac Level 1→2

He quickly Identified the stick.

Test Test Test

Okay, twelve characters at level 1. Let's try this again? Outsider's Almanac. Test Test Test T—

A quick check with Identify showed that there was an additional character on the message, so his limit now seemed to be 13 characters. Applying a new message, accompanied by another check showed that it did change when he reused the Almanac, but the limit hadn't increased. Grabbing another stick, he Identified it, only to see the same message again.

So it ties the message to sticks in general? Hmm. What if I try to focus it on that branch specifically, instead of the branch as a concept?

A bit more experimentation showed that Edwin could indeed make the different sticks have separate messages, but doing so overrode the "default" note. So he could have a message pertaining to all branches, but if he set a message on a *specific* branch, that note wouldn't show up for other branches and at the same time it wouldn't show his generic "branch" message.

Level Up!
Outsider's Almanac Level 2→3

His character limit didn't increase with this level, though he did discover that he could tag different parts of an object as separate from the whole. He could make each of his fingers have different labels, and they would show up if he Identified them, but it wouldn't interfere with a message he had for his entire hand. In addition, by focusing on parts of his body *specifically*, he didn't always see his identity as "Outsider." That was reserved for his entire being, it seemed.

Level Up!
Outsider's Almanac Level 3→5
Identify Level 6→7

Those levels increased his character limit all the way to 15, and Edwin discovered that while he could even give his individual finger segments their own notes, he couldn't subdivide below that. Was it because he couldn't really conceptualize a discrete object for his Skill to work on?

He *had* had trouble Identifying a single gnat in a swarm, so it seemed like a workable hypothesis for the time being. Even with those restrictions, though, Edwin was *ecstatic* with his new Skill. He would never have to memorize something ever again! He could just make a note about it and refer to it later. Like writing on the back of your hand—he rubbed his arm guiltily—only with magic! That made it infinitely better. Time to experiment!

Level Up!
Outsider's Almanac Level 5→6

Hmm ... What was the formula that determined how many characters he could use? This was the first chance he'd had to peel back the literal mathematics of the universe, and he'd be a poor excuse of a physicist if he let this pass him by. Since he had 16 characters at level 6, that meant ... Hmm. He had 12 at level 1, 13 at levels 2 and 3, then increasing by one for levels 4 through 6. Maybe it was an increase of .7 characters per level? And that was just if it were linear ... He'd need more data to be sure.

Level Up!
Research Level 3→4
You have unlocked the Mathematics Skill!
Accept Skill? Y/N

He must have already been *really close* to unlocking Mathematics, if he'd gotten it by merely thinking about a linear progression and not when he was trying to add the modulus of the days he'd spent on Joriah or anything like that. Still, Edwin would *gladly* get magical assistance. He probably wasn't getting back to his calculator any time soon, after all ... And nope.

Not thinking about that. Darn it. He had been doing such a good job of not thinking about Earth until recently. Being in constant danger probably helped with that, admittedly. Still, he wasn't getting side-tracked yet. Uhhh ... Accept Skill!

Mathematics
Useful when counting sheep ... though not like that.
Do advanced calculations.
Improved numerical sense per level.

Even though he really should have expected it at this point, it was still disappointing to get yet another Skill with such a vague description. *Then again, this one might actually be worthwhile,* Edwin thought as he got up to tend to his fire and warm himself by it. *Numerical sense might mean I get better at making estimations, can mentally handle larger and smaller numbers, or can keep track of extra digits beyond ... What was the human average again? Seven? It might be very useful.*

Sadly, Edwin's new Skill brought no immediate insights as to the scaling for his Almanac, but that was fine. He could figure it out himself eventually. That said, he disabled his level-up notifications and started applying notes to *everything.* The range for which he could apply his Almanac messages seemed to be linked to his Identify distance, interestingly, which also enabled him to sense *that* Skill leveling as he could target things farther and farther away.

The general guideline for what he could or could not mark with his Skill seemed to be directly tied to what he could conceptualize as a single object, so not half of a stick or "the atmosphere." Still, there were exceptions to that rule.

He couldn't leave a mark on the planet as a whole—doing so overlapped with him making a note for the mountain he was on—though that may have simply been due to him not being able to properly conceptualize the difference between the two.

On the other hand, he wasn't able to make a distinct note on arbitrary groups of objects, either. He could make a note for a specific leaf, or a type of leaf, or leaves in general, but he couldn't do so for two specific leaves next to each other, or two leaves in general.

That then scaled back around, though, as he could make a pile of rocks have its own note, and disassembling the pile and building up a new one, with some rocks exchanged, still returned the same marker. He could also put different generic messages for rocks and for boulders, because apparently size *did* matter.

Perhaps most interesting, though, was that he was able to focus on the *material* something was made of instead of the object itself. It followed the same rules for generic/specific as objects, but he was indeed able to make different tags for "wood," "not-maple," and "not-cedar," and analyzing branches from the corresponding trees let him see either the message for a branch or the message for their wood, depending on what he focused on. He couldn't make a message for not-cedar branches, though. It was either all not-cedar or all branches.

In this way, Edwin was able to discover that the cliff and the giant boulder that made up his cave were different kinds of stone, though his knowledge of geology wasn't good enough to determine *what* those types of stone were, and the miscellaneous rocks scattered around were mostly the same kind as the cliff, a few that matched the boulder, and a handful, including his broken knife, that came from neither.

As it turned out, Edwin was also able to mark smoke and fire—though only if the former was visible—but not a distinct "cup" of water (held in a concave rock); nor could he make separate notes for fire resulting from different types of wood being burned or different colors of flames. He *could* make a specific note for his campfire, though, and removing a burning stick showed he could mark that, though the mark vanished when he returned it to the greater campfire, and if he left it in long enough that the stick burned up, the note burned up as well.

Overall, a very productive day in his estimation. Sure, he hadn't found any other sources of food for when he inevitably ran out of chears, nor had he explored to try and find a way out of the forest, or really done anything other than sit around and play with notifications. But it was a *productive* day of playing with notifications. He had so many Skill levels now!

Level Up!
Outsider's Almanac Level 6→21
Identify Level 7→12

Visualization Level 12→15
Research Level 4→7

Okay, so he may have gone a *little* overboard and brought his Almanac back to being his highest-level Skill, but he *needed* those levels if he was to complete more Paths, which would give him more rewards, probably Skill upgrades, which could be *very useful* in surviving. Besides, who knows when it might be useful to have—he checked his current maximum—a character limit of 35 letters for his Almanac notes? That could save his life. You never knew.

Perhaps more seriously, though, he should consider what Path he wanted to fill out in the future. While he could complete something like Novice or Beginner right away, what with his 39 Skill Points, Edwin felt it might be better to use them on a longer Path, which would probably give better rewards, going purely on gut feeling. That would logically mean he should go for Realm Traveler, but was that *too* much to spend on a single Path for right now? Hmm. He pulled up his Paths.

Paths
Skill Points: 39
Athlete 0/60
Beginner 0/30
Daredevil 0/60
Explorer 0/60
Linguist 0/60
Lumberjack 0/60
Micro-Biomancer 0/90
Novice 0/12
Outsider 0/60
Path Less Traveled 0/90
Physical Alchemist 0/90
Pioneer 0/60
Realm Traveler 0/120
Researcher 0/60
Stonehide Vanquisher 0/60
Survivor 0/60

Titan Slayer 0/90
Trainee 0/60
Trapper 0/60
Way of the Empty Hand 0/60
World Traveler 0/60

Athlete, Daredevil, Linguist, Pioneer, Researcher, Way of the Empty Hand, and World Traveler all sounded cool, and were 60 points, but he wasn't sure how much they might help him out now.

Explorer, Lumberjack, Outsider, Stonehide Vanquisher, Survivor, and Trapper might help him now, but he also didn't want to specialize himself into surviving in the wilderness too much, which his Class changing as a result of his Path completion seemed to indicate. Though that concern only really applied to Lumberjack and *maybe* Survivor; the others sounded cool enough that he might want them eventually.

Titan Slayer sounded incredibly metal, Path Less Traveled was in a similar vein to his CharLim-whatever Path, and he *absolutely* wanted Physical Alchemist and Micro-Biomancer, but they were all 90 points, which seemed like a lot. He also wasn't doing Trainee. It was too generic in comparison to his other options, which might not be a *bad* thing and could possibly help him get some sort of tutorial-like effect, which he definitely could use.

Hmm. This was tricky. Go safe and take low-cost Paths, or try and risk it for the higher-cost and potentially more potent ones? Well …

Edwin sighed as he looked around at his surroundings. He didn't like risks much, but this seemed like the prime opportunity to take them. In any case, it was arguably the *less* risky option. He didn't know what sorts of things he might encounter, and there wasn't any apparent way to get Skill Points *back*. If he didn't spend his points, he could use them whenever something obviously useful came up!

With a bit of focus, he rearranged his Paths so they'd be easier to parse.

Paths
Skill Points: 39
Very Much Yes-Eventually

Physical Alchemist 0/90, Micro-Biomancer 0/90, Path Less Traveled
0/90, Realm Traveler 0/120
Promising
Stonehide Vanquisher 0/60, Titan Slayer 0/90, World Traveler 0/60,
Researcher 0/60, Explorer 0/60, Outsider 0/60
Maybe One Day
Survivor 0/60, Linguist 0/60, Athlete 0/60, Daredevil 0/60, Pioneer 0/60
Meh
Lumberjack 0/60, Way of the Empty Hand 0/60, Trapper 0/60
No
Beginner 0/30, Novice 0/12, Trainee 0/60

Maybe he should go for the Explorer Path? That or Survivor, he felt. Those stood the best chance of getting him out of the wilderness alive. But he could decide tomorrow. Pushing off major life decisions never went badly, right?

After loading up his campfire with the biggest piece of deadwood he could find, to hopefully give him something to work with in the morning, he retired for the evening.

Hopefully it won't rain, that would be annoying. Does feel a bit like it might be coming, though, Edwin mused as he shifted in his bed, then berated himself for even thinking something that might tempt fate. Fortunately, though, the real world *didn't work like that.* As he fell asleep, he almost believed it, too.

Level Up!
Sleeping Level 4→5

CHAPTER 8

A Stormy Disposition

A crash of thunder jolted Edwin awake. After a few confused moments spent drowsily trying to recall where he was and what was going on, he mentally groaned. *Darn it. I knew I jinxed it. Things were just going* too *smoothly for me, weren't they?*

Peeking outside his shelter, Edwin got just a moment of warning from the pitter-patter of endless raindrops falling upon the canopy. Then, the heavens opened up and an absolute downpour of rain extinguished what few embers were left of his campfire, making him silently curse. He'd never get it started again now. While he vaguely wished that he could have had the fire inside his little cave, there simply wasn't even enough room to stockpile more than a few pieces of dry wood, let alone manage an open flame, to say nothing of the inherent flammability of his bed.

Still, he really couldn't do anything about it now. Just hunker down and hope it blew over by tomor—

Level Up!
Basic Mana Sense Level 8→11

Edwin's *entire body* lit up with the crackling, staticky feeling he'd come to associate with magic, the most he'd ever experienced.

Touching the rock above him, he jolted back after barely brushing it, in a way reminiscent of touching a live wire—his boulder was positively *brimming* with magic. It wasn't *quite* as strong as a live wire, but it was still at the point where it was almost painful to touch. He rushed out from under his cover, trying to get as far away from whatever was making it so hypercharged, figuring he could deal with a bit of rain better than magical rocks. He got out just in time, as the *entire boulder* was wrenched suddenly from the ground it was so firmly embedded in and flew into the air, leaving a gaping hole where it once was. It crashed into the canopy with such speed that the enormous branches it broke off from the trees above didn't fall to the ground but were instead carried along with the massive projectile into the sky.

Congratulations! For reaching level 12 in Basic Mana Sense, you have unlocked the Mage Path!
Level Up!
Basic Mana Sense Level 11→14

Ooh, *Mage* Path? Screw Explorer, he was getting *magic* when he got up to 60 Skill Points.

Far above him, Edwin could just barely make out his former shelter as it joined a handful of similarly sized boulders orbiting a seemingly empty point. Then lightning flashed, and by straining his eyes as much as he could, he was able to just barely make out a tiny black dot in the center of the circling stones.

Level Up!
Seeing Level 8→9

Was that … a person? If so, that was both a *terrifying* prospect—that someone could have that much power—but also thrilling, because it doubled down his desire to get magic. Both to maybe wield that kind of power himself one day, and also just because it was *magic*, and what sort of self-respecting scientist *didn't* want to break the laws of reality over their knee? Oh, something was happening again. Edwin moved to get a better view of what it was, barely feeling the rain pounding down on and all around him as he focused on the mage.

The boulders spun up, faster and faster, blurring together until he could barely distinguish them from one another—

Level Up!
Seeing Level 9→10

Okay, that was getting annoying. Disabling automatic notifications for the moment ...

And then one of the rocks flew forward at a devastating speed, only to be intercepted by a bolt of lightning, shattering the boulder and lighting up the sky. Now that he had a clear idea of where to look, Edwin could just barely make out another speck far up in the sky. Was that *another* person?

Edwin lost track of the second person as the dot darted away, and the sky lit up with lightning. The vast majority of the bolts struck the orbiting shield of rocks, shattering several of the boulders, but a lot of the lightning cascaded all the way to the ground. For the briefest of moments, the entire mountain lit up from the brilliance of dozens of simultaneous lightning strikes; then it went dark and the thunder boomed.

Even with covered ears, Edwin felt as though his eardrums were going to burst. A pressure wave rolled over him, and he came to the snap realization that perhaps watching two insanely powerful mages clash in the skies above *wasn't* the best idea. It seemed as though he wasn't the only thing with the idea to run far and run fast, either, as he saw several other creatures burst from the surroundings and join in a massive wave of terrified animals.

Behind him, he heard more peals of thunder, almost omnidirectionally reverberating through the woods, and he redoubled his sprint to get literally anywhere else. He'd never remember how to get back to his cave, but that hardly mattered now. He was just glad that he had everything important on him already.

Every once in a while, he'd feel the buzz from his Mana Sense, usually followed by a chunk of terrain being ripped from the ground nearby or a bolt of lightning striking too close for comfort. Edwin diverted around a stream too wide to jump over, an assessment the deer-things he was running alongside clearly disagreed with. They cleanly outpaced him and bounded into the air, soaring what must have been twenty feet off the ground and twice as far horizontally only to land effortlessly and continue their prance on the far side of the river. Within moments, they had vanished into the bushes, taking with them any possible lingering doubts Edwin had about animals having Skills. There was no way that sort of thing was possible with normal biology and physics.

Sadly, Edwin was still limited by such things, at least for the time being, and so had to resort to running parallel to the riverbank, doing his best to keep his feet from getting stuck in the mud. He pretty much succeeded, and even when he chanced a glance behind him—another massive bolt of lightning forked across the sky as he did so—he managed to not trip.

He wasn't sure whether to be proud of that fact or ashamed *about* potentially feeling proud of it, but it was proven moot either way a moment later when the ground shook beneath him and knocked Edwin from his feet into a solid face-plant in the mud. A series of further crashes kept him from regaining his footing at first, but he managed to adapt to the series of minor earthquakes before too long.

Edwin, fueled by desperation and a not-insignificant amount of adrenaline, kept running upward until he saw sunlight. The river had shrunk to a small brook, but it was bursting its banks with water. It was well past daybreak—the sun had clearly already risen well beyond the horizon—but it took far longer for the clouds to finally allow a few haggard rays of weak, watery sunshine through. Considering it had been at least a minute since any tremors or peals of thunder had reverberated through the landscape, it seemed the battle had finally stopped. Exhausted, Edwin turned around and let himself look at the scene below.

It looked like a hurricane had passed through, which, Edwin supposed, it sort of had. Plants were flattened, sections of the forest were covered in uprooted and splintered trees, and there were even a few boulders lying here and there, which he could spot if he looked closely. It was a complete and total wasteland, and … trying to navigate it probably wouldn't go very well. If he descended again, he stood a decent chance of having something fall on him or falling into an inescapable hole himself. No, going back down the mountain wasn't a feasible option right now, not with the current condition of the mountainside.

So he was going to stay up here, it seemed. There weren't as many trees this far up, the landscape instead favoring hardy-looking grasses and a few scraggly bushes, and the air was noticeably chilly in comparison to the forest. He wouldn't be able to stay up here for long, though the more open ground meant he might have more luck spotting proper civilization.

While he sat down to recover his breath, Edwin triggered his notifications, letting the numbers wash over him.

Level Up!
Seeing Level 10→11
Walking Level 9→14
Athletics Level 13→16
Basic Mana Sense Level 14→15

That brought Edwin to ... 58 Skill Points, presumably just two shy of getting magic of his own. He couldn't wait. It still left him with the question of where to go now, though. Really, he was back to more or less square one. His chear grove was most likely destroyed, or at least impossible to find again, so he needed to track down more food. His cave, after all that work put he'd into it, was absolutely gone, destroyed before his very eyes, and he needed a new place to shelter.

Not really seeing any other options, Edwin set off on a path toward the sun. There didn't seem to be any mountains that way, and going in a cardinal direction should hopefully help him avoid going in circles.

The view was spectacular from up here. Looking down the mountain, past the devastation wrought by the mages, Edwin could see an entire tapestry of greens laid out before him. Beyond that, it all blurred together, but he could imagine the signs of civilization in the sprawling lands beyond.

It really was chilly up here, but walking at least kept Edwin warm enough. Overhead, a few flocks of birds swooped across the sky. To the south, some magnificently snow-capped peaks loomed high above him, almost seeming to stretch to the sky.

Level Up!
Walking Level 14→15

One more Skill leveling-up to go. It was getting harder to level up his Skills, though he was still making a little bit of progress, he could tell.

Finally, Edwin got what he was waiting for.

Level Up!
Breathing Level 7→8

Bit of an odd one, though Edwin supposed it had been quite a while since it had leveled up. He eagerly opened his Status and dumped all his Skill Points into the Mage Path.

Mana level set to ... 1
You have unlocked a new Attribute!
Mana
Done!
...
Calculating Rewards ...
Class Change!
Outsider → Outsider Novice
You have completed the Mage Path!
You may be an outsider to this world, but that does not stop you from seizing what power has presented itself to you, bringing the world to your fingertips. Your potential has been awakened, and from great heights you will accomplish great things.

For the first time, Edwin actually *felt* the change as it happened, his body beginning to tingle with magic from the moment the final notification came through. While the sensation spread out mostly evenly across his body, it was most pronounced in the space between his collarbones, so much so that Edwin looked down and prodded the skin there just to make sure it wasn't glowing or had otherwise visibly changed.

Despite the lack of visual indication, he felt a bit of mana attached to his fingertips, clinging to it like a film, which quickly faded away. A few more tries yielded the same result, with no obvious effect beyond setting his Mana Sense off. Still though, *magic!* It was like the message said, he had the world at his fingertips—literally.

Level Up!
Basic Mana Sense Level 15→16

This is awesome, Edwin couldn't help but think, disabling level-up notifications for the time being, *I'm magical. Sure, I suppose the System is basically magic, regardless of what my Mana Sense ... Manareception? Arcanoception? Something like that, anyway. Regardless of what my Mana Sense may say, the System is magical, but it still feels different from this. So ... magic! You're a wizard, Edwin.*

Even as he continued his walking, and the day started passing into the late afternoon, Edwin kept trying to play with his brand-new *magic.* Sadly, none of the standard fantasy tropes for mastering magic that he knew about were helping. It didn't pulse with his breath, didn't crackle to the touch, didn't respond to gestures and words. Picking up a stick and waving it like a wand didn't do anything except make Edwin feel silly, and visualizing a fire in his chest made no difference either.

Hopefully, he could figure this out in a reasonable length of time, and once he did, it would be easier to build on. Magic would probably be hard enough to learn without needing some special dance or taking an hour to get his mana flowing each time. The speed at which the two fighters had been throwing attacks out earlier in the day had suggested it would be quick once Edwin was good at magic, but the scale at which they did so also suggested they were very, *very* good at it. Maybe novice magicians needed a half hour to light a candle or whatever.

But okay, magic. His Basic Mana Sense had acclimated to it somewhat, but while he no longer felt pins and needles dancing across his skin, Edwin could still sense the power radiating from his chest into his limbs. He tried visualizing it as a miniature sun, throwing off magic in the form of light.

During one break from walking, he tried sitting and meditating for a while, breathing carefully and trying to feel every part of his body. Granted, he had never done proper meditation before, but as sore as Edwin may have been, he was able to sit in the lotus position, so he was basically doing it, right? Nothing worked. He even tried calling on his magic in much the same way he had unlocked Identify and Status, or how he used his Almanac, but no amount of thinking "magic" really hard made it work.

Why couldn't this stupid Skill have come with a user manual? Edwin mentally groused, even as he started the process of looking around for a shelter to spend the night in.

It wasn't quite dark, but the incomplete night of sleep meant he was rather tired already. Eventually, he settled down under a tiny outcropping of rock, sheltered from the winds but still shivering. There were a few small trees nearby, and after some time working on them with his knife, he had a small pile of twigs that were … probably dry enough to light. Unfortunately, he was having about as much luck getting a spark as the first time he'd rubbed two sticks together.

If only I had my magic working. All I'd need to do then is snap my fingers, and boom. Instant campfire. Even easier with my … Firestarting … Skill. Edwin sat back on his haunches. *Could it be that easy?* he wondered.

Holding his hand out over the stack of sticks, he snapped his fingers, using his Skill in a way he hadn't tried before. Instead of just accepting whatever passive benefit it might provide, he tried triggering it manually, focusing its effects into a single moment of time.

Firestarting.

No response. Undeterred, he coated his fingers with mana, touching his fingertips to his chest, and tried again.

Firestarting.

He felt a bit of heat from his fingers, but that was it. Edwin's eyes narrowed. That proved that he could make this work, theoretically. He just needed to keep at it.

Firestarting.

It felt like trying to pick up a puddle of water. His metaphorical fingers just passed straight through, with nothing to grasp.

Hmm. He could do this.

Firestarting. Firestarting. Firestarting.

Okay, maybe he couldn't. Well, if he couldn't pick up the puddle of water, maybe he could … wipe it up? Could he *de*-activate the Skill, and maybe get some insight from that action?

He marshalled his Skill muscles and tried to wipe away the small puddle that was his Firestarting Skill. Much to his surprise, he *could* move it, though it fought his displacement. The more he tried to push it, the more it tried to return to where it was. It wasn't perfect, but … this was as good as he would get.

Firestarting.

He released his grip on the Skill puddle at the same moment he tried to activate it, his mana-coated physical fingers snapping simultaneously. He felt a *click*, and there was a brief flash of blue between his fingers, then sparks rained down on his tinder like embers, setting it ablaze.

Congratulations! For integrating mana into a Skill, you have unlocked the Skilled Arcanist Path!

Congratulations! For using a mana-empowered activated-fire-based Skill you have unlocked the Novice Pyromancer Path!

You have unlocked the Basic Mana Manipulation Skill!

Accept Skill? Y/N

Heck yes.

Basic Mana Manipulation

Lightning! Fireballs! Teleportation! Eh, maybe one day.

Manipulate your personal mana.

Increased capacity per level.

Level Up!

Firestarting Level 3→6

Survival Level 5→6

Basic Mana Sense Level 16→20

Research Level 7→10

Walking Level 15→16
Breathing Level 8→9

Edwin smiled as he drifted off to sleep, but he knew better than to tempt fate by so much as thinking anything positive. Darn it, that was probably too much already, wasn't it? Yeah, he was totally screwed. Hopefully it didn't ... Nope, not finishing that thought.

Level Up!
Sleeping Level 5→6

CHAPTER 9

A Chilly Reception

Edwin woke up shivering. At some point overnight, the cloud cover had returned, and what would have been a light drizzle, when combined with his higher elevation, was instead a dusting of snow. As he yawned himself awake, he watched his breath steam in the frigid air, caught by faint eddies and carried away. He blew on his hands, rubbing them together in an effort to restore feeling to his fingers. After briefly trying and failing to breathe fire—because why *wouldn't* he?—he went back to rubbing his hands together, this time calling faintly on his magic.

Firestarting.

Level Up!
Firestarting Level 6→7
Basic Mana Manipulation Level 1→2

As he had expected and hoped, now that he had a Skill for it, calling on his *magic* was much easier. And if his Skills were this much more effective with what meager amounts of power he had at level 1— well, level 2 now—he could only imagine what he might be able to accomplish once he was able to channel more than an iota of power. Of course, that may have just been because he knew what he was doing this time, but he liked to dream. That Skilled Arcanist Path was looking quite tempting and was *absolutely* the next one he was filling out. He could survive without dedicated Paths for the sake of breaking physics in half. Only, ah … 46—

Level Up!
Mathematics Level 1→2

—*45* points to go. If he was lucky, Basic Mana Manipulation might even upgrade, and wouldn't that be fun? Edwin did wonder how Skill evolution worked, but with only one data point to go off of, it was impossible to say if it was a regular occurrence, something that happened really rarely, or only happened because of his unique Path.

It was a sad day, when Edwin would get distracted from doing *literal magic*, but in fairness, he was getting distracted by other magic and *math*, so it was probably fine.

He wasn't entirely sure how he was able to hold fire, no matter how small, in his hands and not be burned, but maybe it was because it was his own mana. Or maybe it was just too little to properly burn him. Actually, how did he know if magical fire was as hot as normal fire? What if it was just 30 to 50°C and made light some other way? No, it was able to ignite an actual fire yesterday. Maybe it changed temperature in accordance with some unknown variable. He was dealing with actual, physical magic after all, so anything was possible. Maybe it was some sort of conceptual fire, which warmed but didn't consume what it wasn't supposed to.

Honestly, while the last possibility sounded like an absolute *nightmare* to figure out, it also had the most potential in the future if he could get a handle on it. So he wasn't really sure what he hoped. He could get a handle on it when his *life wasn't on the line*, so *stay focused, Edwin.*

All that aside, though, it was really, really cool to watch phantom flames flicker across his palms, keeping them warm. Edwin felt a slight drain on his mana as he kept the Skill active, though nothing major, and something of an odd strain on his mind as he applied his Firestarting Skill in a manner so radically different from its intended use.

He disabled notifications for the time being, not wanting to be distracted by the level-ups as his storm sense was tingling. The air felt heavy, and a slight breeze was starting to pick up, carrying with it the smell of cold mountain air.

While he'd never been caught out in one, Edwin had some inkling that a snowstorm might be moving in, and he wanted some kind of decent shelter before it swept through. He drummed his fingers on the rock in thought. It was a risk to leave what little shelter he had here, but this wasn't really sufficient as it stood.

Should he try going back down the mountain? Eh ... from where he was now, the ground wasn't as torn up as it had been, but at the same time he wasn't sure if he would be able to descend to the tree line again. The terrain was rather treacherous, and he didn't trust his mountaineering skills enough to pick his way down the mountain again.

Could he backtrack? No ... not really, because then he'd be dealing with the mages' battleground again. He would push on for now, keeping an eye out for either better shelter or some way back down the mountain.

Edwin nodded to himself and stood up, letting the fire die as he stretched and started his hike across the mountainside.

The frosted ground crunched under his feet, and as his footprints receded into the distance, eventually covered by a continued dusting of snow, Edwin seriously wished he was wearing warmer clothes. But why would he have been? So far as he could remember, he had just been in the lab taking measurements, when he suddenly vanished. Really, he should consider himself lucky he was even wearing his jacket, as thin as it may be.

What *really* confused him was how he stayed fully clothed but lost his glasses and everything in his pockets, basically anything that might have possibly been useful in his world-hop. Even his watch had disappeared into the possibly literal ether. But at least everything he did have was in pristine condition.

Around him, the wind started to pick up, knifing through what woefully few layers of fabric Edwin was wearing and leaving him chilled to the bone. He needed to find some kind of shelter soon and was starting to regret having left his boulder to try to find something better. His previous shelter would have been better than nothing, which was what he'd found so far. Why did he ever leave a place where he could have been comfortable?

Reigniting his hands with Firestarting for a moment, Edwin reassessed his surroundings. There were a couple of tiny shrubs and a windswept tree nearby, but nothing substantial enough to provide any kind of cover from what was looking to be the start of a blizzard. There weren't any good ways down, either. The barren mountainside was silent, save for the whistling of the wind, and the one notable feature—usually a trickling creek, cutting through the landscape—was frozen over, further contributing to the auditory wasteland.

The silence was unnerving, and Edwin, for once, actually longed to hear someone's voice. That truly was strange, Edwin couldn't help but think, as he'd never been that keen on other people. Why would he be? They just tended to talk and talk and talk. It could be nice, when he wanted to find out what was going on, but then they usually wanted some sort of *feedback*, and that meant you had to actually pay attention to what they were saying. He much preferred spending time with people in companionable silence, or with people who were content to just use him as a rubber duck, saying things with the understanding that it would all go in one ear and out the other. Not that there were many of those around …

So on second thought, he was fine as he was now. Going a while without talking to anyone was nice! The silence was soothing. No emotional problems to deal with, no shifts in the web of interpersonal connections to keep track of, no professors to appease. No stressful and unpredictable people to manage. Just him and his Skills, standing up to the endless turbulence of the snowy winds engulfing him. Being alone, in a new world, with nothing but his wits to pit against the elements? That was far more satisfying.

Around Edwin, the world slowly blanketed itself in white, and the fallen snow further muffled what few sounds might survive, save the howling of the wind. Even the *crunch, crunch, crunch* of his footfalls barely reached his ears before they were snatched away and flung to the far corners of the earth. Behind him, his tracks were swiftly covered by the blowing gusts and further filled in by the heavy snow, leaving, as usual, almost no trace of his passage. Still, he carried on. Surely, he'd find somewhere to shelter eventually.

Things were so much easier without distractions. He carried plenty of those along with him everywhere he went. Still, Edwin knew the steps to take, the right things to do in the right situations. It was all a dance, making sure you weren't blown off course by outside interference. So long as you stayed focused on a landmark, some touchpoint to ensure you didn't go in circles, you'd be fine.

Just one foot in front of the other until you either reached your destination or failed. Simple as that. A bit of magical fire staved off frostbite, even as the weather around him continued to worsen, forming half-corporeal figures for mere instants before they were torn apart.

He was on his own. There was nobody to count on, no last-minute rescue team, no hiking partner with extra food and water. Not that there ever was, but the simple knowledge that he would do this on his own—and he *would* do this—kept Edwin going. Just him, trekking across the hostile terrain as he looked for any kind of shelter. He even had *magic* helping him. He could do this. Shelter of some form. The snow was somehow too powdery to make an igloo, yet wet enough to weigh down his every footstep.

Edwin made sure to cast a glance upward around every few steps to ensure nothing new loomed in front of him. After a few failed glances, though, he almost gave up. He *wanted* to give up, but he couldn't. So he kept trying again and again, just in case *this* time he'd find what he was looking for. Something, anything to help keep the pervasive chill away before it became a fully fledged blizzard.

It would be so easy to just admit defeat and dig in. The snow was at least a couple feet deep, and if he got started now, he could probably excavate enough of a trench to lie in it with a small break for the wind … assuming it didn't collapse on him.

If he did that, he might survive the coming storm. At least, so long as it lasted hours rather than days. If it lasted for days, then he was dead already. Shelter wouldn't help in that case, wouldn't keep him alive through such biting winds, wouldn't help him if he started to starve, so why even keep looking? Any benefit it might provide would probably be offset by the effort needed to find it and make it suitable for his purposes.

Ahead of him, Edwin thought he saw another potential shelter—a rock sticking up out of the ground. As he got closer, though, he realized it was just a drift, which collapsed as he approached. Kicking it despondently, he discovered it was built around a tiny bush, which he spent a couple of minutes trying to work into some kind of functional shelter, before finally admitting to himself that he'd never manage to get anything from it. Really, why did he even bother? He should have known that nothing out here would actually serve as a windbreak. He figured that out after just a handful of failed attempts; why would the next attempt be any more successful? No shelter would actually protect him, and his attempts to create them were just wasted effort.

Maybe he shouldn't have left his tiny hollow after all. But if he hadn't, that would have meant admitting defeat before even trying, and consigning the entire day of exploration as a loss, a thought that rankled him. Could he stop right here and make a bank for himself? Maybe. He should stop here.

A gust of wind blew over what little shelter Edwin had constructed within minutes of him starting. He cursed and kicked at the snowpile, trying desperately to keep his fingers from freezing. Okay … maybe he couldn't make a shelter, then. Not if he wanted to keep frostbite away, anyway. He couldn't keep Firestarting active while building a shelter, and without gloves his hands quickly became numb and unresponsive.

Every step now was a struggle, and Edwin's feet were freezing. Not wet, fortunately, that would have been really bad, but still insanely cold. They'd need careful tending to once he found shelter, which had to be close, right? He needed shelter. He'd never make it without. He hoped he could somehow magically stumble over what he needed, but that was wishful thinking. Finding shelter required effort; despite the terminology used, you didn't just *find* it.

The only thing keeping Edwin going at this point was his magic. Every time he stopped to look around, he summoned the ethereal fire to fight off frostbite, then pressed onward. The wind practically threatened to carry him away, whipping up snow all around him and drastically lowering his visibility. All he could make out now were vague impressions of his surroundings at best.

One foot in front of the other ... His footprints were filled in with snow the instant his feet left the ground, and there was no way to know if he was going in circles, save his intuition that uphill was still to his right. Who could really tell at this point? Everything was a white blanket, and he could scarcely distinguish up from down.

Then a misplaced foot brought him tumbling down a small cliff, the snow rendering it all but invisible. While the fall was exactly what he had been trying to *avoid* for so long, he was too tired to care. Down here, it was dry and he was out of the cutting winds. No longer was he at risk of losing himself to the storm. Here, he had comfort and the potential for warmth. In fact, it was perfect.

Edwin breathed a sigh of relief. Falling asleep here wouldn't be permanent. As he huddled into a tiny ball—anything to reduce his contact with the frigid air—and summoned the spectral flames of his magical Firestarter, all he could think as he drifted to sleep was how glad he was that, this time, he hadn't given up.

CHAPTER 10

Let It Burn, Let It Burn, Let It Burn

The storm was raging when Edwin came to. He'd gotten used to waking up cold, and compared to what he was anticipating, he was surprisingly warm for being in the middle of a blizzard. His body heat had been almost entirely trapped inside the tiny space surrounding him, it seemed. It was still quite cold, though, and touching the stone walls of his shelter revealed why, as they sapped away any lingering heat from his already chilled fingertips instantly.

At the top of the bluff was a tiny opening, which was presumably where Edwin had fallen through, and the wind played an eerie tune as it danced across the snowbank. The small cliff had accumulated a pile of snow next to it, with just enough of a gap for a skinny traveler to slip through and spend the night. There was no way there was *actually* twelve feet of snow piled everywhere, right?

Eh, that was something Future-Edwin could deal with. For now, it was time for Present-Edwin to try and fight off frostbite and hypothermia once again. A bit of scrounging around in the snow uncovered a few twigs that he was able to light for a few minutes of fire, which he started with a mere snap of his fingers.

Magic made things *so* easy. Hopefully he could figure out how to integrate mana into some of his other Skills, though there wasn't any immediately obvious way to do that. He called up his notifications as the sticks crackled and melted the snow around them.

Level Up!
Firestarting Level 7→15
Basic Mana Manipulation Level 2→5
Survival Level 5→8
Sleeping Level 5→6
Basic Mana Sense Level 20→21
Seeing Level 11→12
Walking Level 15→17
Breathing Level 8→9
Athletics Level 16→17
Improvisation Level 10→11

Lots of levels. It seemed like near-death experiences were *really* good for advancement. *Lucky me*, he thought bleakly. *So many chances to level up. This is probably a pretty good advancement rate considering I've been here for, what, less than a week? Like, five or six days? Status.*

Name
Edwin Maxlin
Age
22 years
Race
Extraplanar Human
Class
Outsider Novice
Attributes
Mana 1
Skills
Athletics: 17
Basic Mana Sense: 21
Breathing: 9
Firestarting: 15

Flexibility: 8
Identify: 12
Improvisation: 11
Mathematics: 2
Nutrition: 3
Research: 10
Seeing: 12
Sleeping: 6
Outsider's Almanac: 21
Survival: 8
Throwing Weapons: 3
Visualization: 15
Walking: 17

Paths

Skill Points: 37

Next Up

Skilled Arcanist 0/60

Very Much Yes-Eventually

Physical Alchemist 0/90, Micro-Biomancer 0/90, Path Less Traveled
0/90, Realm Traveler 0/120

Promising

Stonehide Vanquisher 0/60, Titan Slayer 0/90, World Traveler 0/60,
Researcher 0/60, Explorer 0/60, Outsider 0/60

Maybe One Day

Survivor 0/60, Linguist 0/60, Athlete 0/60, Daredevil 0/60, Pioneer
0/60, Novice Pyromancer 0/60

Meh

Lumberjack 0/60, Way of the Empty Hand 0/60, Trapper 0/60

No

Beginner 0/30, Novice 0/12, Trainee 0/60

Completed Paths (Expand)

More than halfway to Skilled Arcanist, Edwin thought as he tapped
his chin. *I wonder if there's any other easy Skill levels I could get.*

He glanced upward. Unsurprisingly, the storm hadn't abated at all in
the last five minutes. *Not going back out there if I can help it, that's for sure.*

Edwin's fire was starting to fail, the tiny mass of wood barely holding on after just a few scant minutes of warmth. He started scrounging around in the snow for anything more he might be able to use for fuel, and found a bit but nothing substantial. The fire lasted for a handful of minutes longer before it was down to mere embers, and Edwin found himself huddled against the tiny patch of stone wall heated by his tiny flame, trying to stay warm once more.

Level Up!
Firestarting Level 15→16
Basic Mana Manipulation Level 5→6

After quite a bit of trial and error, Edwin had figured out how to mimic fire-breathing. It required breathing through his cupped hands but was still quite fun.

Level Up!
Firestarting Level 16→17
Basic Mana Manipulation Level 6→7
Breathing Level 9→10

Edwin bit off a curse as his fingers went numb, handling ice-cold snow that he was allowing to slowly melt into a puddle of water in his cupped hands. Eating snow when potentially battling hypothermia was a *Bad Idea*, hence his current dilemma. At least he was able to melt snow directly and quickly this way.

Level Up!
Firestarting Level 17→18
Basic Mana Manipulation Level 7→8
Survival Level 8→9

Edwin carefully pulled off his shoes and socks, holding his ethereal, dancing blue flames close to his toes, hoping to get feeling back in them and chase off any potential for frostbite. It was the first time he had really looked at his feet in the past couple of days, and he was somewhat impressed at how calloused they had gotten and relieved he hadn't had to deal with too many blisters. His shoes may be well-loved and somewhat water resistant, but they were still very much *not* made for several days of hiking through mud and snow and it showed. At least he was wearing warm socks. It was the small mercies, sometimes.

Level Up!
Firestarting Level 18→19
Basic Mana Manipulation Level 8→9

It was getting late, but the storm continued to rage outside. Edwin hoped it would die down soon. He wasn't the most nourished, having only eaten chears for the past several days, and would need all the energy he could muster to find his next shelter and next source of food. The battle in the sky had shown him not only that the wilderness was *decidedly* not safe even if he managed to figure out something sustainable, but also that there had to be some form of society nearby.

Or, he bleakly thought, *there* was *nothing anywhere close and that's why the two insanely powerful mages decided to settle their spat out here where nobody would get hurt.* That thought wasn't actionable, though, so it was best left ignored.

Hopefully the snow wouldn't take too long to melt away, either. If it were truly as deep as the wall of snow he kept staring at suggested, he'd never get out. However, if that was just the result of how the wind was blowing, there was no telling how long it would take to go away.

Basically, if this was a snowstorm heralding the start of winter, Edwin was dead. If this snowstorm lasted more than a week, he was dead. If the snow collapsed on him, he was dead. If there really were drifts of snow almost twice his height, he was dead.

However, if this was an out-of-season or perhaps end-of-season blizzard, and it stopped soon, *and* the snow wasn't all that deep, he might still make it out alive. What a way to go, though. To have survived a bear the size of a truck, found food and water, endured a nigh-apocalyptic battle of individuals he may as well have been an ant in comparison to, and found shelter from a blizzard, only to die of starvation because he couldn't go looking for food.

He could also summon fire with a snap of his fingers, though, so coming to a new world wasn't all bad. He hadn't left that many people behind, anyway. And they would most likely think he was dead, what with up and vanishing in the middle of the day, so passing away in a snowbank wouldn't change much as far as everyone else was concerned. Just another face in the crowd, anonymous and forgotten as the tides of people swept by, carrying off any not secure in themselves.

The light in his shelter faded, until only the flickering illumination heralding from his magical flame remained. Edwin sighed. Even if the storm did stop, he wasn't going anywhere in the dark. He melted himself another handful of water and went to bed.

Level Up!
Firestarting Level 19→20
Sleeping Level 6→7

Whatever it was exactly that his Sleeping Skill affected, it did wonders to make Edwin feel more fully rested. Cold, hard ground or not, he didn't feel any more tired than a standard rough night of sleep would have yielded back in his room with a mattress, pillow, and blankets. An actual bed, no matter how poor quality, would probably feel like heaven right now.

The blizzard seemed to have abated overnight, and Edwin could see glimpses of blue sky above. After a quick bout with Firestarter to warm himself up, Edwin used the Skill to melt some holes in the sheet of ice. About a minute of pressing his hands to the wall later, he broke free, stumbling forward and crashing through to the other side, coating himself with a thin layer of powdered snow. After brushing himself off, he was able to look back and assess his temporary shelter in the light of day and with more than two feet of visibility.

As he had suspected, it was indeed the result of snow being pushed off the edge of a small cliff, the precise angle having left a gap between the rock and ice. Around him, the snow was probably at most only a foot or two thick, though in areas not as sheltered from the winds it was significantly deeper. The sun felt *heavenly*, and he just stood and basked in its gentle radiance for a few minutes. It wasn't as warm as his flames, for sure, but he didn't have to constantly fight the sunlight to keep it in place.

As the sun continued to shine across the snow-covered slopes, Edwin found himself having to make sure he wasn't blinded from the bright light glaring off the vividly white banks.

Level Up!
Seeing Level 12→13

The uniform color of the landscape had one extremely beneficial aspect to it, though. It was *incredibly easy* to spot anything that didn't conform to the same dimensionless white as the rest of his surroundings. That was, after all, how Edwin managed to spot an oddly black line bisecting a hill some distance away. He couldn't tell what it was exactly, but it didn't *look* like a river—too straight—and the landscape didn't sit in a way supportive of one.

Of course, there was a big difference between seeing an odd landmark in the distance and then actually *getting* there. As Edwin walked, he amused himself by seeing when exactly his Identify stopped recognizing a handful of snow *as* snow and started returning results for water instead.

Level Up!
Outsider's Almanac Level 21→22

Oh, cool. That hadn't leveled up in a little while, not that he had been using it all that much. A quick test showed his new character cap was at 37, which would … probably … let him figure out the formula if he weren't running on a week of rough sleep, no food, and very little water, and probably suffering from low-grade hypothermia. Numbers floated by his head, and he tried to grab them, but he didn't make much progress, Mathematics Skill or no.

His head was starting to feel fuzzy, but he kept pushing on nonetheless. The cold air was somewhere between bracing and extremely uncomfortable, but Edwin wasn't sure where exactly it fell. Or maybe it was both simultaneously?

Level Up!
Breathing Level 10→11
Walking Level 17→18

Only eight Skill levels to go, then … He'd take Survivor, he decided. His brain was fuzzy, but he needed to prioritize living over magic, as much as it pained him to think. It was a bit strange how often two Skills would level at the exact same time. Maybe there was some form of shared Skill growth between them. Or maybe improving one managed to provide just enough of whatever magical energy made level-ups happen to push the next-closest one over the edge. Or perhaps they didn't actually happen at the same time, just close enough to both be logged at once—he wasn't sure what his System's refresh rate was. Seconds? Minutes? Variable? Probably variable, in all honesty. Though variable based on what?

"Further testing required," Edwin half mumbled, half whispered, his throat dry and vocal cords decidedly feeling their lack of use. He stumbled his way through the wintry landscape, scratches and bruises making themselves known once more, though nowhere near as painful as before, a few good nights of sleep and rest doing wonders for him. His recovery was, admittedly, perhaps equally offset by just how numb his legs and feet were at the moment. Even those blisters he was so happy to have escaped were starting to come out in full force as snowmelt trickled down his legs and left his socks soaking.

Level Up!
Athletics Level 17→18

After hours of struggling through snow that reached almost to his waist at times, Edwin finally found himself in front of the black band that had caught his eye from so far away, and he looked at it with a measure of disbelief.

It was a road. A giant, apparently well-maintained road without so much as a speck of snow to be seen on it.

CHAPTER 11

Roadside Assessment

Edwin couldn't help but stare. It was such a radical departure from everything else he'd seen the past few days, he had to rub his eyes and check again to ensure he wasn't hallucinating. Then, he carefully inched his foot onto the ... road, hoping it wasn't a trap or some sort of illusion or harmful in some other crazy way.

When he did not, in fact, have his foot immediately bitten off, he stepped out onto the surface fully and nearly collapsed as a wave of comfort and warmth washed over him, accompanied by the buzzing of magic.

While Edwin managed to avoid staggering to the ground immediately, his legs eventually gave out from under him enough that he was driven to his knees, before sitting down on the strange, smooth black stone. It felt heated, warm but not uncomfortable. Presumably, that was an antisnow measure, but keeping such a massive piece of infrastructure warm in the surrounding snow must have been *insanely* expensive.

It was a surefire sign of civilization, though, and for that Edwin was thrilled. He was on a new world, and who knew what sort of person he might be able to make himself into, when not held back by his past and people's prior conceptions of who he was.

Edwin tried to stand up, but with his legs acting decidedly nonco-operatively, he instead found himself becoming quite well-acquainted with the road beneath him. On closer inspection, the rock—What was it, anyway? He couldn't place it—had a faint texture on it, presumably to aid traction, and appeared to be a single, continuous stone without a single gap or seam.

Right along the edge, on closer inspection, were nigh-invisible sigils, only visible because Edwin's nose was two inches away from the rune in question. Probably, it was related to whatever magical nonsense made this sort of structure possible to begin with. What kind of Skill would that be, anyway? Runistry?

Level Up!
Basic Mana Sense Level 21→22

Whatever it was, it was impressive. Probably meant to keep the road clear, clean, warm, and in good repair. Edwin couldn't see so much as a speck of dirt on its surface, after all. It was so, so warm. Oh man, that felt good. Ah …

Any reservations Edwin may have had about falling asleep on the side of a road were quickly overruled by a nigh-unanimous veto by the rest of his body. This was the warmest and most comfortable he had felt since he'd fallen out of the *literal sky*, and ironically, the road was probably the cleanest bed he'd had thus far. The buzzing of his Basic Mana Sense was annoying, so he turned it off, closing the metaphorical eye involved. He could practically feel the tension drain out of his muscles as he just let himself … slip … away …

Level Up!
Sleeping Level 7→8

Edwin woke up briefly as the sun was rising, completely warm for the first time in a long time, but he just muttered something, incomprehensible even to himself, and fell back to sleep.

A branch started poking into his side as he slept, and Edwin absently went to shove it away and resume sleeping, but it moved in response to his attempted swat and began insistently prodding into his stomach, which had been exposed by his movement. It took a moment, but Edwin eventually came to, blinking the sleep out of his eyes at first and then scared the rest of the way awake as he became aware he was literally face-to-face with something with a *very* large mouth.

Edwin scrambled back, getting some distance away from whatever thing was so close to his head, and realized he was looking at a goat. A very large, *very* hairy goat but a goat nonetheless. It had to have been at least as twice as big as him and was laden with a lot of heavy-looking bags, which was what finally brought his attention to the figure standing next to the goat.

It seemed the entity responsible for prodding him in the side was a dwarf. That was the *overwhelming* first impression Edwin got of him. Short? Check. As hairy as his goat? Check. Sporting a beard that covered more than half of his face? *Very* check. The dwarf stood looking at Edwin warily, holding a mean-looking pickaxe somewhat loosely as he peered at Edwin through something that resembled smoked goggles, one of the few things visible beyond his *massive* red beard. Honestly, he couldn't have looked more of a stereotypical dwarf if he tried.

"Sa! Solsiniwash! Thas fanishel tankaile lae sorwal!" His tone was quite insistent, though the words he was saying were utter nonsense.

"Wha-What?" Edwin choked out, vocal cords protesting at their sudden usage, as he stared at the first person he had seen in Joriah (the dueling mages didn't count). "I can't understand you."

"Sa thas tankaile lae!" the dwarf tried again, to which Edwin could only dumbly shake his head in response.

"I. Do not. Understand. You." Edwin repeated the words slowly, doing his best to pantomime each word.

"Sa cavelstin? Sorwe shollen cilath." The dwarf seemed less angry now, more confused. "Sa kiltana-shoshal? Sovish? Teltelki? Farsia? Vollok?"

Edwin lamely shrugged at what was clearly a question, and at that, the dwarf sighed and started walking up the mountain, waving after himself in a clear indication that Edwin was to follow him. Without any kind of viable alternative, and excited at the prospect of seeing new people, Edwin followed along. Once the dwarf and the goat were back in range, he Identified the pair.

Inheritor of the Bringer of Radiant Gold and Good Fortune
Adult Torvelk Goat

Huh. That seemed like an … impressive Class name. A bit unwieldy, perhaps, but that may have just been the translation from whatever language the Inheritor spoke. Certainly more impressive than Edwin's. He couldn't help but wonder what kinds of Classes were typical, and how much stronger than him everyone must be.

Hopefully this wouldn't be too long of a walk, though it was *far* easier than the sorts of treks he had been doing recently. The road cut straight through several ups and downs in the terrain, with the ground directly below the road either dug out or filled in at times to accommodate as needed; it was always inclined at what felt like, but couldn't possibly have been, an apparently uniform angle and the surface never had any holes, cracks, slippery patches, or any other obstruction.

It *had* to be magic, Edwin thought as they walked along one stretch of mountainside that hadn't melted yet. The snow was piled up high on either side of the road and perfectly cut off at its edge, without so much as a single snowflake on the black stone. Really, it was eerie just how *perfect* it all was. It would put the quality of nearly any road Edwin had seen back on Earth to shame, though it was really only sized for foot traffic from the looks of it.

The dwarf must have had a high level in Walking, as it had been about two hours of hiking uphill at this point, and even Edwin was starting to flag. He had gotten a level-up in his own Walking Skill some time ago, which was usually a sign he had walked enough to need a break, but his companion hadn't so much as slowed by a hair. Edwin was run ragged, the comfort the road exuded slowly eroding the near-constant state of adrenaline he had been running on for the last week. He was nearly at the end of what he could feasibly accomplish when what had to be their destination *finally* came into view.

Ahead of them, set into an exposed cliff face of the mountain, was an enormous door. On either side of the gate, depictions of snakelike dragons were carved into the same kind of black stone that the road was made of, and carved above the apex of the colossal work of masonry was what looked like the bust of a dwarf, his massive beard captured in intense glory.

Drawing closer revealed that "massive" might have been an understatement. The door was at least a hundred feet tall and absolutely covered in all manner of intricate carvings and inscriptions. From his cursory examination, it looked to Edwin like a story of some form was being told, and the carvings telling it were almost fractal in nature, larger pictures being composed of smaller pieces of art, with those in turn composed of their own smaller carvings until the detail was too small for him to see. The door itself looked *utterly* impractical, and it would be more likely to get an A grade on a Professor Schwer test than for the door to actually open, if physics had anything to say about it.

For a moment, Edwin thought—kind of half hoped, really—that he might be proven wrong, but then the Inheritor moved off to the side of the road, to the base of the doorframe. He knocked on a part of the wall and said something incomprehensible to the raw stone.

After a moment had passed, that section of the wall was drawn up in the blink of an eye, revealing a dark passage behind it. While Edwin was initially hesitant to enter such an ominous-looking passage, a glance from the dwarf and what seemed like a barked order to follow had him hesitantly tagging along behind the goat. What else was he supposed to do, anyway? Stay on the outside?

Right after Edwin stepped past the threshold, the door behind him suddenly ... vanished. There was no sound, no rush of wind, just the sudden cessation of light from behind him, plunging the tunnel into complete and total darkness.

As his eyes adjusted, Edwin realized it wasn't *completely* dark, but instead was lit by some very, very dim magical crystals set into the walls. The stone in here wasn't immaculately carved as was the outer door; rather it was composed of the same smooth, featureless black rock as the road.

Level Up!
Seeing Level 13→14

As he progressed along the winding corridor, Edwin noticed a few tiny holes in the walls. They looked like arrow slits, which he presumed meant this passage was meant to function as a sort of gatehouse in case … wherever this was found itself under attack.

The corridor didn't stretch on too far, and as it rounded the final bend, Edwin was able to see the inside of this stronghold properly and it took his breath away. Everything he could see was carved out of a single piece of black rock, trimmed in gold in several key locations. Stairs, which really shouldn't have been capable of supporting their own weight, stretched to balconies far above. Gems were set into the floor in a handful of prominent positions, causing the room to sparkle with multicolored light.

At first, Edwin wasn't able to tell *where* the orangish-yellow light pervading the entire space emanated from, but then he realized the massive cavern was *lit* by glowing rivers of molten metal, flowing through stone troughs and falling in waterfalls across the space. Most notably, it flowed in a trench right in front of Edwin, between the door and the rest of the citadel, with only a single bridge connecting the two sides. It couldn't have been practical to do something like that, by *any* stretch of the imagination, but what a *sight* it made.

In the distance, Edwin could hear the sound of metal striking metal almost rhythmically, a smithy surely the source of the percussive beat. The air was warm, dry, and smelled like iron, perhaps unsurprisingly given the rivers of molten metal—he just *couldn't* get over that aspect. It was just so *cool* and properly fantasy. There were a few dwarves walking around, though they all moved with purpose and sadly none were within his Identify range.

Was he being called? He was probably being called. The dwarf—the one Edwin had tagged with "The Guy Who Found Me on the Road" using Outsider's Almanac—was gesturing at Edwin while talking to another dwarf with a black beard no less massive than the first's. The goat, for its part, was nowhere to be seen. Still, it seemed as though Edwin was being summoned, and so he joined the two dwarves as they talked, though he kept getting distracted by the architecture, particularly the stone bridge over the molten metal—would it have killed them to include guardrails? He wasn't able to follow the conversation anyway, and all he learned from Identify was that the other dwarf was a "Chief Goldworker." On a whim, Edwin tagged that dwarf with "Welcome Party," because why not?

Level Up!
Identify Level 12→13
Outsider's Almanac Level 22→23

A few minutes of quite animated talking later, the Goldworker tossed a small pouch of what sounded like coins to the other dwarf, then snapped his fingers and motioned for Edwin to follow him. With a shrug (and hoping he hadn't just been sold into slavery), he did so and was led up a fairly prominent staircase, into what must have been the throne room for whatever dwarf king ruled this city.

On either side of the throne, made of wrought silver and gold, were about a half-dozen statues of what were likely the previous rulers of wherever this was. Either they were all male or dwarven ladies also had beards, but the detail on the statues was incredible. Even without his glasses, Edwin could still practically make out individual hairs on their beards. Only one of the statues, one of the two closest to the throne, was made of the same black stone as the city and road, though. Weird. He had thought they had a pretty clear aesthetic going on, but apparently not.

And there was more talking. Great. Edwin didn't have much patience for this sort of thing when he could *understand* what was being said, to say nothing of when he couldn't, and he was practically dead on his feet at this point besides. There were more of the glowing rivers of metal around here, too. It was so cool to watch and— Oh. His attention was being grabbed.

The king, who had suddenly appeared, said something, and then another thing, and a third thing. Each time he spoke, it sounded like a different language, but it was all gibberish to Edwin so he could only shrug in response regardless. The dwarf king, apparently somewhat perturbed by this development, stroked his black beard, even more impressive than any Edwin had seen so far, it must be said—it had various trinkets braided into it—and called out to someone. From off to the side, another new dwarf appeared.

This new dwarf's beard was much smaller than the others he had seen so far, thus gaining an immediate appellation in Edwin's mind, and after skittering into the room and bowing to the king, Smallbeard turned to Edwin and somewhat nervously motioned for him to, once again, follow along.

Edwin had the distinct feeling that he was just getting passed along from dwarf to dwarf until someone figured out what to do with him, but he was warm, mostly comfortable, and saw the potential for an actual *bed*, so he played along. He could really only imagine what he must look like at this point. Scruffy, unkempt hair, dirty and tattered clothing, and even skinnier than usual. At least he *looked* the part of a haggard survivor. Still, where was Smallbeard taking him? A quick check revealed he was a Page of the Graven Word, so maybe going to a librarian or scholar of some sort? Not sure how useful that would be, though. There was no way anyone here would know English; they'd be stuck with pantomimes for some time, until Edwin could puzzle together enough words from Dwarven to explain what had happened, and wouldn't *that* be a fun time …

His suspicions were proven correct as Smallbeard stopped, knocked on a door, then led Edwin into a fairly spacious room, lined utterly with books. Sitting off to one side was a bespectacled silver-bearded dwarf, who turned to the newcomers to the library, adjusted his glasses, and spoke in perfect modern English, without so much as a hint of an accent, "Ah, Thrandin. What have you brought me today?"

CHAPTER 12

A "Talk" with "Friends"

"You speak English?" Edwin blurted out, followed promptly by him choking over his own words and descending into a coughing fit. Small-beard—Thrandin?—said something in Dwarven, and the librarian stroked the tip of his silver beard.

"Lost Outsider, brought in by Soralash, native language of … English, you said?" The last part was directed at Edwin, who managed to pause his coughing long enough to nod.

"Can I get some water?" he croaked out. "Sorry, I haven't talked much lately."

"Certainly. Thrandin, would you fetch a tankard of water for our guest here? He shall need his voice at full capacity. And a mug for myself. Much obliged." He dismissed Thrandin—Edwin made sure to update his Almanac tag for him; no *way* he would remember that name otherwise—and turned back to face Edwin, motioning at a stone chair with some *very* comfortable-looking cushions on it. "Please, take a seat. This won't take long, hopefully. I simply need to ask a few questions, then, Ancestors willing, we can help you however you need."

Relieved, Edwin sank into his chair, his legs in bliss upon finally being given a break. He was about to speak when a knock on the door yielded ~~Thoro~~ *Thrandin* (Almanac already proving itself useful) bearing a metal cup filled with water and a black stone tankard full of some steaming liquid. Edwin gratefully accepted the metal mug as it was offered, and drank deeply, sputtering for a moment but recovering. "Sorry. I haven't been able to get a solid drink in ... I don't know how long."

"Truly? Oh, apologies for my rudeness. I am Rashin, resident diplomat of Clan Blackstone, and you are?" Rashin—whom Edwin took the opportunity to Identify as a "First Inheritor of the Blackstone Tapestry"—prompted. The man's voice washed over Edwin like a warm blanket, reassuring him and allowing the stress and tension of the road to fall away.

"Edwin. Edwin Maxlin. How can you understand me, if you don't even know what English is? Is it a Skill?"

"Very astute of you, young Outsider. Indeed, I have the Polyglot Skill, which enables me to make myself understood in and to understand all languages. Very useful when examining the Records, and similarly excellent to have when, to provide a random example, an Outsider is found half dead on the surface road." Rashin's eyes sparkled like pale emeralds. "May I inquire as to what has brought you to the hallowed Blackstone citadel halls?"

"Well ..." Edwin hesitated, not really sure how much to divulge. "I woke up farther down the mountain a few days ago, sort of wandered around for a little while, fled up the slope from a battle a couple days ago, got stuck in a blizzard, then discovered the road leading to here. I was found on the road and brought up here ... Wherever 'here' is, anyway." He shrugged, then shook his head. "Actually, before we get into that, I have a question. What's an Outsider?"

"You are, are you not? That's your Class, if nothing else, surely?"

"You can ... Oh! That's what Identify returns, right."

"You're a smart one, aren't you?"

"Um, thanks? That's what people tell me, anyway. But I'm not sure I believe them."

"Nonsense! I assure you, all intelligent people feel much the same as you. Myself included, if I might be so bold." He laughed, and Edwin's heart lifted, a grin creeping onto his face for the first time in quite a while.

"Thank you," he said honestly. It was always nice when strangers complimented him. They, unlike people who knew him personally, didn't have any stake in sparing his feelings. "But Outsider? It seems like they're something you've known about before."

"An Outsider is one who comes from, well, outside of Joriah," Rashin explained, and Edwin felt some hope rise in his heart despite himself. "Personally, I thought they were a myth. Useful to explain why some parts of Joriah are the way they are, but not *actually* based in reality."

"I think I follow"—ah, sweet water. Who knew it could taste so good?

"How did you come to Joriah?" Rashin asked, sipping his drink, though Edwin had yet to see the dwarf's mouth. Did the beverage go through his beard? Did he even *have* a mouth? Even ~~Smallb~~ Thrandin's comparatively tiny beard still utterly hid the lower half of his face. How might that ... Oh wait, Rashin was waiting for an answer.

"I don't know. Last thing I remember, I was working on my research project, and the next thing I knew, I was falling from the sky. Crashed in the woods, and well ..." Edwin spread out his hands to indicate *here I am.*

"It truly is fortuitous that you arrived here. Did you know of the existence of Clan Blackstone before today?"

"No. How could I have?"

"I must ask, I'm sure you understand. Do you intend to bring any harm upon Clan Blackstone as a whole or to any of its members?"

What kind of question was *that*? "No. Do you have a Skill that allows you to distinguish the truth from lies, by any chance?"

Rashin didn't respond, though there might have been a smile buried underneath all that hair. Well, assuming he had a mouth, anyway. The possibly-mouthless dwarf took another sip of his drink before continuing, "Well. Such matters thusly dealt with, please, allow me to extend the hospitality of Clan Blackstone unto you. We can speak more of your experiences in the morning. For now, allow us to grant you a bath, cleaner clothes, a meal, and a bed. I presume all those have been in short supply for you as of late?" Edwin mutely nodded. "Marvelous! Please, wait here; I shall make the appropriate arrangements."

The door opening snapped Edwin awake from a doze. He downed the rest of his water and plodded along as *Thrandin* led him to a fairly spacious room, with a bunk set into the wall, a stone table bearing some bread, cheese, and meats, and a large tub filled with steaming water and human-sized clothing sitting on the ledge. His escort, after ushering Edwin inside, turned and left, closing the door behind him.

Edwin tried the door and, satisfied it wasn't locked—fortunately, though he admittedly didn't know what he would have done if it was— proceeded to devour all the food on the table. He paid no mind to pacing himself, which he knew he'd regret, but it was the first real food he'd had in so very long.

Level Up!
Nutrition Level 3→5
Survival Level 9→10

Ooh. Perfect. That put Edwin at just above 60 Skill Points, and as he peeled off his mud-encrusted clothes, balefully eying the many, many holes in them, he dropped all 60 into his Skilled Arcanist Path. As he sank into the steaming bathwater, he looked over his influx of notifications.

You may evolve your Basic Mana Manipulation Skill into the Mana Infusion Skill!
Accept Evolution? Y/N
Done!
…
Calculating Rewards …
Class Change!
Outsider Novice → Outsider Apprentice
You have completed the Skilled Arcanist Path!
You have grasped the endless possibilities that magic makes available to you. Following this Path will make you a force to be reckoned with as your Skills grow in surprising and potent ways. With your every action now filled with the power of the arcane, all manner of possibilities lie within your grasp.
For continuing along a magical Path, your mana has increased!
Mana 4 → 5
For continuing along a magical Path, your mana has increased!

Mana 3 → 4
For continuing along a magical Path, your mana has increased!
Mana 2 → 3
For continuing along a magical Path, your mana has increased!
Mana 1 → 2

Huh. Did that increase every ... 12 Skill Points? Might be worth putting points into Paths even before he could complete them, if that were the case.

Mana Infusion
Is it magical? No? Well, not *yet*.
Imbue magic into an object or Skill.
Density increases with level.

Imbue magic into an object or Skill? That would be worth trying out. Edwin tried pushing magic into his bath and felt a faint trickle of mana flow into the water. It wasn't immediate, though the water did seem to become more relaxing the more mana infused it. Eventually, it seemed to hit some sort of cap, but it was still quite comfortable.

Level Up!
Mana Infusion Level 1→2

Eventually, Edwin started nodding off, but he caught himself before he fully fell asleep in the bath. With an absolutely titanic expenditure of will, he dragged himself out of the tub, toweled off, dressed in clean clothes (a plain but clean, comfortable, and well-made shirt and pants), and collapsed onto his bed.

He was asleep before his head even hit the pillow.

Level Up!
Sleeping Level 8→9

It was heavenly sleeping in a real bed. Though Edwin was somewhat confused when he first woke up as to where he was, that was a small matter compared to what had to have been the best sleep of his life. He felt so well-rested it was *amazing*. Though the magical crystals embedded in the walls gave no indication of what time it was, it *felt* like morning and he was up and ready to go! He stretched and ventured out of his room. The blank hallways offered no suggestion as to which direction he should go, and he hadn't been paying close enough attention last night to remember.

A few minutes of confused wandering later, one of the dwarves (a Skilled Blacksmith) he passed seemed to recognize him and waved him over. Up stairs, down stairs, through long hallways—were they *trying* to get him turned around? This was a maze!—and past many rooms, mostly with closed doors, though some were open, allowing him to see a mix of bedrooms, larger halls, a few smithies, and a few rooms half filled with all kinds of weapons and armor. Eventually, he found himself back in Rashin's library, and the dwarf welcomed him back and beckoned him to sit.

"I trust you have slept well, Edwin? And you upgraded your Class! Marvelous. What Skill did you get, may I ask?"

"I slept well enough, thank you." Edwin was offered a cup of something hot in a stone mug, which he accepted. It smelled a bit like tea. Tasted like it, too, though his efforts to try it scalded his tongue. "I got Mana Infusion."

"You got a magical Skill? Tremendous! Were you a mage back on your home world as well?"

"No. I wasn't a mage. It's a new development, really. We didn't even *have* magic back on Earth."

"There must have been some, surely?"

Edwin shrugged. "Not so far as I know."

"Ah!" Rashin exclaimed. "I'm certain you understand the aching of a scholar's heart to be faced with something straight from myth and legend, with the opportunity to ask questions! Though first, politeness dictates that I ask of your time upon Joriah thus far. It did not sound particularly friendly, though I would be delighted to learn more of your efforts."

Well ... there *probably* wasn't any harm in it, and Rashin was clearly trustworthy enough to be open with some details. After a moment of consideration, Edwin shrugged and regaled Rashin with most of his experiences since landing in Joriah, though, on a hunch, he kept quiet as to the details of his Paths and Skills. It took a few hours, and other than a bit of disbelief and some amusement as Edwin reached his fight against the bus-sized Stonehide Bear, Rashin merely sat back and occasionally prompted Edwin to continue his tale.

As Edwin reached the fight between the two mages, Rashin flinched. "My deepest apologies regarding that. Xares, the neighboring emperor, attempted to make forays into the Highpeaks. I am not aware of the full details regarding what he was attempting to achieve, but King Shoroshal drove him off. They would have been the individuals you saw."

Edwin paused, trying to digest that piece of information. "And the Highpeaks are this mountain range? Are there other dwarven famili—er, clans, living here?"

Rashin raised his hand and tilted his head in a manner that Edwin couldn't quite interpret, then said, "Ah, naturally. You wouldn't know. Indeed, the Highpeaks are where you stand now. Most of the inside is carved out, as is only right, but the Highpeak Kingdoms are the strongest dwarven nation in Joriah. Our borders stretch as far as the Second Deep and to every peak. There are over a hundred clans, each functioning akin to a surface city, and we, the Blackstones, alongside the Skyseekers, Woodcarvers, and Highpoints themselves, function as the border cities."

"I see. And the names?"

"Named for our founders. We are the Inheritors of the True Wielder of Blackstone's legacy, for instance, hence the nature of our halls."

"Oh, is that what all the magical concrete is?" Edwin asked. It made sense that a magical, stone-oriented culture would have forms of the stuff Edwin wasn't familiar with.

"Concrete?" Rashin asked. "I'm not familiar with the name, though that could merely be Polyglot showing its limits. Is that something from your homeland? Could you describe it? That does help on occasion with my Skill."

"It's a sort of ... liquid stone, I guess you could call it? It comes as a powder that you add water to, then you let it set for a while and some reaction happens, makes basically instant stone."

"No," Rashin admitted, "I can't say I do know of it. What is the powder?"

"Uhhh … it was sand, uhhh … cement, and was there something else?" Edwin rapped on his forehead with his knuckles, racking his brain for the appropriate information. "I can't remember, sorry."

"Would you be capable of determining what goes into it, then?"

"Well … probably? It wasn't something I spent that much time looking into; there were some *really cool* variants that were in development from what I remember, like self-healing or porous versions, but while my area of study does—did—overlap slightly with concrete development, it wasn't much of an interest of mine, sorry. Why do you ask?"

"Oh, no reason."

Edwin eyed the dwarven scholar. "You don't have some supersecret monopoly over Blackstone, do you, and you'd have to kill me to preserve the secret about how it's made, do you?"

Rashin laughed, a hearty, full-body chuckle. "No, no. Nothing of the sort at all! Regardless, you are a guest under our full hospitality aegis. So long as you are under our roof and do not move to act against us, Clan Blackstone shall do you no harm."

Seemed like there were some fairly large and obvious loopholes in that statement, but … okay? Edwin was probably just being paranoid. So far, the Clan Blackstone dwarves had been perfectly kind and quite reasonable. This would be a perfect place for him to recover, learn a bit more about the world, and figure out his plans for the future.

What could go wrong?

CHAPTER 13

Pretentious Neighbors

Edwin and Rashin rambled on for a few more hours, mostly about their respective worlds but also miscellaneous topics. It was refreshing, getting to talk to someone about mutual interests. Sure, he had no delusions that the dwarf was really his *friend*—he knew he was just a charge—but at least he seemed entranced and very engrossed in what Edwin was saying. Rashin seemed particularly interested in material science, which definitely made sense for someone from such an apparently crafting-focused society.

For Edwin's part, he greatly enjoyed learning about Joriah! There were apparently two major landmasses, or two and a half depending on how you counted it. He was on Korizan, the "and a half" continent, a big Greenland-like landmass that just barely touched the much larger Tarneis continent up near the Arctic Circle. The other continent, which Rashin literally called "Enigma," was an almost complete mystery, and other than its being mostly covered in jungles, not much was known about it.

Most of Korizan, along with a good portion of Tarneis, was ruled by the "Pretentious Empire," which had Edwin nearly spitting out his drink in surprise. He could only presume it wasn't what the Empire called itself, that the name was just a result of Polyglot's translation effect being overly literal.

The Highpeak Kingdoms were, naturally, in the Highpeak Mountains (Rashin didn't know which was named first), located near the southern tip of Korizan in the middle of what was apparently called "the Verdant," which proved that, even on a fantasy world, people weren't immune to using obvious names. (Then again, what else would you call a massive magical forest? It was definitely better than just "the Forest," so perhaps he shouldn't think too harshly of them.) There was supposedly an elven city somewhere in the Verdant as well, though nobody knew where exactly, allegedly not even the elves themselves. Edwin wasn't sure how much he believed *that*, nor how it might work, but just shrugged and nodded at all the right points in the conversation.

Non-System magic also existed. Due to his Mana Sense Attribute and related Skills, that revelation didn't surprise Edwin too much, but it *did* surprise him to learn that having enough magic to cultivate into actual Skills was really rare. Only those who were somehow born with an innate connection to magic really managed to develop into true mages, as there was no dedicated study of it. Once in a while, some bold individual would try to tap into magic despite no natural talent, only to fail in a frequently spectacular manner.

There were legends of those blessed by gods who developed magical powers, but Rashin emphasized that they were very much just legends, only mentioned for completeness's sake.

In addition, even more rarely, a Skill might develop into true magic, but usually only among the most powerful individuals. Of course, what classified as "true magic" was unclear anyway.

Naturally, the strongest of the strong were those who had begun as natural mages, then developed their magic into earth-shatteringly powerful Skills.

Which actually reminded Edwin to ask, "Oh, right. What exactly does completing a Path do, anyway?"

"Ah, but of course. I forgot you were not raised with such knowledge.

"When you complete a Path, the System selects a reward for you. This reward can either be an evolution to a Skill that you already have or to a new Attribute. Attributes are similar to a Skill in many regards, though they can only be improved via the completion of additional Paths. In exchange, they are frequently more wide-reaching and powerful than similar Skills. The Walking Skill will ease your burden when using your feet to travel, but the Stamina Attribute will make all physical exertion easier.

"However, getting an Attribute is rare. Most commonly, the completion of a Path will result in one of your Skills evolving. The method by which a Skill is chosen follows a few basic rules, though the specifics are unknown. What *is* known, however"—Rashin grabbed his mug from a nearby table and took a drink—"is that no Skill which has already evolved will be evolved again."

Edwin frowned. "You can only evolve Skills once?"

"Allow me to finish." Rashin was patient and kind, but Edwin still felt impatient. "No Skill that has already evolved will be selected again until every Skill you possess has been evolved. Thus, as you possess mostly basic Skills, yes?—yes—if you were to complete a Path, none of the Skills that you've already evolved would evolve again. Only after every basic Skill you have has been evolved will any evolve for the second time."

"Is that a good thing?" Edwin asked.

The dwarf shrugged. "Depends who you ask. The Pretentious Empire thinks it's priceless. They limit the number of Skills their subjects can get to make it faster for them to go up in Tiers."

"How many Skills do most people have?"

"Oh … twelve is fairly common. I myself have ten, such is the Legacy I follow. Many of our craftsdwarves have sixteen, though there is a Legacy that only uses nine."

"Legacies?"

"Well"—the dwarf set his drink aside as he explained—"the System is incredibly complicated. As an individual, it is all but impossible to properly predict what form of Skill you might obtain beyond generalities. Thus, we follow Legacies. These are sets of Skills and Paths that our ancestors accomplished greatness with. Their wisdom helps us succeed where we might have failed otherwise."

"What about just free-handing it?"

"Foolish." Rashin informed him, "The wisdom of our forefathers and their truly wondrous achievements overshadow anything that might be accomplished today. However, as you are an Outsider and a mage, in addition to not being a dwarf, you are perhaps the sole individual who might benefit from attempting to pace your own way."

Edwin sat in silence, processing.

"What do you think I should do?" he asked. He certainly wasn't as qualified as someone decades older than him and with infinitely more experience with the System. "How do I know what Skills and Paths to take?"

"You put a heavy burden upon me, Edwin, I hope you know that."

Edwin flinched. "I'm sorry. I don't want to be a drag. I just ..."

"No, no. It's perfectly all right." Edwin didn't believe him. There was just too much tightness around the words for them to be genuine. Darn it, why did he always have to stress people out? Gah, he couldn't do anything right.

"You want to be selective." Rashin acted unaware of Edwin's internal struggle, thankfully. "Taking every Skill you are offered is inadvisable, though I cannot stop you. Instead, when presented with one, truly consider if it will provide you with something you will use often."

"But what about generally useful Skills? Is there a ... oh, Drinking Skill?"

"There is. It increases the efficacy of imbibed liquids. Popular with those who like their ales."

"How is that not something everyone could benefit from?"

"They all could. But for every Skill you take, there is an additional Path to complete. And not just for that Skill but also whatever it evolves into, and every Skill that evolves from it likewise needs to be leveled in order to be grown. If the Skill that you begin with is only marginally useful to begin with, regardless of its potential, there is no assurance that future evolutions would fare any better, and no one has unlimited time. Best that you instead focus your efforts upon a few Skills of your choice, those which you use frequently and intimately, and master those.

"We have a saying, from the forges. Polyglot does not do it justice, but it goes as such: An apprentice can only wield a single hammer; a craftsman knows how to use a dozen. But a master will use a single hammer in all their work."

"Focus on developing what you know, rather than learning something new?" Edwin clarified, and the dwarf nodded. "Well, I'll consider it, I guess.

"So, what about removing a Skill? Is that possible?"

"It is not, I am sorry to say. There are *rumors*, of course. However, there are always rumors about elves, and I would advise you not pay them any mind. I have heard they ride upon dragons, or perhaps *are* dragons, or yet again perhaps sang dragons into existence. I inform you of the rumor once again to caution you against it."

Fair enough. "What about being offered a Skill you declined already?" The dwarf nodded.

"So accepting a Skill can't be undone, but declining them can be?" Edwin clarified.

Well, that's not going to give me crippling decision paralysis or anything. Okay, new rule: don't take new Skills unless I'm absolutely certain I want them.

"How about Skill evolutions? Can you put them on hold, get them again later?"

"No. You must take or decline the evolution when it is offered. If you seek to merely ignore the notification, that is more of an option perhaps, though I wish you good luck not declining or accepting the offer by accident."

"Can you merge Skills? Like if you have two that are really similar in some way, can you reduce the number of Skills you have in that way?"

"Are you worried about those which you already have?" Rashin inquired, but Edwin just shrugged. Rashin went on. "There is, to my knowledge, no way to combine Skills together. However, it is possible to gain a *new* Skill in such a way that it leaves the originals untouched, though perhaps with a few additional levels.

"In practice, it rarely matters, as few unlock Skills that are exceptionally close to each other in function. Few unlock both Running and Walking, for instance, and as most individuals have Walking from their time as an infant, the Running Skill is usually relegated to an evolution of Walking, for those interested in such matters."

"Really? Why's that?"

"I do not know."

"Huh. Well, okay. So, I have a few more questions …"

* * *

All the talk about Skills made Edwin's Research Skill *very* happy. A surreptitious set of questions led him to believe it was close enough to the more common Learning Skill to gain experience from all this, though he'd probably forget most of the more fiddly cultural and geographical bits as soon as he left the room.

Level Up!
Research Level 10→18

He'd need to start thinking about what Path he wanted to fill out next, Edwin mused as he returned to his room, following directions given to him by Rashin and recorded on his fingers. The way back wasn't nearly as complicated as he'd thought, and the room he found himself in seemed like it might have been slightly different. It had the same layout, the same decorations carved into the wall, and looked all but identical to where he had slept last night, but it just seemed slightly … off, for some reason he couldn't quite pin down. Was it larger? Was it shinier? He couldn't tell. To make sure something similar didn't happen again without his knowledge, he marked everything he could with his Almanac.

Level Up!
Outsider's Almanac Level 23→24

Oh, hey! 41-character limit, nice. Was it exponential? That could get carried away fast if it were. Anyway. Edwin had *no* idea what had happened to his Earth clothes, but considering the state they had been in last he saw them, that may not have been too terrible a loss. He was quite content in his current outfit, though it wasn't as familiar as jeans, a T-shirt, and a light, comfy jacket. Maybe he could get his T-shirt back. It hadn't been *too* badly damaged. Really, it had mainly been his jacket that was full of holes; his pants would probably have been fine with a good wash.

Whatever. He could try to get his clothes back tomorrow. For the time being, his dwarven shirt and pants were adequate. The shoes he was wearing were *incredibly* comfy, though. Maybe he'd be able to keep them. Inspecting them, they looked like they had been perfectly tailored for his feet, which seemed impossible … but then he remembered Skills, and that there was probably a Cobbling Skill out there that improved the comfort of created shoes. If so, this particular cobbler must have had a really high level.

There was more food on the table, too, similar fare to the night before. Edwin wolfed it down eagerly, as he was either hungrier or the food was *way* better than last night's, earning another Skill level in Nutrition and Survival for his efforts.

Before he retired for the night, though, he pulled out a book Rashin had given him—a primer on the local Dwarven, which was used by those who desired to learn the language. Learning a new language was apparently a very reliable way to unlock the Linguist Path, and while redundant for Edwin, Rashin had been hopeful that he could get the Language Skill instead. Apparently, the Linguist Path combined with the Language Skill, or one of its evolutions in many cases, was a well-known combination to grant the Polyglot Skill, which Edwin found very appealing.

Reading the book was a bit of an odd experience, as every single Dwarven word was written by someone with a high Polyglot Skill level (Rashin hadn't *said* it was him, but Edwin had a strong suspicion it was), meaning that he could instinctively understand the meaning behind every single word. It took a fair bit of effort to not just read the thing in English; even the slightly different sentence structure resolved itself seamlessly into an equivalent English sentence.

It was only when Edwin analyzed the words letter by angular letter that he could really parse the fact that it was a different language. For such a harshly written script, though, Dwarven was a fairly flowing and pleasant-sounding language, very few hard sounds like "k" or "t" to be heard.

Two levels of Research and several hours later, though, Edwin finally had his breakthrough when he attempted to sound out what he was reading, exactly.

Language
Tomato, tomato. Potato, potato.

Speak more clearly.
Enhanced pronunciation per level.

By the time he called it a night, Edwin had reached level 3 in his new Skill and was quite ready for rest. As he drifted off, he realized he hadn't done anything to figure out his longer-term plans, but there was always tomorrow.

One fresh level of Sleeping later, Edwin found himself dragged out to meet *Lord* (he had been very emphatically informed he was not to call this person a king) S'fashkchlil Blackstone, which Edwin had tried and *majorly* failed to pronounce. He couldn't even sound it out properly in his mind. Rashin functioned as an interpreter, repeating what Edwin said pretty much verbatim and presumably doing the same for the ki—*lord*, sorry—allowing them both to understand what was being said. Edwin gave a slightly awkward bow as he entered.

"You wished to see me, Your Lordship?" No harm in turning on a bit of charm for the person indirectly responsible for saving him.

"Indeed, little Outsider." Oy now, what kind of dwarf calls someone *else* little? Edwin wasn't even slightly short! Oh, the lord was talking again. "… heard my servant Rashin tell some marvelous stories about the land you hail from. Magical mirrors, horses powered by fire, and strange oils as hard as stone yet as transparent as water?"

"Well, that's not entirely—"

"And you know how to make these wonders?" the dwarf asked, his voice getting more demanding as the lord leaned forward on his chair. "You are one of the crafters who know their secrets?"

"I mean, I studied material physics, but that's hardly—" Edwin defended himself, not sure he liked where this was going.

"Then as is my right as Lord S'fashkchlil of Clan Blackstone, I declare the Outsider Edwin Maxlin to have been found in abuse of Hospitality Rights—"

"Hey!" Edwin interjected. "You can't do that!"

Rashin continued repeating the lord's proclamation undeterred. "… and with what little property he has on him insufficient to pay off the debt, I seize his person to pay off the debt of his stay through labor, until such a time the debt is equalized." The lord narrowed his eyes at Edwin as two guards previously standing at his sides moved forward and locked his wrists in an ironclad grip. "So I claim in the name of King Shoroshal of Highpoint as my gods-given responsibility."

Edwin's struggles were utterly fruitless as his new captors dragged him out of the room. Before he left, they paused to let him hear one last statement from the person he thought he trusted.

S'fashkchlil leaning back on his throne with an avaricious look in his eye. "Make me Blackstone, Outsider, and I will set you free."

CHAPTER 14

There Are Worse Internships

Edwin paced restlessly in his cell. While it may not have looked much like one, furnished more like a luxurious suite than slave quarters, there was no doubt as to the true nature of the arrangement thanks to his latest Path.

Congratulations! For being forced into a nonpaid working arrangement, you have unlocked the Slave Path!

He knew for a *fact* that he was never completing it, and given that even just looking at it made him mad, he dismissed the message with a frustrated slash, dropping onto his new bed in annoyance. If anything, the fact that it was equally comfortable to the previous night's bed just made the situation worse. Really, with two exceptions, his new quarters—complete with bathtub and bathroom, bed and table, the latter of which was already laden with food—was practically the same. The first exception was the metal hatch set just above his table that was responsible for delivering food, and the second was that his door didn't open into a hallway but instead a workroom.

Edwin's new "office" wasn't as comfortable as his room, but he'd be lying if he said it wasn't equally impressive. A large table, attached directly to the middle of the floor, occupied most of the space, but it bore all manner of equipment, ranging from scales and tongs to crucibles, metal beakers, and more.

Along the walls, Edwin had access to a faucet of sorts, fed by a giant basin of water near the door, a furnace and kiln, with corresponding pile of coal, and a couple of additional appliances whose purpose he hadn't pieced together yet.

A noise in the workroom broke Edwin out of his aimless thoughts. Moving to investigate, a none-too-welcome face greeted him. "You. I suppose this is typical for you? Taking half-dead people from the mountain and enslaving them the moment they have something you want?" Edwin spat.

Rashin's face was as unreadable as always as the door swung closed behind him, sealing into the wall without so much as a seam. "Lord S'fashkchlil is fully within his rights to desire recompense for abusing our hospitality."

"Abuse? Ha! I fell out of the sky not a week ago, have been here for two days, and demanded nothing! All I wanted was to not *die* out on the mountain. Just let me go and keep your hairy noses out of my life! You're just slavers, that's what you are."

"You offered no gifts of thanks nor gave any indication when you would leave. Abuse of hospitality can be a serious offense; be thankful you are still alive after taking our clothes and eating such fine food with neither thanks nor indication of intent to leave. Ignorance of the law is no excuse. You are not a slave in the slightest, merely a worker, free to go once your debt is paid. Your task is to develop Blackstone through whatever means necessary, and to do so is to be your only concern."

Edwin glared at the scheming dwarf. "This was intentional. I don't have the faintest clue about your customs nor the value of what you *freely gave* me, *and you know that.* You even provided me with *finer* conditions once you heard about the sorts of things I might—*might!*—be able to provide, which I suppose was just to get me in debt? You're slavers, plain and simple." His eyes narrowed even further. "You're going to keep throwing me deeper into 'owing you,' aren't you? That's why this food is even nicer than before, isn't it?"

"Not at all. We are a hospitable clan; we do not wish for your time in our service to be uncomfortable," the traitorous dwarf lied.

They stared each other down, Edwin glaring at the dwarf with the mass of silver hair, who returned a falsely cheery gaze.

Eventually, the tension was too much, and Edwin broke the silence, "What do you even *need* me to make Blackstone for, anyway? Isn't that your whole thing? Clan Blackstone and all?"

"That is classified."

Edwin glared.

"You are not allowed to know that."

"I know what classified means, darn it! I just … How do you expect me to make the stupid rock if I don't even know where to start? At least give me some of your lab manuals or a paper on the stuff, though I don't know why you couldn't—" Edwin stopped as a thought occurred to him. "You don't know *how* to make it, do you? Someone in your glorious Legacy's past didn't write the instructions down and now you're floundering, looking for any chance you stumble across to try and find it again. You *do* need me, because concrete is the closest thing you've heard of to whatever fragments you know about it. You could have just asked! I would have gladly helped you out in thanks!" As he ranted, he got closer and closer to the dwarf until he was towering over the treacherous man.

"If that is so, Outsider Edwin," Rashin said, glowering as he shoved something into Edwin's stomach, "prove it."

Edwin stumbled back a step in surprise while he scrambled to grab whatever he had been attacked with … a notebook of some sort? "What's this?"

"What I came here to deliver, and conveniently, what you requested. Notes on the properties of Blackstone, copied by my own hand. Teach us how to make it, and you can go free."

No, I won't. That will just make me even more valuable. And if Blackstone is really so important to you, you'll never let me go knowing your secret, Edwin thought as he thumbed through the notebook. "I don't even *know* how to make concrete! Let alone whatever black magic alchemy stuff it'll take to make your stupid rocks. I need to at least learn how to use alchemy if you don't want me flailing around blind."

"Then I suggest you do so."

"How am I supposed to do that?"

"That, Outsider Edwin, is *your* job. We shall keep our 'hairy noses' out of your life. That is what you wanted, no?"

With a wordless cry, Edwin threw the closest heavy object—a metal bowl—at Rashin, but missed the scholar and the dish clanged into the far wall.

"Such a temper. It wouldn't do for you to break anything you might later need, would it? Do let us know what materials you shall require."

Rashin rapped on the wall, prompting the door to swing open and latch shut behind him a moment later, vanishing once more, and Edwin found himself alone with his thoughts again. He vaguely wished he could have rushed out the door and left this whole mess behind, but before he could act on the urge, the moment was gone.

"Stupid treacherous dwarf, stupid alchemy, stupid world," he muttered to himself before regaining his composure.

His burning anger faded quickly, which made Edwin wonder: Did Rashin have some form of emotion-manipulating Skill? It would explain why Edwin felt so trusting of him, and the sudden wave of anger when he was visited just now. How far did that extend? Was there more mind control at play? It would be something he'd have to keep in mind. He *did* feel his thoughts continually drift to concrete, which was … odd. Was that another Skill, meant to keep him "on task"? He could ignore it, but it was annoying. Easier to just go along with what it was prompting him to do, which was admittedly fine for the moment.

Idly, he glanced through the notebook, glancing at Blackstone's specifications.

Sheesh. I can see why they want this stuff. Stronger than steel, barely denser than water, magic resistant, supposedly liquid until set, insanely good insulator, almost entirely scratch-proof. Heck, I want this stuff now! But first things first, I suppose. Start with concrete and see what I can get from there.

Water, sand, and cement, right? Was there something else? Cross that bridge when we get there. What is cement made of, though? Lime? Uh … calcium carbonate? Are those the same thing? Is there lime in limestone? Gah, I wish I had the internet right now.

I need a notebook. And some limestone. And some samples of Black-stone, see if I can learn anything from that … Edwin looked out over his workroom, eyes narrowed and hard. *But they have another thing coming if they think they're getting any Blackstone from me. You locked me in a cave, and I have* way *more than just a box of scraps.*

Edwin's Logbook, Day 1

Analyzed samples of sand, limestone, and Blackstone.

Blackstone sample held up to reported attributes. Unable to scratch or crush with available tools, slightly heavier than water, and did not heat up when exposed to flame nor cool in water, staying at a consistently warm temperature.

Attempting to use Mana Infusion on Blackstone failed, the Skill finding no purchase on the material. Seems to function as a mana mirror? Needs more testing. Basic Mana Sense was apparently disabled. Reenabling it resulted in momentary sensory overload, so disabled it again afterward. Note to self: train mana sense tolerance.

Initial attempts at extracting lime from limestone via crushing probably unsuccessful (no way to check). Crushed samples now soaking in water to see if that helps.

Limestone, when Mana Infused, grew harder. Unable to crush samples postinfusion. Established a second cauldron to attempt to soak Infused limestone.

Sand seemed normal. The magical fires in the workroom are not quite hot enough to melt it (seems close, though), so uncertain if silicon (proceeding under the assumption it is, not that it makes a difference?).

Infused sand has odd properties. Outsider's Almanac recognizes it as a distinct material compared to Noninfused sand. Individual sand grains have no apparent change, but refuse to pile together, spreading out like a liquid. When held in a container, they flow like water.

Hypothesis: Friction on Infused sand has been reduced or is negligible.

Trial: Spread layers of Infused and Noninfused sand out and compare the force required to move an object across the bed of sand.

Conclusion: Infused sand refuses to support weight. Any objects placed on top of Infused sand immediately fall through as though sinking through water. Trial inconclusive.

Hypothesis: Sand has taken on the properties of a liquid.

Trial: Attempt to mix with another liquid (using unspecified oil for nonpolar liquid, water for polar liquid).

Conclusion: Infused sand refused to mix with either water or oil, instead sinking to the bottom of the respective containers. Was wet and oily, respectively, when retrieved, and the two samples had no issues mixing with each other.

Trial: Attempt to measure viscosity and buoyant force.

Conclusion: Viscosity of Infused sand appears to be close to 0, and buoyancy is negligible.

Hypothesis: Each grain of sand has an upward force on it, nearly canceling the weight of gravity on it, like in aerated sand.

Trial: Compare equal volumes of Infused and Noninfused sand on scales to compare weight.

Conclusion: Infused sand has the same weight as Noninfused sand.

***

Congratulations! For conducting rigorous scientific research via the scientific method, you have unlocked the Scientist Path!

Edwin sat back with a sigh, rubbing his forehead as he completed his latest notebook entry, an act more intensive than he would have thought. How did anyone ever write with a feather quill? That thing was impossible to use! The Infused sand was definitely behaving as a fluid, though the "how" was beyond him. It seemed to basically act the way people thought quicksand worked—sucked whatever touched it immediately all the way to the bottom. But he couldn't imagine how that physically *worked*, and there was no way he'd accept "just magic" as an answer long term. He'd have to for now, though, as sand wasn't close enough to concrete for his focus to stay on it for any significant length of time, apparently.

After he had tried and failed to use Mana Infusion on Blackstone, he had wondered if it was just a matter of making concrete with supercharged magical ingredients. He had the second part of that down, at least. Though if he was dealing with an almost-superfluid with sand, he wasn't sure if that would interfere with the concrete-making process.

He'd have to make a nonmagical concrete mix first, then add magic one ingredient at a time.

Despite his frustration with actually measuring its properties, Edwin could barely contain his glee at his Infused sand overall. He'd been at this for less than a day, had really only tried using magic on three (well, four, if you counted his bathwater) different types of material, and he had already found an object really close to a room-temperature superfluid! What else might he find with just a bit more experimentation?

He was done for the day, though. Edwin's body clock was *all* off, but he was starting to feel tired, and the limestone would need to soak overnight, anyway, before any further steps ... probably. He could be totally wrong, for all he knew. Maybe concrete didn't need lime, or lime wasn't actually in limestone and it was just some weird linguistic quirk. Most likely, limestone wasn't water soluble but, well ...

Only one way to find out, I suppose.

Edwin flopped onto his bed with a loaf of bread and his Dwarven dictionary. He didn't have anything better to do; might as well try and learn the language. Perhaps he'd be able to get a book on alchemy at some point. That would be a huge help. There was no way something as incredible as Blackstone didn't involve it in some way. He was running blind in far too many directions, and he didn't like it. In any case, he was going to complete his Physical Alchemist Path next. He'd put it off long enough, and he needed *something* to do with alchemy. It would help him escape ... and also work on Blackstone.

And that was all without even *touching on* what he would do post-escape. He'd require a whole host of tools to survive in the wilderness again, and he needed some way to break out of his room. Plus, he'd have to do it while under an unknown level of surveillance *and* with an inability to directly think about it for extended periods of time, because it wasn't hard enough already. Any weapons he created would have to be not only essentially untested but also made using materials and methods similar to those for producing concrete, unless he wanted to risk the clan finding out he wasn't just working on Blackstone.

All Edwin could really do was hope that he happened to stumble across something weaponizable in his research, which was a ... dubious prospect, but he also knew that compounds could have all sorts of unexpected properties.

Heck, was it even so bad to be only researching concrete, really? He got to do magical research, didn't have to interact with anyone, and had food and shelter basically for free! The thought of being a slave, though, even if the work wasn't too bad, was not the life he wanted. No. He needed to get out, and the sooner the better. All that, though, required him to be stronger, to complete more Paths, to advance his Skills. He could do all that during his research, probably. It was a long road ahead of him, but honestly?

Level Up!
Language Level 1→4
Research Level 20→26
Nutrition Level 6→7
Mana Infusion Level 2→12
Outsider's Almanac Level 24→25
Improvisation Level 11→12
Basic Mana Sense Level 21→23
Throwing Weapons Level 3→4
Breathing Level 10→11

He'd be lying if he said the compulsion was the only thing making him look forward to it.

CHAPTER 15

End of the Lime

Edwin was lying on his bed, playing with his latest notification. Sleeping wasn't his highest-level Skill by any measure, but it did have a fairly steady growth, which was appreciated. Maybe it would start to taper off in time, but for the time being, a level-up every time he slept was *so* satisfying. Though he had no real way to measure the passage of time, he suspected he was sleeping for around eight hours but getting rest equivalent to ten or twelve. He hadn't felt this well-rested since, well ... uh ... Actually, when was the last time he had managed to get a lot of sleep regularly? Certainly not college, not really high school either ... Middle school, maybe? Or over a summer where he didn't have some internship or job ... So, back in early high school? That was kind of sad. Not that he could do much about it save try to make up for it now.

It was nice to just fidget with the floating text, though, contorting it into different configurations and display formats. Hmm. It had been a while since he'd last checked his full Status. How close was he to his next Path, anyway?

Name

Edwin Maxlin

Age

22 years

Race

Extraplanar Human

Class

Outsider Apprentice

Attributes

Mana 5

Skills

Athletics: 18

Basic Mana Sense: 23

Breathing: 11

Firestarting: 20

Flexibility: 8

Identify: 13

Improvisation: 12

Language: 4

Mana Infusion: 12

Mathematics: 2

Nutrition: 7

Research: 26

Seeing: 14

Sleeping: 11

Outsider's Almanac: 25

Survival: 11

Throwing Weapons: 4

Visualization: 15

Walking: 19

Paths

Skill Points: 46

Very Much Yes-Eventually

Physical Alchemist 0/90, Micro-Biomancer 0/90, Path Less Traveled 0/90, Realm Traveler 0/120, Scientist 0/60

Promising

Stonehide Vanquisher 0/60, Titan Slayer 0/90, World Traveler 0/60, Researcher 0/60, Explorer 0/60, Outsider 0/60, Linguist 0/60

Maybe One Day

Survivor 0/60, Athlete 0/60, Daredevil 0/60, Pioneer 0/60, Novice

Pyromancer 0/60
Meh
Lumberjack 0/60, Way of the Empty Hand 0/60, Trapper 0/60
No (expand)
Completed Paths (expand)

More than halfway to Physical Alchemist, very nice. Hmm. A few of his Skills were starting to fall behind; maybe it was worth trying to work on them, get a few easy Skill Points. Mathematics couldn't be that hard to level up; whatever standards the System used, it couldn't count stuff like calculus as low level.

Edwin didn't have a lot of paper, though. Maybe Outsider's Almanac could be used for that sort of thing? He was up to 43 characters at this point, which should be plenty for most equations. Grind two Skills for the price of one. Hmm ... What level of grinding might be best suited for concrete creation? Shoot, it was acting up again. Maybe if his mathematics improved he might be able to determine proper ratios for his experiments better.

That seemed to work, and Edwin mentally cheered. Apparently, whatever compulsion he was under was no match for the justifications of a college student used to explaining away their procrastination. Now he just needed to imagine montage training music playing while he did calculus in an imaginary text box ...

Level Up!
Mathematics Level 2→31
Visualization Level 15→18
Outsider's Almanac Level 26→27

That ... was a lot of levels, all at once. At a certain point, tossing around huge numbers and keeping track of a dozen different values in his head became almost trivial, and Edwin was able to stop using the Almanac without slowing down. He doubted he'd get that much of a level spike in anything else, though. He was just good at math, hence his field of choice, and was hitting his limits for complicated formulas he could use to show off to the System for easy levels.

Doing matrix multiplication with two three-by-three matrices entirely in his head was strange, but then again that was basically par for the course. Still, his excuses (and his patience) for doing math instead of directly working on his research was wearing thin, so it was probably time to actually do his work.

Pulling himself out of bed and doing stretches—he had to get himself limber for what was probably going to be a lot of crushing rocks, after all—netted him a level in Flexibility, selecting food to make a balanced meal upped his Nutrition, and throwing a mana-filled piece of bread at the wall got him a level in both Mana Infusion *and* Throwing Weapons.

Eating a mana-infused roll got him another level in Nutrition. He tried to juggle, hoping that it might count as "throwing" practice, but his attempt was apparently pathetic enough that he didn't get so much as a single notification.

All that effort still left Edwin five Skill Points short of completing Physical Alchemist, though. *Maybe tomorrow*, he mused, *though maybe I should start being more selective about when I fill out Paths. If early levels for things like Mathematics are so easy to come by, I wouldn't want to waste that opportunity. I do absolutely need some kind of Alchemy Skill, though, and I* think *it's not just the compulsion.*

He ran out of procrastination excuses, sadly, so Edwin found himself dragged back to his workbench. Looking into his basins, he wrinkled his nose in annoyance. Fishing out one of the crushed limestone chunks, he turned over the wet stone in his hand. It didn't seem to have shrunk in the slightest. Still, he needed to be sure. With a heave, he moved the cauldrons—mentally cursing his lack of foresight; he should have had it in position before he filled it with water—atop a magical heating stone (somehow made of Blackstone, despite the material's alleged antimagical properties) and waited for the water to boil off.

There wasn't enough water in the cauldron to appreciably change the humidity in the room, but the steam that billowed from his cauldron definitely raised the temperature in his lab, leaving Edwin lightly sweating until he retreated to his bedroom.

* * *

There might have been some slight residue on the inside of the cauldron, though Edwin wasn't entirely sure if it was just his imagination. It wasn't enough for the Almanac to pick up on it as distinct from the metal if it was there.

So, attempting to soak limestone was a bust. Then again, it was never likely that a common type of rock would be water soluble, but he needed to check to be sure. Still, that left him without much of an idea as to where to go from there. Crushing it, maybe? Limestone dust? It would still be insoluble then, though. Maybe if he burned it? He pulled out a blowtorch, triggering his Firestarting Skill as he did so, and held it to the pile of dust.

There was a sudden *flash*.

**Congratulations! For creating an improvised explosive, you have
unlocked the Bomber Path!
Level Up!
Improvisation Level 12→14
Firestarting Level 20→21**

Right. Dust explosions were a thing. That was *not* his proudest moment, but Edwin didn't think he had done much worse than just singe some of his eyebrows. Interestingly, no dwarves rushed in to see what the sudden burst of flame was about, which suggested they had limited surveillance over his activities. In itself, that fact made his escape plans far simpler, though he couldn't assume they wouldn't be looking at any given time, just that they weren't right now.

A lot of powder was still lying around, now dispersed as a thin coat across every surface, which Edwin was able to gather together and identify as limestone. Did it not just burn up in the explosion? Ooooh. He had swept up a big pile of dust from the counter, without caring much about keeping it pure. There had probably been something else that had burned, causing the explosion. Maybe coal dust? Wouldn't surprise him. That would have been *much* worse if the limestone had been combustible. He probably wouldn't have survived in that case, if just whatever traces of flammable materials that had gotten mixed in had resulted in that much of a fireball.

* * *

Edwin's latest attempt at burning limestone was going much smoother, though he hesitated to even *think* such a thing, lest it mess everything up. The powdered limestone was being heated inside a kiln, which was *probably* meant for metals but worked just fine for rock dust this time. The kiln itself was really interesting and Edwin's first real magical item to play around with. There was, of all things, a knob to control the temperature protruding from the wall next to the kiln's opening, and Edwin didn't know how hot it could get … but it was pretty dang hot. If limestone did need to be heated, the magical fire-box could do it.

The dust was at minimum now a pale yellow color and even registered as a different substance to his Almanac, a Skill he rapidly was coming to love more and more. Once it had cooled, weighing it revealed the new powder, hopefully lime, had lost roughly half its weight from the heating process. Both promising signs, though the *real* test would come with him attempting to make something with it. If concrete required more or different active ingredients than just lime, Edwin didn't know what he'd do, but first he divided his mound of powder in two, infusing one with magic, and leaving the other as a control.

Next, he carefully measured out an equal amount of water for his two batches, then mixed it into his mundane batch, followed by doing the same for the magical one. He was *not* expecting his cauldrons to heat up so quickly, causing him to snatch his hand from its surface just in time for the mana-infused batch to outright *explode*, sending superheated water all over the room.

Okay, that's it. Proper PPE for me when dealing with unknown chemicals and magic. What the heck just happened?

By the time Edwin returned to his workstation, he was fully equipped with a thick leather lab coat reminiscent of a trench coat, safety glasses (the *quality* of the glass left something to be desired, but it was at least mostly see-through), a breathing mask made of some kind of fabric Edwin didn't recognize, and surprisingly pliable leather gloves.

The vast gulf between the quality of his leather and cotton clothing and that of the glass in his goggles was somewhat surprising, but then again, would dwarves really need that much in the way of glassworking expertise? They only seemed to have a few implements made of the stuff, and they wouldn't exactly need windows. Heck, if the smoked goggles he had seen on the dwarf who found him were any indication, maybe they intentionally didn't want superclear glass. Did daylight or generally bright light hurt their eyes? If they were mostly subterranean, it would make a fair amount of sense …

But anyway! There was *science* to be done! He'd been away from actively working on the mixture for too long, and it was showing. The nonmagical lime mixture had hardened in the intervening hours into a stony, though somewhat brittle, coating that reminded Edwin vaguely of dried plaster.

While that may have been an excellent indication he was at least on the right track, it was the second batch that had him most excited. It was still a powder, but a thin layer of some kind of *different* powder was on the surface, centered where he had poured his water onto the lime. Very careful addition of a few drops of water to the unreacted powder gave off intense waves of heat, boiling what little had been added away and leaving another thin layer of the reacted substance.

Presumably, dumping too much water into the Infused lime had caused a steam explosion, which in turn got rid of all the extra water, leaving the lime reacted with nothing to spare.

Adding water to the reacted Infused lime powder yielded a white puttylike substance that was, oddly, mostly devoid of mana, and which hardened into something approximating solid rock the moment he Infused it. Edwin wasn't really sure initially how to tell if it would revert to the paste form once he removed mana from it, and a few minutes of struggling involved trying to reach inside and use his Basic Mana Manipulation to pull the magic from the rock, but once he did manage it (strangely not getting any Skill level-ups for his efforts), it returned mostly to its uncured state.

Edwin's Logbook, Day 2

Result of prior attempt to make lime from limestone: Failure. Limestone is not water soluble.

Hypothesis: Limestone needs to be heated, then forms lime.

Trial: Expose limestone powder to flame.

Result: Dust explosion. Probably due to other contaminants, but I lack the proper safety equipment to try and replicate it for the time being.

Trial: Set limestone powder inside of a kiln. Set to maximum heat to see if any reaction occurs.

Result: Success! Resulting powder is yellow-white and registers as a different material than limestone to Outsider's Almanac.

Hypothesis: Formed substance can be used as a basis for concrete.

Trial: Mix water into Infused and Noninfused "lime;" see if resulting mixture dries into something resembling concrete in any way.

Result: Noninfused "lime" dries into a plasterlike substance after mixed with water (exothermic reaction). Apparent success.

Secondary Result: Infused "lime" is incredibly exothermic when mixed with water. Risk of steam explosion if not careful. Resulting mixture is a paste initially, but cures instantly into a white rock when Infused.

Hypothesis: Removing mana from cured Infused lime will revert it to a paste.

Trial: Attempt to remove mana.

Result: Decured Infused lime is pliable and malleable though still solid. Acts similarly to a putty.

Material notes:

Limestone: Produces lime at high temperatures. Infused limestone has increased toughness.

Lime: Mix with water to create something like plaster in an exothermic reaction. Infused lime has the exothermic reaction *strongly* enhanced (possible steam explosion grenades? Investigate further).

Plaster(?): Cures into a rocklike substance that isn't terribly tough. Infused plaster is itself barely magical (where did the magic go? Was it used up in the reaction?), and when water is added, it turns into lime putty.

Lime putty: Slightly elastic, not bouncy, deforms easily, highly malleable. Hardens over time. Denser than water. Cures instantly when Infused, or naturally over time, and removing mana from the putty removes the curing. When cured, it is very hard (comparable to Infused limestone) and is even capable of holding a cutting edge, though not an especially sharp one.

***

Level Up!
Research Level 26→27

Now that he had a vague idea of what to do, Edwin was more than capable of setting up a new batch of limestone inside his kiln, but he tried varying the size of chunks included somewhat. Heck, he could do this sort of iterative production-run process in his sleep, what with all his internships and on-campus research classes back on Earth.

Limestone dust, which was *so* exhausting to make (he hoped he'd find a method that bypassed its need, but wasn't holding his breath); limestone pebbles, from the size of pea gravel to as big as a tennis ball, lined the furnace as the magical flames powering it fired up and got the process underway.

Hopefully he wouldn't have to grind all the limestone he needed by hand, but as always, only one way to find out. While his rocks were cooking, though, he had some time to kill. The result of his efforts to remove mana from the Infused plaster was interesting, and he wondered if something similar might be possible with Blackstone.

While no amount of prodding, coaxing, or anything else in Edwin's power and imagination managed to induce even the barest hint of mana from the Blackstone it resided in, he wasn't entirely discouraged. Sure, that could mean he was mistaken, or possibly he just wasn't strong enough to pull it off, Blackstone likely being on an order of magnitude more complicated than anything he could make. So instead, it was time to change tack slightly. It was time to leverage the natural world around him to do his work for him. It was time to turn rocks into weapons.

It was time to do *science*.

CHAPTER 16

Shedding Some Limelight

Due to the incredible amount of heat the Infused plaster powder (he needed a better name for his Infused materials) generated during its creation, Edwin wasn't able to physically get close enough to the reaction to feel where the mana Infused in it went. He knew that it was full of mana before the reaction and mana was drastically reduced afterward. Unless it was somehow absorbed by the powder (could something magical turn into something nonmagical?), that meant it had to be released in the process. Or maybe magic didn't follow the laws of thermodynamics, but that possibility was nonactionable so he ignored it for now.

There was one obvious product of the reaction; namely, heat, and it was obviously related to how magical the substances were. Measuring the amount of water and lime before and after mixing them (nonmagical in this case, Edwin didn't have any way to compensate for the flash-boiling of the magical reaction, so a lot of water would be lost) revealed there didn't seem to be any weight loss, so there probably weren't any secondary products involved, gaseous or otherwise, at least not in any appreciable amount.

While he didn't have any precise method of measuring mana content beyond metaphorically eyeballing it, the plaster powder seemed to have about half the mana content of the lime, and that in turn was reduced once he turned it into putty. However, he couldn't detect a release of heat, light, or anything else as he made it.

Turning on his Basic Mana Sense Skill while creating the plaster allowed Edwin to feel a small pulse of magic during the reaction, corresponding with the wave of heat, though it was only barely noticeable above the background mana content. Certainly, whatever was released was not enough to account for the difference in mana between the reacted and unreacted compounds. He tapped his chin and spelled out the formula for the reaction so far as he could tell.

Water + Lime + Mana $\rightarrow$ Plaster + Heat + Less Mana

Hmm ...

Edwin turned his Skill back on, and despite a little fight against a bit of a headache from the initial sensory overload, he managed to adjust in time. Hopefully it would give him more insight into the mechanics of what was going on.

This time, when doing the reaction, Edwin tried to monitor the entire batch constantly, to see if he could catch the exact moment the mana content dipped. It stayed the same as he added a drop of water, fell ever so slightly after the flash of heat, and then lowered when ... when ... Huh. It should have dropped by now. He took a sample of the plaster powder and compared it to an equal amount of lime. Yep, it had definitely dropped. But the mana content had ... stayed ... the ... same.

Edwin removed his goggles and gloves, massaging his forehead and unsuccessfully suppressing the urge to scream into his hands, *I'm an idiot.*

Yes, the mana *density* in the plaster had dropped, which was all he had been measuring. He kept comparing the mana content of equivalent-mass samples of plaster and lime, which of *course* would be different. Making the powder required nearly as much water as lime, and because he was using entirely mundane water, half of the *contents* for the plaster was nonmagical. He had entirely forgotten to account for good old dihydrogen monoxide, despite knowing *full well* that it could be Infused.

Edwin sighed. At least he had caught his error after only a couple hours of work, not days. He'd done worse before. It still was annoying to overlook something so obvious, though. Hmm. He should check his notifications. That would probably make him feel better, especially if he could finish the Physical Alchemist Path now.

Level Up!
Research Level 27→29
Mana Infusion Level 13→14
Basic Mana Sense Level 23→24
Identify Level 13→15
Outsider's Almanac Level 27→28
Skill Points: 96

Excellent. Who even needs life-or-death situations when you can do science? Or … alchemy?

You have completed the Physical Alchemist Path!
Alchemy, that strange and long-derided practice, has for so long been a mild curiosity, something for practitioners of the healing arts and craftsfolk, not meriting study nor prominence. And yet to the eyes of an Outsider, it is a Path without equal as you rend reality to its base components and rebuild them to your whims.

That sounded quite awesome. Though it did bring up the question of whose knowledge these messages were based on. It couldn't have been custom-made from the System administrators; Edwin's previous experience indicated they would be trying to communicate with him more directly if that were the case. It couldn't be generic; his messages referenced things that were *distinctly* from Earth. It also couldn't just be his own thoughts, either, as *he* didn't know the state of alchemy practice on Joriah. Maybe some sort of combination? Generic messages, filtered through his own knowledge? More notifications had been piling up, though, so Edwin shifted his attention toward them.

Alchemy
Spin moonlight into threads as strong as steel, forge weapons as light as air, brew life itself.

Create magical materials.
Proficiency increases with level.
You may evolve your Improvisation Skill into the Alchemy Skill!
Accept Evolution? Y/N
Done!

...

Calculating Rewards ...
Class Change!
Outsider Apprentice → Outsider Chemist

The rush of satisfaction from completing a Path wasn't getting old anytime soon. Edwin felt the distinctly odd sensation of a second set of instincts settling in next to his half-remembered quantum physics class, not enough to really tell him anything, just enough for him to get a vague idea of what he needed to do in order to use the Alchemy Skill more effectively. There was more to it, as well. What he was doing—chemical reactions with magically infused materials—was just the surface of what Alchemy could accomplish, though he had no idea how to do anything else. Maybe with more levels, maybe with more experimentation, but just not yet.

Unbidden, a thought rose to mind. Limelight. ... That was a thing, back in the 1800s. That used lime, right? If it burned brightly enough to be used as a spotlight, Edwin could only imagine how brightly the magical version would be. His next batch of lime was ready, after all. May as well give it a go.

He yawned. Tomorrow, then.

The next day, Edwin, armed with full lab equipment getup and a set of long tongs, took a pebble-sized chunk of lime and carefully set it on a stiff piece of mesh. Then, with goggles firmly in place, he set the burner beneath it to maximum heat and spun around. The first trial was only the control, to see if nonmagical lime burned at the temperatures he had at his disposal, and how bright it was. That said, he didn't want to blind himself, hence making sure to turn around before it started to burn. The precaution proved itself quite valuable as the entire workshop was lit up by a harsh white light, casting sharp shadows on every surface.

Well, that seems to have been a success.

The light didn't seem to be fading, though. Why wasn't it burning up? Through squinted eyes, he turned around and groped blindly at the limelight's source, eventually managing to knock it off its pedestal, and when it fell onto the counter, its glow began to fade. Once it was dim enough to look at comfortably, Edwin studied the white pebble. Hadn't it burned at all? A quick Identify confirmed it was still made of lime. Where did the light come from, then? Something to look into, he supposed.

Edwin made a quick note of lime's luminance before taking the pebble and Infusing it, then putting it back onto the pedestal and starting the burner again. This time, the light was utterly blinding. If he thought the previous trial was bright, it was nothing compared to the *mana-powered continuous flash-bang* levels of brightness he was currently dealing with. Even the reflection from the walls was enough to blind him. Through his Mana Sense Skill, he was able to feel the magic radiating off the glowing rock until it ran out a few seconds later, and the light returned to the comparatively *much* more bearable levels it was at before.

So he had managed to find a substance that gave off mana as it reacted. He could use that. His next step was to create a dome of uncured Infused putty, place it over the recently re-Infused lime pebble, and start up the fire again. The covering managed to contain both the light and the mana admirably, and neither radiated uncontrollably across the room. Testing the dome, he found that it had mostly, though not completely, cured from the mana given off by the light. It made sense now why it cured over time, if it passively absorbed ambient mana.

Edwin was mulling over possible ways he could use the materials he had at his disposal to escape, when he was startled by the door into his cell slamming open. In came two gruff-looking dwarves, wearing almost full plate armor and open-faced helmets.

"Hey! What's going on here?" Edwin demanded, only to receive no response, the newcomers instead marching over to where he was standing and grabbing his arms, twisting them until he was in front of the dwarves; then they half marched, half shoved him out of the room and into the hallway. "Hey! Let … me … go!" Edwin struggled, but the grip of the dwarves was absolute.

As Edwin was dragged along, he kept an eye on the layout, which he hadn't quite managed to memorize as he was being pulled into his cell the first time. His room was near the end of a hallway with no other visible doors, and the single guard posted nearby joined in the march. The hallway itself was essentially featureless (though the walls continued to be intricately carved) and about fifty feet long. It then opened into what appeared to be some kind of mess hall, with hundreds of dwarves milling about at masses of long tables. Was that *iron ore* some of them were eating? Did they eat *rocks*? What the heck was going on with their physiology that had them eating literally raw iron? Oops, don't get so distracted that you miss which archway is yours. Oh, the one directly opposite the main entrance. Well, that was easy enough to remember. Hopefully it wasn't always this busy, though.

Out the main entrance to a huge stairway (with dwarf-sized stairs, no less; those were a pain to climb) going up and up and up … A few individuals were here, though not too many coming and going from the seeming feast below, and then the staircase opened out into the main cavern of the citadel, complete with still-flowing rivers of molten metal. Edwin didn't get a chance to stare more at the spectacle, though, as he continued to be yanked along, this time up a short flight of stairs to where the dwarven Lord S'omethingorother sat upon a Blackstone throne.

"Where is my Blackstone, human?" he asked, and Edwin blinked.

"You speak English now as well? Oh wait, is this that Polyglot thing again?"

"I require no such Skill to comprehend your pitiful language, Outsider. Now I ask again. Where is my Blackstone?"

"What? It's been like three days!"

"I told you to make me Blackstone. Do you not understand your position here?"

Edwin struggled futilely against the grasp of his dwarven escort. "What the heck? I've barely had any time to even reinvent *concrete*, let alone your stupid supermaterial! I have to reinvent an entire *branch* of material science with nothing but half-remembered linguistic tricks and *then* discover a wholly unique branch of science with no assistance! I—"

"Enough," the dwarf said, cutting him off. "I will not hear your excuses. You promised me Blackstone; I intend to collect."

"I didn't promise you anything! And I've been working nonstop on this stuff. It's not easy. Honestly, you're worse than my professor."

"Oh?" S'limeball let out a bark of mocking laughter. "You claim to have been working on Blackstone when you have in truth been working on weapons to use against us? We know your tricks, saboteur. We should have never accepted your aid."

That statement left Edwin blinking in confusion. Accepted his aid? What? Also, weapons? Was it the limelight? So, *could* they see into the room? They were either negligent or didn't think his accidental explosions yesterday were worth worrying about. It *had* to have been the limelight, then. Sensitive eyes, perhaps? If they were a subterranean race, that could be their weakness …

S'laver noticed Edwin's confusion and seemed to willfully misinterpret it. "You admit to your wrongdoing! Why should I not have you executed where you stand?"

"Because you … want the Blackstone really badly and I'm the best chance you've had your entire life? Because I've already gotten farther in three days than you did over the course of years?" Edwin guessed wildly. *Something* clearly drove the dwarf to near madness in his obsession with the material, so it had to have been really valuable and made the clan desperate. Sure, it was a shot in the dark, but what else was new?

Something he said must have struck a nerve of some kind, as his captor fell relatively silent, before speaking up again, this time in Dwarven. As Edwin was dragged away, S'nob switched back to English for his last threat: "Hear me, Outsider. Your Task is, and continues to be, to make me Blackstone. Fail, and you are worthless to me. Plot against me, and I shall keep your head to myself. It is possibly the only useful thing about you. Now, begone and resume your Task."

Edwin's last glimpse of the dwarf as he was turned around and dragged off showed him looking unbearably smug.

CHAPTER 17

The Time of Our Limes

Edwin fumed in his cell, peeved about his "meeting." He wasn't a miracle worker; he didn't even know what Blackstone was made of! It was presumably some variant of concrete, but that was still a colossal assumption. For all he knew, it was magically transmuted water or something. Or cooled magma. It *did* look vaguely igneous in nature, but Edwin didn't even know how to *begin* determining that sort of thing. Its being volcanic in nature would actually make a lot of sense ...

Escaping had become a much higher priority now, but he was still nowhere close to managing that. He needed more Skill levels, more experience, more materials ... More everything, really. The dwarves all probably had Skills of their own, and he'd need to combat that somehow. What might he even be dealing with? Darksight, Iron Teeth, probably weapon and armor Skills. ... And he'd have to somehow figure out how do it while only able to really focus on Blackstone/Concrete. That was fine. Some experimentation with lime would probably yield impressive results.

Edwin moved back to his lab bench. He'd have to keep working to make his Task-compulsion lord happy, and it sounded like trying to defy him might cost Edwin his life. Rashin's earlier words had suggested that Edwin was still under some level of protection from the host, but Edwin wasn't about to risk his life by calling a bluff. Besides, if the actions of the dwarven lord so far were anything to judge him by, the lord probably didn't care much for hospitality rules, at least not in spirit. Maybe in letter? Who knows. Someone with a more complete picture of the forces at play and a grasp on dwarven psychology might manage it, but not Edwin. All he knew was he needed to be on his toes and at least pretend to play nice.

So that meant work. Lots of work. They didn't micromanage him, at least. Small mercies and all. He had a system down, which was also nice. *Still doesn't make it easy, though*, he thought as he brought his sledgehammer down, crushing another chunk of limestone into rubble.

That rubble was loaded into his kiln, heated for a couple hours, pulled out (putting in a new set of limestone), and pounded into dust. Mix the powder with a bit of water (carefully, trying not to make it into a paste) and repeat.

Another batch of plaster was produced.

Another day passed; more lime was made and pounded into dust.

More experiments had their results jotted down.

Edwin practically ran on autopilot as the days turned into weeks, interrupted only once every few days to be dragged out to Lord S'Fishkill, yelled at for a few minutes about his lack of results, told his Task was to make Blackstone (or concrete, which was added later), and returned to his cell. After a few times of returning to find his notebook or other tools *decidedly* not where he had left them, Edwin realized that his workshop was being searched, presumably for any "weapons," like the limelight, he might be creating to try to escape.

Sure, having his only real "human" contact be a self-important dwarf with anger management issues probably wasn't healthy in the long run, but Edwin could just stay silent in the meetings and it wouldn't make a difference. So, he tuned out all of S' … S'ineedbetterinsults's ranting and it all worked out.

Rashin started making an appearance at one point, coming in as Edwin was summoned from his cell, walking alongside him to the court, where Rashin stood off to the side, and escorting Edwin back. The scholar tried striking up a conversation a few times, asking Edwin more about himself, but his charge never obliged.

* * *

Edwin's Logbook, Day 24

Notes on plaster creation: Infusing small amounts of mana (rate of 1 second of infusion per estimated 10 kilos) into lime prior to mixing in 5 kilos of (nonmagical) water would give the reaction just enough energy to seemingly completely react while still leaving no excess moisture in the plaster. This powder form seems to be stable and nonmagical.

No noticeable variation between plaster made of Infused powder and that made of nonmagical powder Infused after mixing it with water. Namely, higher mana content stiffens the plaster slurry, allowing it to be set quickly. Mana can be removed from this set plaster to return it to uncured form. However, over several hours, this latter aspect fades as the plaster sets via the natural method.

Mixing magical water into nonmagical plaster resulted in a very watery slurry that solidified via crystallization, curing in patches rather than all at once. The process seems to mimic freezing.

Using magical water and magical plaster resulted in a magically saturated plaster that automatically cured at a rate comparable to mundane water and mundane plaster.

Notes on mana infusion: It seems as though mana is infused at the atomic or subatomic level, but the effect of said mana is variable depending on what molecule said atom is bound into. Some mana is released during a chemical change. Some experiments seem to contradict one another. Further research is required once I have proper measurement tools.

On mortar creation: Mixing sand into plaster creates a mortar mixture much more structurally sound than mere plaster (which is hard but breaks under sustained force).

N-N-N: A nonmagical mixture of plaster, sand, and water creates a basic mortar mixture. Functions basically as my memories of mortar on Earth, just not as high-quality. Infusing it with mana causes instant curing.

N-N-M: When using nonmagical plaster and sand but magical water, the sand seems to slide out of plaster mix as it cures, condensing at the bottom into a form of sandstone.

N-M-N: Using nonmagical plaster and water but magical sand results in the sand refusing to interact with the plaster and water, sliding directly off. Resulting mixture is just plaster mix.

M-N-N: Depending on the ratio of magical plaster to nonmagical sand used, this can result in making something like permanent sand structures (such as sandcastles), which can be sculpted and harden without gaining much strength, or by Infusing it once set but before cured, it can mimic M-M-N mortar (below).

M-N-M: Creates a very sticky mortar, which readily adheres to almost anything. When cured, it remains attached to whatever it was in contact with but loses its stickiness.

N-M-M: Creates a substance when cured that looks and acts similarly to wet sandstone in most respects but has a very low coefficient of friction (lab equipment not precise enough to properly measure, but its comparable to ice). M-N-M does not adhere but does not slide freely across it either.

M-M-N: Seems to function as standard magical mortar, being supernaturally tough, capable of supporting at least twice the weight a comparable amount of N-N-N mortar is capable of holding.

M-M-M: Cures slowly into a substance resembling concrete. Is difficult to shape properly but much stronger than M-N-N, with the current best sample withstanding an additional 50% additional force before breaking.

I need a better naming scheme, Edwin thought as he updated his notes with his latest test, the cracked M-M-M cement. *Gah, it's even bad in my head*, resting on the tabletop in front of him. *Maybe slipstone for N-M-M? Supermortar for M-M-M and magical mortar for M-N-M? M-M-N isn't distinct enough for its own name, and maybe sandsculpt for M-N-N? I'm no good at this. Still, at least the way it currently is doesn't take many characters.*

Edwin sighed, removing his gloves and setting his notebook to the side. It was getting late, and he was hungry. That was enough work for today. As he settled into his chair, eating the food provided for him, he decided that he'd look over his Skill level-ups today. It *had* been about three weeks since he had last done so, after all. At first it was just because he was too mad at Lord S'tupid to want to give himself a distraction, then it was a way to make the days go by faster. Regardless! It was time to change that.

Level Up!
Alchemy Level 1→15
Research Level 29→32
Outsider's Almanac Level 28→34
Mana Infusion Level 14→26
Basic Mana Sense Level 24→29
Identify Level 15→27
Athletics Level 18→21
Nutrition Level 9→14
Language Level 4→12
Walking Level 19→20
Firestarting Level 21→23
Sleeping Level 11→16
Breathing Level 11→13
Throwing Weapons Level 5→8
Mathematics Level 31→35
Visualization Level 18→23

Whew. That was a lot. It put him at 97 Skill Points, which was enough to fill out almost any of his Paths, but Edwin held back on assigning them right away. He'd need to think about what he wanted next, and what would help him in his current predicament.

Still, that was practically all his Skills getting in on the action there. Apparently, he had been walking around enough just in his tiny workshop to get a level in Walking, and breaking enough rocks for three levels in Athletics. Throwing Weapons would probably have leveled up with that one incident last week that he didn't want to think about, Language from studying his Dwarven dictionary regularly, and the others probably just from routine use. Sleeping must have slowed down somewhat, though. That was a shame, though if it hadn't it might have been too easy a source of Skill Points.

Edwin was getting close to the end of his time here. After nearly a month of work, he had fairly good ratios for his strongest mortar, though it still wasn't Blackstone. He was still nowhere close to understanding the stuff, and despite constant reminders from Mr. "Give Me

Blackstone" telling Edwin he had better hurry up if he wanted to live, it was too alien a stone for Edwin to even have a clue where to start. Honestly, he wasn't sure why the dwarf was so convinced that Edwin *could* provide. Simple denial, perhaps?

Edwin's Alchemy instincts only helpfully provided that it didn't seem Alchemy related in the slightest but was more likely the strange product of some form of highly evolved Skill. In other words, he wasn't going to replicate it this way, using the sort of alchemy he knew. Well, at least not the kind he knew so far.

So he wasn't getting out that way. Which only left fighting his way out, not that he'd ever really anticipated otherwise. His weapons were limited basically to whatever was closely related enough to cement and concrete for him to focus on for more than an hour, so only things he could make out of limestone. Still, that meant he had limelight, slip-stone, quick-drying mortar, steam grenades, and powdered lime, which would *absolutely* cause chemical burns if it got on someone, especially if it were Infused.

But if he were to escape, he'd still need to get somewhere. Which brought up what he was going to spend his Skill Points on. He pulled up his Paths to check his options.

Very Much Yes-Eventually
Micro-Biomancer 0/90, Path Less Traveled 0/90, Realm Traveler 0/120, Scientist 0/60
Promising
Stonehide Vanquisher 0/60, Titan Slayer 0/90, World Traveler 0/60, Researcher 0/60, Explorer 0/60, Outsider 0/60, Linguist 0/60, Bomber 0/60
Maybe One Day
Survivor 0/60, Athlete 0/60, Daredevil 0/60, Pioneer 0/60, Novice Pyromancer 0/60
Meh
Lumberjack 0/60, Way of the Empty Hand 0/60, Trapper 0/60

Micro-Biomancer probably wasn't going to be helpful either in combat or helping him get away without being recaptured unless he made some sort of bioweapon, which Edwin was *not* keen on doing even if he somehow got that kind of Skill. Path Less Traveled and Realm Traveler were wildcards. He had *no idea* what they would do (teleportation, maybe? That would definitely be cool, if unlikely), though they might at least help him survive the wilderness better this time. Scientist was cool, but again, he wasn't sure how much it would help.

Stonehide Vanquisher was apparently a Trophy Path, from what Rashin had said, and would give him a cool item of some sort, possibly a cloak made of the train-sized beast's eponymous hide. Titan Slayer would probably give him some kind of combat-based Skill, so it went on the shortlist.

World Traveler and Explorer did as well, as they would help him after he escaped. Researcher was discarded for the time being accordingly, and he was about to do the same to Linguist when he reconsidered. If Rashin hadn't been lying—and would he have been lying?—it was likely to give Edwin the Polyglot Skill, which would be really useful when interacting with anyone.

Outsider might do any number of things, so it was similarly too risky to try. Survivor and Athlete ... were both possible. Either would most likely help him in some way after he got out, and maybe even in the meantime depending on what they did.

Way of the Empty Hand, then? Ehhh ... Edwin was no master of martial arts, and even on Earth there was a reason that unarmed fighters weren't really a thing. He might get some sort of unarmed combat Skill, sure, but he'd be against armed foes who *also* had Skills. He didn't like those odds.

Bomber, though ... Bomber would probably be the most beneficial overall. It would most likely make his steam grenades, his most potent weapon, more effective, evolving either Firestarting or Throwing Weapons to do so. That would help him get out, and then he'd need some way to survive once he did.

The Blackstone road leading down the mountain would keep him from getting lost, so whatever benefit Explorer or Survivor would have once provided would probably be redundant, so long as he brought along enough food. It would be risky traveling in such open space should the dwarves try to pursue him, but Edwin was more focused on not getting lost in the wilderness again. If he did get lost in the wilderness somehow, he could always just complete the Path then. Not like he'd get much chance to level up a wilderness-survival Skill while he was in here.

Still, he couldn't just stay away from civilization forever. Some people might enjoy making everything they used from absolute scratch, but not Edwin. So that meant it was inevitable that he would want to interact with other people eventually. Plus, if dwarves were chasing him, he'd need to … be able to persuade other people that they were in the wrong and they should help him instead of them. That meant communication, which meant Polyglot, which in turn meant the Linguist Path. Also, he totally wasn't just desperate for meaningful human interaction with people who *weren't* trying to exploit him. It would be just like the first few weeks of college again, but now he had better social skills and knew once again what not to do.

Nope … That definitely didn't factor into his calculations at all.

Bomber and Linguist combined took 120 Skill Points, so he wasn't quite there yet. Also, with how low his Throwing Weapons Skill was, he should probably try to get a few more levels in that before taking a chance with Bomber advancing it and wasting his chance for easier Skill Points. How to level it, though, was the question. Hmm … Following his gut, Edwin picked up a piece of relatively smooth limestone that fit into his hand and threw it at the corner of the room. It hit slightly off-target and clattered across the floor. With a slight groan of exertion—he'd been sitting down for too long—Edwin picked himself up and went to retrieve it. A dozen tries and a quick diversion working on cement production later, and he had what he was looking for.

Level Up!
Throwing Weapons Level 8→9

Perfect. Twenty-two levels to go.
He'd be out of here in no time.

CHAPTER 18

What's Left of Bare Arms

It took Edwin three days of throwing rocks at the wall whenever he could and five levels in the Skill before his complete lack of talent was offset by whatever bonus he was receiving from Throwing Weapons and he was able to start juggling. Once he did so, he swiftly confirmed his suspicion that constantly keeping three balls in the air *did* help him level up his Throwing Weapons Skill, and the near-constant use of his Skill (juggling was fun when you could actually do it!) meant it rose steadily. By the time he hit level 24, he could keep four rocks in the air or juggle two one-handed. That wasn't the only benefit, either.

Congratulations! For reaching level 12 in Throwing Weapons you have unlocked the Warrior Path!

Attempting to juggle rocks while working hadn't gone well at all, which slowed his practice down some, but Edwin found that he *could* toss things from one hand to the other without his attention getting mad at him. Integrating his Skill training into his every movement had paid dividends.

After several weeks, Throwing Weapons, once his lowest-leveled Skill, was now at level 47, which, while not quite as high as Almanac—which had hit level 61 two days ago—was nonetheless quite respectable. Yes, his initial idea had been to just raise it high enough to afford the Bomber and Linguist Paths with it, but further reflection had him doubting if that was a good idea. It was, after all, easier to improve a lower-leveled Skill's level, and if he wanted to evolve all his Skills eventually, that meant he would similarly want to *level* all his Skills to the 60–90 range.

That realization made him want to bang his head against the wall for trying to advance Basic Mana Manipulation at level 9, when he had only been at level 14 and 22 for his other evolved Skills. Gah!

Well, that was all in the past and there was nothing he could do about it now. At least he kept the benefits of the base Skills so he technically didn't *lose* anything beyond some easy Skill Points and additional System power.

Hopefully, Edwin would be able to get Throwing Weapons and Language up to half-decent levels before he had to break out. His last audience with Lord S'fashkchlil (hitting level 24 in Language had gotten him to the point of being able to barely pronounce the tongue-twister of the name, though most of the time Edwin still preferred to use whatever insult came to mind when thinking about his captor) had been even rougher than usual, and overhearing the chatter of other dwarves made him realize S'tinker was under pressure due to ... something. Edwin hadn't caught the details. Research seemed to combine well with his Language practice, and he was able to at least catch the gist of what was being said in Dwarven most of the time, even if his ability to speak it was rudimentary at best.

Hmm. Actually, if he wasn't mistaken, he would probably be getting an audience with the "esteemed" head of Clan Blackstone today. It had been a few days, after all. Edwin wondered what insults and threats he'd be subjected to today. Would he stick with the digs against humanity, or would it return to the tirade against extraplanars? He couldn't *wait* to find out.

Almost on cue, the door opened and his guards—the same two Blackstone sentries as always—entered, then stood aside for a third figure to enter. Rashin, for his part, stepped past the two mostly alert figures and swept into the room. Edwin raised an eyebrow. That was different. As Rashin snagged Edwin's notebook from the bench, he got *very* suspicious. In the past, the dwarves had always been careful to not make it obvious they were disturbing his stuff; what had changed?

As Rashin left the room, notebook in hand, Edwin shrugged and followed along. He knew the whole song and dance like the back of his hand by now, no need to rock the boat. To his surprise, the sentries barred his way with their spears.

"Wait," one of them said in Dwarven, and Edwin looked at him dumbly.

"What's the holdup?" he asked, in English naturally. No point letting his *captors* know he could understand them. It was, after all, the only way he had caught what little information he had from them. The guard merely grunted in response, and Edwin shifted from one foot to the next impatiently.

After about a minute, the dwarves uncrossed their spears in perfect unison (was there a Skill involved in those sorts of coordinated movements?), turned, and led Edwin out the door and down the hall, through the (currently empty) mess hall, up the stairs, up the *other* stairs, and into the throne room. There, flipping through Edwin's notebook, was S'Fashkchlil, wearing the perhaps most displeased expression Edwin had yet seen on the man.

"For the longest time, *Outsider* ..."

Ah, so it was an Earthling-insulting day. Good to know.

"... I have allowed your behavior to slide. I believed you indeed had some form of reasoning behind your endless repetition and inane work. You recorded so much in your journal, which I had believed held countless insights and notes to the process you seemed so insistent would provide results ..."

The dwarf was half yelling now, and Edwin's eye itched. It was really annoying; he wanted to rub it but figured His Blusteriness wouldn't be amused. Oh, he was still talking.

"... that whatever you were writing was unreadable even by Magistrate Rashin due to poor *handwriting* ..."

Well. That was a bit harsh. In his defense, the quill and inkwell they apparently expected him to write with were *impossible* to use. He would have to make a fountain pen as soon as he had the chance and remembered how to ...

"... find out that you have been writing nothing but *actual* nonsense interspersed with insults toward not only myself ..."

In hindsight, it may not have been the *smartest* idea to actually write his thoughts about Lord S'fishkill down, especially as his quill-work was half legible by that point, but Edwin had *really* needed to vent at the time. The drawing may have been a bit much, though. Hmm. Did the dwarf lord have a Skill pertaining to volume? Shouting, maybe. Could Edwin go deaf from overexposure to this loud of a voice? Could *S'houter* go deaf? Was that why he was always so loud?

"... so you have three days to give me something I can actually *use* in this Gor'kcha-damned war ..."

They were at war? Interesting. And was Gor'kcha a god? Were there gods on this world? Edwin probably should try to find out.

"... swear to you, I will have your head cut off and mounted upon a stake. Do you understand me?"

Edwin nodded vaguely, then caught what exactly was said. "Wait, what?"

The dwarf's face somehow grew even more thunderous, which Edwin hadn't thought possible. "I said, your Task is to, within three days, show me the results of your work, and they had best be impressive, or I will cut off your head and mount it upon a pike."

Edwin was taken aback. Well, beyond the fact that he had never promised *anything*, what was more surprising was the direct threat to his life. Sure, ominous-sounding warnings and insults were par for the course, but never before had he been *actively threatened with death* if he didn't produce results. This was probably serious, then. Darn it. He was nowhere *close* to ready, but it sounded like he was out of time. This would be a few *very* busy days.

Edwin was snapped out of his musings by his notebook impacting his shoulder with a very painful *smack*. Gah, that hurt. It didn't feel like it broke anything, but it would probably leave a welt. He tuned out something about "getting out of my sight" as he picked up the slightly battered notebook. Flipping open to a random page, he checked to make sure it still was working properly.

Identify.

No noticeable variation between plaster made of Infused powder and that made of nonmagical powder, Infused after mixing it with water. Namely, higher mana content stiffens the plaster slurry, allowing it to be set quickly.

Okay, that was a relief. The damage to the notebook hadn't affected his Almanac entries at all, not that he had really expected it to. Sure, he had most of his critical notes saved on other things—materials or generic items like spoons, generally—but the notebook's pages were where it was most organized.

Sure, his adviser would probably throw a fit about these records being editable, but he didn't need to sign and date the pages to deal with possible patent disputes anyway, and there wasn't a Carbon-12's chance of decay that he'd write out everything using a *feather quill*. So Edwin had just used Almanac and Identify for his notes. His Skill levels *loved* it, and he was at 273 characters these days, so he could actually fit most of a paragraph in a single entry.

As his cell door slammed shut behind him, his feet having walked him back to his room nearly on autopilot, Edwin caught himself absently tossing his notebook from hand to hand. With a sigh, he tossed the slightly tattered tome onto a small patch of empty counter. Checking the kiln, he found that his latest batch of lime was done, so he scraped out the rubble and replaced it with fresh limestone. The next few days would be *crazy* busy, but he needed to start slow. He had done enough odd things that making a few spheres out of mortar wasn't that strange, but if he was too blatant, the dwarves might notice what he was doing and that would be Very Bad. Also, he'd have to work around his Task's compulsion, which … Wait.

Edwin had gotten pretty good at recognizing and dealing with the limits imposed on him by the lord's command to "make Blackstone/ concrete," but that was completely gone. What had … oh. OH. His Task had changed! It wasn't "make concrete" anymore, it was "show me something impressive that you've been working on"! Edwin couldn't help but chuckle as a smile spread across his face. Oh, he could *absolutely* do something impressive. Just you wait.

It was time to get to work.

* * *

Knowing in advance that he was likely to get some kind of Skill that benefited bombs had led Edwin to develop a sort of grenade casing made purely from mortar. The trick was finding some setup that wouldn't go off or crack on its own but would do so quite easily once thrown.

For most of his arsenal, the answer was two hollow hemispheres of M-N-N mor—no, *sandsculpt*—which he would fill and then fit together with a tiny coating of M-N (magical lime, nonmagical water) plaster. The plaster kept the seemingly loose sand from being rubbed away and the two halves together, and the sandsculpt helped keep the plaster in shape and prevented it from cracking open. The trickiest part was just keeping the sandsculpt from becoming magically infused when he insta-cured the plaster, which would harden it and make it almost unbreakable.

Some of his grenades, though, required more delicate treatment. His steam bombs, which would be the deadliest of his entire arsenal, were entirely encased in a full (if thin) supermortar casing. Those Edwin made by carefully pouring a bit of Infused lime inside, coating it with a tiny, tiny amount of plaster, and filling the rest with water, once the plaster was cured. It was a nerve-racking procedure, and the first few times he did it, he was worried that the moisture in the plaster would react hyperexplosively with the Infused lime it was covering.

Then Edwin realized he had been an idiot and he could just wait to Infuse the lime until he was ready to use it. It would still be dangerous before then—even mundane lime's reaction was exothermic enough to boil water—but the casing should keep it from outright detonating. He made sure to test that he could prime the lime even through its coating—he could, but doing so also Infused the water inside the grenade, which *should* be all right. Sadly, he wasn't able to test his grenades, for obvious reasons, but there wasn't much of an alternative.

The next two days passed in a blur, as Edwin set casings, mixed mortar, and entertained himself via tongue twisters and juggling, managing to net one last level in each of the Skills. *Actually*, he realized, *I don't need to fill out my Linguist Path right now, just Bomber. If I encounter more people, I can just complete the Path then. Sure, the Polyglot Skill will be a lower level, but I doubt it would level up much before then anyway.*

Edwin also managed to rework a couple of discarded sacks, brought in with loads of limestone. When he had first seen the burlap-looking bags, he was stunned at the fact that they held up to what must have been two hundred pounds of rock while slung over the shoulder of a Blackstone Laborer. Close inspection with his Basic Mana Sense Skill had shown the fabric was interwoven with some kind of magic, present but barely noticeable. Infusion hadn't done anything, but some experiments had shown that nothing short of his full weight behind a knife could tear the material.

A few attempts at improvising them into a form more conducive to carrying yielded sad-looking, barely functional backpacks and a couple of somewhat-better book-bag-like containers.

There was one last pleasant surprise waiting for Edwin as he packed his arsenal away (his backpack was filled with food, a metal flagon of water, and some other odds and ends). As he placed a gingerly wrapped explosive inside a rag and packed in some excess space with sand, a notification popped up. He almost ignored it, not really caring about a level-up, but it wasn't formatted like one.

You have unlocked the Packing Skill!
Accept Skill? Y/N

Most Skills Edwin had been offered in his time with Clan Blackstone—Baking, Sand Sculpting, Shaving, Small Blades, Geology, Writing, Mixing, and more—he had rejected with varying degrees of regret, not wanting to clutter up his Skill list too much.

They'd provide Skill Points, sure, but they would also make it harder for him to evolve all his Skills, which from what he had gathered, was important. Unlocking a Skill let you do something you were already capable of, just better. Evolving a Skill would let you do something new. So he had always pushed off the decision—a rejected Skill could still be offered again, if the number of times he had to decline Rock Breaking was any indication—to Future-Edwin. The nice thing about Future-Edwin was that he was older and therefore wiser, so automatically more qualified for this kind of decision than Present-Edwin.

Packing, though? Packing was immediately useful *and* useful long term as well. Edwin could only haul around some fifty pounds of stuff over extended periods of time, and his arsenal, being mostly more or less solid rock, weighed *far* above that. He hoped the Packing Skill would help his carrying weight so he wouldn't be quite as slowed by all his gear during his escape, and further help him as he … did whatever he was going to do after he escaped. His straining while he lifted his mostly full bag settled it in his mind, but first Edwin decided to complete his Bomber Path, just in case something strange happened.

Bomb Throwing
You're the bomb. Not *completely* literally, but close enough.
Throw bombs.
Power of weaponized explosives increases with level.
You may evolve your Throwing Weapons Skill into the Bomb Throwing Skill!
Accept Evolution? Y/N
Done!

…

Calculating Rewards…
Class Change!
Outsider Chemist → Alchemist Outsider
You have completed the Bomber Path!

Your way has taken a fairly explosive turn. Fortunately, you have survived, yet those who stand against you may not. You are beginning to show some of your potential, though you still have a long way to go before you are a true force to be reckoned with.

Perfect.

Packing
Useful when trying to bear the whole weight of the world on your shoulders.
Carry heavy loads easier.
Strength when carrying objects increased per level.

Status.

Name

Edwin Maxlin

Age

22 years

Race

Extraplanar Human

Class

Alchemist Outsider

Attributes

Mana 5

Skills

Magical

Basic Mana Sense: 29, Firestarting: 23, Alchemy: 41, Mana Infusion: 53

Physical

Athletics: 23, Breathing: 15, Flexibility: 11, Nutrition: 16, Packing: 1,
Seeing: 15, Sleeping: 20, Survival: 12, Walking: 20

Mental

Identify: 27, Language: 33, Mathematics: 37, Research: 40, Outsider's
Almanac: 61, Visualization: 23

Combat

Bomb Throwing: 1

Paths

Skill Points: 206

Very Much Yes-Eventually

Micro-Biomancer 0/90, Path Less Traveled 0/90, Realm Traveler 0/120,
Scientist 0/60

Promising

Stonehide Vanquisher 0/60, Titan Slayer 0/90, World Traveler 0/60,
Researcher 0/60, Explorer 0/60, Outsider 0/60, Linguist 0/60, Warrior
0/60

Maybe One Day

Survivor 0/60, Athlete 0/60, Daredevil 0/60, Pioneer 0/60, Novice Pyromancer 0/60, Warrior 0/60

Meh

Lumberjack 0/60, Way of the Empty Hand 0/60, Trapper 0/60

CHAPTER 19

Stupid Cheating Skills

Today was the day.

Edwin had had a hard time falling asleep, even when he activated his Skill, but he managed it eventually and woke up well rested. He didn't have much of an appetite but made sure to eat as much breakfast as possible to keep his energy up anyway. He'd taken a bath, shaved, and changed into clean clothes the night before, so he would start this trek into the wilderness off fresh. His boots, as comfortable as ever, were laced up tightly. His backpack was filled to the brim with food, knives, various heating plates, a pebble of Blackstone, a chisel, his notebook, and more. His gloves were concealing a miniature blowtorch hot enough to melt iron. His twin bags filled with ammo and his backpack were hidden behind piles of rock.

There was nothing else he could do to get ready, and Edwin's heart was racing. He was *not* ready, but he had to appear calm and like nothing was unusual. He hefted his sledgehammer and brought it down on a chunk of limestone.

This is going to fail, I'm going to die, what am I thinking, I'm going to die, I'm going to die, I'm going to— He closed his eyes and took a deep breath.

He could do this. If he didn't do it, he was dead anyway, so there was nothing to lose. He would survive. He had *Science!* to do. He was a proper Alchemist, too! It even said so in his Status. Edwin took another calming breath and had to set down his hammer due to how much his hands were shaking. Another breath. In and out. In. Hold. Out. Hold. In. Hold. Out. …

Level Up!
Breathing Level 15→16

Oh, right. He should turn off his notifications now. Edwin didn't want them distracting him during his escape run.

Breathe in, breathe out.

Focus.

Stay calm.

Grab on to the edge of the counter; that should help keep his shaking hands steady.

Breathe deeply. He closed his eyes and counted to one hundred. Another deep breath. He mentally multiplied three 3x3 matrices together. Another deep breath. Recite the alphabet. Now do it backward. Another deep breath.

Edwin opened his eyes, hands barely trembling and breathing mostly under control. He picked up his hammer and continued to crush limestone, careful to not put too much effort into the activity and wear himself out.

Down the hall, up the stairs, to the left, he promised himself. He could do that. He didn't need to beat every dwarf in the mountain; he just needed to get *down the hall, up the stairs, to the left.*

Some sixth sense alerted Edwin to his company before they entered, and he positioned himself near where his packs were located. The door swung open, and Edwin saw Rashin enter in his peripheral vision, followed closely by the two guards.

"Guess it's time, then?" Edwin asked, of nobody in particular, trying to sound resigned. He sighed, heart racing, and before any of his foes could react, he threw his sledgehammer as hard as possible at Rashin's head.

The heavy iron head connected with the scholar's skull with a clang that sounded more like the hammer had struck a helmet rather than a skull, and the dwarf collapsed. The two guards were stunned, too shocked to properly react at first, and by the time they were in motion, Edwin already had two grenades in hand and a third at the ready.

The first was M-N-M mortar, the superadhesive, and it struck the base of the door, breaking open and sticking it in place. Edwin wasn't about to let them just close the door on him, after all.

The second was N-M-M, slipstone, and it hit right in front of the two guards, spreading its payload in front of them. It wouldn't do much in its wet state, but if cured ... Edwin quickly threw the third bomb at the ceiling. It struck and exploded in a powerful flash of magical light, exposing the slipstone to just enough mana to initially cure it.

Just in time, too. The guards' feet came down, found no purchase on the nearly frictionless material, and were thrown off-balance. By the time they recovered, shouting for help, Edwin already had his bags on, straining under the weight.

At least it was going to get much lighter very quickly. He could already hear the sound of approaching footsteps, and the third guard outside his cell was blocking the doorway.

As all his enemies were so kind as to be right next to each other, though admittedly right in front of the door, Edwin decided it was time to pull out the big guns. He primed a steam grenade and threw it directly at the third guard, ducking behind his lab bench and plugging his ears.

After a resounding *boom*, Edwin emerged from his hiding place to see all three dwarf guards mostly motionless, collapsed in various positions. The one he had struck with the grenade was bleeding from somewhere in his beard but they seemed otherwise fine, which was just *unfair*. Rashin didn't look to be in good shape, though, and Edwin moved on before he could get distracted.

All good so far; hopefully, his luck would hold out.

As he made it out into the hall, Edwin grabbed a spear from the ground but discarded it immediately. It was too cumbersome to use with his massive bags of ammo slung around his shoulders. Speaking of which, a group of dwarves was coming down the hallway at a decent clip. Perfect setup for a slipstone grenade. Edwin quickly withdrew and threw one, which landed perfectly in front of the squad, almost exactly where he'd aimed it ...

The sphere broke open, and a marble of cured slipstone rolled down the hallway, easily avoided by his advancing foes. Edwin bit back a curse as he threw another three in an offhand toss. One more broke open to reveal a dud grenade, but the other two worked properly, spreading liquid slipstone across the ground. He didn't have enough time to throw another flash-mana grenade, so he had to go with his backup plan.

Firestarter paired well with his favorite magitech blowtorch, and Edwin's gloves worked *just* well enough to protect him from the magical lime, heated up to thousands of degrees centigrade and emitting a light that threatened to blind Edwin even through closed eyes. More important was the rate at which he could pump mana into the substance.

A barrage of curses got Edwin to cut the heat and mana, allowing the light to fade to "mostly bearable" in brightness, and he was treated to the sight of a half-dozen dwarves covering their eyes and tripping over their own feet.

Unfortunately, the hallway was still covered in slipstone, and Edwin would fall on his back just as surely as the dwarves if he tried to cross it as he was, but he had at least thought about that in advance. He broke open a tiny plaster container and carefully applied a dot of superadhesive mortar to the toe of his shoes as he prepared to walk onto the frictionless surface.

Despite himself, Edwin felt the corners of his mouth twitch upward. *Assume a spherical grenade on a frictionless surface. ...*

By the time Edwin made it across the self-made hazard and managed to scrape off the mortar he had on his shoes (using a shard of slipstone made specifically for that purpose), it seemed as though the dwarves in his cell were starting to recover. Fortunately, they were on the wrong side of the slipstone, so he should be fine.

Down the hall, he thought with satisfaction, *up the stairs, to the left.*

As Edwin continued forward, he broke open about half of his remaining slipstone grenades to coat massive patchwork areas of the hallway, curing them as he went. He couldn't use all of them—they'd be too useful on the stairs for that—but any level of slowing down his enemies was welcome.

The mess hall was fairly empty again. A few dwarves were milling around, but some of them somehow didn't seem to notice what was happening, and most of those remaining were decidedly *not* looking at Edwin. There were a handful left, though, who seemed to take umbrage with his existence and charged at him, hefting various weapons. Okay, eight foes. Hopefully he could manage.

The first dwarf, right ahead of him, got entangled in a batch of super-adhesive and tripped, gluing even more of himself to the floor. Edwin threw a primed steam grenade to his right, which took care of one more but left the dwarf right next to him mostly unharmed, despite *surely* taking a few fragments of supermortar to the face—*dang, these guys are hardy*. Fortunately, the dwarf paused to check up on his fallen friend.

Two and a half down, five and a half to go.

The other dwarves were more wary now, having seen the sort of firepower Edwin had at his disposal, though one hefted a bench as a shield—the thing had to be twice as long as he was tall—and continued his advance. Edwin backed up until his leg bumped against another bench, and the others seemed to take that as encouragement and continued to approach slowly.

On the bright side, he now had a clear shot at the shield dwarf's legs, as he had moved into the center aisle ahead of Edwin. Withdrawing two more slipstone grenades and an instant-cure bomb, he threw them all at Shield dwarf's feet, then mentally changed targets.

To Edwin's shock, despite both the slipstone spreading properly and the cure going off as it should, Shield just grunted and planted his feet solidly on the utterly frictionless surface, as though it were just another patch of Blackstone. Edwin grimaced and prepared to throw a different kind of bomb

Stupid cheating Skills.

Edwin's reminder that other Skills were in play was driven home when a dwarf seemed to materialize from thin air and grabbed Edwin's arm. Sneaky (or teleporting?) dwarf probably regretted his decision instantly, though, as he drew breath to speak just as Edwin jerked his grenade-holding arm in surprise, which broke the plaster directly on Sneaky's forehead. Edwin looked in horror as the lime powder burst into the dwarf's face, getting all over his skin, into his beard, in his eyes …

The screaming started a moment later and made Edwin *exceedingly* glad he didn't have any exposed skin and his eyes were covered by his goggles, as Sneaky fell to the ground clutching his eyes even as the lime probably boiled them whole.

That certainly got his assailants to pause for a moment, especially when Edwin withdrew a matching grenade from his bag, and he spoke up in Dwarven for the first time, "Stay back, I pass. I don't want to hurt."

Okay, so he didn't really know the grammar, but he at least probably got the words right.

All but one of the remaining dwarves backed off at that, and when a solidly thrown grenade just bounced off his pursuer's head before rolling onto the ground (it was *supposed* to be a superadhesive, but apparently more than just slipstone had cured), this dwarf only got more bold. Another steam grenade followed, but it was batted from the air by the dwarf's axe, cut in half and unexploded. Clearly more Skill nonsense, and the stone crashed against the ground.

A quick barrage of different bombs—Edwin was frantically backpedaling, throwing whatever he could pull from his bag, his opponent blocking each throw with an impenetrable defense, falling more and more into a rhythm and blocking the attacks with more and more ease. Each clang of metal on stone rang out across the hall, but the dwarven cries for backup and help were barely overpowered, the elongated syllables of their tongue rarely drowned out by the sudden impact of steel on mortar.

Edwin was running out of bombs in his first bag, now, and while his second bag was almost full, it didn't have many of his adhesive and slick bombs, consisting mainly of his steam grenades, and the axe dwarf was too close at this point to risk one. Then the dwarf *blurred* and appeared right next to Edwin with his axe midswing.

Edwin barely managed to duck out of the way to keep the strike from hitting his head, but it still cut a painful line across his shoulder and down his chest, leaving him bleeding from what was a thankfully superficial cut.

Edwin almost breathed a sigh of relief, until he realized the strap on his mostly full bag had been severed by the attack. He could only watch in horror as the bag, stuffed to the brim with powerful explosives, fell seemingly in slow motion, dropping and cracking hard against the stone floor.

CHAPTER 20

Out with a Bang

Time seemed to freeze as Edwin's bag of high explosives clattered to the ground. He spared a panicked glance at the axe-wielding dwarf, who looked at him uncomprehendingly. Freed of some thirty pounds of ammunition, Edwin dove away from the bag as fast as he could.

A moment of clarity made him twist in midair so as to not land on his *other* bag of ammunition. Mostly empty it may be, but any bombs breaking open directly against his stomach would *not* be survivable. Once he was on the ground, though, Edwin rolled over to present as slim of a profile as possible, covering the back of his neck with his hands and screwing his eyes shut.

A massive explosion followed a moment later, as almost all Edwin's steam and flash grenades went off in unison. The axe-wielding dwarf responsible for the mess was still in one piece, amazingly, but his front was covered in fragments of stone and mortar and he'd been blown off his feet. Edwin couldn't tell if he had survived, but the dwarf wouldn't be happy even if he had.

Edwin scrambled to his feet and beheld the greater carnage. Fragments of stone were buried in the tables around him and, as Edwin realized when he tried to put weight on it, in his foot. Stifling a scream, he yanked out the offending piece of shrapnel and carried on as fast as he could limp.

From beyond the hall, Edwin could hear more dwarves approaching. He managed to make it to the bottom of the stairs all right—if any remaining dwarves had been considering attacking him before, they seemed to be quite dissuaded after the last explosion. But as another squad of dwarves came around the corner, and he heard movement and shouting above, he checked his stocks to see what exactly he had to work with.

Edwin's bag still held three each of sticky and steam bombs, four slipstone, one flash, four just filled with water, and one extralarge grenade entirely full of infused lime. He also had a decent amount of putty-hard supermortar. Overall, it was nowhere near enough. He had seen dwarves all but take a full-powered steam grenade to the face, and given the mix of Class names—none of which had seemed that impressive, being variations of Miners, Smiths, or Combat Miners—Edwin probably hadn't run into any actual high-level elites yet, who may well be able to shrug off his entire arsenal for all he knew. Scary thought.

Up the stairs, to the left.

Edwin started climbing the stairs three at a time, wincing every time the ball of his injured foot came down at the wrong angle. He didn't let that slow him down any, though, pushing forward through every shot of pain. He was perhaps a third of the way up the staircase when dwarves came into view at the top. They had pretty obviously been hastily called from being off-duty (which made Edwin wonder where the on-duty ones were), as half weren't wearing full suits of armor and the other half looked confused.

When they saw Edwin on the stairs, though, they seemed to come to some sort of consensus at remarkable speed, and two dwarves, one on each side of the group, pulled out crossbows and fired at him. Edwin hit the ground, but the bolts actually *curved midair* to follow him. Fortunately, though, they weren't able to turn enough to strike him head-on, and so while one cut through his leather lab coat and gave him a long cut along his back, the other just struck his backpack and stayed there. Edwin hissed at the pain, but he couldn't stop now.

There wasn't any cover on the stairway, so as the crossbow dwarves reloaded, Edwin began to frantically think of some way to survive the next pair. Below him, another set of dwarves began to climb the stairs.

Fortunately, the latter problem helped solve the former, as the marksmen at the top of the stairs seemed unwilling to shoot Edwin while their allies were in the line of fire, and they lowered their crossbows instead of taking aim. Edwin was more than happy to take advantage of the time provided to keep climbing the stairs, pulling out his supermortar putty to try and fashion himself a shield. Not like he had any other option. Unfortunately, the momentary reprieve was broken by a familiar, bellowing voice.

"What are you doing? Shoot him! Throw things at him!" S'Fashkchlil had arrived, apparently, and was yelling in Dwarven at his minions. Something was said in response, but too quietly for Edwin to understand it. He certainly heard the reply, though: "To the deep depths with them! They'll live! Just don't let him escape! Get that Skill if you must!"

Real inspiring leader there, Edwin thought, preparing himself to try and block the incoming shots. He hefted his makeshift shield, hiding his head and upper torso behind the magically strengthened mortar. The first shot clipped him in the shoulder, making him involuntarily release his grip on his shield with that hand. His right hand, not strong enough on its own to hold up the solid rock, dropped just enough for the next quarrel to strike the center of his makeshift creation instead of the edge. The entire block of mortar just *shattered*, covering his hand with cuts from the fragmented stone.

How the heck— NOT THE TIME, EDWIN.

Fortunately, Edwin had a slight reprieve as they reloaded, so his momentary distraction didn't kill him. He fumbled for a moment as he pulled out his limelight pebble and turned the heat on his blowtorch to the absolute maximum, boosting it and his Firestarting Skill with as much mana as he could manage (admittedly, not much). He couldn't hold the torch steady due to his left arm being out of commission from the *crossbow bolt sticking out of it*—at least Edwin was so high on adrenaline he barely felt it—so he broke open a grenade of sticky mortar and used that to glue the blowtorch to his glove, needing only to twist his hand to make it glow.

From the cries above, he gathered they were blinded by the light almost entirely, and before they could get the chance to accustom themselves to the brightness through whatever other unfair Skills they had,

Edwin charged up the stairs, head down and peering through heavily squinted eyes, as fast as his bruised and battered body would let him—which wasn't all that fast.

After a moment, the chaotic shouting became more organized and Edwin cut off the light, angling the pebble of lime so it wasn't in the flame anymore. There was a momentary delay, but everything was quickly plunged into inky blackness. The lime was making it as bright if not brighter than a sunny day, after all, and the halls were dimly lit. Eyes, whether human or dwarven, presumably, just couldn't adjust that fast.

Of course, Edwin wasn't taking the chance they somehow *could*, so he brought the lime back into the flame, returning daylight to the underground cavern. Then he pulled it out, flickering the light to make it almost impossible to adjust to the changing conditions. Naturally, it affected Edwin as well, but all he needed to do was judge how far it was to the next step. It wasn't exactly *easy* to do, with just a single eye left barely a hair open and the other tightly shut, but it was manageable and helped Edwin maintain his night vision.

Then he was at the top of the stairs, and Edwin cut the light one last time so he could get his bearings. *Up the stairs*, he mentally checked off, *and to the left*.

There were perhaps a dozen dwarves, only two armed with crossbows, in various states of disarray—Edwin's light must have been even more effective than he was anticipating—surrounding him, and another ten to twenty arranged in a loose semicircle around him. Behind the line stood Lord S'wordfish himself, staring Edwin down.

"So this is how you repay my hospitality? Attacking my citizens?" he asked in English, and Edwin scoffed.

"Hospitality? Hah! Don't make me laugh," Edwin knew the lord was just stalling for time to get his soldiers readjusted to the current light level, but that was fine. Edwin needed time to think as well. "I just want to leave. If I am truly a guest, let me walk out of that gate"—he indicated the massive door—"and we can go our separate ways."

"After you assaulted my kin? You have an interesting sense of humor, Outsider. You've violated hospitality. You shall never see the light of day again. You will—"

Edwin didn't let him finish. Instead, he darted forward and to the left, trying to break through a portion of the semicircle. Behind him, he broke two of his slippery bombs—one was a dud—and cured it with a tap of his foot. The dwarves around him surged forward, but without knowing that particular trick, they didn't know to avoid the slipstone, and it caused the first dwarf to fall flat on his back, triggering a cascading effect of his fellows almost comically tripping over him.

Every step sent daggers of pain into Edwin's foot and up his leg—there must have still been a bit of rock stuck in either his shoe or foot—but he couldn't stop now. Guards moved to intercept him, but Edwin fished out a steam grenade and threw it at the closest dwarf. It detonated with a bang and sent its target staggering back. It didn't matter how many times he had seen it. It was just flatly *unfair* that the dwarves could survive a grenade to the face. This time, though, there were marks on its target, and his face was a bloody mess. Maybe Edwin's Skill levels were finally getting high enough to help counteract whatever defense the dwarves had. Would be nice if that was what was happening.

His bomb had created just enough of a gap for Edwin to slip through the line, and he threw his last two steam grenades at the next-closest dwarves. He missed one—the bomb arcing off into the distance—but still bought himself enough time to pull out a sticky grenade and glue the next dwarf to the ground. Edwin vaguely realized he must have somehow poked a hole into his bag, as a stream of sand started pouring out the bottom, scattering across the ground. Interestingly, the guards still pursuing him halted their advance, avoiding the scattered sand. Edwin, now on the narrow bridge crossing the channel of molten metal, was momentarily confused, until he realized what happened and bit back a laugh. They didn't *know* he was all but out of tricks and that the sand spread across the ground had only been used as packing material. They just knew he had disabled a bunch of their kin with what looked like rocks and didn't want to take the chance that this was something similarly harmful. Perfect.

Edwin was so distracted by the sight of the dwarves avoiding some scattered sand that he didn't notice S'fashkchlil until the dwarf had Edwin's forearm in a vise grip, glaring daggers at Edwin. "No more tricks." He yanked on Edwin's arm, and Edwin yelped as he felt and heard something crack. "Your escapade ends here." The dwarf's grip kept tightening, and Edwin felt like the bones in his arm were about to shatter under the pressure. "You will regret not completing your Task; you will—"

"See, that's where you're wrong." Edwin's mind was racing at a mile a minute, and his mouth was running basically on autopilot. Hopefully it was saying something clever; he couldn't keep track of it. "I'm doing *exactly* what you Tasked me with."

Desperate for any kind of escape, Edwin's free arm blindly groped in his almost-empty bag, and his fingers settled around an extralarge sphere. He broke his final weapon over the head of his captor, scattering Infused lime dust all over S'fashkchlil's hair and beard. Sadly, none got in the dwarf's eyes, but Edwin could manage anyway.

"You Tasked me with impressing you."

The dwarf just snorted derisively, wiping some of the lime out of his beard. "Ha! Is this the best you have, Outsider? I knew you wouldn't be any sort of threat. Your kind needs far more time to—"

Edwin wasn't listening, his hand moving once more. His fingers closed around one of his final two slipstone spheres, and he crushed it against the ground, curing it in a blink and rendering the bridge almost frictionless.

The next thing he grabbed was one of his water grenades, and while it was snatched out of the air and crushed like a paper bag by the enraged dwarf, it did get what powder remained on the lord's hand *thoroughly* wet, and Edwin felt the Skill he had been pushing to employ finally get a bite.

Firestarting.

As S'fireface's hand ignited into brilliant white flames, he yelled in anguish, involuntarily releasing Edwin's arm from his death grip. He staggered back, trying to smother the magical flames, but he only managed to spread the chemicals to more parts of his body, and his feet flailed, trying and failing to find traction on the slipstone all around him.

Edwin broke his final sticky grenade on his own foot, giving him enough traction to throw all his weight against the dwarf. He barely managed to budge his captor and his shoulder felt slightly singed from coming so close to the infused lime midreaction, but it was enough. A last barrage of water-filled casings, Infused with as much mana as he could summon, caused S'firebeard's torso and head to erupt into more flames, only intensifying his struggles and making him susceptible to one last push by Edwin.

"Are you not impressed?" Edwin asked, eyes hard as he toppled the dwarf, who fell into the river of molten metal below.

Edwin dashed for the exit, ignoring the lord dwarf's tortured screams, and made it thankfully unaccosted to the massive door. Unfortunately, it refused to budge, even when he put his (uninjured) shoulder into it as hard as he could. Looking around, he saw an archway built into the wall and ran through it. On the other side was a younger-looking dwarf clearly terrified of him. Glancing behind him, Edwin saw that several dwarves were trying to pull out their lord from the molten metal river, but a pair was still pursuing Edwin (trying to avoid the sand, from the looks of it). He didn't have time for anything clever, so he took the fastest route.

"Open the door and I won't," he threatened the dwarf in Dwarven, hefting his second to last grenade, a flash bomb. The dwarf seemed reluctant to heed him, but Edwin mimed throwing it, and his target quickly ran to … an unmarked portion of the wall? Ah, it was a hidden door. Made sense they'd want to have a quick entrance or exit. The terrified dwarf pushed it open, and it swung outward, letting daylight, actual daylight, spill into the tiny room.

"Good dwarf," Edwin absently said in English, blinking as his eyes adjusted to the blessed sunlight. Behind him, he heard the first of his pursuers curse in Dwarven as the light once again shifted. He threw his flash bomb at them as a final farewell present and was about to do the same with his last grenade—a slipstone bomb—when he looked out at the massive Blackstone road in front of him, dipping and running down the side of the mountain. It would be an absolute pain to try and run down that, especially under pursuit, unless …

A smile played across Edwin's lips, and it grew into a full smile and then a laugh.

Freedom.

CHAPTER 21

Assume the Physicist
Ignores Air Resistance

It had seemed like such a good idea at the time. Edwin needed to get away, really fast, from the Blackstone citadel, before any sort of pursuit could assemble and apprehend him. All he had left of his armory was a single capsule of slipstone, and since he had a long, constant-incline path ahead of him, the solution seemed obvious. He'd just coat the outside of his lab coat with slipstone and use it for a sled. It was the perfect way to escape from the dwarves really quickly!

Well.

He certainly was going very quickly. Very, *very* quickly.

AAAAAAAAAAAAAAHHHHHHHHHHH!

The Blackstone road stretched out before him, hurtling by at a speed far faster than he was comfortable with, and as a bend rapidly approached, Edwin hastily pulled up on one of the sleeves of his coat-sled to try and turn without flying off into the undergrowth. The landscape had changed a lot from his start up at the top of the mountain. The small shrubs and grasses had long since merged back into the forest he had been lost in, and he had *no* desire to careen into a tree at these speeds. It *felt* like he was going a hundred miles an hour, but it was in all honesty probably closer to thirty or forty. Still *more* than enough for him to break every bone in his body if he didn't— OH SHOOT, ANOTHER TURN.

Edwin hugged his transport tightly, not wanting to even have the chance of letting go and falling off as the coat banked around the turn. It wasn't as bad as that one section of the road bordering the cliff, at least. Edwin had nearly passed out, going so fast that close to a massive drop. This thing needed guardrails. And *he* needed brakes. He was bound to be far enough away from the Blackstone citadel to be safe from any immediate pursuit by now, or at least he hoped so.

Unfortunately, that fact was of limited use when he had built up so much speed on his way down that a sudden stop would send him tumbling, break his bones—a twinge on his shoulder reminded him, break *more* bones—and possibly not even bring him to a complete stop. At least the road seemed to have mostly leveled out, so he wasn't speeding up anymore. Small mercies and all that.

Okay, time to think.

A physicist is on a constant slope. Assuming there's no friction, calculate the speed at which … Shut up, me.

Edwin was sitting on his lab coat, sleeves turned inside-out and used for reins and mostly coated with slipstone, which was for most intents and purposes, frictionless. His backpack was sitting next to him, one loop half-heartedly hanging over his right arm. He had an arrowhead stuck in his shoulder (most of the shaft having broken off already), a bleeding foot, and a probably broken arm. He couldn't wait to stop on his own, and if he didn't slow down, he *would* eventually miss a turn.

It would be hard enough to do this on a normal day, never mind with only one functional arm. It was not, however, the most suicidal thing Edwin had tried today, so at least it had that going for it.

But anyway. Slowing down. Edwin had stuff, mainly food, in his backpack. Probably not useful. He had decently sturdy boots, but not enough that he trusted them to stop his current speed without breaking or wearing down to the point of uselessness. He still needed shoes! Hmm. One of them did have the adhesive mortar on it, but it had cured back when he set the dwarf lord on fire so wouldn't be much help in this situation. He had glass goggles that would probably hinder his vision but also allowed him to see without his eyes being dried out in moments. He still had his gloves, but they wouldn't … Hmm. Actually. It worked for ziplines; could it work here?

Though how could he manage to both steer and slow himself down using his gloves while only having a single free hand? Could he put it under his shoe, perhaps? Then he could spare his shoes while still braking? Eh, no. Odds were much more likely it would be ripped away from him in seconds, leaving him no better off.

Edwin gritted his teeth. There was no way around it, but this would *hurt*. Might permanently injure him, too, but hopefully not. First, after making another turn anyway, he slowly rotated himself so he faced primarily to the left, leaving his right hand steering, his left slowly creeping off the end of the tattered hem of his coat until his gloved fingertips skated across the smooth-yet-rough Blackstone paving.

Thankfully, the motion didn't hurt *too* badly, so Edwin pressed slightly harder. The application of force was enough to make him drift ever so slightly to the left, and he corrected at the front, then de-corrected as the road itself began to angle to the left. How far did this road go, anyway?

The world streaked by, the woods a blur of color as Edwin slowly increased the pressure his hand was applying. With every additional touch, though, the pain in his arm increased and he started to doubt if he could manage his plan. A tiny bump in the road made his sled jump and *crunch* back into the road, jolting his arm and sending pain shooting through Edwin's shoulder. Hmm. That gave him an idea, though. Maybe he could crack the slipstone in half, letting him slowly trap debris in the gap and accumulate friction that way? Once there was a bit of slowdown in this out-of-control descent, he could probably manage to stop the rest of the way.

As Edwin carefully maneuvered back to his original position, he waited for a decently long straight stretch in the road to arrive, then lifted up the front of his ride as far as it could go—well, as far as he was willing to lift it, anyway—and brought his foot down hard on the portion lifted into the air. He felt a little give, but not enough. He kicked again. A bit more give. Again. And again …

The slipstone splintered, sending fragments of mortar in every direction. Several got caught under the coat, jamming up what slipstone remained on the outside and *severely* slowing the ride. Edwin, not adequately prepared for the extreme change in speed, lurched forward, his bad shoulder impacting the coat and exploding with pain. The jolt also threw his legs up in the air, where they caught the force of the wind full-bore.

He screamed, waves of agony radiating across his entire upper torso, and rolled over on his back, trying to relieve the pressure.

His weight pressed down on the front half of his sled, introducing a fairly large new force involved in this free-body diagram of a physics problem. Suddenly, the front half of Edwin's former coat was not moving *nearly* as fast as the back half, and the discrepancy pulled him into a head-over-heels tumble, just like he was trying to avoid. Well, at least this way he had the … mostly intact leather coat to help protect him. His backpack went flying off somewhere, slipping from his arm as he lost his grip on the reins during his descent. Even his gloves flew off at some point, the left one getting caught against the road at some point and yanking painfully on his arm as it was wrenched off, the right glove just getting lost in the tangle.

All Edwin knew was pain and confusion as the world spun. At least the road was almost entirely smooth, so there weren't any jumps or rocks crashing into him. Just a very long tumble, wrapped up in an almost-smothering blanket made of tattered leather.

How long has it been since I had to just stay lying down because of how sore I was? Edwin mused. *I was with the dwarves for like a month, month and a half, so about that long, I suppose. Didn't feel that long, though.* He tried to move but was met with only pain. *Pity I couldn't bring my bed along. That would feel heavenly about now. …*

Eventually, Edwin woke up enough to get his bearings. He didn't throw up, though for someone who never got motion sick, he came pretty close. That was not fun in the slightest. Ugh. At first, he tried rolling himself over and pushing himself into a sitting position, but his left arm told him in *no uncertain terms* that was not going to be an option. Instead, he settled for grabbing his legs with his right arm and pulling himself upright in what proved to be a very painful sit-up. His wounds, as minor as they might have been—aside from his left arm, anyway—were still tremendously uncomfortable as he contorted himself into place.

Once Edwin had successfully sat up (it was the small victories that got him through), he looked around, assessing his latest situation.

Pro: He was alive, free(!), and (mostly) unharmed.

Con: His coat looked like a dishrag, his backpack was nowhere to be seen, his gloves were probably *long* gone, one of the lenses in his goggles had a giant crack running through it, and *mostly* unharmed was not the same as completely unharmed, even discounting his preexisting injuries.

It felt like half of his body was one giant bruise, and the other half had been run over by a truck. His face wasn't too badly scraped up, fortunately, though his back was definitely bleeding again. With a pained groan, Edwin removed the goggles from his face, feeling the indentation they had made around his eyes, and tossed them to the side. The crack in the lens grew bigger, but at this point Edwin couldn't bring himself to care. All his dwarf-made PPE was pretty much ruined, anyway; he'd need to replace everything somehow before he could resume any sort of lab work.

He'd made some *really cool* stuff, after all, and that was literally just using rocks and his own Skills. Edwin couldn't wait to see what he could make when not under the threat of death, forced to focus solely on concrete and lime, and able to use more potentially magical components.

Before he could get too carried away by the fantasies of the Alchemists of old, spinning lead to gold and brewing the elixir of life, Edwin dragged his excitement back down to earth, chaining it to his current predicament. He was back in the middle of the wilderness, and he was arguably in worse shape now than he was a month ago. At least a month ago, he still had two unbroken arms and didn't have a *really sharp* arrowhead buried in his shoulder. Then again, he now had the Blackstone road, both as a guide back to civilization and as a way to stay somewhat warmer, and finding food and water would be as easy as figuring out where his backpack had gotten to.

Also, I have better shoes. And it's time to put them to good use, Edwin thought as he pulled himself to his feet, wincing as he did so.

It took a little while, but Edwin eventually managed to track down his left glove and thankfully full backpack, both tossed to the side of the road a good ways back from where he had eventually stopped. His right glove, sadly, was nowhere to be found. Pity. Presumably, his blowtorch was still attached to it wherever it had landed, but after about a half hour of searching he had to give it up as lost.

He may have gotten a sizable lead over anyone following him, but he wasn't about to assume that meant they would never catch up. After all, they presumably didn't have a limp and likely would have some sort of Skill to help them go faster. No, he needed to press on as much as possible, keeping an eye out for places he could stop for the night and get this *stupid arrowhead out of his shoulder*. Ahem.

Edwin ran through a mental list of the things he was fairly certain he had brought with him. There should be a hotplate and metal bowl in his bag, along with some burlap rags, so he could make some bandages for himself at least. He hadn't brought soap, though, which he mentally cursed himself for forgetting.

Cleaning out his injuries would be way harder without it, and he wouldn't be able to do it nearly as well. Still, boiling water and cloth should go a long way. He also had a couple of knives, so he might be able to fashion a makeshift splint for his arm. He hoped he would find civilization soon and would be able to get proper medical attention. Supposedly, the "Pretentious Empire" should be nearby, though what exactly "nearby" entailed, and what might count as proper medical attention were far less certain.

The Blackstones seemed basically standard pseudo-medieval fantasy from what limited glimpses he had seen, and that meant a medic in a local town might prescribe leeches and bleeding, or tap his shoulder and magically close all his wounds. Well, worst-case scenario he might be able to walk someone through bandaging his injuries properly. In the meantime, would doing a temporary job help level up Survival or would it unlock a First Aid Skill?

Oh yeah. That reminded him. He had notifications to check. Mentally preparing himself for an utter wall of text, Edwin called them all up at once.

CHAPTER 22

Just Follow the Black Stone Road

Level Up!
Seeing Level 15→16
Flexibility Level 11→15
Athletics Level 23→25
Visualization Level 23→24
Alchemy Level 41→43
Mana Infusion Level 53→55
Firestarting Level 23→27
Bomb Throwing Level 1→9
Walking Level 20→21
Survival Level 12→14
Language Level 33→34
Packing Level 2→3
Breathing Level 16→17

Congratulations! For leaving your lifelong home with no intention to return, you have unlocked the Wanderer Path!

Congratulations! For being driven from your home on threat of violence should you return, you have unlocked the Exile Path!

Congratulations! For freeing yourself from captivity you have unlocked the Escapee Path!

Congratulations! For managing to defeat multiple trained soldiers of

Clan Blackstone against all odds, you have unlocked the Blackstone Conqueror Path!
You have unlocked the Intimidate Skill!
Accept Skill? Y/N
Congratulations! For lighting a powerful political figure on fire, you have unlocked the Pyromaniac Path!
You have unlocked the Shield Block Skill!
Accept Skill? Y/N
Congratulations! For surviving a powerful explosion, you have unlocked the Unkillable Path!
Congratulations! For killing a sentient creature, you have unlocked the Killer Path!
Congratulations! For blinding an opponent through severe chemical burns, you have unlocked the Alchemical Warrior Path!
Congratulations! For killing an unarmed sentient creature, you have unlocked the Assassin Path!
Congratulations! For attacking your mentor, you have unlocked the Traitor Path!

Edwin was *really* glad he had updated the way his leveling-up notifications were displayed. There was already a lot to parse here, never mind if it were interspersed with ... thirty Skill increases. Huh. Counting that had been surprisingly easy. Apparently, Mathematics was paying off.

Each of the Paths got a brief look-over, and the Assassin, Killer, and Traitor Paths, a great deal of concern. Who did he kill? He wasn't exactly hoping to kill anyone, though with how sturdy all the dwarves. ... Oh. It was probably Rashin, wasn't it? He was also likely the "mentor" attacked for the Traitor Path.

Edwin's excess mental chatter fell silent for a moment. Sure, Rashin had arguably been the one to sentence him to slavery, but that wasn't really accurate. Really, he had just been tasked by Lord S'fishkill to keep an eye on Edwin, and as a result he was now dead.

It was sobering to think that he had been directly responsible for the death of someone. Did Rashin have family? Edwin hadn't thought to ask initially, and, out of spite, he had ignored the few attempts at conversation Rashin had initiated while Edwin was captured. He couldn't say that he regretted what he had done, not really. But he still wished that he hadn't needed to kill anyone.

Had anyone else died as a result of his escape? He hadn't thought so, but then again, he had thought that whatever kept Rashin's skull intact when it was struck with a sledgehammer would have let the dwarf survive as well, when that was ... apparently not the case. Maybe not the dwarf that he had dumped Infused lime on?

Edwin felt *emotions* well up inside of him—regret, sadness, a hint of self-loathing—but he steeled himself, locking that whole bundle of screwy feelings inside a solid box right next to where he was keeping his thoughts about being worlds away from everyone he knew. He did *not* have time for that right now. Okay, maybe he did. He *absolutely* had time to process being on Joriah in his monthlong imprisonment, just ... No. He clearly didn't have time. Besides, his emotions were securely locked away, there was no time pressure, he could deal with them *later*. *Later*, Edwin. Not now. Once he was safe and secure somewhere, then he could deal with his emotions. Might not be the healthiest idea, but ... Nah. It'd be *fine*. He had loads of practice keeping his feelings separate from everything else because ... And nope! He was *absolutely* not opening *that* box right now. One day, maybe.

Oh look, something to distract him! More Paths!

Alchemical Warrior sounded incredibly fun, but at 90 points was a bit much. Pyromaniac, Exile, and Escapee were all 30 points, cheap Paths with ... debatable value. Edwin wasn't sure if he wanted whatever they might bring to his Class. Wanderer, at 60, was more promising.

Sure, calling the Blackstone citadel Edwin's "lifelong home" might have only been technically correct, and only from the System's perspective, but at the same time, the sentiment wasn't totally off.

Under further consideration, Edwin kind of liked the idea of being a wandering Alchemist, traveling around and seeing everything Joriah had to offer. He couldn't really settle down, not with Clan Blackstone dwarves likely willing to follow him to the far corners of the earth—far corners of Joriah? English expressions weren't really made with other worlds in mind—to drag him back to enslavement. Granted, he could probably manage to avoid them by making political allies until it would be too complicated to pull Edwin back, but … considering what had *just* happened, he was hesitant to run to another person in power and trust that he'd get away totally fine. Heck, he might even be used as a way to get cheap political favors if he wasn't careful! And Edwin had no clue how to *be* careful, or even how to get political allies.

No, he would need to keep traveling to avoid his pursuers. Alone, preferably; then he wouldn't have to worry about anyone selling him out. Besides, he liked being alone. No emotional baggage or social intricacies to worry about. Just him and his thoughts. Yeah … he liked that idea. Maybe he could be an adventurer! Show up, kill a monster, get rewards to fund his trek to the next town, repeat ad nauseum. Sounded good to him. What had he been thinking about? Oh yeah! Paths.

Wanderer sounded good to him, though when he would take it … Eh, at some point. Unkillable sounded very appealing, but at 90 points fell slightly behind the other Paths with a similar cost. Blackstone Conqueror was probably a Trophy Path like Stonehide Vanquisher. From what Rashin had said, it might give him a Skill with a physical manifestation. Something made of Blackstone, perhaps? That would be cool, if unlikely. Blackstone was seriously magical stuff, and it had sounded like that sort of effect only started appearing at higher Tiers.

Also, Edwin had Skills to reject! This always hurt a little bit, but if he were offered them again he might reconsider. At least Intimidation and Shield Block were both easy rejections—he had no desire to scare people to get them to cooperate; it just wasn't his style, and he had no real intention to use a shield in the future.

He could have taken them, anyway, of course, but then he would just be dealing with extra Skills that he wouldn't be using and thus not providing the Skill Points needed for their own evolutions. Rejecting was temporary, after all, whereas accepting was permanent, and he didn't feel committed enough to either of the Skills to make that choice.

He seriously needed to sit down and figure out some long-term plan. Blindly stumbling through things and accepting all Skills offered might have worked for him up until now, but that could only take him so far. Failing to plan was just planning to fail, after all. The only problem with devising a Build was that he didn't know enough about the System to make informed decisions, and he doubted that he would trust anyone enough to share the details of what he could do any time soon. Not after that last fiasco.

So … blindly stumbling around looked like the name of the game for the foreseeable future. Still, it had worked out decently well so far. After all, Edwin liked roughly what sorts of Skills he had—an eclectic mishmash of abilities that worked together well. Sure, he might have unintentionally crippled his mana usage, but what he could still do was clearly enough to take down really spectacular odds.

It is a pity, Edwin mused, *that I probably won't have access to any workshops near as nice as what the dwarves provided. They had a really nice kiln and lots of tools, way more than I could reasonably carry around even if Packing gets really high-leveled. Just too cumbersome. Ooh! I wonder if spatial bags are a thing. That might be helpful in terms of carrying stuff around, not to mention all the physics-breaking fun that could be had with something like that.* Edwin shook his head to clear it. *Anyway, I wish I had been able to take more tools with me as I left, all that sort of thing is bound to be even more expensive here than on Earth, so I won't be funding a lab for myself any time soon. Heck, I don't even have the right protective equipment anymore…*

Edwin was broken out of his thoughts by a branch falling somewhere off the path, not terribly far away. He froze, not wanting to attract the attention of any kind of predator that might be lurking nearby as he carefully scanned his surroundings for something that might have knocked a branch down or made a sound that was really similar to that. They might still be invisible, though. He never did rule out the possibility that predators might well have insane Stealth Skills. If anything, running into a bear the size of a train just made the possibility of invisible panthers hanging around somewhere all the more likely.

Still, scanning the woods carefully had its own benefits. Off the path a little ways, Edwin caught sight of a trickling brook, cascading off the edge of a small, rocky bluff. It looked close enough to what Edwin was hoping for that he decided it was worth a try, and given he would have never noticed it without looking closer specifically here, it was probably hidden enough for his purposes.

Sure enough, the area by the brook did seem to suit Edwin well enough. A tree had grown up right next to the exposed rock, creating a small, sheltered space beneath its branches that was just large enough to hold him if he was curled up. While there may have only been a trickle of water flowing by, it was better than nothing, and Edwin settled in for the night.

His first step was to dig through his backpack to find his water canteen, which he gratefully gulped from. Then, he dug out a heating stone and his bowl. Unfortunately, it seemed as though a stray crossbow bolt had struck the heating stone, cracking it and rendering it useless.

Well, at least he had a crossbow bolt now, he supposed. Not sure what he might do with it, but it didn't seem like anything else was *ruined*—a couple loaves of bread had a hole through their centers, but that wouldn't really make a difference. A bit more digging turned up another heating stone. While it wasn't as nice as the broken one, it still got hot enough to boil the water Edwin had collected in his bowl. Once it was boiling nicely, he took a handful of rags from his bag—well, they *had* been sacks, but a few cuts with his knife tore them into strips—and shoved them in the water, hopefully sterilizing them. He was pretty sure this would work, anyway.

The bandages were dripping wet when he removed them from their bath, but he dried them out by laying them directly on the heating stone, where they started steaming. While they were drying, Edwin turned his attention to the real problem at hand, or more accurately, at shoulder.

Fortunately, the quarrel hadn't gone too deep into his shoulder. Unfortunately, that was because it seemed to have hit his shoulder bone, which Edwin was pretty sure was Very Bad. At least the arrowhead hadn't been fully enclosed by his flesh, which should make it easier to remove, especially as it wasn't serrated or barbed in any way, just a leaf-shaped tip on a broken, slender wooden shaft. After sterilizing his knife blade via a quick application of Firestarting, Edwin carefully poked at the wound, opening it up just enough to let some blood out, then attempted to slide the crossbow bolt out. He had to abort that attempt when he was left seeing stars, same with the next and the next and the next and … Eventually he worked it all the way out, but it left his shoulder bleeding at an uncomfortable rate. He brought up a handful of bandages to stem the flow. It was … half successful. Still bleeding an uncomfortable amount. Gah. *This* was why everyone always said to not remove the puncturing object, because it would just bleed more. That worked *great* when you had 911, but out here? Not so much.

Edwin knew what he should probably do: use Firestarting to try and fuse the skin together, but he didn't want to. For one, it might not work. Two, it would hurt a heck of a lot, and three, *setting himself on fire* didn't strike him as the smartest idea. Still, it would also probably sterilize the wound, which, if he wanted to avoid infection, he would need to do. He still couldn't believe he'd forgotten to bring soap.

He took a deep breath. Maybe because it was magical fire, he could somehow tune it so it wouldn't hurt as much? It was magic; anything was possible. That thought was enough for him to set out on a course of action. He'd do it, hoping it went all right. Hey, he'd done stupider stuff in the past, right?

The first thing Edwin did was prep the surrounding area, Infusing his bandages and shoulder with as much mana as he could. He hadn't tried Infusing *himself* before, and it ... didn't really take. He might have Infused the bone or something, but he didn't get the sensation that he had Infused "his shoulder."

With a deep breath, Edwin imagined a spark of fire alighting on his severed blood vessels, cauterizing them. Elsewhere, he imagined fire dancing along the surface of his skin, scorching right outside of it without touching or burning his actual flesh. Above all, though, he saw the fire *not* going inside of him, but instead staying purely topical. Then, with a few deep breaths to calm himself, he poured as much mana into the forming Skill idea as he could and *pushed*.

Firestarting.

The pain was intense; it felt like his shoulder was briefly lit on fire ... which, Edwin supposed once his wits returned, it was. Fortunately, the majority of the pain went away decently quickly, leaving only a lingering burn and ... *AAAHHH THE BANDAGE WAS ON FIRE!*

Once the burning rags had been thrown into the brook, where they now sat smoking, Edwin turned his attention back to his shoulder. The skin, now a painful shade of red, was definitely burned, but the cut seemed to have closed enough to slow the bleeding and just a fresh set of bandages was able to stem it. He'd have to keep a close eye on the burn to make sure *that* didn't get infected, though.

Tying bandages around his shoulder with a broken arm was ... awkward, to say the least, but Edwin managed eventually with comparatively little pain, then shrugged his shirt back on. All that finally taken care of, he checked the notifications that had been tugging at his attention this entire time.

Congratulations! For successfully closing an open wound on your own in the wilderness, you have unlocked the Field Medic Path!
Congratulations! For earning the Cauterize spell, you have unlocked the Mage Path!
You have unlocked the First Aid Skill!
Accept Skill? Y/N
You have unlocked the Cauterize Skill!
Accept Skill? Y/N
Level Up!
Firestarting Level 27→29
Mana Infusion Level 55→56
Visualization Level 24→25

Wait, the Mage Path? Hadn't he already completed that? Huh. He had. Could you re-earn Paths? Was it only completed Paths? It had to be that. Edwin couldn't imagine not re-unlocking the Daredevil Path after his sledding incident if you could have multiple of the same Path at the same time. That was interesting. Granted, he didn't know what he might be able to *do* with that information, but it was still interesting.

Also, even *more* Skills to choose between? Cauterize being a spell sounded really, really cool. An actual spell! Were they different from normal Skills in some way? If so, how? Gah ... Edwin felt torn. On the one hand, he would hopefully never need to use it again, so it would be a wasted Skill. On the other, it was a System-recognized spell! Then again, like with Reflexes, if he somehow needed it again, he knew how to unlock it. First Aid, though, was an absolute *necessity*. He needed something like that, if his misadventures so far were any indication. Plus, he'd need all the help he could get for his arm.

Level Up!
First Aid Level 1→4
First Aid
You've had one, yes, but what about Second Aid?
Patch up wounds.
Effectiveness improves with level.

Edwin vaguely wondered what the dwarves would think about him, not following any particular legacy, just grabbing whatever Skills he thought sounded useful. He did really need the help, though. A couple of half-remembered classes about first aid was *not* enough when there was nobody to go to for a better job after he first patched himself up.

Level Up!
First Aid Level 4→7

I miss Improvisation, Edwin thought as he tried to work one-handed with his swiftly dwindling stock of cloth. *I don't think I'm any worse than before, but I could have gotten so many levels if I still had it.*

Edwin's forearm was wrapped up tightly now, the swelling on his arm mostly manageable, and with a few more minutes of work, he even had a makeshift sling to help keep it immobile. With no way to set the bone, or even the knowledge needed if he could, all he could do was hope that his bone would heal correctly on its own.

Curling up while trying to avoid disturbing a broken arm wasn't easy, but Edwin managed it eventually. It had been a long, exhausting day, so pretty much as soon as he had himself situated in a half-decent position, tucked beneath the tattered remains of his coat, he was fast asleep.

CHAPTER 23

Foreign Exchange

It took Edwin nearly a week, but he eventually managed to limp his way out of the forest. It hadn't been easy, not by any stretch of the imagination, but he had done it. Every day, he'd walk as far as he could manage, eat enough food to keep himself going, find a spot to hunker down for the night, clean his bandages, and repeat.

Whenever he needed water, he'd find a stream to fill his canteen and boiled it with either Firestarting or a heating stone, and he had found enough sources that he'd never gone too thirsty. He would have expected that he might have run out of food by now, but he just ... didn't need to eat that much. Not that he had ever eaten that much, but usually when he was physically active, he'd need a hefty amount of food to get by, but not at the moment. In any case, he was in *great* shape. His legs were getting stronger and stronger by the day, the hole in his foot had healed (it was still sore, though), and he'd gotten a bunch of Skill levels just through constant use.

Level Up!
Walking Level 21→28
Packing Level 3→5
Language Level 34→36
First Aid Level 7→13

Survival Level 14→17
Athletics Level 25→27
Sleeping Level 20→21
Outsider's Almanac Level 61→62
Identify Level 27→28
Seeing Level 16→17
Breathing Level 17→20
Mana Infusion Level 56→57

Things had slowed down recently, though. Language had barely leveled up despite Edwin having spent nearly the entirety of each day devising and reciting the most twisty tongue twisters he could imagine, something that used to net him about a level per day. His Almanac continued to level, naturally, as he would mark any discrete object in his fourish meters of range with a message. If someone was able to read his messages, they'd probably find some very confused ramblings, each in the form of a single sentence-length blurb covering branches, twigs, and leaves on either side of the road.

It wasn't all good, though. Edwin had yet to see so much as a hair of his pursuers, which in some ways just made him more nervous. How many were they sending that it took them *this* long to get organized? He knew they'd be coming after him; it was just a question of how hard it would be to evade them. If they sent an army, he'd have no chance. If they sent a specialist who was just taking their sweet time setting off on their hunt, he would also have no chance. His only real chance at this point was to get into civilization proper before his pursuers showed themselves, and … it looked like he had finally made it!

The Blackstone road ended with a massive archway, made of two giant Blackstone statues of dwarves with pickaxes raised and crossed at the peak, in an utterly superfluous yet really impressive construction. On the other side of the arch, the road changed abruptly to packed dirt, barely muddy even with the current drizzle making everything ever so slightly wet. Just as sharp of a change was the shift from the wild, untamed forest he had become so familiar with to farmland. If he looked off to the side, he was able to see a section of the forest that extended into the farmland, but it looked like it was some form of logging camp. Of most interest to Edwin, though, was what appeared to be a small town a little ways farther down the road, next to a bend in a fairly large river meandering its way through the fields.

Edwin may have been dead on his feet by the time he got close enough to properly see that what he had thought was a small village was, well, calling it a *small* village was … He wasn't sure. There were plenty of buildings, mostly made of what appeared to be living trees with branches woven together intricately to make walls, but they were all built in miniature. As were the people. There was lots of activity going on, bustling through the town square as the … halflings carried around bags stuffed to the brim and a few carried around timber and logs twice the size of themselves. The entire place emanated endless chatter in a rapid, staccato-sounding language of which Edwin couldn't understand so much as a single syllable. Time to change that.

Polyglot
You can understand me, right?
Make yourself understood.
Increased comprehension per level.
You may evolve your Language Skill into the Polyglot Skill!
Accept Evolution? Y/N
Done!

…

Calculating Rewards…
Class Change!
Alchemist Outsider → Foreign Alchemist
You have completed the Linguist Path!
Your way has brought you far afield from where you started. To call
you an Outsider is simplistic and incomplete. You are truly an Outsider
wherever you find yourself, a Foreigner to all. Yet with that status of
standing on the outside, you are nonetheless capable of seeing what
others cannot, yet often incapable of seeing what they do.

Edwin had mixed feelings about losing the Outsider tag on his Class description. For better and for worse, it marked him as different, something he had always loved and hated simultaneously. Being on the outside was much less painful if he were different, yet to be different was to set himself on the outside. Granted, "Foreign" wasn't that much better, but it was probably less exotic? Eh, it didn't sound quite as cool, but it was what it was.

What was *definitely* painful was spending more points on a Path than the Skill had for levels. These days, he definitely wanted each of his Skills to at least pay for itself, but … Yeah. Future-Edwin could deal with that problem; for now he needed to understand people.

Edwin was drawing close enough to the town that he could tell a fair level of attention was being directed his way. A few glances were tossed at him, children stopped and stared for a moment before continuing to run around, and a couple of people looked at him directly. Edwin wanted to shrink away from the attention, and very nearly did, but he pushed through and continued toward the bustling crowd. He must have been quite the sight, with one arm in a sling, a backpack over his shoulder, and wearing a coat with more holes than leather. Now that he was closer, Edwin could see that the halflings weren't *quite* just "humans but smaller." They had proportionally larger heads and eyes and seemed to have an extra joint on their fingers, giving their fists an oddly fluid and unsettling appearance.

One of the halflings staring at Edwin—a "Watcher of the Community," according to Identify—approached him, saying something in the staccato halfling language. While he couldn't understand the words, Edwin was able to get the gist of what was being asked—who was he, and what was he doing here?

In response, and with a voice that hadn't spoken in a week, Edwin spoke in Dwarven, gesturing to the forest, "Lost in there. Can I get help?"

The halfling cocked his head and responded in halting Dwarven of his own, "Lost in … Verdant? Come, will give help." He grabbed Edwin's hand—the extra joint felt *weird*—and pulled him along the edge of the town to a grand-looking building, the trees that it was built from seeming to emanate age and strength. It was also one of the few structures that seemed to have a second story, the canopies of its corner … Not corner*stones*. Cornertrunks? The canopies of its cornertrunks were interwoven in a similar way to the walls on the ground floor, overall giving the building a vaguely mushroom-shaped profile.

As Edwin was led inside, ducking inside the door and preparing to hit his head on the ceiling, he was pleasantly surprised, and more than a little confused, to find that the inside was far taller than it should have been. More Skill nonsense, clearly, but one that messed with space. Seemed like his wish for a spatial bag wasn't just a dream after all, but decidedly possible. Oh, his guide was talking about him to an important-looking halfling sitting on a finely crafted wooden seat.

Level Up!
Polyglot Level 1→3

After some discussion, for which Edwin was almost *completely* zoned out—his legs were killing him and he really wanted to sit down, not to mention the fact that he couldn't understand a word of it—the important-looking halfling, a Village-Community Elder Head, stroked her chin, speaking in perfect Dwarven, "So you were in the Verdant? For how long?"

"About a week"—Edwin racked his brain for the Dwarven word for ma'am, but came up blank—"lady. Before that I was with Clan Black-stone until I could escape."

"Escape?" Her interest was piqued.

Telling the truth was a risk, but Edwin would have to take his chances. After all, a lot of his wounds were pretty clearly caused by weapons, so if he wanted them treated he'd need to answer questions about where they came from. "I was … held against my will. I took what I could as I ran."

"A thief, then? You were arrested for stealing?"

"No … no. They … kept me wrongly. Made me work, shot me when I left." Edwin shrugged off his jacket and shirt from his wounded shoulder, showing his bandage.

Halfling lady narrowed her eyes at him, assessing his wounds, examining his expression, and Edwin felt his pulse quicken. She clearly wasn't buying his story, Edwin could tell. She didn't believe him and was no doubt going to contact the dwarves to return a thief—he could sense it. Ahh. He was in no position to fight his way out, to look for another village to get help at. Okay, he could probably make it to the door, at least. Once he was there, he could—

"We will help you. Your wounds need healing and you came with no motive beyond seeking some way to survive. Taktalai will escort you to Sisi; he will help you."

Level Up!
Polyglot Level 3→4

Whew. So, he was at least going to get healed first. He could escape hopefully before whatever messages they would need to pass to ship him back to the Blackstones would be exchanged. That was of course assuming they didn't keep him under lock and key, but Edwin didn't think that they would do something so obvious.

No, their sort clearly liked to pretend to be nice while secretly plotting something. There were other roads, and hopefully he could make it to wherever the next town was. Another one had to be relatively close, right? This looked like farmland, and the halflings wouldn't want to have to tend to too large of an area outside their village, right? That was probably how it worked?

Edwin ducked into the house that—Taktally? Tactically? Taktala; Edwin quickly Almanaced his guide with what Edwin was pretty sure was his name—Taktala led him to. He was pleasantly surprised to find that this building, too, was larger on the inside. The ceiling wasn't *quite* high enough for him to stand up straight, but it was close enough. Another flurry of words was exchanged—Edwin marveled slightly at just how *incredibly* different the language the halflings were speaking was from the Dwarven tongue—about him again, and then he was directed to lie down on a rolled-out mat on the floor, next to a bed far too small for him.

Edwin removed his backpack and gratefully lay down. At the silver-haired Sisi's (an Experienced Community Healer) mostly mimed directions, he also removed his shirt, as bloody and cut-up as it was (he was going through clothes fast). Once Edwin was shirtless, Sisi knelt down next to him, slowly unwrapping his bandages to reveal his swollen shoulder, tutting softly. No, wait, Sisi was saying something about him doing something stupid. Or maybe that's what the tutting was? Polyglot wasn't very clear in its clarifications, not that *anything* with this System was.

It really was cool, seeing Skills at work from people, who had clearly practiced them their whole lives, when they *weren't* actively aimed to kill him, and Edwin, despite constantly waiting, never felt any mana coming from the halfling as he took a damp, clean cloth and just … wiped away Edwin's burn. Wait, *what?* He blinked, trying to clear his eyes. What was *that?* That injury had been bothering Edwin for days, but carefully poking his shoulder still had him hissing in pain. The burn was gone, but the underlying wound was still there.

Sisi, who was examining Edwin's broken arm, looked up at Edwin's exclamation, and he carefully set Edwin's arm down before examining his shoulder more carefully, gently admonishing him again.

Polyglot was *weird*. Edwin could understand the intention behind statements, but only so long as he didn't try to focus on the individual words. The more he focused, the better he could understand fragments of words, but the less he comprehended the statement as a whole. Concentrating let him identify the word *tikil* as meaning some form of wound or injury, but he had no idea what context it was being used in.

Level Up!
Polyglot Level 4→5

If he broke his concentration on the individual words, all the similar-sounding syllables just started to blend together again. Actually, no. Apparently *tikil* also meant the "torso"? Wait, now it was used again as an admonishment. Did the halfling language just have a half-dozen words with a hundred different meanings, or what? Still, Edwin felt compelled to defend himself.

"Sorry." He shrugged—earning a shot of pain from his still-injured shoulder, making him flinch. "I was bleeding out. Didn't have a choice."

Sisi narrowed his eyes at him—the halflings' large eyes made all their expressions seem cartoonishly expressive—and lightly cuffed Edwin's head, accompanied by a muttered statement regarding "idiot children." Hey, a more complex idea! Polyglot was improving! Sisi didn't notice Edwin's excitement, though, shaking his head and leaving Edwin's shoulder with no further ministrations, instead turning to his broken arm. He nodded contentedly to himself and wrapped up Edwin's arm tightly in fresh bandages, but to no apparent change.

"Thanks," Edwin said with a nod. "It's a big help."

He started to ask about what Sisi had done when the halfling moved up to his forehead, tapping it and saying, "Tikil."

Wait, now it meant *sleep*? What the heck was … yawn … this … language …

CHAPTER 24

Birds of a Feather

Edwin jolted awake as shouting penetrated his unconscious state, yanking him to wakefulness. At first, he panicked at the noise, thinking he was about to be attacked or shipped back to Clan Blackstone, but as the initial scare faded and his rational mind asserted itself, he realized it sounded more like celebration than an attack or anything negative.

It didn't rule out the dwarves coming through, though, so he stayed wary as he got up, preemptively wincing as he put weight on his left arm, then became relieved as the expected jolt of pain never came. The bandage on his forearm had been removed at some point; after inspecting his shoulder, he also saw that the swelling there was completely gone and it was apparently completely healed. He had a fairly nasty scar on the shoulder from some combination of the bolt-wound and his subsequent cauterization, but it didn't seem to impair his flexibility at all.

Edwin stretched gratefully at his newfound health, and casting his gaze around showed that he was alone in the healer's building, but his shirt, repaired and cleaned to such an extent it looked brand-new, was lying on the tiny bed next to him. Another few seconds of searching unveiled his backpack at the foot of the bed, but his coat was nowhere to be seen. Ah well, not like it was going to do anything for him.

As Edwin got to his feet, his stomach rumbled, which made him wonder how long he'd been asleep. It had to have been at least a day, given the light streaming through the leafy roof. Interestingly, the light coming through the canopy wasn't strongly tinted green, just the normal warm glow of sunlight, which made him suspect magical shenanigans. As though the whole trees-woven-into-houses wasn't a giveaway on its own, anyway.

Ducking under the low doorframe, Edwin peeked outside to see the commotion. To his relief, he didn't see a battalion of armor-clad dwarves waiting for him. Instead, he saw what looked to be a caravan of sorts, a train of covered wagons hooked together just outside the town, and a flood of intermingling halflings greeting one another and embracing as though they hadn't seen each other in some time. Standing on the outside, milling around the caravan, was a group of humans and what looked to be approximately humanoid birdfolk, with talons in place of feet and seemingly prehensile wings in place of arms.

Most of the talking was utterly unintelligible even with Polyglot, a thousand different conversations happening all over one another, but Edwin caught vague snippets of something that sounded like English. Someone else with Polyglot, perhaps? He saw one of the bird-people talking to the village elder from yesterday, which seemed to be the only instance of a nonhalfling talking to a halfling and therefore a decent place to start.

Edwin waded his way through the crowds of tiny people, reminding him of a sea of children. By the time he arrived at the discussion between … uh … what was her name again? Did he ever know? It was probably lost in the flood of incomprehensible halfling jibber-jabber. Anyway, by the time he arrived at the discussion between the two of them, they had taken note of his approach and seemed to be waiting for him.

"Can we help you?" the bird—a Caravan Merchant Leader—asked. It was weird seeing Polyglot in action, so to speak. Edwin had never been able to see Rashin's mouth, if he even had one, as he had spoken, but now that he was able to see the bird's beak, it looked like a bad dubbing job in real life, as the sounds that Edwin heard didn't correspond to the motions made while speaking in the slightest.

"Sorry, didn't mean to intrude—" Edwin started, only to be cut off.

"Well, you are. So, spit it out and get it over with, *Adventurer.*"

Edwin's expression soured. "I just heard speech in my native language, and—"

"It's a Skill. Polyglot. Get it yourself and stop bothering us." The bird was clearly not in a good mood, but the halfling said something that got him to roll his eyes. "Fine. What do you want? Get on with it."

"... and as I was saying, I thought that someone with Polyglot might be able to help me understand what's happening. You see, I—"

"Look, Ritian and I—"

Oh, Ritian. Let's just mark that with Almanac ...

"... are discussing payment, which is a private matter and of no concern to your type, so if you could just dive off, that would be appreciated." When Edwin didn't move, the bird flicked one of his feather-fingers at him. "Shoo."

Ritian said something, which caused the bird to grumble in such a manner that Edwin couldn't quite catch what he said.

"Fine. Go bother Forala; he's got Polyglot, he can help you."

Though he wouldn't normally heed such a dismissal, Edwin figured he probably *would* be more likely to get his questions answered by someone inclined to actually listen to what he was saying. Actually, what even *was* he wondering? He had a vague idea about wanting answers, but no concrete questions. He should probably figure that out. It was likely a safe assumption that the bird was talking about one of the nonhalflings milling around by the caravan, so he headed that way.

Now that Edwin was outside of the crowd, it was a lot easier moving around, and as he approached the small group, he drew a few curious gazes, but most simply didn't appear to care. One being, a bird with brownish-bronze plumage similar to the Merchant Leader's and leaning with his eyes closed against the side of the wagon, spoke up, "No, yican't climb on ta wagons." Unlike his previous experiences with Polyglot, there was a distinct accent associated with the newcomer, but Edwin could tell the Skill was still at work.

"Forala?" Edwin guessed. At that, Forala jerked into attention, standing up straight and looking at Edwin with a sharp gaze.

"Whatdya want? Who sentya?"

"Your, your, uh"—Edwin gestured vaguely in the direction he had come from—"your leader sent me?"

"Mum? What for, ten?"

"Well, she didn't want to be bothered and I had some questions."

Forala—Edwin made sure to tag the Formational Caravanner with his name—looked to the sky and muttered something Polyglot didn't translate. "Fine. Just get it over wit, wouldya?"

"What's going on? Who are you guys and where are you from? Where are you going, and can I come along?" Edwin inquired.

"We're traders, yaknow. We give rides at times ta those witout a Class ta defend temselves, and so we took allta loggers back ta home." He yawned, or at least did the avian equivalent of a yawn, before continuing, "We came from Port Torveil and are on our trade route. Drop off ta loggers, pick up some wood fer inland, caryon as always. Wishah could be in ta wagon, but Mum always says, 'Nah, Forala! Yagotta make sure te kids don't climb on ta outside. Wouldn't want tem to break! Not tat tey could anyway. Wha wasyer oter question?"

Edwin wasn't sure if Forala's accent was somehow getting *worse* as time went on or if he was just saying more words affected by it, but he was getting harder and harder to understand despite Polyglot presumably leveling. Edwin was able to manage, but it wasn't easy.

"If I could come along? I wound up around here through what I can only assume is some kind of powerful magic shenanigans and I'm kind of interested in not spending the rest of my life—"

"In ta middle o nowhere? Ahgetya. Ya can talk ta Mum about it, but we don't do charity. It'd never be allowed, yaknow? What'syer Class, anyway?" Forala cocked an eye open, looking at Edwin. "Pah. Adventurers. Well, good luck wityer try, not sure whya tink anywhere else'll be better forya."

"What do you mean by that? Why am I an Adventurer and why does it seem like that's a bad thing?"

Forala gave him a side glance. "Ya aren't from around here, areya?"

Edwin shook his head. "That's what I said."

"Well, it's easy ta tell tat you're an Adventurer, what kinda Class is 'Foreign Alchemist,' anyway? It sure as tois ain't a proper Alchemist Class, anta Foreign part is a dead giveaway, yaknow? But who would ever wantan Adventurer ta work for tem anyway? Cripplin' their Build just cause tey don't wanta play by da rules. Really, tey should be punished way harder if yeask my mum, but eh. If ye want ta wreck yer life, I ain't gonna stop ye, yeknow?"

Edwin blinked, trying to process that influx of information. "So … an Adventurer is someone with an unusual … Build? Like Class? And that's bad because … they aren't effective?"

"Are ya daft? Yeah. What even gotya ta do such a stupid Build, anyway?"

Edwin shrugged. "Getting dropped in the middle of a forest. Needed every bit of help I could get. Took Skills and Paths that seemed like they'd help."

"Eh, yer funeral. Looks like Mum is near done wit her trade; ye can asker what ye can do ta get passage once she comes over."

With that, Forala returned to his relaxed lean against the wagon, leaving Edwin to awkwardly stand around while he waited for whatever was next. He needed to get away from here, but all the attention his conversation had drawn from the other members of the caravan made Edwin want to shrink away and run off from the caravan, never mind that it would be needed to actually leave. He Identified the closest members, finding a Sword Marshal, Hired Guard, and Experienced Marshal (all human) and a Highquarry Hauler and Windblown Merchant (both birds). The rest of the … twenty-one members were out of his fourish-meter range so he couldn't tell what they were, but the birds did narrowly outnumber the humans, with nine featherless members in total.

Level Up!
Identify Level 28→29
Polyglot Level 5→6

After what seemed like ages, but was probably only about five minutes, Forala's "Mum" returned to the caravan, fluttering down from the sky. "Okay, you lazy lot! Lumber's by the river, go earn your keep!" The small crowd dispersed quickly, the birdfolk doing an odd sort of skipping jump or flying instead of walking. She turned to Edwin and said, "What are you doing hanging around, Adventurer? Get."

"I was hoping I could tag along as you headed to a bigger city. I got stranded out here and I—"

"Don't need your kind helping. I got my guards already, and I'm not risking my license for you. You want a position as a guard, find someone with bluer feathers. I don't want you."

"I just want a ride. I'll work doing whatever or offer what I have in trade, but it's not much. Look, I just want to get out of here, and fast. I'm not good in a fight anyway, so no worries there."

She assessed him with an appraising eye. "You aren't to quarrel with any of my crew. You do, you're gone. Don't care if we're on a bridge over the Rhothos, you're out. Can you set up a camp, start a fire? Cure a wound? Fix a broken wheel? Make a Cure? What do you have to offer?"

"Understood." Edwin shrugged. "I can set a fire with the snap of my fingers, have a Skill for wound tending, but I'm a bit of a miserable Alchemist unless you want to know how to make Blacks—" As soon as the last words left his mouth, Edwin instantly clamped down on his tongue, glaring at the bird. What the heck was that? He wasn't about to say *anything* about that, not after the last time. "Are you using a Skill on me?" he asked accusingly.

Birds couldn't smile, but she certainly seemed to give a predatory grin. "Just a bit of Honest Negotiation. Leads you to being open with what you have to offer and keeps you from lying. You must have your head in the clouds to cut off where you did." She stroked the top of her beak with a feather. "I don't suppose you were about to say you know how to make Blackstone, do you? Ha! No wonder you're in such a hurry to get away from here. Those dwarves refuse to give anyone even a hint of the stuff."

She clicked her talons against the ground, an action that surprised Edwin. He didn't know you could make that sound against dirt and grass. "Tell you what. You give me the formula for Blackstone and help around the caravan as we travel, setting up the fire at night and so on, and we'll give you a ride to Vinstead, next big city over, couple weeks away, and give you food and such on the trip. If you want to go farther than that, we can renegotiate then; deal?"

Edwin cast a wary gaze on the merchant. He couldn't help but feel like he was being taken advantage of, but he didn't really have any other options at hand. Also, it wasn't like he *really* had that much to give away, so would he be taking advantage of them? "I don't know how to make Blackstone."

"What do you know how to make, then? It's gotta be something good if you want to keep it so secret."

Edwin warily eyed her, sizing up how much he trusted her. He didn't have much of a choice, but that was how he ended up in the *last* fiasco, and he was not letting something like that happen again. Still, it was the only thing he had to bargain with, and he couldn't say he *really* cared about the "secret" of concrete getting out. "It's a sort of liquid stone. Once it dries, it's all one piece, as hard as rock."

Her posture instantly shifted. "I'm interested. Tell me how to make it and you've got a deal."

"I'll tell you how to make it *after* we arrive, not before. And if you so much as try to pull any sort of trick to keep me from leaving, deal's off entirely and I'll ... I'll see if I can get your license revoked. Hiring an Adventurer or something, you said?"

She shrugged. "We have a deal; no need to threaten me. You wouldn't be a hire, just a passenger, and they don't care much about Adventurers in Rhothos anyway. But if you behave, I'll even see about getting you some practice for your Polyglot Skill."

Edwin was taken aback. "How could you tell?"

"Once you get good enough at the Skill, you can tell when you're talking to someone with it as well. Hells, you're speaking a language I've never even heard of, yet I could understand you better than Ritian herself. That's as sure a sign as any that you've got Polyglot. It can be a lot easier to level up when speaking with someone else with the Skill themselves. Forala could use the practice, anyway. He's gotten a bit brown-clawed as of late." She started fiddling around with something invisible, presumably something System-related.

Edwin scowled, then was taken aback as an unexpected notification popped up.

A Contract has been extended!
Caravan Merchant Leader Aerfa Tallfjaer offers: Passage to Vinstead and accompanying amenities.

Foreign Alchemist Edwin Maxlin offers: Aid setting up nightly camp, instructions for the Blackstone knockoff, not to cause any trouble. Accept Contract? Y/N

"What's this?"

"You've never seen a Contract before? Where are you even *from*?"

"What does it—"

"Just accept it."

"Tell me what it does, first."

Aerfa looked to the sky and said, "Heavens help me." Then she looked at Edwin, who had just been proven wrong about birds being able to look exasperated. "All it does is let the other know if the terms have been breached. It's not an Unbreakable or Punitive, don't worry. Just accept it so I can go yell at my IDIOT SON, who DOESN'T KNOW HOW TO CARRY A LOG!"

Edwin winced at the volume and tentatively accepted. It was a bit of a risk, but he figured the System probably wouldn't lie to him. Aerfa nodded and jumped into the air, soaring over Edwin's head, displaying a capability for flight that ... shouldn't have worked with the length of her wings. What was going on there?

Probably magic, Edwin grumbled to himself. Aerfa reached where the caravan crew was returning, the humans carrying comically massive stacks of lumber on one shoulder from around the village, and started yelling about how incompetent they all were, focusing specifically on a few key individuals. The birds didn't have as large of loads but were still bringing some smaller logs as they hopped back over.

Edwin sighed. Great, loud people. Just what he wanted. He was ... vaguely starting to remember why he was content being alone. Still, at least now he had a ride.

CHAPTER 25

Settling into the Roost

Edwin found himself milling around awkwardly as the caravan crew started loading up frankly ludicrous amounts of lumber into the wagon train (turns out the covered wagons also had spatial shenanigans going on), feeding stack after stack of milled logs into vehicles that looked shorter than the logs being fed inside, but that was magic for you. It looked really strange, and all he could do was gawk until Aerfa dropped by to show Edwin where to go, namely the second wagon in the train, apparently for passengers.

There was only a single other person in "Edwin's" wagon, a tiny sleeping bird-person, and upon laying eyes on the individual, Aerfa started screeching, "Is *this* where you've been, young miss? Get your lazy tailfeathers out of here and do your chores before your talons go brown! Come on, Faera, we don't have all day! Get, get, get!"

The poor child—presumably one of Aerfa's ... Wait, were their names anagrams of each other? Huh—literally flew into the air, jumping with a squeak as she tried to fly past Edwin and escape the wrath of her mother. Edwin stepped to the side just in time as Faera darted out the door.

Identify.

Avior Child

"Get back here, you ungrateful fledgling! You have chores to do! Hey! Don't you give me that tone!"

Edwin unconsciously shrank away from Aerfa as she took off after the fleeing Faera, the two avior entering a midair dance reminiscent of an eagle trying to catch a songbird. He shook his head at the spectacle—not that he had *that* much room to judge—and put his meager possessions and assigned bedroll off in the corner of the fairly spacious wagon. While the outside was probably about ten feet wide by twenty feet long, the inside was at least triple that in each direction, there was even a second floor of sorts, but climbing up the ladder to it didn't uncover anything noteworthy.

Once he had gotten as situated as possible, Edwin returned to the outside, where he saw Aerfa dragging her struggling daughter with one talon through the air. After depositing Faera, who just sat and pouted for the moment, on the ground near where a handful of horses were milling about, Aerfa returned to talk to Edwin.

"Apologies. She loves to shirk her duties, even though she knows they're why I let her come along on the route. It looks like you were able to store your belongings? Good. We leave first thing in the morning; don't be late. You don't have any duties today, so go have fun and enjoy doing ... whatever it is you Adventurers like to do. Kill ten rats or whatever."

Edwin heard the clatter of wooden boards from behind one of the halfling house-trees, and Aerfa's head snapped up, staring in the direction the sound had come from, and she jetted off without so much as a word.

...

Well, she *did* say that he should enjoy himself. The village folk seemed to be busy greeting one another, lots of chatter driving its way into Edwin's skull. Nothing there, not that he really wanted to interact with people anyway. Hmm. Edwin pulled up his Status. He hadn't looked at the whole thing in a while.

Name
Edwin Maxlin

Age

22 years

Race

Extraplanar Human

Class

Foreign Alchemist

Attributes

Mana 5

Skills

Magical

Basic Mana Sense: 29, Firestarting: 29, Alchemy: 43,
Mana Infusion: 57

Physical

Athletics: 27, Breathing: 20, Flexibility: 15, Nutrition: 16, Packing: 5,
Seeing: 16, Sleeping: 21, Survival: 17, Walking: 28

Mental

Identify: 29, Polyglot: 6, Mathematics: 37, Research: 40, Outsider's
Almanac: 62, Visualization: 25

Combat

Bomb Throwing: 9

New

First Aid: 13

Paths

Skill Points: 223

Very Much Yes-Eventually

Micro-Biomancer 0/90, Path Less Traveled 0/90, Realm Traveler 0/120,
Scientist 0/60, Alchemical Warrior 0/90

Promising

Stonehide Vanquisher 0/60, Titan Slayer 0/90, World Traveler 0/60,
Researcher 0/60, Explorer 0/60, Outsider 0/60, Unkillable 0/90, Blackstone Conqueror 0/60, Mage 0/60, Field Medic 0/60

Maybe One Day

Survivor 0/60, Athlete 0/60, Daredevil 0/60, Pioneer 0/60, Novice
Pyromancer 0/60, Warrior 0/60, Pyromaniac 0/30, Wanderer 0/60, Exile
0/30, Escapee 0/30

Meh
Lumberjack 0/60, Way of the Empty Hand 0/60, Trapper 0/60

When he first pulled it up, Edwin wasn't sure where he would put his First Aid Skill. It wasn't magical, it wasn't really mental, it certainly didn't fit into combat, and physical didn't fit either. Eventually, he just created a new "Utility" category, which on further reflection also expanded to include Almanac, Identify, Firestarting, and Alchemy. They weren't *quite* mental/magical Skills, just sort of related.

He also looked at his Skill Points saved up ... There were a lot of them. Should he spend them on something? He was definitely itching to get more Skills, but ... he didn't know enough. Not yet. Once he found someone who would be able to explain stuff about the System to him, then he would decide. But who? He definitely didn't want to reveal the fact that he wasn't from Joriah to anyone, but how else would he be able to bring up the fact that he had no idea what this apparently ubiquitous part of life was or how it worked? He'd ... need to think about it a lot more.

Anyway, he had time to kill. And no need to worry about keeping his strength up, or what various overly nosy prison wardens would think. That meant he could experiment with his Skills! Hooray! The first and most obvious thing that Edwin could think of to try and push his Skills' limits was using Mana Infusion to improve their capability. It had been a long, long time, but Edwin faintly remembered the Skill description for Infusion mentioning that it worked on his Skills. All he needed to do was figure out how.

Firestarting was easy. So easy, in fact, Infusing it had become almost second nature at this point, making it hard for him to tell exactly how the Skills interacted. After a fair bit of experimentation, Edwin felt that he had figured it out. It worked by Infusing both his fingers and *the air around them* simultaneously, and also triggering Firestarting at basically the same time. Even that wasn't quite enough to actually ignite something, though pairing the Skill activation with a snap of his fingers seemed to be sufficient.

Okay. Now that he had established a baseline, all he needed to do was apply the same logic to his other Skills!

…

How the heck was he supposed to do that? Firestarting was a bit of an unusual Skill, so far as Edwin could tell, as it allegedly had a passive benefit, but he could also use it actively. The fact that it was a passive Skill let him Infuse it, but it wasn't until he used it actively that the mana seemed to actually *do* anything.

Okay, what about Almanac, then? It had an active effect—namely, entering a new message—but also had to have been passive for Identify to key off it, right?

A fair bit of experimentation later, Edwin didn't feel any closer to a solution. Why was it so easy for him to "feel" the passive aspect of Firestarting, yet so hard to identify the passive portion of Almanac? Just using Mana Infusion at the same time as Almanac maybe did something? His mana went somewhere when he pushed it at the Skill, but he couldn't figure out any difference in the Skill manifestation. Even his Basic Mana Sense seemed to tell him that the mana just left, with no apparent destination or direction. It was … puzzling.

Edwin eventually found that he could get his success rate of Infusing Almanac up significantly if he first "primed" his mana by using Firestarting. It helped him get his mana flowing in a way that he could then grab and feed into Almanac … It was weird. It felt in some ways like he was somehow manually controlling the beat of his heart, yet not quite.

At some point during his experimentations, he suddenly felt Almanac bite into something new, and in some indefinable way that felt decidedly different from his normal messages. Confused (he had already gotten virtually every last board in the wagon tagged by then), Edwin gave it a simple message of just "This is something new and strange," then started hunting all over the wagon for what it was that he had tagged.

I'm Board 1.
I'm so very board.
Lalalalalalala.

Supercalifragilistic …
Uhhhh. I'm out of ideas?
Level63lengthtest:20222426283032343638404244464850525456586
06264666870727476788082848688909294969810110410710110213
16119122125128131134137140143146149152155158161164167617
01731761791821851881911941972002032062092122152182212224
22723023323623924224524825125425726026326626926272275278
8129429730030
I'm Board Too.
3.1415926535897932365 … something.
Something something clever statement.
Look at me, I'm important maybe.
Reminder to drink water.
whittles innocently

And on and on it went. Eventually, Edwin glanced down at his hand at just the right moment, his gaze drawn by something, and his Identify locked onto the phantom flames produced by his Firestarting.

This is something new and strange.

Edwin nearly jumped as he found the message. He confirmed it wasn't just his hand—it wasn't—and then reconjured his Firestarting flames.

This is something new and strange.

He could sing! Not actually, but if he were to ever sing for joy it would be right now. He was able to Almanac magical effects! He had tried before but it hadn't worked, but apparently Infusing his Outsider's Almanac let him tag at the very least magical Skills, maybe all magic, maybe all Skills!

Level Up!
Outsider's Almanac Level 63→64
Identify Level 29→30

Mana Infusion Level 57→58
Research Level 40→42

Oh! He could tag sections of his Status with this! There wasn't much he could really do with it at the moment, but in the future he could use it to save his Skill descriptions so he could refer to them easily. Between that and being able to Almanac the Skills in use, this changed … ! Well, okay. Not everything. Maybe not even some stuff, honestly. It was cool, but when would it actually be useful? Edwin had yet to encounter any magical spells or anything thus far, but maybe being able to Identify Skills would be useful? Or did it have to be magic? Sigh. His momentary excitement significantly dampened, Edwin moved on with his experiments, hoping another Skill would have better luck.

Now that he had an idea of what to do, Edwin was fairly easily able to determine that Infusing his Identify Skill just allowed him to have more than one Identify box open at the same time. Normally, using Identify closed any preexisting results, but if he Infused the Skill as he used it, it wouldn't close until he chose to dismiss it. Handy.

Using it with Packing required Edwin to Infuse whatever he was carrying in addition to the Skill itself, and made whatever he was carrying stronger, but only so long as he was in contact with the object. He found that out the hard way when his grip on his last remaining spare sack slipped while he was trying to cut it with a knife, resulting in a fairly lengthy tear in the fabric.

Trying to Infuse his eyes while utilizing Seeing had one of the absolute *coolest* effects. His eyes glowed! In a really nice shade of blue, too, just a bit brighter than his natural eye color, and with just a hint of green. He couldn't see (heh) any other effects, though, sadly. Still totally worth it.

Edwin wasn't sure if he was Infusing Breathing correctly at first, his mana not going anywhere nor having any apparent effect when he tried, until he realized that he had been involving it every time he had successfully breathed fire using Firestarting. Realizing that confirmed he was Infusing it correctly, but otherwise didn't help him figure out what, if anything, Infusing only Breathing did. It did, however, give him the idea to try and use multiple Skills at the same time to combine their effects.

The first combination he found with an obvious use was Seeing and Basic Mana Sense. Not only did his eyes still glow, but also the buzzing sensation that normally accompanied his arcanoception was replaced with the ability to see faint, ghostly halos of light around magic. It was really imprecise; Infusing his fingernail (he couldn't Infuse his finger for some reason, just the nail) made his entire arm and a fair bit of surrounding air glow, but it was perhaps even better than just the glowing eyes.

Congratulations! For imbuing a part of your body with mana, you have
unlocked the Physical Arcanist Path!
You have unlocked the Fire Breath Skill!
Accept Skill? Y/N
You have unlocked the Mana Reinforcement Skill!
Accept Skill? Y/N
Level Up!
Seeing Level 16→19
Basic Mana Sense Level 29→30
Mana Infusion Level 58→59
Research Level 42→43

Edwin didn't take either of the offered Skills. They were both tempting, sure, but he could already mimic their effects. And sure, actually taking them might have helped him do them *better*, but he could always choose to get them later, when he was more informed about the System and had talked to some other people whose strategy wasn't "do what worked for the last guy."

Poking around at his Skills more gave Edwin a general sense for a handful of them that had a sort of synergy, where he would be able to use Mana Infusion to combine their effects, even though he wasn't able to determine what those effects *were*. Athletics/Walking, Seeing/Identify, Sleeping/First Aid, Mathematics/Visualization, Breathing/Sleeping, Research/Alchemy, Survival/Nutrition, Packing/Athletics, and Research/Polyglot were the ones he was able to find before the light started to fade outside, as each combination took quite a bit of fiddling to actually tell if it worked or not. He didn't even want to *think* about testing combinations of three or more Skills. That was a (sometimes literal) headache for another day.

Outside, the caravan's members were sitting around a campfire, chatting and laughing in what must have been the avior language, given its resemblance to some mix between birdsong and the cries of a hawk. Edwin naturally couldn't understand a word of it, save the occasional out-of-context snippet that either Aerfa or Forala spoke loudly enough for him to hear. It looked like they were having a great time, which Edwin might have normally enjoyed being a part of, but they certainly wouldn't appreciate his presence, and he quite literally didn't understand what they were saying.

So he didn't go out. His bedroll was still more comfortable than what he had been on more often than not, anyway. Besides, Edwin wanted to see if he could get the Breathing/Sleeping combination to work.

He didn't get the chance, though, long-accumulated exhaustion pulling him to sleep before his head even hit the pillow.

CHAPTER 26

Chitter Chatter

Edwin woke to a beam of sunlight worming its way through a minuscule gap between two boards on the side of the wagon and directly onto his closed eyelids. He grumbled and tried to fall back asleep at first, but the damage had already been done, and he was, if not wide awake, awake enough.

As he sat up, Edwin rubbed the sleep from his eyes with a yawn, casting his gaze around to regain his bearings. It was interesting how, even with over twenty levels in Sleeping, there was still time each morning where he was all but dead to his surroundings, at least until he got his heart going. Magically potent rest didn't prevent morning grogginess, it seemed. He was just glad he hadn't been one of those people who needed a cup of coffee to get started in the morning. Tea, sometimes, but he didn't like coffee, even when it was filled with all the stuff people told him made it "barely" coffee. He wasn't sure why that always seemed to be phrased as though it were somehow meant to *encourage* him to try black coffee, not that it ever worked anyway.

"Who's laughing now, huh, Ryan?" he muttered. "You'd have headaches for weeks without your"—he yawned—"caffeine fix. Hmm."

It took him a couple minutes of yawning and stretching, but Edwin eventually got himself up, hopping outside of the wagon to stretch his legs. All around him, the members of the caravan were at work, busily making what appeared to be last-minute preparations before their departure, hitching up horses to the train of wagons, moving a few bags of supplies around, and he even saw one human walking toward the caravan with a stack of six dripping-wet barrels in his hands.

The town, too, seemed to be back to a normal set of operations, with individuals bustling every which way, halflings darting around at high speeds, some so high that Edwin could barely track their movement. A few were carrying around entire *trees*, or at least their trunks, which brought a smile to Edwin's face. There was something humorous about a single three-foot-tall individual carrying around a fifty-foot-tall solid log as though it weighed no more than a couple of pounds. There must have been some Skill involved in just keeping them from having the trailing ends of the log hit anything, or even just walking into one another or their surroundings in general.

How can I get that Skill? I want to stop running into things, Edwin thought, rubbing his shoulder. Was it *really* his fault that he didn't notice how far he was from the edge of the wagon? Okay, fine, maybe it was. But he still wanted that Skill; he didn't care that it broke his promise to himself.

Hmm, okay. Where was the village elder? He should probably try to at least offer his thanks for the help ...

"Dive, you brown-taloned chicks!" A screeching voice broke Edwin from his thoughts. "Daylight is wasting; let's get this on the road! Faera, stop messing around and get inside! Sorahna! Get those horses bridled! Come on, dive! Dive! We want to be over the Thardil by nightfall! Edwin! You're in the front wagon today! Enjoy it! Forsish, why isn't the water secured? You should already be done with that! Get diving! Sharaf and Rosil! You're first in the sky! Get up there! Now, do it!"

Wait, he heard his name somewhere in there. And that sounded urgent.

Sorry, guys, and thanks for the help I suppose.

Uhh ... front wagon, was it? He made his way up the connected chain of wagons until he got to the front, admittedly only a few away, and after staring at the six horses that were apparently supposed to pull the entire train of ... twelve wagons, Edwin pushed aside the curtain separating the interior from the exterior and went inside.

Really, he should have expected something to surprise him. Sure, while the casual space-warping that seemed to accompany all buildings he'd entered so far was surprising—especially given how casually everyone treated it, suggesting that it was completely normal for them—and had somewhat lost its initial shock factor, it still required a touch of mental recalibration to see how large the lead wagon was on the inside compared to the outside. But no. That wasn't what surprised him. What was more surprising was that everyone inside was lounging on *beanbag chairs*. They were just so utterly modern, and in such stark contrast to the distinctly semimedieval aesthetic the rest of Joriah had thus far displayed that Edwin couldn't help but stare, and he walked over to investigate one. It looked … just like a beanbag chair. On closer inspection, it was, well, a beanbag chair. A sack of some sort made from thick cloth, stuffed with … something, Edwin couldn't tell. Probably straw, though maybe feathers? Would avior feathers be good for something like that? Would they *want* to use their own feathers, or would that be like having something made out of human skin?

Anyway, people were lounging around on beanbag chairs. Edwin supposed it made some sense, certainly more than normal chairs on a wagon, and they clearly weren't hurting for space. It seemed odd that they had at least two wagons basically empty of goods for what was apparently a merchant caravan, but who was he to question their strategy? They'd know better than he would, and asking Aerfa would probably not go over well. He liked his eardrums in one piece, after all, and even now, he could still hear her flying around outside screeching orders to everyone else with some decidedly inventive language, including a few phrases that Polyglot just had no clue how to properly translate. Where was he again? Oh yeah! The interior!

There were nineteen other people in the front wagon. While Edwin had initially drawn some attention, most of their gazes had wandered again, a couple to dice games and some others to poring over paperwork. One person seemed to be doing something System-related, swiping a feather through the air to interact with some unseen screen. Most of the passengers were avior, though there were six humans off in one corner. Of the avior, about half were the same burnished brown/bronze of Aerfa and Forala … Forala was *part* of that group, actually. Three of those remaining had dark gray plumage, two had glossy black feathers and beaks that resembled more a crow's than an eagle's like the others, and the final one was a pure white. That one was busy literally preening, straightening its feathers.

The humans were either fairly tanned or just had slightly darker skin naturally, but they stuck together for the most part, not mingling with the avior as they rolled dice, speaking some language just as unfamiliar to Edwin as the literal birdcalls of the avior. If he were to compare it to some language from Earth, he would have said it sounded vaguely Asian. Trying to tune Polyglot to their conversation led Edwin to an interesting realization: he could only try and interpret a single language at a time, and, at least at the moment, he couldn't direct his focus away from the racket outside as Aerfa continued to wrangle the caravan into motion long enough to switch what tongue it was attempting to translate. So, what the humans were discussing remained a mystery for the time being. He was close enough to Identify them, though. Two were Junior Pack-Laborers, one was an Experienced Packer, and the final three were just Strong Laborers. It was a surprising degree of homogeneity compared to the avior Edwin was in range for, who numbered two Junior Travelers, four Skyguards, a Feather of Wealth (that was the white one), an Experienced Medic, and Edwin caught the tail (heh) end of a Pack Beastmaster as they left out the back in response to another loud screech for a "Sorahna" (Edwin made sure to Almanac the name).

It didn't take too much longer before Edwin felt the wagon begin to rumble under his feet, setting off slowly at first but gradually building momentum as Edwin imagined the six horses straining to somehow pull *twice* their number in wagons. His beanbag felt quite comfortable as Edwin sank into his thoughts, musing idly about what Paths he might want to complete next.

He was pulled out of his thoughts as Aerfa swooped in through the entrance, the curtain parting as she entered, landed perfectly, and started looking around. She immediately zeroed in on Forala, who seemed to be dozing in his beanbag, lying on his back. "Forala! Quit bending your tailfeathers. Edwin has Polyglot. I want you to hit level forty-six in it by the time we reach Vinstead!" Following that, she seemed to find some reason to give everyone in the wagon at least one instruction, which everyone moved at least half-heartedly to fulfill. Content, Aerfa leapt back out the entrance, off to do something else, namely ... Ah. She was looking for her daughter Faera again, judging by the yelling.

Forala, for his part, dragged his chair over and plopped back into it, sitting more like a bird would sit in a nest. "So Mum letya come along, I see. Whatya haveta promise her ta let ya?"

Edwin shrugged. No real harm sharing that; it would be public knowledge soon enough. "Minor help setting up, and a formula for concrete, a kind of liquid stone. What's even the big deal with it? Everyone seems to freak out about it whenever it comes up."

Forala cocked his head. "Liquid stone? So it'd all be one solid rock whenits dry, ya?" Edwin nodded. "Well, surely yaknow tat ta big ting for sometin tats all one object is tat Skills are harder ta use on it, yaknow? Ya need a red sky of power ta try and break down a wall tats all one ting, specially for any kinda magic Skill, but if it's small pieces, any ol' Destructive Strike or Move Stone could make te ting break, one piece at a time. Ye just can't use Skills on a part of a whole. How dontya know *tat*?"

Edwin nearly spoke up—his Mana Infusion could affect part of an object, couldn't it? No, wait. It had seemed like that when he Infused his eyes, but he was really just Infusing his Seeing Skill, wasn't he? His fingernail? Eh, that was arguably a separate object, if each rock in a wall made of stones was counted separately. It *would* explain why he wasn't able to Infuse his finger, though.

Hmm. He could Infuse a bit of the air when using Firestarting, but that probably didn't count as a single object ... Huh. It seemed like an arbitrary restriction, especially when delving into the subatomic scale, but he'd have to test it out at some point to see if he could get around it, or what exactly the limits were, though there was no reason to doubt that it was a general guideline for Skills.

With that in mind, though, the dwarves' obsession with concrete made a *bit* more sense. Edwin offered something revolutionary after a sense, and they wanted to control it. They still seemed a bit desperate for it, though, all told. Eh, people. They probably thought they had some reason for it, and Edwin wasn't going to try and understand people who might have a totally different thought process than humans did. He had enough problems trying to figure out how *his own* thoughts worked.

"Just ... slipped my mind, is all," Edwin lied unconvincingly. He could tell his conversation partner didn't believe him, either, but chose not to follow up on it for whatever reason. "So, ah, what's your story? Tell me about your life. Where are you from? What brings you out on the road?"

That was standard conversation stuff, right? What else was there? Oh, Forala had started talking.

"Eh, hatched and nested in Farport, yaknow? Along ta water. So many great winds, perfect fer flying. Mum always pulled me alongon her trips, but Da would take my clutch sis out to sea for his trips. Tried te water once, didn't agree wit me. Give me a solid rock ta perch on after a good fly any day over sometin bein tossed around so much. Farisel always liked te sea air, toh. Tey've been preening us ta take over when tey retire. Divin up in a couple years now, bu' Mum says I need ta get all my Skills Advanced at least one more time afore she'll let me take point, ten I'll haveta do a full round wit her as *my* aide, before she finally retires. 'Parrently she thinks I'm still her liddle kid though I'm ta Third already! Mum likes ta say tat I may have been set as her successor, but she sure won't let me underflap even once. Personally, I tink tat ..."

Edwin couldn't really say he *cared* about what Forala was talking about, fantasy gossip being just as boring as nonfantasy gossip, but he made sure to at least pretend—*that* was something he didn't even need a Skill for, after long years of practice—as the bird prattled on.

And on.

And on.

This might have been a mistake.

By the time the caravan started winding down in the late afternoon, Edwin had been subjected to a good ten straight hours of chatter from Forala, mostly about his plans for the future and stuff about his hometown and *all sorts* of interesting facts Edwin could have learned about Joriah if he was capable of actually giving someone talking to him more than about thirty seconds of attention at a time.

After that, Edwin's focus would just wander off to some corner of the wagon for about a minute, only to snap back to Forala long enough to realize nothing immediately interesting was being said and have the cycle repeat. Even what few potentially interesting tidbits Edwin *had* heard went mostly in one ear and out the other. He knew they were possibly important, but his attention just … wasn't there. It was frustrating. This was a chance to make a friend, and his brain just *wasn't cooperating.*

Still, Edwin did glean enough information to know that this caravan was on a fairly long loop across the southern half of Korizan, starting in the harbor city of Farport, going up the coast to Port Torveil, then skirting along the edge of the Verdant on their way to Sheraith, Vinstead, Tyra … and … there were more, he knew it … Kinea, and … ah, forget it, it didn't matter … then back again. Each step of the journey they'd pick up a set of goods and then slowly sell them off over the course of their trip, taking the excess back to Farport, where it would be loaded on ships and sailed elsewhere. Edwin was *really* glad he wouldn't need to take any tests on it, because he'd fail without a doubt. It was all long and complicated, and sometimes they'd pick up passengers and sometimes they wouldn't, and there was a whole *hour-long tangent* about them needing "better horses," which Edwin found hard to believe given how insanely strong their pack animals already seemed to be.

Forala's monologue was thankfully brought to a close when the wagon slowly clattered to a stop, and everyone began filing outside to get the camp set up for the night. Edwin didn't fully understand at first why they didn't just sleep for the night in their wagons, but he quickly realized they probably did, and this was just to cook dinner. A few avior flew off and returned quickly with fresh game, some deer-looking creatures clutched in their talons. While they were being prepared, Edwin was tasked with starting a fire, which was simple enough. A tap on a few of the piled-up logs was all it took for the fire to start blazing, no need to even use kindling. Not long after that, the designated cook—the human Experienced Worker—had the prepared venison on a makeshift grill, filling the campsite with the appetizing smell of roasting meat.

It tasted fine. Bit of a surprise, really. Edwin half expected something utterly sublime once Skills got involved, but maybe not? Or did nobody here have a Cooking Skill? Either way, Edwin dug into his provided food with gusto. He wasn't *too* hungry, as, despite not having eaten all day, he hadn't been very active and his Survival Skill meant he needed less than half the food he would otherwise require. He kept waiting for a notification that his Nutrition level had increased—it did pretty much any time he had a new kind of meal, so long as it was at least somewhat healthy—but when it didn't come, he remembered he'd turned off notifications earlier in the day.

Level Up!
Nutrition Level 16→17
Research Level 43→44
Polyglot Level 6→13

Huh. Pretty nice gains, considering all he had really done today was sit around and half listen to the ramblings of a regular chatterbird.

Edwin sat as a silent part of the giant circle around the fire, listening slightly as everyone chatted in their own strange languages. Every once in a while, he was able to pick up on the odd word spoken, neither Forala or Aerfa speaking loudly enough to monopolize his Skill this time. Nobody struck up a conversation with him, not that he expected anyone to. Still, it left a strange melancholy resting deep within him, as he longed for the social interactions he had ... well, never really had back on Earth. But memory was a funny thing, and so it tried to tell him that he actually did have friends who would talk to him in this sort of situation, and it really hadn't been that bad.

His memory was such a liar at times.

CHAPTER 27

All That Glitters Is Silver

The next two days passed in essentially the same way as the first. Edwin kept being invited/sent to the front carriage, where Forala would spend the next eight to tenish hours talking at him; then it would be dinnertime, with Edwin igniting the fire, followed by bed. Not once did anyone other than Forala and Aerfa speak to him or address him in the slightest, which was honestly fine by Edwin. Fewer people, fewer problems, so far as he cared. He didn't need anyone else. He was an introvert, after all. Loneliness wasn't a problem for people like him.

Not at all.

The fourth day they were on the road, Forala was interrupted mid-sentence as he was going on about something or other involving one of his friends from back home and the girl said friend was interested in, and it was all Edwin could do to avoid falling asleep altogether. Why couldn't the avior have been more interested in economics, or something. He was a merchant, wasn't he? Edwin would *legitimately* prefer to hear about invoices than this ... pointless gossip.

Their wagon suddenly stopped, though, which snapped him back to attention. From outside, he heard voices faintly yelling, both incomprehensibly muffled. About half the people currently in the wagon went to investigate, dropping from the wagon onto the cobblestone road below and looking around the side. There, Aerfa was animatedly discussing something with a raggedy-looking man with a drawn sword just off the road. Behind him stood a group of similar-looking people, mostly human and a couple of avior, all with weapons drawn.

Whatever Aerfa was saying, though, the bandit leader (what else would they be, really?) didn't seem happy and started to raise his sword in some sort of signal. As he did so, the two Skyguards on duty swooped down from above, talons extended and ready to strike. However, they were each intercepted by an arrow piercing their wings, which brought about a sympathetic wince from Edwin. That was bound to hurt. Still, they weren't content, and a sudden sword swing by the bandit leader— the blade seemed to lengthen midswipe before returning to its normal size—chopped down Aerfa as she attempted to flee, leaving her on the ground with a giant gash in her back. The Experienced Medic dove forward, trying to reach their fallen boss but had a wing severed with another casual swing from the bandit leader's blade; the wing fell to the ground in a swiftly growing puddle of blood.

The man looked around pensively for a moment, seemingly waiting for something; then, when whatever it was didn't happen, he let out a bark of laughter. As he wiped off his bloody sword on the fallen wing of the medic, he directed his followers forward with a few hand signals toward the small crowd of onlookers, who scattered, rather appropriately, like a flock of birds. The only one left, standing dumbfounded at the scene, eyes fixed on the blood pouring over the grass, was Edwin.

Edwin's mind immediately went to how he had managed to take down a bunch of fully armored soldiers, whereas the bandits seemed lightly armored at most, before mentally berating himself. He was unarmed beyond a small knife in his pocket and absolutely did not have a bunch of alchemical bombs just lying around.

Okay, what could he do? Think, think … As one of the bandits got close enough for Edwin to Identify him as a Cruel Swordsman—what kind of Paths led to a Class like *that?*—he began to slightly panic. He didn't have time to come up with some intricate plan, he just needed to move enough to avoid *dying*. As Edwin scrambled backward, trying to keep out of range of the intimidating blade, he found himself literally backed up against a wall, pressed against the side of a wagon. So he did the only thing he could think of. He breathed fire, channeling mana into Firestarting and Breathing.

The torrent of flame was somewhat less impressive than Edwin had hoped for, but it still got his attacker to back up a couple of steps, enough for Edwin to slip away and start running down the caravan train. A protruding board caught his eye, and he grabbed it, using it to swing himself up onto a ledge, then farther up, clambering on top of the second wagon in the train.

From above, he was able to see as the last of ... one, two ... seventeen bandits emerged from the woods, spread out slightly as they approached the wagon train in a loose collection. Most were congregated near the front of the train, on some small plants and grass near the edge of the road. A few smaller rocks were scattered here and there, but other than them and a handful of larger bushes, the area was a clear battlefield. In the back, Edwin noticed an additional pair of bandits, two avior archers on an elevated bluff, roughly equal in height to where Edwin was perched. Fortunately, they either didn't notice or care about him, but he still dropped onto his stomach on the wooden roof to reduce his profile. No point in inviting another arrow to his shoulder, after all.

Okay, so they're all on the one side. If I drop down on the other side and make a run for it into the woods, I might be able to get away while they're busy plundering or whatever, Edwin strategized. He was just about ready to put his plan into action when his eyes widened. *Shoot! My bag! I need that.* It had his notebook, after all, and he still needed that to access his Almanac, alongside what few other odds and ends he still had from the dwarves. He also snuck a guilty look at the bleeding form of Aerfa. *Sorry. I wish I could help, but not with all these— Wait, what was that?*

A flash of silver caught Edwin's eye, and he saw a blur of brilliance leap from the other side of the road, land *on top of* one of the wagons, and then jump down from there, touching down next to one of the bandits a moment before the bandit in question's *head* fell with a thump, leaving the rest of the body to slump over.

"He's here!" Edwin's Polyglot managed to pick up a snippet from one of the bandits, though still with a hefty accent.

"Lay down your arms and surrender, so you may face justice! Your crimes end here!" the silver figure called out in a crisp, clear voice.

Now that the newcomer was stationary, Edwin was able to tell that he was clad head to toe in shining silver plate armor, with a crimson eagle emblazoned on his front the only section of his regalia not a uniform shining silver. In his hand was a reflective blade the same color so radiant it almost glowed, only the trickle of blood slowly running down its length marking it as an actual, physical object.

The overall impression Edwin got was that someone had forged literal moonlight into a blade and suit of armor, but that didn't stop the bandit leader from pointing his sword at the knight and shouting, "There … kill him!"

Okay, so Polyglot wasn't perfect yet. So what.

A spear-wielding bandit reached the knight first, charging at the armored figure and trying to stab him, the tip of his spear bursting into flames as he did so. The knight sidestepped the blow, moving with an almost contemptuous ease that belied the weight of what must have been nearly a hundred pounds of solid steel on him. The spearman, overextended from his own strike, tripped over his own feet and was swiftly disarmed. His severed forearms thudded to the ground, still gripping his spear, but before he could even fully collapse to his knees, the silver blade was buried hilt-deep in his chest.

Two more bandits, siblings from the looks of their matching hair, skin, and battleaxes, were the next to assault the warrior. One of them was knocked off his feet when the corpse of the spear wielder was kicked off the end of the silver blade, serving as a makeshift, but very heavy projectile. His sister kept up the attack, though, attempting a powerful downward cleave at the knight's head. But then it … missed? Edwin had barely even seen it, but the armored figure had taken a half step backward, putting him just out of reach of the attack. As before, getting knocked off-balance for even a split second proved a death sentence, as the woman's head went flying a moment later, her axe still stuck in the ground.

Her brother managed to escape from under the corpse lying on top of him, wrenching his sister's axe from the ground and wielding it alongside his own, the twin battleaxes forming a deadly rhythm and forcing the knight to give ground. The silver blade flickered out, and one of the axes was turned from its course just enough that it hit its pair, severing the head and disarming the man from one of his two weapons. Before the knight could follow up on his advantage, though, a pair of arrows were shot by the archer bandits some distance away. The first arrow glanced off the knight's helm, doing nothing but drawing his attention. The second was met by a shimmering silver wall that sprang into existence, intercepting and reflecting the shot such that it took a bandit trying to sneak up behind the knight in the throat, causing him to fall with a gurgle.

At this point, the rest of the bandits had haphazardly surrounded the knight, trying to attack from all manner of flanking positions. They didn't seem to be very *good* at it, though, as even Edwin could tell that they were just getting in each other's way. One's attack forced another to duck, another bandit with a shield was positioned directly in front of another with a sword, and so on. As obvious as it was to Edwin, it was certainly not lost on the knight, who simply moved out of the way of the next pair of arrows, allowing one to hit a bandit behind him in the side, the victim collapsing in a heap, and the other to embed itself in the side of the wagon Edwin was on.

Three bandits took the opportunity of the opening provided by the quick dodge to strike in unison, two spears and the same axe wielder from before. In response, the silver barrier that had deflected an arrow so easily sprang back up, causing each of the attacks to stop dead in its tracks, rebounding off as though it had struck a steel wall. The bodies of those affected fell to the ground a moment later, bisected just below the ribs.

There was a bit of a buildup of corpses at this point, with only a single opening in what was otherwise a complete circle of bodies around the knight, who, for his part, had barely even moved. The remaining bandits looked at the silver figure, unmarred save for a few drops of blood, saw the mutilated bodies of their companions, and took off running into the woods. The knight merely watched them as they fled, head turning as though noting each of them and where they went.

The bandit leader cursed at their cowardice, then looked at what he still had available to him. Of the original nineteen members of the bandit group, only he, the two archers, and the Cruel Swordsman remained. He barked an order, and the Cruel Swordsman tried to disengage from fighting the knight but was stymied slightly by virtue of being backed up against a knee-high rock. The two archers firing additional shots

gave him the opening he needed, and he slipped away from the engage-
ment to stand by his boss's side.

"Fine ... myself," the bandit leader said, brandishing his sword in a
clear challenge to the silver knight. The knight, for his part, turned his
head to affix his gaze on the bandit, not even flinching while he caught
a new arrow in his hand, crushing the shaft to splinters.

The two advanced toward each other, and sparks flew as their blades
crossed.

It became immediately apparent that the bandit leader was both a
league ahead of his peers and several steps below the knight in martial
prowess. His probing strikes were effortlessly batted away with almost
contemptuous parries, his attempts to feint utterly ignored. Some unseen
signal passed between the bandit leader and the Cruel Swordsman, and
they attacked in unison, the leader taking a broad swing at the knight's
head, the swordsman trying to stab at the base of the breastplate. In
response, the knight raised a gauntleted arm, a phantasmal silver shield
akin to the walls from before flickering into place to intercept the head
shot, and his sword darted down, knocking the lower strike away such
that it struck the center of his armored thigh instead of his torso.

The two bandits circled around the knight, taking advantage of the
distraction brought on by another pair of arrows to flank him. After
cutting one of the projectiles out of the air, the knight pivoted, dodging
the second shot while also trying to keep both his opponents in front of
him. A new arrow clanged off his helmet, shot faster than the previous
volleys, which proved to be a mistake on the part of the archer, as the
knight used his foot to retrieve a spear from among the fallen bodies,
throwing it like a javelin at the bowman. It passed clean through the
archer's chest, exploding out the back with a spray of blood, and continuing in an almost flat arc into the woods beyond. Even as the other
archer realized it might not have been quite so safe for him to have
stuck around and he started to fly off, it was too late.

In the intervening seconds, the knight had crossed swords with the
Cruel Swordsman, sliding their blades together until they met at the hilt,
and grabbed the forearm of the swordsman. With a solid yank, he pulled
on the bandit enough to give him a headbutt with his armored helm,
sending the swordsman reeling back with a crack, and giving enough

of an opening to disarm the bandit, retrieving his sword such that the knight held one blade in each hand. He didn't keep the second sword for long, though, throwing it end over end at the fleeing bandit archer, handily impaling a wing and sending the avior plummeting to the ground, where they landed with a crunch on the grass next to the road.

That just left the knight against the bandit leader and the disarmed Cruel Swordsman. As the swordsman went after a weapon lying on the ground, the knight disarmed him at the shoulder, his blade gleaming with a silver light and passing through flesh and bone with barely any resistance, the limb falling to the ground next to its gripped longsword. The Cruel Swordsman screamed, but was cut short a second later as the blade swung once more.

At the sight, the bandit leader's face contorted into an expression of rage, and he shouted a word that Polyglot didn't provide a translation for but Edwin still pretty much understood.

The armored face of the knight was unperturbed as he responded in a soft voice, "Tolra Revashs"—he intercepted a wild swing by the leader, Tolra's, sword—"you have committed crimes"—he moved almost imperceptibly to dodge a stab, even as the blade lengthened—"against the Empire, including but not limited to"—the shield made another appearance, stopping an overhead slash glowing with crimson light dead in its tracks—"banditry, murder, defilement, assault of an officer, assault." Each word was accompanied by the casual deflection of another rapid strike as Tolra was pushed back farther and farther. "… incitation of violence, rejection and incitement of rejection of Citizen Status, and obstruction of a criminal investigation. Have you"—he blocked a two-handed strike, the glow present for the attack guttering out in an instant, the sword returning to its normal length—"anything to say in your defense?"

Tolra grunted, and said something, Polyglot switching languages midsentence: "… kill you!"

"Allow the Log to show that the Ravenous Sword-Reaver Tolra Revashs presents no defense," the knight said, a final swing of his sword splitting Tolra down the middle and sending his blade catapulting through the air, where it embedded itself, sinking to the hilt, in a nearby rock.

And then there was silence.

CHAPTER 28

A Long Day's Knight

As soon as the fight was over, Edwin started scrambling down from the top of the wagon. It had only been a minute or two at most. Aerfa would probably still be alive, and he might even be able to save her if he acted quickly. However, as soon as he hit the ground, the knight spun around, bloody blade still in hand, pointing it at him. The knight—Edwin was close enough now to Identify him as a Silver Blade—started to say something, but Edwin hastily raised his hands to show he was unarmed and blurted out, "I'msorrypleasedon'tkillmeIjustwanttosaveher." He vaguely tried to indicate he was talking about the fallen avior, which was trickier than anticipated given his attempt to keep his hands above his head.

"You are not a Citizen." It was a statement, not a question.

"… Correct?" Edwin hazarded. "I'm kind of just passing through. Needed a ride."

Even though his face was completely obscured by his helmet, Edwin got the distinct feeling the Silver Blade was narrowing his eyes at him. "You do not have a Healer's License." Another statement.

"Yes? I have the First Aid Skill, though. I can help! She'll die otherwise!" Edwin protested, not liking where this seemed to be going.

"It is forbidden for any without a Healer's License to use medicine-related Skills on another individual. As an Enforcer for the Empire, I cannot stand by and allow you to break the Empire's laws."

At this point, a few other members of the caravan returned from where they had fled off to, and those who had remained in the first wagon were slowly peeking out to see what was going on. Most seemed to immediately make themselves scarce once they noticed the Silver Blade, though.

"We have laws for a reason. People like you always think themselves above them and do more harm than good. Allow the medic to tend to the merchant." Edwin could *feel* the knight's gaze even through his helmet.

"She'll die if nobody does anything! Look right there!" Edwin protested, pointing to the wingless avior lying near Aerfa's barely moving body. "That was the medic! There's nobody else! What could I do that would be worse than just letting Aerfa die?" He nervously shifted from one foot or the other. Hopefully, that sword wouldn't come any closer to him …

The helmet implacably stared at Edwin. How was he supposed to tell what the knight was thinking? "I cannot allow you, Adventurer, to break any laws of the Empire under my watch, foreigner or no."

The sword wasn't moving. That wasn't good, but it wasn't bad, either. He still had a sword pointed at him, though …

The blade was withdrawn in an instant. "I shall return!" Silver Blade called out. "Some of the bandits fled into the woods and it is my duty to track them down and end the threat they represent. Empire Ever Strong!" The Enforcer spun around to some confused, scattered cheers, then fled into the woods in a flash of silver.

Edwin stood still, blinking in confusion. What had just happened? The knight was clearly mad at him, yet ran off? Gah, people. Oh, right! People! He scrambled over to where Aerfa was bleeding out, Forala panicking next to her. The knight saying that Edwin wasn't allowed to help Forala "under his watch" and then immediately running off painted a pretty clear picture, and for once it was one that Edwin was in favor of.

He tuned out the frantic cries of the avior; they wouldn't help him. A quick Identify proved that the medic was indeed dead, also that Edwin could apparently use Almanac using "avior" as a material … Focus!

Okay, so he was dealing with a fairly deep cut along her back. After getting a bit of space by shoving Forala to the side and sending him on a task to get clean bandages, Edwin gingerly started removing a few severed feathers from where they had fallen into the wound.

By the time he had finished, Forala returned with some linen strips of cloth, handing them off to Edwin before resuming his panicking. Honestly, what was that supposed to accomplish, anyway? Applying the bandages slowed the bleeding, at least, and Edwin found after a bit of frantic trial and error that if he Infused the cloth through First Aid *and* Firestarting, it would cause it to heat up and stay in place, stopping enough of the blood flow to make him feel comfortable while also hopefully sanitizing against any infections. Still, Aerfa had lost a lot of blood, but Identify kept returning "Caravan Merchant Leader" rather than his hastily tagged "Avior corpse," so at least she was still alive.

"Forala."

"Mum! Mum, wakeup! You can't die here; you aren't ready ta pass it on ta me yet. Comeon, Mum, comeon …"

"Forala!" Edwin slapped the shoulder of the panicking avior. "I need your help. Give me a hand carrying your mom inside. She won't die, but we need to get her somewhere sheltered and more comfortable."

It took a bit of coaxing, but Edwin was eventually able to calm Forala down enough that the two of them were able to transport Aerfa into the first wagon, where they carefully laid her on top of two bean-bags pushed against the wall. Once done, Edwin breathed a sigh of relief, dropping into a beanbag of his own.

Notifications.

Level Up!
First Aid Level 13→17
Visualization Level 25→26
Identify Level 30→31
Polyglot Level 13→21
Congratulations! For putting yourself at risk to save another's life through medicine, you have unlocked the Steadfast Medic Path!
Congratulations! For defying an Enforcer of the Empire, you have unlocked the Rebel Path!

Huh. Interesting Paths, there. Decent Skill levels, too. Edwin had to wonder what sort of Skill the Rebel Path—why were all the ones he didn't want only 30 points?—would give him. No new Skills, though that wasn't really a surprise. He hadn't done anything particularly novel, after all.

The clatter of armor outside the wagon led Edwin to want to get up and investigate, but he decided he was far too comfortable in his seat to actually do so. It also seemed that he didn't need to, as the Enforcer, whatever he said his name was, appeared in the doorway.

He addressed the carriage as a whole: "The bandits have been vanquished. May the Empire be ever strong. I will be joining your caravan for the next two days until you reach Vinstead; thank you for your service to the Empire." His tone brooked no argument. "Where is your leader? I will speak with them." A few fingers hesitantly pointed at Aerfa, which brought only a quickly suppressed flinch to the Silver Blade. "Very well. Carry on as soon as you are able. There is no damage to your wagons, and thus you ought to be able to leave posthaste. You, Adventurer"—he pointed to Edwin—"come with me. I will speak with you."

Edwin didn't want to get up, and he really didn't want to speak to some official Empire Enforcer—when was someone with *that* title ever good news?—but he also didn't want to be on the bad side of someone capable of going through almost twenty armed combatants like butter, so he dragged himself upright nonetheless, following behind the knight as he left the wagon. Outside, the bandit bodies had been dragged into a pile, and the fallen Caravan Medic was being wrapped in some kind of cloth by two avior. Edwin almost stopped to see if the two injured Skyguards needed help; he was hardly qualified, but it didn't seem like there was anyone better on hand. A glance from the Enforcer brought him to heel, though, as the knight looked inside the next wagon in the train. Whatever he saw inside seemed to satisfy him, and he indicated for Edwin to follow as he climbed inside the passenger cart, empty save for Edwin's small collection of stuff.

"Sit," he commanded, once Edwin was inside, and he obliged, leaning against the wall, sitting on his bedroll. He was kind of curious how the Enforcer would sit. That was full plate armor; no way would it have enough range of mobility to let him— The thought was cut off as the suit of armor began to dissolve into silver sparks, fading like one of the silver walls he—no, *she*—had employed in her fight with the bandits.

As the last of her armor faded away, revealing a crimson uniform embroidered with silver thread, she sat down facing Edwin with a pointed expression on her face, brown hair pulled back tightly, presumably to help it fit under her armor. Was the armor one of those "Trophy" Skills the dwarves had mentioned? A Skill with a physical manifestation? Her sword had undergone a similar vanishing act earlier, so was it all just a Skill? Would armor like that automatically tailor itself to you? Would you need to wear your hair in a specific way to get it to fit, like with normal armor, or—

The knight cleared her throat, making Edwin snap to attention. "Answer the question."

He shook his head. "What?"

"I asked you a question. Answer it."

"Look, if this is about earlier when I—"

She cut Edwin off. "I hope you are not planning to do something unwise, such as admitting to a crime directly to an Enforcer."

Edwin immediately clamped his mouth shut. "No! No, of course not. I'm sorry, what did you ask? I got distracted by your armor."

She raised an eyebrow. "By the armor itself? That's not what I typically hear."

Wait, what did she typically hear? "Um, yes? It was just really cool— I hadn't seen a Trophy Skill used before."

She raised an eyebrow. "You're telling the truth. How have you never seen one before?"

Edwin winced. He hadn't meant to say anything hinting at his background. "It's been happening a lot lately, but ... do I ... have to answer that?"

The Enforcer's gaze turned hard as she seemed to stare into his very soul. Heck, she might well be doing that literally, if she had a Skill for it. "We shall see. Now, my original question?" Edwin shrugged, slightly embarrassed, which prompted a slow exhalation from her, as she closed her eyes in a slow blink, then said, "What is your name, and what is your purpose here."

"I'm ... Edwin. And honestly? I just kind of want to get somewhere else. I had a disagreement with the dwarves of the"—he tapped his knee, trying to remember the name of the place. "Highpeak Kingdoms?" he ventured. "Anyway, I just want to get far away from there. What was your name, if I may ask? I know you said it at one point, but I'm just awful when it comes to names, I have to"—he stopped himself before he blurted out—"mark people with their names with a Skill I have." It was probably innocent enough, but then again, mentioning concrete to a bunch of dwarves *who lived in a city made of magical concrete* had seemed innocent as well. No sense taking that risk. He wasn't going to give *anything* to her if he didn't have to.

Her gaze was fixed back on him, unwavering and strong, making Edwin want to shrink backward from it, but his retreat was foiled by him already sitting against the wall. Underneath him, he felt the wagons begin to move forward, the cobblestone road rattling the floor and wall just enough for him to wish he had a beanbag again. After what seemed like an unbearably long time, she spoke once more: "My name is Tara Lisana. It is my duty as an Enforcer to ensure that the Empire does not fall to threats internal or external. I would advise that you cooperate with me and are honest when answering my questions, lest you be deemed a threat to safety."

Edwin took a deep breath. "Okay. What do you need to know?" Hopefully she wouldn't ask anything too direct.

"Tell me what precisely the nature of your disagreement with the dwarves was, how you got your Class, what your previous Classes were, and how you got to the heart of the Rhothos Province without once visiting any city within the Empire?"

Well, darn it.

"Can I ... not?"

No sooner had the words passed his lips than the sword was back, its very sharp tip resting directly under his chin, forcing him to make eye contact with the Enforcer as she took to her feet, looming over him. Edwin shrank back. He didn't like the look in her eye.

"Let me make this very clear. My job is to deal with threats and potential threats to the Empire. You show up in the middle of my jurisdiction as an Adventurer, speaking a language I have never heard of before, apparently escaping some conflict with the dwarves. If I kill you here and now and ship your body back to the dwarves, I'll probably get commended for heading off a diplomatic incident and dealing with an unknown threat, showing tremendous initiative. You *will* answer my questions, or you will die. I do not wish to kill you, but if you force my hand I *will not* hesitate."

Edwin whimpered, "If I'm not a threat"—he swallowed, throat suddenly dry—"can I get some help? I'm kind of just lost and confused right now. And I have dangerous secrets. Not to you or the Empire! Just, last time I told them it … didn't go well. Mainly for me."

He tried to back up, but already being so pressed against the wall prevented him from budging more than an inch, which distance was in turn closed by the blade advancing just as far, until he could feel the point against his throat. He'd never thought he was afraid of dying, but … he was being proven wrong, it seemed.

Tara assessed Edwin. "If you truly are not a threat to the Empire in any way or form, and indeed need my aid in some manner that I can provide, I will uphold the principles of my office and do everything in my power to help you. I shall keep these secrets of yours unless my duties have previously and directly required me to disclose such information. This I swear on the Honor of the Empire."

A notification popped up.

**Silver Blade Tara Lisana has sworn an Oath of Aid, Duty, and Secrecy.
Silver Blade Tara Lisana has broken no Oaths.**

"Are these … common?" Edwin asked, poking the message away. "I didn't see any of these 'manmade' notifications before this week, and now I've seen two. Also, what sort of things are you 'required' to not keep secret?"

Tara assessed him again, making Edwin shut up quickly before he said something else that gave away his secrets. Keeping quiet about something so *huge* as his entire life was hard!

"Common enough. Are you now content? I would certainly not wish to break an Oath for you. I'm certain that whatever secrets you may have, however dangerous you may think they are, would not be worth the future stain of having an Oath broken. So long as your secrets do not directly threaten the Empire itself or its citizens, you have nothing to fear." She chuckled slightly, a tiny smile creeping onto her face before it turned serious once more. "Now, speak. You've said many strange things and I demand an account for your odd behavior."

Edwin opened his mouth to speak, closed it, took a deep breath, and spoke. Tara had a sword to his throat and could apparently tell when he was lying. Plus, she *had* been pretty reasonable about him treating Aerfa, so she might actually be trustworthy? This was still close to the last thing he wanted to do, but when the alternative was certain death … "I'm from another world. I fell out of the sky about a month ago, but before then I had never set foot on or even heard of Joriah."

That got a reaction, and her entire body recoiled as she looked at Edwin in a new light. "Well. That certainly is a secret worth breaking an Oath for."

CHAPTER 29

A Discussion with "Friends"?

At her declaration, Edwin immediately started panicking. He just escaped captivity; he didn't want to go back into any other kind of forced working situation! No. He would run into the woods and take his chances in the wilds before he let that happen to him again. Even still, he did not want to be on any kind of Empire watchlist, no thank you! Sensing his distress, Tara immediately made a placating motion with her hands—some things transcended planets, it seemed.

"Calm yourself. I understand your plight more now, Out—" She cut herself off, clearing her throat. "Edwin. Rest assured, as I swore, I will still not disclose your origins to any you do not grant me leave for."

She sat back, looking into the distance with a starry look in her silver eyes—wait, her eyes were silver, too? "An Outsider, then. A living legend. One who came from the heavens themselves." She looked him in the eye. "You did well to tell me; there is much I can do to aid you. However, your hesitance to do so is a tremendous asset. You must never tell anyone else of where you come from. They will seek to exploit you, to kill you, to enslave you." She caught a hint of a flinch on Edwin's face. "That is why you sought escape from the Highpeak Kingdoms, then? They found out and attempted to use you?" Edwin hesitated before giving a tiny nod, and she continued, "Blasted greedy dwarves!

They'll be the death of us all, angering Outsiders." She breathed deeply, then continued, "Tell me your story. Leave nothing out."

Edwin hesitated at first, but the ferocity of Tara's gaze managed to persuade him to recap his adventures thus far. It had nothing to do with that *very* sharp sword in her hand. Not at all. In time, he skimmed through his arrival in the forest, his fight against the Stonehide, his arrival at the Blackstone citadel and subsequent capture by the dwarves, his forced debtor's position and eventual escape.

At first, he made sure to never give any specifics about his weapons or what he was trying to make, instead saying that "he fought his way out" and that "he was doing research." That position changed with another glance at Tara's sword, though, and he went more into detail about his weapons, not explaining how they worked, just what they did.

As soon as he finished, though, he started regretting it. He had absolutely said too much. Why was he so trusting? Never mind that he had been threatened with death; he should have just taken his chances with ... Well, no. That was a terrible idea. But was this really any better? She'd sell him out the first chance she got, he knew. He could see it in her eyes, already calculating how best she could profit from knowing he was an Outsider. Well, at least he had managed to change his Class tag, or else everyone would know. But still, did *she* have to know? Aaarrghh. He was such an idiot, he was so ...

"I see. Well done, I must say. You need not explain further regarding your methods; I would not glean anything from them myself, and I understand the secrecy Alchemists like to exercise over their work." This remark prompted Edwin to roll his eyes. Tara said, "Yes?"

"No, no. It's just ... in my old world, we had giant webs of communication, of sharing information. It let people on one side of the planet benefit from experiments that others had done on the other side. I should have figured that it wouldn't be quite the same way here, but it's still sad." A thought crossed his mind, and Edwin sat up straighter. "Wait, Alchemists? I got a message from the System saying that Alchemy isn't highly regarded. What's up with that, if the Class is common enough to have a stereotype?"

Tara thought for a moment. "Fascinating. I must admit uncertainty, though it is not my specialty. I've never heard of the System being wrong before, though a Registrar might be better informed. What did the message say?"

Edwin stared blankly at her. "Uhh ... I don't know? It was like a month ago that I got it, my memory isn't that good."

She returned the stare. "Just scroll back. Status Log is one of the first Skill upgrades anyone ever gets; don't you have it?"

"How would I have gotten it?"

"The Beginner Path, naturally. It almost always upgrades Status, lets you review previous Skill unlocks, Path notifications, and more. Ah. Right. It happens from time to time, where either a particularly bright or dim child doesn't get Status until after the Management comes into effect, so they don't know not to blindly spend points on whatever Path they can unlock. Something similar happened to you, didn't it? Well, can you upgrade now? Not much upgrades Status; go ahead, do it."

"Well ..."

She cocked her head. "Is there a problem? Do it."

"I already have my Status evolved."

"Do tell." Her words were clipped and no-nonsense. He'd clearly done something to annoy her, but what?

"It's an information-storing Skill. It lets me take notes and see them later with Identify."

She rolled her eyes. "And here I thought you might have actually gotten something useful. A notes Skill at the second Tier? So how many Skill Points was that Path? Twelve? Twenty-four?"

"A hundred and twenty."

That seemed to break her, and Tara just blinked, staring blankly at the wall. "Say that again?"

"One hundred and twenty points."

"A hundred and *twenty*, what the *hells*." She shook her head and looked incredulously at Edwin. "And it's a *note-taking* Skill? What sort of flightless Skill is that? How did the System ever justify such an obscene price?"

"Hey, hey, hey!" Edwin felt suddenly quite defensive of his favorite Skill. "It's really cool! I can do all sorts of things with it, and it's an absolute *lifesaver* for remembering na— For encoding my notes! Nobody can see what I've written. Great for experimental safety; you said that was popular, right?"

Tara just looked at him in bewilderment. "I know not what you must have done to anger the System so much, but you utterly wasted enough points to get two to four good Skill advancements. At the very least, your other Skill advancements must have been worthwhile. You must have Alchemy and Polyglot at the very least, yes? What else?" Edwin hesitated, which just annoyed her. "Oh, come on. We'll be here until Vinstead if you stop every time I ask you a new question. I swore on my Duty that I wouldn't tell your secrets; that includes your Class, private or not."

"Fine. I also have Bomb Thrower, an evolution of Throwing Weapons, and Mana Infusion, evolved from Basic Mana Manipulation."

She jerked her head up at that. "You have a mana Skill?"

"Uhh ... two, actually. Mana Infusion and Basic Mana Sense."

Her eyebrows danced once more. "Alchemy would be wasted on you if you already have both of those. You'll make a fantastic mage. So, your Skills are Walking, Identify, Seeing, Eating, Polyglot, Mana Infusion, your useless Status advancement, Alchemy, Basic Mana Sense, and what else?"

Edwin pulled up his Status. "Breathing, Flexibility, Sleeping, Survival—"

Tara interrupted him with a wave of her hand. "Wait. Not only do you have more than twelve Skills, you wasted them on things like *Sleeping*? Dear gods. I retract my statement. You're hopeless."

"Hey! I didn't know any better," Edwin defended himself. "I was lost in the middle of really strange woods and trying to survive. I've only picked up two Skills since I *did* know any better. Packing, because ... ah, my arsenal was really heavy and I needed the help, and First Aid, because I needed to not die."

She seemed unconvinced. "Very well. I perhaps know someone who might be able to advise you on your Class, but you've already set yourself down a Path that ensures you'll be mediocre in all you attempt. You see, by surpassing the twelve Skill limit the Empire advises, you will spend far more time than is required to bring all your Skills to a level in which they can evolve. That will repeat with every successive Tier and only grow more egregious with each one. Particularly since, as your Skills are so disconnected, you will only be capable of focusing on a Skill or two at a time instead of leveraging them against one another for greater leveling rates. You will, in short, be totally outclassed by proper specialists at every point in your career."

Edwin sat in silence for a few seconds, staring into space, then said, "Well. I suppose that's what I was before. I can stand being average again. Do you have to always make sure your Class is the best it could possibly be? What about just … doing what you want? Why can't you be a generalist?"

She chuckled. "There have always been a few people who share your philosophy. They think that doing just whatever, not following the wisdom of those who've walked their Paths before, is the best way to go. They inevitably fail, as they can't keep a job and find themselves just wandering around, throwing themselves into suicidal situations just to make a living. Others turn to banditry or a life of crime. Those with ill intent are a scourge on the Empire, and even those who want to help … Bloody *Adventurers* just make my job harder. It is my duty to ensure they are protected just as surely as they ought to be, yet they do everything in their power to bring me cause for regret in that decision.

"They always think they know best, interfering and getting their grubby hands all over everything, totally wrecking the standard call-response order of the Guardsmen and Army." She muttered more uncharitable statements about Adventurers, but Edwin mentally tuned them out.

After a moment, when it seemed like she wasn't about to leave her current thought track, Edwin stepped in. "Hello?"

Tara's attention snapped back to Edwin. "Yes. Adventurers. They cause more problems than they solve. Everything works far better when following official Class formulas. Thousands of years of slight iteration has determined the optimal combination of Skills and Paths for any conceivable occupation."

That made sense, though Edwin couldn't help but wonder: "What if someone thinks they want to be a blacksmith, but later decides they want to be a baker, or whatever?"

She scoffed. "Please. People are given Builds according to any Skills they might have obtained prior to Management, and they may select what they desire from there. The amount of training you need to even become competent in a job is far more than anyone could manage to undertake on a mere whim."

That seemed … not great. *Well, then again,* Edwin thought, *I suppose the ability to change careers is a pretty modern concept. Not like a blacksmith could have become a baker back on Earth in the early days anyway. No real change there. I guess it makes sense.*

"I see."

"Now, you said you hadn't taken any of the Beginner, Novice, or Trainee Paths?" she asked, and Edwin nodded in response. "Good. Complete them all. Upgrading your Skills is important. Do you even have Common Knowledge?"

Edwin's first instinct was to recoil, but then his curiosity got the best of him. "Common Knowledge?"

"Basic Identify upgrade, usually comes alongside the Beginner Path. Allows you to use Identify on things other than creatures."

That sounded actually kind of useful, but still … "I'd rather not? My Identify is only level thirty; I wanted to get it to sixty before I evolved … er … upgraded it."

"Thirty? That's plenty. That should give you about twelve spans, yes? More than enough. You always want to upgrade a Skill as soon as possible; the improvement is always worthwhile."

Edwin really wasn't comfortable with the degree of authority Tara was trying to display over something like his Skills. They were *his* Skills, darn it. He wasn't going to let someone boss him around over them. He looked for some kind of conversation diversion. "Didn't you say you'd point me to someone else to help with my Build, as it's already completely screwed up? Like you said, something about Adventurers."

She saw right through his effort, but conceded, "Very well. I shall abstain from further comments in such matters for the time being. You are correct, in that a Registrar would be more suitable for this discussion. Is there any other matter in which I can aid you for the time being?"

"What's the name of the Empire? The dwarves just called it the 'Pretentious Empire,' which I don't think was right. What's your job exactly? Actually, could you give me a brief rundown of what I can expect?"

She scoffed. "Blasted dwarves. They like to think they're superior to us and act like we're the stuck-up ones. Maybe if the cavers didn't spend all their time singing while smacking rocks around with steel, they'd ..."

Even after her rant about dwarves, including a fairly long tangent complaining about a few Empire officials who acted more pretentious than the Empire had "earned the right for, which is already a lot," Tara continued on unabated answering Edwin's questions. Amazingly, he kept himself from getting distracted or zoning out as she talked for the next several hours. He felt slightly vindicated by that, proving to himself he *could* do it; Forala was just really boring.

Tara seemed to get more comfortable as time went on, and he realized that she couldn't have been much older than him. She bore herself with a lot of formality, but even that seemed to be slipping away as she continued talking, filling Edwin in on new and old information.

The Liras Empire was a massive, mostly avior-controlled supernation that stretched across two continents and was the result of their emperor, Xares, unifying countless small, warring nations under his wing some two thousand years ago; he had swept forward on an expansion campaign until he controlled everything east of "the Spine of the World," an absolutely massive mountain range on the "main" continent that served as a natural border against their jealous neighbors.

From what Edwin could gather, Tara was a huge personal fan of the Emperor himself, who in turn seemed to be some immortal, magic-wielding combination of Alexander the Great, Julius Caesar, and Napoleon. He combined brilliant military might with literal centuries of study, a magnetic personality, and a keen political mind to form what may as well have been a living god, and, at least according to Tara, he was absolutely perfect, had never lost a battle, and remembered the name of every soldier who had ever died in his service. If he was even half the man she made him out to be, Edwin kind of had to agree that there likely wasn't a better monarch to possibly exist.

Tara, for her part, functioned as an Enforcer, which was part of a chain of command set aside from the normal chain, but was just a few steps under the Emperor himself. Her area of jurisdiction was massive, and within it, she had, from the sounds of it, complete and total say as judge, jury, and executioner, exemplifying the Law of the Empire and bringing order to most of the continent. When there was a giant monster roaming around, a crime spree, or, yes, a bandit group making trouble, she was dispatched to track down the disturbance and end it, by any means needed. If she came across something that might develop into a problem, she was to deal with it similarly.

While apologetic, she claimed to be unable to disclose her Class details, as doing so would potentially grant future adversaries the ability to exploit chinks in her metaphorical (and physical) armor. She was able to tell Edwin that it was an advanced variant of standard Guard Skills, namely including Identify, Status, Language, Seeing, Walking, Eating, Swordplay, Heavy Armor, Reflexes, Athletics, Teamwork, and Authority, which made Edwin curious.

"Wait. If this is supposedly the most advanced possible combination of Skills—"

"It is."

He waved her off. "… Skills for a Guard, why does it include Eating? Wouldn't there be a better Skill to use than that?"

She gave him a quizzical look. "Because it's one of the Basic Six. Oh right. You wouldn't know that."

Edwin gave a flat stare in response. "Yes. I know nothing, remember?"

"Yes, yes. The Basic Six are the six Skills that everyone has from their childhood, before they become Citizens of the Empire and Management can be put into place." She counted them off on her fingers. "Eating, Seeing, Identify, Status, Walking, and Language: the six things that any infant can try to get and practice enough to be rewarded with a Skill for it."

That seemed reasonable enough, but … "Wait, what if—" An ungodly loud screech cut Edwin off, a torrent of swearing filtering its way through Polyglot as his train of thought was discarded.

Tara cursed as well, and her helmet materialized over her head. Maybe it helped block out sound. "What in all the storms is *that*?" she asked.

"It sounds to me," Edwin responded, lightly covering his ears to help block the noise, "as though Aerfa just woke up."

CHAPTER 30

On the Road Again

Tara rose, her full suit of armor materializing around her. It took longer than dematerializing the armor and wasn't as fast as the silver walls that had been in her fight against the bandits, but it was unmistakably the same Skill. Actually, Edwin could test that! He quickly targeted the rapidly forming armor with an Infused Almanac: *Armor conjured by a Skill of some sort, can be used for magical wall formation, too.* Identifying the armor once it had finished appearing gave the same result, so he guessed it worked.

"Are you going to check on her?" Edwin asked. "Why?"

"It is my duty to ensure Citizens of the Empire are in good health, and I must discuss matters pertaining to my transportation. Come, I need to keep an eye on you," Tara replied, all the informality she had slowly accumulated over their conversation falling away in an instant. She walked to the opening in the back of the wagon and just ... dropped out.

The wagons weren't going that fast by Earth standards, perhaps about a brisk jog in pace, but it was still a little strange to watch someone jump out of a moving vehicle, and while Edwin followed a few moments later, it felt even stranger than to just watch. He stepped his pace up to a light run, following behind the armored figure as she outpaced the caravan and jumped inside the first wagon. Looking overhead,

Edwin saw two avior circling in the sky above the wagon, the light forest they were traveling through giving way for the road and leaving the path open to the heavens. Once he turned his attention back to what he was supposed to be doing, it wasn't hard for Edwin to likewise reach the front wagon, though his legs, enjoying their break from constant use, did get annoyed at him.

"… One of my flock is dead, two more grounded, and you '*apologize for the inconvenience*'? You could have saved them, you bastard! If I had died, would that have been a 'slight inconvenience' as well?"

Edwin flinched, nearly falling back out the opening to the wagon as Aerfa's ranting hit him full bore upon his entry. She was not happy, but it was somewhat amusing seeing the avior look so murderous while still draped over two beanbag chairs.

"Yes." In sharp contrast to the venom Aerfa was spitting, Tara's voice was measured, calm, and also noticeably different while in her helmet. More commanding and authoritative, though still soft and gentle in tone and cadence. "I needed to ensure that I could exterminate all the criminals in a single strike, else they would return and continue to harry others while I was not around."

"So you just stood by as they massacred my flock?"

"Yes. Though I note that you suffered only a single casualty."

"You! Your job is to protect Citizens! Was Rellis not enough of a Citizen for you?"

"All Citizens are equal in the eyes of the law."

"Oh, don't you give me *that* nonsense again, I—" She was cut off as Tara continued talking, her mere presence seeming to dampen Aerfa's complaints.

"Acting sooner than I had would have endangered others, both present and future. Had I stepped forward upon the first arrow loosed, the bandits would have retreated, returning to harry another group for which I was not present. I cannot ignore such consequences."

"Your actions endangered others now, you incompetent—" Aerfa's rant was suddenly cut off by Tara's sword appearing, tip at the avior's forehead as the Enforcer loomed over her prone figure.

Huh. She definitely had continued speaking past that point; why wasn't Polyglot translating? Did it just not work if the word suddenly stopped? Edwin was pretty sure he had heard otherwise, but he couldn't remember any specific instances.

"Watch your words."

"You wouldn't, you—" The sword moved faintly closer.

"Do you truly wish to test that?"

Aerfa said nothing, but clearly remained furious.

"As I thought. I will be departing in two days, when you reach Vinstead. Until that time, you are to leave me in peace. Understood?"

The avior sighed. "Understood."

"Good." Tara finished the conversation, dropping out the back of the wagon. As she left, a silence Edwin hadn't even realized existed was lifted from the wagon, and chatter resumed.

"That lousy, inept ..."

"Mum. It's all right. Not her fault. You eard er. She's been at tis for a long time," Forala spoke up, laying a wing on his mother's back. "I don't want ta lose you too."

That seemed to mollify the enraged merchant somewhat, who breathed out, slumping back into her resting position. Edwin, for his part, felt kind of awkward standing around and wasn't entirely sure why he had been brought along, but it definitely felt like he was intruding, so he started to quietly sidle away but was stopped by a resigned call from Aerfa.

"Edwin. Wait." He turned around. "Thank you. If it weren't for you, I ... Thank you."

Edwin just gave a bit of an awkward smile and slipped away, letting the mother and son have their moment. When he returned to "his" wagon, he found Tara sitting in one corner, quietly meditating. Not wanting to disturb her, Edwin just lay down on his bedroll and tried to sleep.

The rest of the trip was fairly uneventful. Sure, things happened, though nothing particularly notable. People talked endlessly about all kinds of stuff, but none of it really stuck with Edwin, who spent most of the time on his own bedroll or in a beanbag chair, just dejectedly thinking. He had had enough of people for the time being, anyway, so he kept to himself.

A few times he attempted to perform some experiments with his Skills but found he just couldn't focus, and he had to pull himself back from the brink of completely shutting down multiple times. Something about the scene of the bandits, lying in pools of their own blood, the lifeless body of the medic, whatever his name had been, and Aerfa bleeding out kept returning to the forefront of his mind, and while he didn't think it had traumatized him nor that it was wrong for them to die ... it was just distracting. He hadn't hesitated back when escaping the dwarves, hadn't worried about killing them, and this was much the same. It just hit different, seeing the aftermath.

It also brought into focus just how different Joriah was from Earth. Edwin hadn't really expected anything else, though. Most historic civilizations had harsh punishments for banditry, usually death, and they had been actively trying to kill Tara, so it was even self-defense. He *agreed* that it was needed and justified.

But what about the bandits who had fled? Sure, Tara said that they would just return to marauding once she had left and that would put more people at risk, but would they really, with their leader killed? Or would they have just run as far as they could and tried to reenter society? *Could* they reenter society? What even turned them to banditry in the first place? That wasn't the sort of thing normal people did, was it? But then again, they chose banditry over other options, whatever those were. No matter their circumstances, being desperate didn't excuse attacking other people and robbing them or worse. Or maybe ...

Edwin sighed. This sort of thinking wasn't productive. Still, he wished he could have asked Tara what happened to people who just by chance weren't *able* to follow the Paths needed for a specific Empire-approved Class. Were they able to take alternate Class options for their own circumstances? Did they just do their best, knowing that they'd forever be second fiddle to people with a more optimized Class? Were they forced to turn to banditry? Sadly, Tara hadn't so much as opened her eyes since she started meditating, at least while Edwin was around, and there was no way he was about to bother her. He'd had enough of that sword of hers threatening him for the time being.

Regardless, he didn't feel bad about the bandits being killed. They had been the aggressors—must have been causing a disturbance for some time if there had already been an Enforcer in the area—and had killed one member of the avior caravan, wounded at least three others, and threatened him. They deserved to die. He would have killed them himself if he hadn't been so worthless.

...

So why did his brain keep dwelling on it then, darn it?

Was it because he had been so helpless in the face of all of them? Because he had no Weapon Skills to his name that would help him in that sort of situation, because he was a scientist, not a fighter? Because, for all his time spent trying out fencing and HEMA back on Earth because martial arts are cool, he never *liked* hurting people?

Or was it also related to the other image that kept coming back to him, of Tara standing over him with her sword drawn and pointed at him, forcing him to spill his secrets once more? Was it just him being weak that was the issue? Edwin had never really felt fundamentally unsafe back on Earth, but it was a regular occurrence here. Between being dropped in the wilderness, facing a bear bigger than a train, getting lost in a blizzard, being captured and enslaved by dwarves, and now the bandits and his first real interaction with Lirasian law enforcement? He'd yet to actually feel like his life wasn't in someone else's hands. It wasn't a pleasant feeling. As nice as Tara was, and as much as he felt she had legitimately had her hand more or less forced, he still didn't want to be so powerless ever again.

He'd taken a wager, venturing back to civilization. He knew that. Admittedly, his only other real choice was to wander around the wilderness with a broken arm and a burned shoulder that was bound to get infected, but it was still a choice and a hope that he could find actually helpful people. Surely not everyone would be awful, would they? And it was true! He had gotten help from that one halfling leader, Ritina or whatever, and Aerfa. Even Tara had helped him out. There were good people here. There might even be people he could befriend, and that by itself was enough reason to pull him back to civilization, if he was being honest with himself.

But Edwin had never felt safe, never felt secure. To do that, he would have to become strong. How could he do that? He wasn't sure about trying to expand and get even more Skills. He should focus on what he could already do and build on that. Okay, so what did he even have?

Magical
Basic Mana Sense: 30, Mana Infusion: 59
Physical
Athletics: 27, Breathing: 20, Flexibility: 15, Nutrition: 16, Packing: 5, Seeing: 19, Sleeping: 21, Survival: 17, Walking: 28
Mental
Polyglot: 21, Mathematics: 37, Research: 44, Visualization: 26
Combat
Bomb Throwing: 9
Utility
Firestarting: 29, Alchemy: 43, Outsider's Almanac: 64, Identify: 31, First Aid: 17

... Well, it certainly seemed to scream *SCIENCE!* to him, at the very least. First Aid was Biology, Mathematics for Physics, Alchemy for Chemistry. So he could lean into that. Maybe he should really try and make Alchemy his primary Skill? Using it a lot would probably also help him level up all his apparently ungodly number of Skills.

Yeah, he liked that idea. He would be an Alchemist. After all, what was an Alchemist if not a magical scientist?

And from what his Alchemy instincts were telling him, he would need materials. Lots of materials. Sure, he could make some basic magical ingredients with his Mana Infusion, but they were insufficient for some reason. He'd need the blood of monsters, the leaves of magical plants, metals whose very essence was permeated with mana. That would be where his Skill would shine; that would be where his strength could come from. And hey, as a bonus, he got to do his favorite things in the world: see cool stuff, especially if he went to find his own ingredients, and uncover the mysteries of the world. Science back on Earth was exciting and cool, and so well-established he could never make any sort of meaningful discovery on his own merits.

Here, though? The sky itself may not even be the limit. Maybe he would revolutionize the world!

Edwin sighed. Or maybe not. He remembered what Tara had said, and what Rashin had said. To try and forge your own Path, blind to the efforts of others, was foolish. Like back on Earth, anyone who tried to figure out how the world worked from just their own experimentation was doomed to fail. The people here had centuries of practice, centuries of trial and error to determine what sort of Classes were good at what they did, and what sorts simply underperformed. It was, after all, only by standing on the shoulders of giants that we could see beyond the horizon. What if he was ignoring those giants by foolishly thinking he knew better?

But then again.

For centuries, it was common knowledge that plagues were the result of "bad air." Everyone "knew" that Earth was the center of the universe. That excess blood caused disease. That stuff burned because of "phlogiston." It wasn't until someone took those theories under the microscope, until they examined the "infallible" wisdom of those who came before, that such theories were revealed to be nonsense. Why should it be any different here? Any of the wisdom he had heard might be wrong, or overly simplistic, or an intentional lie.

But, the little voice in his head said, *they probably aren't. You'll never find a place here, just like back on Earth. You'll never fit in, and you'll never stand out. Nobody here will ever accept you. You saw how Tara looked at you when she found out what you are. Like you were a monstrosity. If anyone finds out, you will be just as shunned here as back in college, as back in school. You're just going to be—*

Edwin cut off the voice, pulling himself back from the brink once more. No. He wouldn't let his doubts get in the way. He wouldn't let fear rule his life.

Isn't that exactly what you're doing? It had returned, mocking him. *You want to gain power because you fear being at the mercy of others.*

That was different. This was a different world. He *needed* strength, he needed security. He—

Is a scared little kid, clinging for any sense of normalcy. You'll never outrun your own nature, Edwin. It's who you are.

He took that pessimistic voice of doubt and chained it up, locking it right next to his box about his feelings about leaving Earth. Something to deal with another day.

Fortunately, Edwin was spared further wallowing in self-pity by a noise outside. Poking his head out revealed massive stone walls directly ahead of him, stretching as far as he could see in each direction. Figures the size of ants patrolled the top, and flocks of birds—no, not birds, avior—circled far above him. On either side of the road, plain but sturdy-looking and well-constructed buildings and homes stretched along the wall. The smell was nowhere near as bad as he had expected, but still quite potent, the scent of thousands or hundreds of thousands of individuals living in close quarters.

Vinstead. They had made it.

CHAPTER 31

Seeing Is Disbelieving

Vinstead didn't look much like a proper fantasy city, in Edwin's clearly expert opinion. While they were waiting to enter the gates, he sized up the nearby buildings. They seemed mostly uniform in architectural style, with four wooden posts driven into the ground serving as the corners of the mostly single-floor buildings, with the walls made of cobblestones stacked so closely together there wasn't even room for mortar between them. The roofs were mostly either wooden planks or thatching, though Edwin couldn't discern any pattern for which one would be used over the other. Overall, other than the oddly well-fit stones making up the majority of the walls, it was a decidedly mundane look, which if he had seen back on Earth, he wouldn't have so much as batted an eye at. Kind of disappointing, really.

There was a clatter of armor from the side of the wagon, and Edwin ducked back inside. A moment later, an armored figure, a human in a chain mail shirt and open-faced helm, entered his wagon, taking a look around. As soon as he laid eyes on Tara, he immediately saluted. "Apologies, ma'am ... back."

Oh hey! Edwin mostly understood that. He hadn't tried Polyglot with normal people lately. Tara dismissed the guard with a nod (wait, when did she open her eyes? She'd been seemingly dead to the world for days, was she aware that entire time?), who climbed back out of the wagon, said something to another person outside, and then moved on to the next wagon in the train.

About fifteen minutes or so later, the wagon finally started moving again, and Tara rose to her feet, effortlessly keeping her balance even as the floor rumbled and bounced slightly over the paving stones. "Gather your things. Once the caravan reaches the merchant's block, we will return to the garrison. There, you will be licensed and introduced to an individual who can help you with your ... unique Class."

"Wait, licensed? What's that?"

Tara cocked her head at him. "Did I not ... Ah, I suppose I did not. *Adventurers* may be a scourge upon the face of the Empire, but they are not without uses." She wrinkled her nose in distaste. "Adventurers may insist on throwing their lives away, but such suicidal determination can still be useful. As an incentive to not cause too many problems or turn to banditry, we license some individuals to report on their Skills, Paths, and Classes. In exchange, they are given many of the legal protections offered to Citizens."

Edwin hesitated. "But what about my Status Skill upgrade? I got that one from my ... origin, after all."

Tara stopped, thinking. After a moment, she finally spoke up: "I can grant special dispensation for you to keep a handful of Skills secret, but you will need to report to me to document any future Paths that relate to that. You said you had a couple of other Paths with similarly Outsider natures?"

"Outsider and Realm Traveler, yeah."

She nodded in agreement. "Wait some time before completing them. Particularly Realm Traveler. Outsider, used outside the context of your origin, may pass unremarked upon. You will be exempted from having to give details about how you obtained those Paths, as well. For the purposes of explaining away your oddities, we will say you came from Fierisal through secret magics. It is true enough for the Registrar."

"Fierisal? Also, what about your superiors? Won't they want to know details?"

She winced. "Yes. However, they are aware of the value of my unbroken Oath, and I can swear to them that the knowledge is best left secret. Fierisal is"—Tara paused, then said the exact same word—"the Unknown Lands."

"Oh! Is that what the dwarves call Enigma? That continent on the other side of the world?"

Tara nodded approvingly. "Indeed. Now, it seems as though we have reached our destination. Further questions you may have can wait until you meet your mentor. He can apprise you of the state of the world; your cover story ought to provide enough in the way of explanation for him."

"Who is this mentor you have in mind for me, anyway? How are you so certain he'll help?"

A mischievous smile played across Tara's face. "He'll help ... if he knows what's good for him. Don't underestimate him, either."

That wasn't ominous at all, but what was that saying about trusting the expert or whatever? Did he imagine that? Eh, whatever. He'd find out when he found out, and he didn't have many options at the moment regardless. Edwin hoped that whoever it was understood the value of peace, quiet, and alone time. Hey, he could dream.

Tara conjured her armor and left out the back, followed closely by Edwin, his backpack slung over his shoulders. It was really uncomfortable, though. He'd need to try and find something that was actually made to be used as a backpack and not secretly cobbled together in a cave. Really, it was kind of surprising it had held together this long, and with that thought, he quickly Infused his bag through Packing, which should keep it together for the time being.

The market section was thriving. While there didn't seem to be many civilians around, or even market stalls, hundreds of individuals—avior, human, halfling, even a few dwarves, and others besides—were all hustling around like ants, hauling comically large loads from one place to another. Forala directed a group mostly made of humans, who were unloading lumber from wagons in the back, alongside other goods Edwin hadn't seen before. Crates, bags, and a few pieces of furniture all streamed out of the wagon train, being carted off to places unknown, vanishing into the crowd. It was all happening so *fast*, too. People were practically sprinting all over the place, even burdened under their loads.

Tara seemed to be impatiently waiting for Edwin, tapping an armored foot on the stone while he looked around, and he gulped. "Sorry. It's impressive around here."

While her voice was distorted by her helmet again, Edwin could still hear the smile in her response. "You've barely seen anything and yet this is already impressing you? Your world must have been fairly dull, wasn't it?"

Edwin immediately glanced around, hoping nobody had heard that, breathed a sigh of relief that everyone seemed to be too preoccupied to listen. "Not dull. Just ... different. We had machines to do all this sort of thing, though at similar if not even greater scales. I'm sure you'd have much the same response as me if you ever ... made it there yourself."

Nope! Get back in your box, homesickness. Shoo. Look, a fantasy city! Stop pining after Earth.

Tara didn't seem to notice the hesitation in his voice. "Well, come along then. The sooner the better."

"Wait, I need to complete my transaction with Aerfa. I agreed to pay her afterward."

"You're my charge now. She's not allowed to require me or any of my traveling companions pay for fare. She will be reimbursed for her expenses by Governor Shash'falara."

Edwin said, "But I like following through on my deals."

Tara stayed silent for a moment. "Fine. Just don't take long."

Nodding his thanks, Edwin checked the front wagon. If Aerfa had sent Forala to oversee her workers, she must have still been resting. Sure enough, she was still lying on her front on a collection of beanbags haphazardly arranged into something resembling a mattress. Faera, her young daughter, sat next to her mother, singing a song that, so far as he could tell, didn't have any actual lyrics but was just a songbird-like melody. There was nobody else in the wagon beside the three of them, so Edwin sat down next to the avior on one of the many plush chairs.

"It's good to see you resting. I would have thought you'd try and push through the pain to work."

Aerfa stirred as he spoke. "I would greatly like to," she replied, "but my husband, Risarn, bless his heart, forced me to make a Contract that I would take care of myself, which includes lying around while I wait for a proper healer to come and finish fixing me. You kept me alive, but I won't be flying until I'm treated. Damn Adventurer cut me to the bone, and I'm lucky it wasn't more."

"Adventurer? The bandit?"

"Eh. Adventurer. Outlaw." She fluttered a wing dismissively. "It's all the same— Ah, present company excluded."

"It's fine." Edwin waved it off. "I'm just here to complete my end of the Contract."

"You didn't have to," she countered. "You managed to keep me from dying, defying an Enforcer in the process. We're even, so far as I care, even if the Enforcer took you as a Charge."

"But I wanted to," Edwin pressed. "You helped me, I help you. It's how things work."

The avior relaxed somewhat at that statement, and her tone became a little less sharp. "If more people thought like you do, then the world might be a much better place. Very well, tell me."

"Do you need to write it down, or …?" he asked, only for the merchant to shake her head. "Okay then."

Edwin quickly outlined the steps needed for making concrete, explaining his method for producing mortar. "Oh, and then mixing it with sand and gravel is how you make something that stands on its own, and I think adding volcanic ash is how you make it really strong. Or something. That part is half remembered at best."

"It will suffice. I know many who would be very interested in what you've already told me. I find myself once more in your debt."

"You really aren't. I'm just upholding my end of the deal. And it's not even that complex of a process," Edwin awkwardly deflected, as he stood up to leave. "Honestly, I just want the knowledge to be out there. Stuff like this, the world is better off knowing. It's not like I'm in a position to make use of it, anyway."

"Be that as it may, thank you. May the winds lift you high."

Tara didn't seem too displeased with how long he had taken, which Edwin counted as a win. As she led him along like—*no, not like a meek little puppy; shut up, brain*—as she led him along, past the insanely crowded merchant square into the city proper, Edwin got a better look at the buildings within the walls. Most were of a similar basic style to the buildings outside, wooden posts on the corners, walls made with stone, but here the stone blocks and cobblestones were much larger and there was more variety in their coloring, particularly among the nicer-looking buildings. There were also a lot more two-story buildings, though Edwin had yet to see any that were three or more.

He did his best to not just stare at every little thing, but to instead keep his head forward and follow after the shining silver figure of Tara. Suddenly, she did a face-heel turn and grabbed *something* from the air next to Edwin.

"No," she said to the empty air, and Edwin looked on in confusion. What was she talking to? He strained his eyes, trying to see whatever it was that caused the reaction.

Level Up!
Seeing Level 19→21
Visualization Level 26→27
Identify Level 31→32
Outsider's Almanac Level 64→65
Polyglot Level 21→25
Visualization Level 27→28
Sleeping Level 21→22
Breathing Level 20→21

Suddenly, he could see. Well, not *see* exactly. More like his Skills were interacting in some strange way, with Seeing letting him notice everything he *could* see, Visualization filling in the empty space, and Identify and Almanac giving him an actual lock on what he was seeing.

Phantom Pickpocket

It was a kid, probably in his early teens, trying to twist out of the viselike grip of the Silver Blade, and even though Edwin could see exactly where he was, he still struggled to actually keep his attention *on* the kid, his gaze constantly sliding off in every direction. It figured that the *one time* he was actually beset by an invisible attacker was when he wasn't expecting it.

"You should have known better. Turn it off," Tara said, voice hard, and Edwin found that he was finally able to focus on the pickpocket. He wasn't wearing *clean* clothes exactly, but he wasn't wearing rags, either. After a moment of looking at the subdued boy, she literally tossed him off to the side. "Now get." The would-be thief twisted in midair and reactivated his Hiding Skill, meaning Edwin lost track of him before he hit the ground. He felt like he saw a flash of silver from the back of the boy's shoulder first, though. Had Tara used some Skill on him?

Actually, did Tara have some kind of vigilance Skill? That was impressive, and also highlighted just how far Edwin had to go if he wanted to be able to protect himself. If he could be looking directly at a pickpocket and not be able to focus on him, he had no chance if there was an assassin or something dangerous sent after him. Scary thought.

As they progressed through the city, the stones making up building walls gradually grew larger and larger, until they were massive blocks, oftentimes with no wooden corner posts. Finally, Tara slowed to a stop in front of a relatively empty square made of smooth white stone, with a massive inset pattern of an eagle with wings spread, matching Tara's coat of arms, composed of black stone (not Blackstone) in the center. On the far side of the square, a white stone wall made of massive blocks loomed. At the dead center, a pointed arch, resting on smooth pillars, left a single aperture into the courtyard beyond. The entire wall had shining copper lines tracing the gap between blocks, but it was especially prevalent in the archway, where there was a thick web of copper lines in various arcs, crisscrossing the entire area.

Beside him, Tara looked up at the construction, armored helm tilting back. "I never get tired of this. Come now, I've been gone far too long."

CHAPTER 32

Protagonist Syndrome

The interior of the ... What was the right word? It was clearly a multi-functional complex, but Tara had called it a garrison, so Edwin would go with that. So ... the interior of the garrison was even more impressive than the outside had been. Once he passed the outer walls and through a small courtyard, the building itself was revealed to be a massive, cathedral-like structure. Inside was, unsurprisingly at this point, even bigger, and the vaults above seemed to stretch almost forever, to the point that he could barely see the ceiling above. Avior ascended and descended like flocks of swallows, swarming to balconies on the sides of the garrison or out what Edwin could barely make out as openings to the sky. In the center of everything was a massive statue of an avior—no, *the* avior, he felt certain, though he couldn't pinpoint why—holding aloft a staff and a triumphant expression. Everything, from the tip of the statue's golden staff to its gray plumage to its taloned feet, was colored and detailed to such an extent it looked like an actual, flesh-and-blood avior, just a hundred-foot-tall one.

No time to marvel at it too much, though, as Tara and Edwin made their way over to an arch set into a nearby wall, venturing up a spiral staircase until it opened onto a rail-less balcony-like area. Sitting at a desk off to one side was a halfling-sized "Lirasian Registrar" with bright blue hair and skin just a little too pink to be human, consulting stacks upon stacks of papers and what had to have been a System notification.

"Rizzali."

The gnome looked up, then spoke with a bit of a scratchy and high-pitched but enthusiastic voice: "Tara! Welcome! Back in Vinstead at last, I see?" He pointed at Edwin. "... this?"

"This is Edwin. He got on the wrong side of a continental teleport and needs an Adventurer License."

"I see, I see ... Polyglot?" he asked.

Edwin nodded. "Yes. Level"—he checked his Status—"twenty-five."

"Not bad! Not bad!" Rizzial—Edwin tagged the gnome—nodded. "... Ccan understand me! Right?"

"Yeah, at least for the most part. I have to lean on a few other Skills to help me, though."

The gnome instantly perked up. "Synergistic Skills? Tell me, tell me! I ... know!"

Tara chuckled. "Good luck with him. I'll be back shortly, once I file my report on my mission. Rizzali, Edwin is cleared to keep a couple of his Paths and his Status advancement confidential."

Rizzali's—Edwin corrected his tag—eyes literally sparkled before returning to normal. "Aww. But Tara ..."

Tara sighed. "Not this again." She headed farther up the stairs. "Let me know when you free Edwin. I'll try to not take too long, but you know how the Administrator is."

Then she vanished, leaving Edwin alone with a very eager gnome.

"And last ... 'Micro-Biomancer' Path?" Rizzali asked, and Edwin sighed.

They had been here for what felt like hours, and for every single one of his Skills, Edwin had been quizzed on how he had unlocked it, what its effects were, what its description was, and what it improved. Then, a similar set of questions for his Paths. How many points they took, how he had gotten them, if he had completed them, and if so, what benefit did they provide.

Most of the time, what Edwin had was apparently fairly typical, and despite his initial reservations about not wanting the Empire to know his exact capabilities, he had gotten a little carried away by talking to someone who clearly loved learning. It had been fun for the first hour or two; then Edwin's throat had started to get dried out, and his social batteries were drained. Now, he was just happy to finally be done with the whole thing, though he couldn't say he regretted it.

"I got Micro-Biomancer the same time I got Nutrition, by thinking about what makes up food. Takes ninety points to complete," he replied. Earlier in the discussion, he would have gone into more detail, but now he was just *tired*.

"Fascinating, fascinating. What does make up food?"

"Oh, lots of stuff. Sugars, fats, oils, fibers, and all kinds of things I don't have the time to explain and I also think I'm not allowed to tell you about."

"Hmm. So be it. Ummm"—the gnome checked a piece of paper, fishing it out from a massive stack of freshly filled sheets—"Very well. That seems to be the last of your … System abilities, which I … our time together. Here is your license. Rizzali handed him a small stone token on a cord. "Don't lose this. We can remake it, but … tricky! It … quite enjoyable speaking to another academic; please do return sometime!"

Edwin had mostly tuned out Rizzali's voice by then, his mind turning to his notifications before shutting down in protest.

Congratulations! For becoming officially licensed by the Liras Empire, you have unlocked the Adventurer Path!
Congratulations! For explaining the basics of science, you have unlocked the Lecturer Path!
Level Up!
Polyglot Level 25→27

He was oh so very tired, his brain run through the wringer with all his speaking and in *desperate* need of some alone time, but he was at least *done* with it all. "So, where do I go now?"

"Wait … wait. Lady Tara will be back! Soon!"

Great. Well, at least he had a bit of time to kill. Wouldn't quite be alone time per se, but he could manage the next-best thing. Edwin settled into his chair, closing his eyes and lightly tugging on his Sleeping Skill to take a quick nap.

* * *

Edwin was woken by someone jostling his shoulder, slowly bringing him back to wakefulness. It took a moment, but he eventually opened his eyes to see Tara's stern face impatiently waiting for him to rouse himself. As he stood up, trying to work out the crick in his neck, he yawned and grabbed his bag. "Am I good to go now?" he asked. "Can I meet this mentor-person yet, or did something go wrong there?"

An amused smile flickered onto Tara's face for a brief moment before vanishing. "No, Lefi will be … eagerly awaiting your arrival."

Something was clearly going on—was she pulling a prank on a coworker or something?—but Edwin quickly decided he didn't care enough to ask. He'd find out in a few minutes anyway. He groggily followed Tara down a couple flights of stairs until he was in an underground section of the garrison, lit by heatless torches shedding an oddly steady light.

She rapped on a door and opened it, motioning for Edwin to enter. He hesitated, not wanting to go through an unknown doorway in an underground dungeon, which only prompted Tara to sigh.

"Xares above, you're impossible." She reached out, grabbed Edwin's forearm, and yanked him through the opening as he yelped in surprise.

Inside the room was a guy who both seemed incredibly familiar and Edwin was sure he had never seen before. He looked basically human, but his hair, flickering animatedly like tongues of fire, was a bright gold in color and so utterly alien, even compared to what Edwin had seen so far, the guy almost certainly couldn't have been *actually* human, right?

Anime hair, Edwin amusedly considered. *He literally has anime hair.*

"Wake up!" Tara kneed the chair the man was snoozing in. "What is it with men and sleeping every chance they get?"

The jolt to the chair got the man—an "Adventurer-Mage"—to start awake, his head snapping around to determine what had disturbed his rest; he quickly found the appropriate target.

"Tara!" he excitedly exclaimed, his voice rich and intriguing, though also annoyingly loud. "And here I thought you didn't care!"

"Shut it, idiot. It's your lucky day. I've settled on your sentence, now that I've come back. Community service, as usual." She shoved

Edwin forward, making him stagger into a position between Tara and the Mage from his previous location, solidly hiding behind the Silver Blade. "But different than normal. This is Edwin. Your job is to ... You're not listening."

"Oh?" The man seemed eager, sizing up Edwin. "So lightly? And I get a baby Adventurer to take care of?"

"Well. It's only fair. I picked up a stray after I sent you back, thanks in large part to your meddling. He is officially now your problem. I solve two problems at one time, and ... Would it kill you to pay attention to more than half of my sentences?"

Edwin ducked behind Tara to avoid Lefi—actually, he may well have been a couple years younger than Edwin—and his intense scrutiny.

"So you found some poor sap and figured you'd 'punish' me with him?" The statement made Edwin feel decidedly uncomfortable, but Tara ignored it. Lefi continued, "What's your name? How'd you end up with an Alchemist Class? Do you have *any* idea how long I've been trying to get the Alchemy Skill?" He got a far-off yet greedy look in his eyes. "You can help me!"

"No. Edwin is forbidden from helping *you* get more Skills. You are in a strictly consulting position, and your monetary fee is going to take the form of kitting him out. Two gold minimum, and I *will* find out if you try to shortchange him."

"Edwin, eh? Where are you from?"

"He is also not to tell you anything about his background save what you already know; he was caught in a teleport mishap, finding himself here instead of Fierisal."

"Pity. Can he at least tell me about his Skills from it?"

"No."

"Could somebody please tell me what's going on?" Edwin protested. "I am so very lost."

Tara huffed, "Very well. Lefi?"

"You honor me, dearest Tara." Lefi turned back to Edwin. "I"—he bowed dramatically—"am Lefi Forolova! Adventurer-Mage extraordinaire! As a mere child, I managed to gain the Exceptional Skill, which showed me that I was never destined to be another mere farmboy. No, I gained Skill after Skill and managed to accumulate so many Skills they didn't know what to do with me! So I became a brave Adventurer"—he puffed his chest out—"righting wrongs and slaying brave monsters! Er, slaying monsters bravely!"

Tara sighed. "He managed to somehow get past the Management as a six-year-old and took a ton of Skills; now nobody wants him around so he goes about killing predators and interfering with Empire work."

"And yet I do so magnificently!"

"He also has a head bigger than his Skills list. Yet somehow, he isn't a completely hopeless buffoon. Well, in terms of efficacy. He's still an idiot, and not a real Mage, so he can't help you there. Rizzali is his Registrar as well and has no idea how he got his current Class."

Edwin raised an eyebrow incredulously, dying internally at the prospect of being trapped with an *extrovert* for the near future. "And I'm supposed to learn from this guy?"

Tara sighed again. "He somehow manages to avoid ever interfering with anything extensively enough or important enough for me to do any worse for him than drop him in prison for a few days and give him a community service project"—Huh. Apparently Tara wasn't the complete rule of law in this province, if that were the case—"but the idiot just takes it as a challenge and seems to *enjoy* being sent into the Verdant to chop down a few trees, and unfortunately, he keeps surviving."

"Well, but of course, my fairest lady. I could never possibly fail such a monumental quest when I have your faith behind me!"

"I've been trying for three years, yet having faith *against* you doesn't do anything," Tara muttered, which Lefi seemed to be wholly oblivious to. She took a deep breath. "But yes. He's quite good at what he does." Turning to Lefi, she very pointedly cleared her throat until he was actually paying attention to her. "You have until tomorrow evening to get Edwin all kitted up; then I don't want to see you back in Vinstead for at least two moons. Give him some pointers, help him optimize his Skills, assist him in getting his feet."

"Are you *sure* this is a good idea?" Edwin warily asked. "You think he'll actually be able to help me? You don't sound confident in his capabilities. Am I really able to tell him my Skills and be fine?"

Tara rolled her eyes, "I've yet to see him fail a task—"

"... a Quest!"

Huh, so he was listening.

"… a *task* that I've given him. I figure, best-case scenario, he might actually learn how to be responsible, but that's not about to happen any time soon. Still, you will be in safe hands. He can also keep a secret, can't he?" The last part was asked very pointedly, and Lefi nodded furiously.

"Indeed!"

"See, Edwin? You'll be fine. I imagine I'll be seeing you around at some point. Please try to not make me regret this." Tara's voice took on an almost pleading tone as she started to move out of the room. "I already have to deal with *him*."

After the door latched behind Tara, Edwin had a blessed two seconds of peace before the extrovert switched his attention from the now-absent Enforcer onto him, and it was far too short.

"So! Edwin! My dearest friend. You are an Alchemist, yes? From the long-lost continent of Fierisal."

"I don't think it's really—"

"From the long-lost continent of Fierisal! And what sorts of secrets have you brought to this side of Joriah, pray tell?"

"I think that's the sort of thing I'm not allowed to tell you."

"Ah, but that's the mentality of one who cares! They don't care about us; why should we care about them?" Lefi asked with a ridiculous grin on his face, clapping his arm around Edwin.

"In this instance? Because I want to keep quiet about it, too," he responded, ducking out of the half hug. "And, besides, I don't want to annoy Tara."

"Ah, that softie!" Lefi flicked his hand. "She likes to talk a big talk but she really isn't as tough as she acts! All protocols and formalities, it was only a little bit of an obstruction, no need for her overreaction."

"… Right. Anyway, I need help with my Skills. I'm seriously behind the curve, so far as I know."

"Sadly, you will never be as Exceptional as I. I have tried many times to share my greatness with others, yet none are as destined for greatness as I!" Lefi looked off into the distance (really just at a stone wall) and his hair's motion changed from being like tongues of fire to blowing in an imaginary wind. It wasn't quite long enough to flutter properly, but it certainly tried.

"Whatever you say. I mostly bumbled my way into having a lot of Skills, and you're supposed to be good at that sort of thing?"

"Naturally! Let us leave this dreary hole and find a more suitable establishment for our magnificence. Though perhaps Skills must wait until morn. Today, we shall prepare for our departure!" Lefi strode to the door and grasped its latch, finding that it wouldn't budge. He deflated slightly before propping himself back up. "After you, fine sir!" He sheepishly motioned for Edwin to open the door. "It seems as though I haven't been properly keyed out of the locks, if you would do the honors?"

Edwin sighed but swung the door open anyway, letting out Lefi, who immediately turned to the right, before swinging around and going to the left. "This way! I must retrieve my possessions!" Then he changed his mind again, heading back once more to the right, confidently striding down the hallway.

Edwin let out a low whine. This was going to be *great*, he could tell.

CHAPTER 33

Packing Up

In the end, it took about an hour for Lefi to successfully bungle his way through enough of the underground corridors to find where his gear had been kept. Once he *had* found the pile of his belongings, though, it still took another ten minutes for him to actually gear up properly, putting on a seemingly endless array of pouches and accessories.

There were even two magical objects that Edwin spotted among the pile, one a short sword whose hilt held a glowing ruby and the other a seemingly plain, ordinary golden necklace with a tooth of some sort strung up on it. While the tooth itself was nonmagical, the chain was most *certainly* not, and Edwin had to "squint" with his mystic senses to avoid being arcanoceptically blinded by the jewelry. He couldn't even feel the sword's obvious magic simply because of how overwhelming the necklace was. Fortunately, as soon as Lefi had put it on, the aura faded away until Edwin could only barely sense it when he was specifically looking for it. Edwin still wasn't able to feel the sword's aura, but that was likely because Lefi was also wearing the blade, so whatever was concealing his necklace's mana must also be affecting the sword.

By the end of it all, Lefi looked like a proper fantasy Adventurer. Bold and colorful yet well-made, well-worn, and durable fabrics supported a few metal plates of armor, all complementing his array of weapons: sword at his left hip, quiver full of arrows on his right, a spear and unstrung longbow slung on his back, pouches all along his belt, two fairly large daggers, one with a black pommel, the other shining silver, strapped to his calves and a very full backpack with what looked to be a gray blanket rolled up underneath. Edwin had also spotted a shield at some point in the process, though he couldn't tell where that had ended up.

"Right then! Far better!"

"How can you ... move in all that?"

"What, this?" Lefi flexed and even jumped into the air, showing off, before returning to his neutral pose, dopey grin and all, as his hair flickered in time with his breathing. "This is hardly anything! And besides, I could never go anywhere without my kit."

"We're ... going to be walking around a city?"

"And? We shall not always be in the bounds of civilization. And once we brave the untamed wilds, you need to have everything at hand."

"Well, sure, but—"

"I'm glad you understand now! Come along now, friend Edwin. Let us equip you for the adventures ahead!"

"Wait, but I wasn't ... Oh, why do I bother?"

It took the rest of the day to track down everything Lefi apparently wanted to get for Edwin. For his part, Edwin had no say in what he would be getting beyond some details, like what color he wanted for his cloak, and was for the most part just pulled along for the ride. Lefi also constantly deflected all his questions about his Skills and Paths, much to Edwin's annoyance, but he always accompanied the refusal with a promise to tell Edwin once they were on the road. It wasn't entirely satisfactory, but Edwin just didn't have the motivation needed to try and combat Lefi's decisions.

It was interesting. From what Edwin had seen, most places weren't terribly inclined to sell to Lefi, and there were even a few that categorically refused to serve him. Nonetheless, the Adventurer seemed to still wrangle everything he wanted, though it seemed like it was usually at exorbitant rates. Then again, maybe it *did* cost a silver piece for a few loaves of travel bread. Who could say? Edwin didn't have a grasp of the economics at play.

By the time the last item—a thick, deep green woolen cloak—had been found and purchased for a silver coin, it was starting to get late, and Lefi brought them to a fairly large building, spoke quite enthusiastically with whoever was there, and something something god of travel providing free beds to travelers, something something they qualified and so got a free bed for the night. Edwin was tired in more ways than one, though, and between the social and physical exhaustion that came from walking around a big city with an extrovert all day, he was out before he could even properly appreciate being on a mattress again.

***

Level Up!
Sleeping Level 22→23
Polyglot Level 26→28
Level Up!
Packing Level 5→7

Edwin couldn't help but feel awesome. While he wished that he had a mirror to properly see what he looked like, he was also slightly worried it would spoil the effect. He still had his clothes from the dwarves—they were apparently high enough quality they weren't worth replacing, though he had acquired a spare set, and gotten his boot fixed at long last—but he now had a gambeson (cloth armor apparently reinforced by Skills) and a proper backpack, with his cloak rolled up beneath it like a bedroll would be.

He also had a bunch of pouches on his new belt, mostly empty but containing enough rations for ten days and a filled canteen. In his backpack, he had carefully packed his remaining three heating stones, his lime pebble (though it no longer registered as made of lime and resembled the material making up a seashell), notebooks (including the Dwarven dictionary), and his metal bowl (Lefi had questioned his insistence on keeping it, but Edwin wasn't about to give up one of the few things he actually had). Last, he had a fairly full coin pouch, with half a gold coin, forty-six silver coins, and seventeen copper, which was apparently the change for the mandated "two gold minimum"

Tara had set for Lefi. Other than that, his only earthly—Joriahly?—belongings were his knife, strapped as it was onto his left hip, and a walking stick.

"Still not sure why I don't get any kind of weapons, or potions, or even some rope."

"Ah! But that is because such things you must accumulate yourself. An Adventurer must be prepared for anything, yes, but if you do not know how to make use of what you have, it is less than worthless. If you don't know how to fight with a sword, carrying one is simply dead weight. Surely you can already feel the difficulty of carrying what you have upon you now, despite most of your bags being empty?"

Edwin shrugged, trying to feel out the weight of his gear. It was maybe … forty pounds or so? Normally that would have been a lot, but at the same time … "Not really? Maybe if I didn't have the Packing Skill, though."

"You already have Packing! Marvelous! What are your other Skills? Paths as well. What are you working with?" Lefi waved cheerily to the guards keeping watch at the gate as they left. Edwin couldn't exactly read their expressions, though he couldn't help but imagine that they were relieved to see them go.

Edwin hesitated, waiting until they'd passed through a throng of people crowding around the side gate before giving Lefi a brief run-down of his Skills and Paths. Unlike Tara, Lefi never cut him off as Edwin went through his twenty Skills, though every once in a while, Lefi would ask further questions about what a Skill did. A few times, he tried to ask Edwin about his history, but he always declined. Without knowing anything about the continent of Enigma, he didn't want to say anything that would give away his ruse.

By the time he finished, they had made it beyond the sprawl of buildings outside the city walls, which were in turn disappearing into the distance as the pair walked along a hard-packed dirt road that had split from the main cobblestone road to meander through endless farmland. Edwin didn't recognize the crops being grown there, but he also didn't know enough about botany to know if they weren't similar to plants back on Earth. It all seemed to be really lush and verdant, though.

Lefi didn't say anything right away, instead simply stroking his chin in thought for a short while. "An adequate start for a true Adventurer! What of your Status evolution?"

"That's one of the things I can't tell you about too much. It allows me to take notes, though. Cost a hundred and twenty points, so apparently that was wasted."

"Hm. Well, don't allow yourself to let it slip by unused. Such a Skill is bound to have hidden depths! Some aspect of its use you have yet to determine."

"I'll keep that in mind, I guess. It's my favorite Skill, though. I use it constantly, so I think I'm using it fully?"

"Perhaps! Or perhaps not. Sometimes, parts of a Skill may be hidden for quite some time." Lefi thought for a bit, keeping blissfully quiet, as they continued on their journey, before eventually speaking up once more: "You have a good initial range of Skills, though more is always better! We must ensure your Skill base is as comprehensive as possible!"

"Yeah, actually, I've been meaning to ask about that. Tara seemed adamant that I had far too many Skills to possibly be any good at anything. How do you manage that?"

"Well! As I have told you, I gained the Exceptional Skill in my youth, and it has enabled me to grow in level faster than others. Any Skill that I attempt to gain or improve levels up at incredible rates! I manage to match any whom I face at their own Skills!"

Stupid XP cheats, Edwin thought. *Aren't I supposed to get the superspecial Skills or whatever as the world-displaced guy?*

"However!" Lefi continued, unaware of Edwin's musings. "Though you cannot be as Exceptional as I, we can still cultivate your arsenal of Skills. You have tapped a small amount into the true strength of any half-competent Adventurer. Versatility! The fine Lady Tara may be the fiercest combatant this side of the Verdant, but could she use a week-old game trail to find the lair of a manticore? Patch herself up after a battle gone poorly? Grow crops to feed a village? Not in the slightest! Even if she had the knowledge, she doesn't have the Skills needed for greatness. But you and I? We can do all of that! You might never match a guardsman blow for blow, but you'll give them blows they can't hope to respond to, run and hide better than they ever could! Lure them into traps you've made, knock them down, deprive them of the handful of tools they need. They're strong, but they aren't flexible. They're brittle!" Lefi drew his spear in the blink of an eye. "And if you're brittle, well ..."—in a blur of motion, the haft of his spear *cracked* into Edwin's walking stick, splintering it into two halves, sending him stumbling as his support suddenly wasn't there—"you break easily!"

Edwin shot Lefi a glare, and the Adventurer-Mage motioned for him to hand his broken staff over. Edwin obliged, and Lefi held the two splintered ends together for a few seconds, then handed them back to Edwin. He couldn't tell where the break had happened upon inspection, the stick having been wholly repaired.

"Okay, so I ... guess that's impressive. That whole speech, is that rehearsed? Do you give it often?"

Lefi winked. "Ah, I'll never tell."

"So, which is better? More Skills or fewer Skills? You said that the guardsmen are good at fighting; isn't that exactly what they want to be good at?"

"Always more Skills! If you wish to specialize, simply take all your Skills such that they are all related and help one another. The more Skills you have, the better you are at what you can do. The more times your Skills have evolved? The more things you can do with those things. You know how else you can get an array of effects? More Skills!"

Edwin nodded. "I think so. But evolved Skills seem to be good; how does that work in all of this, then?"

"Simple! An evolution expands what you can do with a Skill or grants a new ability. However, it will not give you an effect you already have. Leaves behind the old effect—Running will never help you run farther, just faster, that's what Walking does—but expands it into a new direction."

"Wait, but couldn't you just get a Running Skill on your own? Why is that an upgrade?"

"I knew one brave individual who achieved getting the Running Skill as a base Skill. I have attempted myself for quite some time. Not sure how, but he had both Walking and Running leveling up all the time! 'Twas truly impressive. I think he became a Courier of sorts. They weren't thrilled with his honestly better Skill set, but he's still one of their best messengers, last I heard from him. Can run all day so fast you can't even blink if you want to see him." Lefi paused for a breath at long last before continuing in his booming voice—Edwin was so glad there was nobody nearby—"And that is why you must get more Skills! The more Skills you have, the more Skills you can evolve! If you have lots of Skills already, your evolution will always give you something exciting and new!"

"But what about being mediocre at everything?"

Lefi shrugged. "That is simply if you attempt to generalize. Specialists with lots of Skills are masterful at their specialty, even better than the Empire's Classes."

"So then are the Empire's Classes just awful, then? If having more Skills is always better?"

"Not entirely. They have their place. That place is very narrow, but you will never find a squadron of Adventurers who fight together as well as a squadron of Empire Legionnaires! The uniformity of their classes allow them to coordinate and benefit from Tacticians far more than any Adventurer. However! Any single one of them is almost useless outside of that narrow area. Attempting to mimic them will only fail you. You must embrace what makes you unique to make it as! An! Adventurer!"

"And if I don't know what that is?"

"That! Is what *my* aid is for! I have aided countless poor, lost children, outcast from their home for not having the right Skills to fit into the Empire's instructions. Many have gone on to do marvelous things!"

"I see … Well, I suppose before we begin, what are Attributes, anyway?"

"Attributes are where we Adventurers truly shine! Some Paths, such as Mage, Scout, and Athlete, grant you Attributes. They enhance you in ways that Skills cannot quite manage. Or not much, anyway. Scout will grant Perception, which benefits your awareness of your surroundings. Athlete provides Stamina, which makes all physical exertion easier. Artisan grants Dexterity, for greater bodily control. They work with many Skills and can be vital to improve your overall capabilities. The most useful of all is Health, which improves your resilience to all injuries. It is a staple of Classes across the Empire! Also, the only one many might have!"

"Wait, why is that? They sound really useful."

"Because they don't have the Skill Points to spare, my young pupil!" Oh come on, if anything, *he* was older than Lefi. The guy had to have been like eighteen at the most. "When you ration every last Skill level to evolve your Skills as soon as you can, what use is a Path that does not aid you in evolving a Skill?"

"So should I try to get Attributes?"

"Indeed! More Skills, more Paths, more Attributes. However! You must follow *your* heart! Only you can know what is most effective for your capabilities." As the conversation continued, Lefi gesticulated more and more. At this point, he was practically putting on a full theater performance for the wheat field on the side of the road.

"So just ... do whatever feels right? And get lots and lots of Skills?" Lefi nodded, and Edwin took a breath to steady himself. "Right then, I suppose I should at least hear what you have to say."

Lefi grinned, his hair blowing in a faint breeze.

CHAPTER 34

What Lies Ahead

"Just for the record," Edwin hedged, "I'm not going to just do everything you suggest. I know you think that the more Skills the better, but I've had luck evolving my Skills so far and I kind of want to keep doing that."

"Do you insist?"

"Yes." Edwin stayed firm. Hopefully he wouldn't have to be too pushy.

"Very well!" Lefi clapped Edwin on his back, sending him stumbling until he recovered. "I suppose it would be rather hypocritical of me to insist that you must take certain Skills, wouldn't it?"

Edwin was taken aback. "Just like that, you agree?"

"Just like that! Why, did you expect otherwise?"

He shook his head. "No, no. Just ... people tend to be a lot more insistent about that sort of thing in my experience."

"Ah! But those people were not me! I am Exceptional, after all! It's right in my Class!"

Edwin scoffed. "No it's not. You're an Adventurer-Mage, not ..."

He trailed off as he Identified Lefi again.

Exceptional Adventurer
**Lefi Forolova—the guy that Tara stuck me with so I wouldn't immedi-
ately die and as a punishment for him.**

"Wait, what? You can change your Class name? Or can you just fool Identify?"

Lefi winked at him. "That's the benefit of having many, many Skills. You can gain some truly exceptional results!"

Edwin frowned. "That doesn't answer my question. Though I suppose it does explain why a 'mage' had so many weapons, if you aren't actually one."

"Oh, that? No, weapons are always excellent! Anything is better than nothing. Even if you don't pick up a Skill for it, I expect you to be able to use that staff for a weapon by the time we're done."

"It's a stick! A *literal* stick!"

"And with your Mana Infusion, it will be a very strong stick! Perfect for keeping a wolf at bay or blocking a low-level sword strike. But that!" He punctuated each statement by striking a pose, somehow not breaking stride. "Is not what you are here for! Skills!"

Edwin groaned but, mentally tuning down the volume of the Adventurer, nonetheless prompted, "Okay, what do you recommend?"

"Well, a mere twenty Skills is far too few! I advise ..."

The next several hours passed by both really quickly and so, so slowly. Quickly, because Edwin was getting actual details about Skills and being passionately informed about why he should take more and more Skills; Lefi's opinions on the matter were radically different from Rashin's or Tara's, that was certain. His opinion of "grab every single Skill" made more sense in the context of him never expecting to evolve all of them, and the variety of Skills that Edwin had available to him meant that even fairly straightforward evolutions provided a wealth of new options. Then, he'd just figure out some way to combine evolved Skills to create a new basic Skill and start over again. While most of it was useless, Edwin also kind of wished that he had some way to take ...

Actually, Edwin realized midconversation, *I can take notes.*

Edwin's Logbook: Lefi, Day 1—Skills

Eating: Increased energy from eating food. Improved calorie efficiency, perhaps? Worth considering. Possibly too similar to Nutrition to unlock.

Stealth: Reduces noise made when in use. Possible invisibility evolution? Tempting.

Hearing: Increased sensitivity to noises and better ability to tune out sound. Useful for awareness. Probably not worth it, though more useful than the other senses. Spatial Awareness does not seem to be a Skill, or at least Lefi does not know of it.

Reflexes: Reduced reaction time. Difficult to level. Tempting.

Improvised Weapons: Increased "proficiency" and "damage" with random objects. A walking stick might count. Interesting, but no.

Staves: Akin to Improvised Weapons, but focused around sticks and staves. Added focus brings greater bonuses. Similarly not worthwhile.

Learning: Enhanced ability to remember things memorized with the Skill. Possible overlap with Research? *Get.*

Block Strike: Active Skill. Aids in interposing something (shield, staff, etc.) to stop a physical blow. Less efficient than something like Shield Block but wider use. Potentially lifesaving, but still too situational.

Small Blades: Enhanced proficiency and damage with knives, daggers, etc. Popular among cooks, apparently. Slightly interesting.

Cooking: Food tastes better and is more filling. Possibly synergy with alchemy for potions? Worth considering. Also, apparently a possible evolution of Eating/Nutrition.

Speaking: Reduced strain when talking. Can evolve into yelling, which increases maximum volume. Neat, but not worth it.

Reading: Increased reading speed. Potential synergy with Polyglot. Worth considering.

Writing: Enhances ability to write neatly and quickly. Interesting, but probably redundant with Almanac.

Archery: Weapon Skill with bows. Note to self: not worth keeping around as a note. Delete later like the others.

Wrap Wound: First Aid-related Skill, focused on those injuries which need bandages (which might be all of them?). Specifically focuses on increasing the efficacy of the bandage as a protection for the wound and immobilizing/stopping blood from the injury. Amusing possibility that it might be usable as an Armor Skill at higher levels (mummy armor).

Disguise: Makes it harder to recognize you. Possibly useful in the future, but not notable enough to require it at the moment.

Sleight of Hand: Enhanced dexterity for stuff like magic tricks or precision work. Possibly very useful if I can't get proper lab equipment for precision work.

Sprint: Active Skill. Drastically increases speed for a short time. Very exhausting. Might be worthwhile.

Repairing: Fix broken objects. How Lefi restored my walking stick. Worth getting at some point.

Knot-Work: Knots are sturdier/looser/generally better. Might be worth getting purely for research purposes, but probably not.

Cleaning: Makes it easier and faster to clean objects. Possibly useful for sterilization purposes. Worth considering.

"Do you have *all* these?"

"I speak from personal experience!"

"That's … I suppose that sort of answers my question, though I'm not sure if I trust that answer now." Edwin thought for a moment. "Are there Skills that let you copy other Skills?"

"There are Skills for everything!"

"I suppose that's a yes, then." Edwin sighed. "Do *you* have one of those Skills?"

"Alas, I do not." Lefi cocked his head, looking into the distance as he struck a pose. "Such a Skill would be truly exceptional, though, so I ought to!"

"And how, exactly, do you get that sort of Skill?"

"I believe that would be some form of evolution."

"Yeah, I've been wondering about that. Don't you miss out on evolved Skills? Aren't they supposedly better in every way or whatever?"

"They are!" Lefi caught his statement just in time. "Slightly better. And primarily of use in providing more options with your Skills, beyond your normal reach. The higher in Tier you go, the more esoteric the result can be. However! They are less useful when you can already do everything. And have no need of crutches for esoteric effects. I have heard tales of mighty mages of the past whose grasp upon magic allowed them to have hundreds of basic Skills! They barely reached Tier two! Such secrets have been lost, however."

Edwin frowned. "How could something like that be lost?"

"Because it was accepted that fewer Skills were better. The more Paths you complete, the better your Class becomes and the more tailored your Skill evolutions become to you and the Paths you walk. Such thinking is nonsense! Focusing all your Skills on a single point restricts you in other areas!"

So, *politics*. Got it. No more wizards (come on, what else would you call someone with hundreds of spells at their beck and call?) because "common knowledge" dictated that a one-size-fits-all approach was better. Given how poorly that idea had worked back on Earth even just in public schools, Edwin couldn't imagine it would be any better in the place with literally magical diversity.

Something else tickled the back of his mind. "Oh yeah. Tiers. I've heard them mentioned a couple times. What are those?"

"That is how many times each of your Skills has evolved. You are Tier one, most competent individuals your age are Tier two or three, generally finishing at Tier three or four. The best of the best are usually in the six to seven range. That's likely where Tara is at. The Tier of Royals such as Xares is unknown! It is said that they are Tier twenty or even higher."

Tier 20. Sheesh. Even if Edwin assumed that a Skill evolution was no better than a basic Skill, that was still the equivalent of Tara having more than seventy Skills or the Royals having two hundred and forty. That was ... difficult to wrap his head around. "And you are?" he asked, but Lefi just grinned at him in response. "Guess I should have expected that." Edwin sighed. "Though wouldn't you just be Tier one or two, if you have so many Skills?" He realized that was probably the case, though he didn't get any confirmation.

"So ... what, I should just accept that I'll never be high Tier and always underpowered?" Edwin asked, downcast. Well, it wasn't like he really should have expected anything different. He supposed he didn't really mind, but it was still a bit sad to know he'd never even have a *chance* to excel.

"Not at all! You see, the secret of higher Tiers is that the further you go along, the more your Skills support one another and grant you more impressive powers! As an alchemist and a mage, you will be more than capable of leveraging your strengths at any Tier. Particularly early on, you could utilize your magic to create an array of effects that others might see only at Tier five or beyond. Then, all it would take you is a few evolved Skills to aid you in expanding your capabilities even further."

Edwin felt a sudden flood of confidence wash over him with Lefi's words, and he pulled himself from his depression. "Okay, so I'm not totally lost. I'll stick with my current trajectory, then. Though I suppose I should ask: What sorts of Paths should I try to go for?"

Lefi thought for a moment, then spoke, amazingly, softer than normal. Still rather loudly, though. "The Beginner, Novice, and Trainee Paths can all provide good, cheap evolutions of Skills. I don't know what Novice would evolve for you, as it usually provides Status Log, though that wouldn't apply to you. Beginner provides Common Knowledge, which allows you to see more than the type of animal something is or what type of Class someone has. It is an oftentimes invaluable Skill, and the higher level it is, the more detail you can learn!"

That *did* sound useful. Especially paired with Almanac; Edwin could save space in his notes by not having to include what everything was called and a basic description in each generic tag. More room for his experiments! Plus, with both Tara and Lefi, what with their totally opposite approaches to Skills, having advised him to take it, it was really tempting.

… So why did he feel so hesitant to do so? Edwin just had a hunch that it would go wrong, and the gnawing in his stomach wouldn't go away.

"You're sure this will work? I just have a bad feeling about it."

"What's your Identify level? Thirty or so, you said? You'll be fine! You don't need much more than a dozen spans of range most of the time, and you'll be essentially even on Skill Points if that is your concern!"

"I guess? Does it ever upgrade anything else?"

Lefi shrugged. "Not from what I have heard of. Only if you somehow evolve Identify beforehand, and then you usually get some small tweak to another Skill. Perhaps Walking to Running at the most?"

Hm. Well, his Walking Skill was coming close to hitting level 30. It was 28 last time he had checked, and it would probably level up once or twice over the course of the day. Lefi was taking *really* big steps—there had to be a Skill involved—and Edwin had to struggle to keep up. He might even net an Athletics or Breathing level or two today.

"I'll ... complete it tonight, I suppose. When we stop to rest."

Lefi nodded, and Edwin continued, asking, "What about my other Paths? You've dealt with a lot of them, surely. What sorts of things can I expect to come out of them?"

"Ah! I'm glad you asked! Well, you see ..."

Edwin's Logbook: Lefi, Day 1—Paths

Note to Edwin—These are apparently common results, but Lefi seems to think I'd get alchemy-related variants for some Skills like Fire-starting should they evolve while I have my current Class.

Micro-Biomancer: Uncertain, but would likely affect First Aid, possibly changing it to Disease Prevention.

Path Less Traveled: Lefi had never heard of this Path.

Realm Traveler: Didn't ask.

Scientist: Would evolve Research. Lefi seemed certain, though that may have been a result of me having to explain what a Scientist was and eventually settling on calling them a type of researcher. He didn't know what it would result in, though.

Alchemical Warrior: Possibly Firestarting, though Lefi advised waiting until it might be able to affect Alchemy and give a weapon Skill of sorts.

Stonehide Vanquisher: Trophy Skill, though what exactly was unknown. If I had an Armor Skill, likely that.

Titan Slayer: Lefi got annoyed about my lack of combat-related Skills. Guessed possibly Athletics into some sort of Leverage Skill.

World Traveler: Walking. Possibly changing it to Hiking, or something pertaining to keeping my footing and improving traction.

Physical Arcanist: Likely to grant some sort of body-centric magical Skill in combination with Athletics.

Researcher: Research, obviously. Though Lefi didn't know what the result may be for something so closely aligned. He offhandedly speculated it had a slim chance of giving an Attribute, but said most likely not.

Explorer: Most likely Seeing, with Walking being a possibility. Seeing would probably result in an active zoom-in Skill of sorts, like Skill binoculars. Walking would result in something similar to World Traveler's Hiking.

Outsider: Didn't ask.

Unkillable: First Aid or Survivor, probably making either a damage-resistance or healing ability.

Blackstone Conqueror: Trophy Skill. Lefi once again ranted about me not having any Weapon or Armor Skills.

Mage: Basic Mana Sense into Mana Sense.

Field Medic: First Aid into Battlefield Medicine, making patching up wounds faster. Lefi claims to know someone who got this.

Steadfast Medic: First Aid or Athletics into a kind of self-heal, though Lefi is purely guessing.

Rebel: Some kind of anti-Skill restriction resistance Skill. Quite possibly useful, if niche.

Adventurer: Packing into Bag of Tricks, making it easier to pull things from my belongings.

Survivor: Survival into some kind of damage resistance.

Athlete: Would unlock the Stamina Attribute. Highly advised I complete it.

Daredevil: Athletics, maybe granting a Reflexes-like Skill or increased toughness.

Pioneer: Mathematics, apparently. This was based on the logic of it being a "signature Skill" of sorts for me.

Novice Pyromancer: Firestarting into Basic Pyrokinesis. This was apparently something Lefi had personally experienced and was used to unlock a lot of other Skills.

Warrior: Would unlock the Health Attribute. Highly advised that I complete it *soon*.

Pyromaniac: Firestarting into Persistent Flames or something else that would make fires harder to control and extinguish.

Wanderer: Walking into Longstrider. This was apparently well known and would let every step taken be longer. Highly tempting.

Exile: Walking into Running, which increased maximum speed.

Escapee: Breathing into Breath of Freedom, an active Skill that made direct mind control and usurpation of abilities harder, though offered little protection against more subtle threats.

Lecturer: Research probably into something like Teaching, which functioned like Research but for people he taught.

Lumberjack: Lefi didn't know, but guessed possibly something involving Athletics, possibly evolving it to Climbing.

Way of the Empty Hand: Athletics into something like Unarmed Combat.

Trapper: Either Survival or Firestarting into some variant of a Trap-setting Skill.

Novice: Strong possibility of Walking into Running or something similar.

Beginner: Identify into Common Knowledge.

Trainee: Similar to Novice, possibly evolving Nutrition to Eating or Sleeping to Napping (reducing the time needed for a full night's rest).

Slave: Would have evolved Status to make it out of his control, would instead probably make Walking into Fetters, making it hard to leave a certain area (would be countered by Breath of Freedom).

Assassin: Flexibility into Stealth, or something similar.

Killer: Would make *something* into a weapon Skill.

Traitor: High possibility of Sleeping into something like Sleepless, allowing him to sleep less.

"So Skills can evolve into a Skill that you could get on its own?"

"Yes! That's a major contribution to my dislike of the 'upgrade' terminology. Granted, a higher-Tier Skill with the same effects as that same Skill at a lower Tier usually is ever so slightly stronger, but it is barely worth noting. Far better to just get the other Skill and gain a different effect with your evolutions. Also, if you can accomplish it, you can get a Skill for it! If you were a natural mage, you might be able to get Basic Pyromancy as a basic Skill instead of needing to evolve something."

That made enough sense, Edwin supposed. It was starting to get a bit late, though, so they stopped at a small roadside shelter made of wood and stone. It wasn't much, but there were a couple of bunk beds inside, affixed to the wall, and a small shrine with a statue depicting a leaf inside of a circle.

"What is this place?" Edwin asked as they settled in. "I saw a couple others as we were walking, but I guess I didn't question it."

"This!"—it was a bit strange, hearing Lefi whisper-yell as he actually wanted to stay quiet—"Is a shrine to my god, Curicna, patron of Wanderers, Travelers, and Adventurers, one of the few to actually take an interest in the commons. His church establishes them along roadsides as a form of worship, and his presence keeps them safe and clean!"

"Ooh. Did we stay in a church of his last night?" Edwin's comment prompted a nod from Lefi. "I understand."

As he sat down on his mattress, delighting in the feeling of relief for his ever-sore feet, Edwin munched on one of his rations and pulled up his notifications for the day, ready to get to work.

CHAPTER 35

Starstruck

Congratulations! For attempting to peel back the intricacies
of the System, you have unlocked the System Scholar Path!
Level Up!
Flexibility Level 15→16
Walking Level 28→31
Research Level 44→50
Packing Level 7→9
Athletics Level 27→30
Breathing Level 21→23
Outsider's Almanac Level 65→66
Identify Level 32→33
Polyglot Level 27→28

Huh. That was an oddly good result for only a single day of walking.

"Hey, Lefi. Are there Skills that let you gain Skill levels faster?"

"Of course! My Exceptional Skill is exactly one such!"

"Does that affect people near you? I got a ton of levels today for … not much effort at all."

"It does! I am simply so incredible that simply being near me can make you grow at inconceivable rates!"

That struck Edwin as rather odd, and he frowned. "So wait, if that's the case, why can't you just, like, I don't know, hang around people and help them level up faster? Surely Tara would enjoy these sorts of benefits when she's training or there are soldiers training or whatever."

Lefi froze for a moment before regaining his composure. "Ah! Uhhh. Ah! It is because they already are affected by a similar Skill that does not interact with my Exceptionalism. It is an evolution of Leadership or Teaching and is quite desirable among those in authority, trainers, and teachers to aid their subjects and students. However! It often requires sole dedication to their tasks and that they are completely under their authority! My Skill only affects those who meet none of the criteria."

So Lefi was pretty clearly lying about *something* in that statement. He must not have had a Lying Skill, somehow, but assuming he was truthful about rulers and teachers having Skills that aided Skill growth, maybe that was both how Edwin had gotten so many levels while under the Blackstones, and also a possible reason for why he had to be "in the service of" Lord S'fishkill. Though why wouldn't they have just hired him, then, instead of enslaving him? Ah, whatever. That was all in the past; Edwin should have a pretty hefty head start on whatever pursuit was heading his way, and politicians did stupid things *constantly*. That was both metaphorically and— Edwin took a moment trying to visualize where he was relative to the Blackstone citadel—and, yes, literally behind him.

There was nothing to be gained dwelling in the past, so it was instead time to get excited for the future!

Edwin's current primary problem was that he had a Skill Point "debt," so to speak, of over *300* Skill Points. If he didn't deal with that soon, then he might find himself in the unenviable position of having Skills whose levels were too high to get additional Skill Points in, but not enough points to complete a Path and evolve the Skill. That would practically softlock him out of the System altogether unless he wanted to pick up dozens of new Skills if he wasn't careful.

He had *slightly* offset that problem thanks to how many points he'd gotten from Almanac and Mana Infusion, at 66 and 59, respectively, but he couldn't continue to borrow from his future forever. That was just a personal Ponzi scheme. That debt was also a big part of why he was so hesitant to pick up new Skills at the moment. Anything new he picked up would need to be raised to at *least* level 30, more likely level 60 or beyond, before he would want to complete a Path and evolve it. Plus, there were the Stamina and Health Attributes to get, not to mention Perception if he could get the Scout Path, and he was quickly spiraling out of control.

But in any case! He could complete Beginner right here, and even get 3 points toward his debt! A couple of bookkeeping things first, though. Edwin wanted his notifications to display chronologically, making it easier to parse, and then he was due for some reorganization of his Status, showing and hiding different information. Once he was done, he lay back in satisfaction and dropped 30 points into Beginner.

You have completed the Beginner Path!
Your route has been circuitous and slow, with both your origin and destination unique from your peers. Though you have yet to fully come into your own, you nonetheless possess nearly limitless potential and shall one day be a true force in your own right.

Wait, what? His origin and destination were unique? That didn't sound good. Edwin really hoped he hadn't just screwed himself over *again*.

Class Change!
Foreign Alchemist → Hedge Alchemist
Calculating Rewards …

…

Done!
You may evolve your Research Skill into the Memory Skill!
Accept Evolution? Y/N

He should have *known* something would go wrong. Actually, he did. He just should have trusted his gut. Still, he couldn't say he was *too* upset, certainly not enough to decline the Skill. *Memory!* That was one heck of a Skill, possibly even better than Common Knowledge. Also, it netted him a positive twenty levels to his debt!

"Hey, Lefi, what happens if you decline a Skill evolution?"

"The Skill does not evolve."

"You don't get any points back, right?"

"Correct. However, your Class still changes and if you obtain any Attribute increases, those remain with you."

"Okay, thanks."

Memory
It's the ... whatchacallit. Something or other.
Recall with greater detail.
Improved clarity and timespan per level.

Now *that* was a solid Skill. Maybe he could use it to recall more science stuff in time! That would be so helpful. Edwin looked through his current Status, content with his decision.

Name
Edwin Maxlin
Age
22 years
Race
Extraplanar Human
Class
Hedge Alchemist
Attributes
Mana 5
Skills
Magical
Basic Mana Sense: 30, Mana Infusion: 59 (Basic Mana Manipulation: 9)
Physical
Athletics: 30, Breathing: 23, Flexibility: 16, Nutrition: 17, Packing: 9, Seeing: 21, Sleeping: 23, Survival: 17, Walking: 31
Mental
Polyglot: 28 (Language: 36), Mathematics: 37, Memory: 1 (Research: 50), Visualization: 28
Combat
Bomb Throwing: 9 (Throwing Weapons: 48)

Utility

Firestarting: 29, Alchemy: 43 (Improvisation: 14), Outsider's Almanac: 66 (Status: 22), Identify: 33, First Aid: 17

Paths

Skill Points: 266

Current Plan

Wanderer 0/60, Stonehide Vanquisher 0/60, Titan Slayer 0/90, Path Less Traveled 0/90, Scientist 0/60, Athlete 0/60, Outsider 0/60, Warrior 0/60, Blackstone Conqueror 0/60, Mage 0/60, Novice Pyromancer 0/60, Unkillable 0/90, World Traveler 0/60, Researcher 0/60, Explorer 0/60, Adventurer 0/30, Field Medic 0/60, Physical Arcanist 0/60

Save for Tier 2

Micro-Biomancer 0/90, Realm Traveler 0/120, Alchemical Warrior 0/90, Pioneer 0/60

Maybe

Novice 0/12, Trainee 0/60, Trapper 0/60, System Scholar 0/60, Survivor 0/60, Daredevil 0/60, Escapee 0/30, Lecturer 0/30

Probably Not

Lumberjack 0/60, Way of the Empty Hand 0/60, Pyromaniac 0/30, Exile 0/30, Rebel 0/30

No

Slave 0/12, Assassin 0/60, Killer 0/30, Traitor 0/60

Completed Paths

CharLimitCanttalkmuchNocluewhathappenedDidmybesttohelpyouli, Mage, Skilled Arcanist, Physical Alchemist, Bomber, Linguist, Beginner

Gah … He had so many expensive Paths. He'd want to bring basically every Skill he had up to at least level *60* before he started completing Paths, and with the latest mishap with Lefi's prediction about what Beginner should have upgraded, he wouldn't be able to trust his advice on other Paths until Edwin knew it couldn't go badly. At least he wouldn't need to get the Learning Skill, not if Memory worked the way it claimed to. Sure, they might have overlap and make his memory truly spectacular, but literally assigning himself homework wasn't worth an additional Skill.

"Well, I did it," he told Lefi.

"Marvelous! Have you used Common Knowledge yet? Using it upon the shrine can be quite enlightening!"

"Well, that's the thing. I didn't get it. Research evolved into Memory for me."

"Truly? That is … most puzzling. Even with your unusual Class, it should have still evolved Identify, even if the result were different. Most curious. But regardless! Memory is a … most excellent Skill!"

"I guess, yeah. Well, good night, Lefi. Bedtime, I suppose."

Lefi started to say something, but Edwin wasn't listening. Maybe he'd have a Memory of what it was in the morning, but for now?

Sleeping.

Well, traveling with Lefi was certainly effective, if nothing else. Over the next week of travel, Edwin managed to accumulate levels at an incredibly rapid pace, almost to the point where it made up for Lefi's constant chattering.

As it turned out, Visualization could be paired with Memory to let Edwin vividly recall scenes from his past, helping him thoroughly tune out the talkative Adventurer. Curiously, despite the clarity of the Visualized Memory, Edwin found he frequently wasn't able to remember things like the precise shape of various runes on walls and the like. He could tell, because the shapes changed slightly with every recollection. Perhaps with a higher level, that aspect would diminish, but it was still plenty for his current purposes.

Between his ability to tune out Lefi's constant talks about all his grand adventures in the past—after the third time he'd told a story about slaying a demon lord, Edwin was pretty sure Lefi was just making it all up as he went along—and the rate at which he was able to level his Skills, it was actually tolerable!

Level Up!
Basic Mana Sense Level 30→32
Walking Level 31→38
Athletics Level 30→34
Breathing Level 23→26
Identify Level 33→35

Flexibility Level 16→19
Seeing Level 21→24
Sleeping Level 23→27
Outsider's Almanac Level 66→73
Survival Level 17→19
Visualization Level 28→41
Firestarting Level 29→34
Nutrition Level 17→22
Memory Level 1→23
Mathematics Level 37→39
Mana Infusion Level 59→61
Polyglot Level 28→33
Packing Level 9→16
First Aid Level 17→18
Congratulations! For reaching level 24 in the Seeing Skill, you have unlocked the Scout Path!

Even First Aid had leveled up just by treating a blister he had gotten on the fourth day traveling; it was *great*, Edwin was doing so well. At the same time, though, he didn't know how much longer this would last. Lefi had been pretty clearly getting more and more annoyed with him as time went on. Edwin wasn't afraid of the Adventurer, but he still didn't like bothering him.

It wasn't there explicitly in Lefi's tone of voice or how he treated Edwin—no, the act that he actually liked Edwin held as firm as ever—but just in the tiny things: how readily he cut off Edwin's sentences and questions, the curt way he'd provide responses, and just how he'd never look at Edwin if he could help it. It made Edwin sigh. It seemed that even in a fantasy world, the same things still happened to him. Nobody ever wanted to be around him for whatever reason, and he was never able to figure out what exactly it was.

Must have just been some subtle aspect of his behavior that people found annoying, but while it wasn't ideal, he could ... he could live with it. So what if another person didn't like him and wanted him to go away? He'd had decades of practice dealing with that sort of thing back on Earth.

It was better that way, anyway! If he was alone, it would be harder to track him down and he'd have blissful peace to work stuff out at his own pace. It had been *too long* since he had been able to do Alchemy, after all, and he was getting restless. They'd spent the last week doing nothing but *walking*, after all.

Sure, the scenery was spectacular, but they never stopped in any of the towns they passed through. In fact, the two times that their path had crossed through a village were also the only times they hadn't slept in a shrine, instead camping off the side of the road in a cave or something.

They didn't even seem to have a destination in mind! Whenever he had asked Lefi where they were going, the adventurer would always laugh it off with some variation of "Oh, the journey is the destination," which frustrated Edwin *to no end*. Really, the more he thought about it, the more transparent Lefi's scheme became. He had been tasked with taking care of Edwin, so he was doing his best to drive him off so he'd no longer have to deal with the superannoying human. Typical. Well, if he wasn't wanted, he'd just leave and make it easier on the guy.

Yeah! He could tell Lefi. He would speak his mind and confront the man! What did he even need Lefi for, anyway? He could survive just fine on his own.

He wasn't entirely sure *where* this certainty came from, but as he thought, the clearer it became. Edwin was an Alchemist; he could make his own way, do his own stuff. He didn't need to be led on some wild goose chase with some guy who, while useful, wasn't *needed*. Heck, he could level up his Skills on his own. He didn't need the easy-EXP guy.

"If you don't want me around, you can just tell me, you know, and I'll leave. You don't have to pretend to like me," Edwin blurted out one day. Lefi was in the middle of one of his tall tales, a story about three sets of identical twins messing with people.

"What?" Lefi was taken aback, clearly not expecting to be called out on his act. "What are you talking about? You are a most excellent companion! If Tara knew how much I would enjoy this, she would have never tried to give me such a task!" he blatantly lied.

For a moment, Edwin faltered, then his confidence redoubled. No, he *knew* he was right. "Sure, sure. You can drop the act whenever you want. I've had a lot of practice seeing when people don't want me around."

"You are mistaken! I do enjoy your presence!"

"Uh-huh. Okay then." Edwin ostensibly acquiesced, but inside his resolve had set.

Fine then, if Lefi wouldn't admit to it, Edwin would just have to sneak off overnight at some point. Maybe even tonight. There was nothing worse than someone trying to persuade him that, no, they really did truly like him, and it was a total coincidence that every time he walked into the room they stopped talking and changed whatever they were doing, that he was always "accidentally" not invited to events, and that they'd *totally* add him to the group chat. No. He wasn't dealing with that. He'd be better off just leaving. Maybe he'd leave a note of some sort. He could char the end of a stick and use it as a makeshift pencil from a torn notebook page.

Lefi,

I appreciate your efforts in informing me about Paths and Skills, though you needn't worry about pretending to like me as you put up with me. I'm not going to be a bother for you anymore. I'm confident I can manage this on my own.

Edwin

Edwin nodded in approval at his handiwork, the writing messy ... but legible. As he had been writing it, he'd tried to Infuse Polyglot and his stick simultaneously, so it should hopefully be readable by the Adventurer once he woke up. His task done, he pretended to go to sleep, waiting until he heard Lefi snoring softly before quietly tearing out the page and setting it on the bed, putting on his shoes and wrapping his cloak around him.

Edwin stole quietly out of the shrine, the door closing without so much as a click while he ventured into the chilly darkness. Sure, his legs were somewhat sore, but between his ever-growing Walking and Sleeping levels, it wasn't too difficult to push onward.

The world was so quiet and yet so loud, Edwin couldn't help but notice as he followed the hard-packed road, winding through seemingly endless grasslands. Beyond the standard night noises—an owl hooting in the distance, crickets chirping, and wind snaking through the tall grass—it still just seemed so peaceful. There were no planes flying overhead, no hubbub of city life in the background, no cars driving by to spoil the natural tapestry of sound. While it had been slightly cloudy at first, it cleared at some point, and the lands were bathed in heavenly light, instinctively drawing Edwin's attention to the Great Above.

As he glanced up, Edwin stopped in shock. It struck him all at once that in all his time on Joriah—about two months at this point, by his reckoning—he had somehow never seen the night sky. His first few nights were deep in the Verdant, with the tree cover too thick to see through; then he'd been underground in the Blackstone citadel for a month and a half before escaping and immediately camping under trees once more. Then the caravan, where he'd also slept indoors, and finally on his walk with Lefi, where they'd usually slept indoors once again. Sure, he'd seen the occasional star, but he'd never seen much beyond that.

What was painted across the night sky was truly wondrous. The moon, a luminous crystal-like orb glittering with pinks and blues, set among a carpet of stars of all shapes and sizes, and even with a lone orange star radiating glorious color across the sky, that was somehow the *least* impressive aspect of the heavens above. Across the night sky, vivid nebula-like formations were twisted into shapes vaguely reminiscent of galaxies and … something else he couldn't quite remember. It looked familiar, though. Most of the sight consisted of luminous, brilliant emerald nebulae, but there were several radiant gold clumps of gases, and even a handful of red-purple clouds that stood in direct contrast to the rest of the sky, providing highlights to frame the rest of the view in even more wonder. Words failed to properly capture the majesty present above, and Edwin could have stood there for hours.

Maybe he *did* stand there for hours, actually, entranced by the sight above. He stood a very good chance of remaining there until the sun came up, at least. Or he would have, had he not been sent stumbling to the ground by a sudden blow. He spun as he fell, catching a glimpse of two silhouettes against the bright night sky as one of his assailants drew back a club, preparing to strike him again.

CHAPTER 36

Clubbing All Night

"Whoa!" Edwin cried out as he stumbled, regaining his footing with the aid of his walking stick, its end digging into the hard-packed ground as he whirled, trying to Identify his attackers. He wasn't *worried*, of course—he was confident he could take them—but he still wanted to know who they were.

Outlaw Laborer
Brutish Minion

So they probably weren't professional fighters, at least. This would be *far* too easy then. Given their Classes, he didn't need to feel bad about responding with force, either. From a half-remembered conversation with Tara, nonlicensed Adventurers—Outlaws, rather—were simply not protected by laws of any sort. Their life had no value, so he wouldn't need to worry about any retributions should he kill them. Heck, the licensing program was a relatively recent—Tara's words, not his, given it was almost a century old—attempt to ensure *more* Outlaws didn't turn to banditry.

"[...] na, am the greatest *aver* [...] and then ya missed!" one voice mocked.

"Shaddap," his partner snapped. "He moved. It's a lat harder ta hit a moving tahget."

"Oh really? Ya don't say, now. Guess what, ya Tares. Tha's how fightin' works."

Edwin cut off their banter by jabbing the end of his walking stick into the face of the Brute, snapping his head back and making the bandit stumble back, voice distorted as he swore about his nose.

That galvanized his partner into action, and the Outlaw tried to sneak up on Edwin—there was clearly some Skill involved, though not a high-level one—and deliver a Skill-empowered blow to his head, though with the speed of the club, it may as well have been through molasses. If not for the magical nonsense that accompanied Skills, it couldn't possibly have any level of force behind it. However, once it *did*, that slow attack was probably *quite* dangerous.

Edwin casually tried to step back to avoid it, but his assailant just sort of … moved, staying in perfect lockstep, gliding across the ground to keep the blow still aimed at Edwin's face. He frowned at the sight— what was this, some sort of Inevitable Blow? Slow, but can't miss. Hmm—but thanks to the speed of the strike, Edwin was able to bring up his walking stick to block it, reinforcing the structure with Packing and Mana Infusion, in the hopes that it would stop the blow.

As soon as the club connected with his stick, it started moving at more normal speeds, bouncing off the empowered wood and sending a shock wave down its length, giving Edwin a painful jolt. He nearly dropped the staff, though he managed to recover before his body carried out that very Bad Idea. Pitiful or not, he didn't want to fight them with his bare fists. That said, he was confident he would be *able* to if he tried.

Slow down there, Edwin. Don't get cocky.

He disengaged in an effort to get a bit more distance between himself and his attackers, but once he turned to run, he was violently shoved by the Brute, knocking the wind out of Edwin and sending him flying off the road, where he landed in a painful heap in the grass. He groaned and got to his feet, expecting to have broken something but not finding any obvious candidates as he scrounged around in the brush for his baton, managing to grab it just in time.

A rustle in the grass to his right made him sweep his stick out horizontally, trying to trip up whoever was next to him, and while he wasn't quite able to knock out the man's feet, he did manage a solid blow against the ... Brute's shin, causing him to swear and recoil, the grass swishing to accommodate his bulk.

It wasn't much, but it bought Edwin enough time to stand up, and he gave a follow-up swing in an attempt to strike about where the back of the brute's knees should have been, but his assailant had moved without him noticing, sending the blow swishing through empty grass. His strike overextended his reach and he fell prone once more as his balance fled. Edwin's sudden lurch did save him, though, a club blow whistling mere inches over the top of his head an instant later.

Hah. Just as planned, a part of him confidently declared, but that thought was fought back by the extreme skepticism of the rest of his mind.

He was alive, at least, but he was also back on the ground, which was a problem. He used his arms to lunge forward, trying to escape, but his backpack caught on something as he did so. Edwin bit back a curse as his advance was suddenly halted, and he made a snap decision to try and shed his backpack.

It took a moment and required enduring a few painful seconds of kicks raining onto his side, but he managed to finish dumping his bag just in time for a particularly solid blow to connect. Edwin tried to roll with the blow, succeeding enough to block the next kick with his hastily recovered stick braced against a slightly protruding rock.

"He's here!" one of the voices called out as Edwin tried to pull himself to his feet. Another blow of the club thudded into his shoulder, the thick fabric of his outfit blunting the strike such that it didn't feel like he'd broken anything. Heck, it was probably the main reason he was still in one piece.

Although Edwin was certain it wouldn't stop him from getting one doozy of a bruise, he was able to use the impact to tuck into a roll and spring to his feet a short distance away. He whirled around—he hadn't even seen where that one was coming from. Gah, he couldn't see anything. It was really through just luck and occasionally a bit of good hearing that he was able to—

Edwin narrowly dodged a club blow from the Outlaw Laborer, the attack impacting his cloak instead of his arm, and he bit back a curse. If only he could see what was going on. How was he supposed to ... His eyes narrowed. He had an idea, and it just might work.

Yeah. This would work. His confidence was back, and he knew *exactly* how to deal with these morons.

Backpedaling wasn't terribly easy, and he was certain that he would have tripped if not for one or more of his Skills, though which he didn't know—actually, hmm, probably Walking, maybe Flexibility and Athletics, possibly Visualization, was ... No, stop it. *Focus*, Edwin—but he put enough distance between himself and the two robbers for him to start messing with his Skills.

Mana Infusion-Identify.
Mana Infusion-Identify.
Outsider's Almanac: Club-thing. Avoid.
Mana Infusion-Identify.
Mana Infusion-Identify.
Outsider's Almanac: Different kind of Club-thing apparently. Still avoid.
Mana Infusion-Identify.

Outlaw Laborer
Tares(?)
Brutish Minion
Club-thing. Avoid.
Different kind of Club-thing apparently. Still avoid.

Edwin grinned in the darkness as his Skills took effect. Thanks to Mana Infusion, he was able to keep up several Identify windows at once, which also moved appropriately with their corresponding objects. It wasn't perfect, sure, but he at least now had giant glowing blue signs letting him know where the robbers were and, more importantly, where their weapons were.

Speaking of which, now that he could see, he was able to fairly easily step out of range of the latest clumsy blow from the Outlaw Laborer, but that opened him up to a strike from the Brute, which thudded into his gut and knocked him back a good ten feet. There *had* to be a Skill involved, the physics otherwise just ... didn't work out. Still, Edwin's body responded with supreme grace, Athletics and Flexibility working together to let him land on his feet.

"So, what do you guys even want? My money? I don't have much of that, and *threatening* people is more effective than attacking them, I'll have you know. Especially when you're this *bad* at it," Edwin taunted. "And besides, I promise I'm not worth ransoming."

"Shaddup!" the Brute Minion yelled, telegraphing his blow so clearly that even *Edwin* could fully predict its path. "Da boss will wanna see you."

"Oh? And why's that?"

"Well, ya see, ya— Hey, waidaminute! I shouldn' be […] you dis! Issa secret!"

Pity. So much for exploiting the morons. Then he was back to trying to deal with two attackers, and incompetent or not, most of Edwin's attention was immediately refocused to avoid becoming flanked. Gah, even with a clear view of what was going on, and against two people who clearly had no clue what they were doing, he hadn't managed to deal any kind of substantial blow and had taken a couple himself. He was still confident he could win, but if this went on much longer, he wouldn't like the conclusion. So how could he finish this off quickly? Hmm.

Well, fire had worked against S'uchanidiot …

The next time the Brute lunged at him (they couldn't decide if they wanted him close or far away, could they?), reaching out with a hand to try and grab his cloak, Edwin allowed it, stepping in close until he was able to return the grip of the hulking figure, holding on to the hem of the bandit's shirt.

Mana Infusion-Firestarting.

The effect was immediate. The front half of the bandit's shirt immediately burst into flames, illuminating the area and nearly ruining Edwin's night vision (only quickly screwing his eyes shut allowed him to avoid losing it altogether), and the Brute Minion understandably started screaming bloody murder, his grip on Edwin completely forgotten as he frantically tried to pat out his flaming clothes.

Somebody forgot Stop, Drop, and Roll. Hmm. Would they even have that here? Edwin wondered, then looked around at his surroundings. *Oh, shoot. I really hope it isn't the dry season.*

Even as the thought crossed Edwin's mind, some drifting embers of the Brute Minion's swiftly burning outfit floated to the ground, where they fortunately guttered out a moment later. Upon seeing that, Edwin breathed a sigh of relief that he hadn't just started a wildfire.

That still left one bandit to go, though, so Edwin made sure to grab the club the Brute had been using—no point in letting it go to waste— and a quick Firestarting later, it, too, was on fire and being threateningly waved at the Outlaw Laborer, keeping him away. Then, before it could burn his hands, Edwin hurled the burning weapon at the man, illuminating a terrified face before it crashed solidly into his chest.

Edwin felt a triumphant grin creep across his face. Throwing Weapons was such a *great* Skill, and while he was sad it no longer leveled, at least he'd kept its effects. Throwing things was such a useful ability to have, and given how the Outlaw was starting to run, it was exactly the sort of thing Edwin needed to stay safe.

For a moment, Edwin merely watched the fleeing figure as he retreated into the distance, before he narrowed his eyes. A quick glance at the Brute Minion showed that he was lying on the ground moaning in pain, only smoldering a little bit. He might be fine; he might not be. It wasn't Edwin's problem.

He wasn't about to waste any emotions on someone who attacked him. Live or die, it *wasn't his concern, so stop thinking about it.*

Ahem. Anyway, the already-dispatched attacker wasn't his concern, but the one running away? Yeah, that could be more of a problem.

They did mention a boss, one side of him thought. But if he hit the road, he might manage to get far enough away that even if they came after him again, they wouldn't be able to catch up. It was a dangerous assumption, though, because they might really want him specifically. But why would they want him so much? He couldn't be that valuable … right?

I refuse to believe that I radiate that much specialness that just looking at me means people want to kidnap me.

The dwarves had been bad enough. Honestly, he was probably just a target of opportunity for the bandits, and escaping them meant that they'd never bother him again. He'd recovered his backpack; he could turn and walk on, leaving it all behind him.

But …

Edwin didn't want to feel weak anymore. He'd resolved to make himself stronger, and that meant that he couldn't just let them get away with trying to sneak up and attack him. It had been supereasy to fight them off, so either he had gotten way better at fighting or his assailants were superweak. Either way, he could deal with them.

Plus, this would protect future people as they traveled, too. There was no way this attack was a one-off thing, with nobody else having ever or never being at risk, and hey! He could be a proper Adventurer, clearing out a bandit camp or whatever. Besides, if these two were indicative of the quality of the rest of their group, this would be *easy*.

Edwin narrowed his eyes at the fleeing bandit. He was getting away, but not for long.

CHAPTER 37

A Towering Ego

It ended up being pretty easy to trail the fleeing Outlaw Laborer. Although Edwin's tagged Identify boxes faded at some point (was it distance or time related? He'd need to experiment), the bandit wasn't trying to hide his trail at all, instead crashing through the grass and panting loudly enough that it was audible over the quiet-yet-loud nighttime noises as they returned to Edwin's awareness in the aftermath of his fight.

As an added bonus, the Outlaw's single-minded focus on running away along the path Edwin had traveled, presumably fleeing toward the bandit's home base, meant that it was simple for Edwin to follow him unnoticed and even check his notifications at the same time.

> You have unlocked the Mana Reinforcement Skill!
> Accept Skill? Y/N
> You have unlocked the Block Strike Skill!
> Accept Skill? Y/N
> You have unlocked the Hearing Skill!
> Accept Skill? Y/N
> Congratulations! For successfully combining several Skills in an inventive manner in a high-pressure situation, you have unlocked the Skilled Arcanist Path!

You have unlocked the Stealth Skill!
Accept Skill? Y/N
Level Up!
Seeing Level 24→26
Mana Infusion Level 61→62
Flexibility Level 19→22
Athletics Level 34→35
Identify Level 35→38
Outsider's Almanac Level 73→74
Firestarting Level 34→36
Walking Level 38→39

Edwin nearly scoffed when he saw he had unlocked the Stealth Skill. *This* counted as stealth? Please. He didn't need a Skill for this! He could do just fine without it, and he didn't need to make his Skill list even *longer*. He was already going to take forever to properly evolve all his Skills, something he did really want to do, if nothing else to see what sort of awesome Skill either Almanac or Alchemy would evolve into. They were bound to be good.

The battle had even gotten him Skilled Arcanist again! He'd have to incorporate it into his plan, maybe in place of … Hmm. Maybe Mage? Or Outsider. Probably Outsider; he didn't want to risk his Class dipping back into showing his true origins. If not that, though, then maybe Path Less Traveled, or maybe Titan Slayer. He'd have to mull it over. There weren't any obvious candidates to exclude.

The sun was barely peeking over the horizon, bathing the landscape in so much golden light as the rays spilled across the grasslands, when the Outlaw finally seemed to get where he was going. Though it took Edwin a bit of time staring at an empty, ivy-covered hill to notice where the Outlaw Laborer had gone, once he succeeded, he couldn't help but do a double-take in surprise, which was enough for him to lose track of the bandit's destination again.

Namely, it was a massive, solidly built stone tower jutting out from the top of a low hill, stretching a good fifty feet into the sky and overgrown with ivy, the top forming a battlement-like structure around a twenty-foot brass spike that was *bound* to function as a lightning rod, intentionally or not. The strangest part of the thing, though, was how the entire building seemed to vanish if Edwin stopped looking at it, or even if he let his focus wander for a second. It was still *there*, he could tell; his brain just sort of edited it out, like it wasn't worth noting. Like that one pickpocket, actually. It was more Skill nonsense, clearly. But it was just his luck that his target was inside of what had to have been a wizard's tower. This was going to be *awesome*. Unless he would have to fight a wizard. Hopefully, it wasn't an actual wizard. That might be the one thing he *couldn't* take.

Edwin yawned. You know what? He could deal with this after some sleep. He'd been up all night, after all. Now, he just needed to find some secluded place where he could hide during his snooze. Wouldn't want to be found by the bandits during his nap, after all. But this was going to be *great*.

He'd— Yawn—

He'd ...

He'd think of a battle plan in the morning. Evening. Whatever. Hmm. It looked like there was a clump of bushes large enough to hide in over yonder. It would do.

Edwin had to work out a bit of a kink in his neck when he next woke up, but he was grateful that he had still managed to sleep undisturbed. He squinted and peered up at the sky, trying to ... Ah, okay. About noon, then. He had gotten *enough* slumber—he wasn't tired at least—but it wasn't the almost supernaturally good rest he had started to become accustomed to.

Information was power, and at the moment, he had neither. If he was going to properly have fun storming the castle, he'd need to do a bit of recon first. Actually, first he'd have to *find* the darn thing again. Its unnoticeability was a bit annoy— Ah, there it was. Stupid invisible giant tower, if he wasn't right in front of it, he'd never have seen it.

...

There seemed to only be a single entrance at ground level, there were no windows on the ground floor (the first was about twenty feet up), there were at least two balconies at different heights with a *second* level of antino-tice effects layered on them, and the entire thing was made of well-fit large and smooth stones. Edwin judged that the tower, with its crumbling holes in the otherwise smooth stones that made up its structure, and naturally the all-pervasive ivy, was in at least minor disrepair, hopefully indicating that whoever lived there now were just squatters. It would make an easy job even easier if that were the case, but he wasn't really worried.

Part of him felt like he *ought* to be worried, but why? He knew what he was doing. The tower was so covered in leafy vines of ivy that he could probably climb up the whole structure as easily as if he were on a ladder (assuming it held his weight), anyway.

The only complication in his current luck and general plan of attack was what seemed to be a lone sentry on the lower of the two balconies. It was hard to tell for sure, though, and given how hard it was to see past the attention effect, he was almost surprised he hadn't gotten some kind of Focus or Mental Resistance Skill yet. Still, insofar as Edwin could tell, the sentry may well have been asleep. He certainly hadn't moved in the past hour and was leaning against the wall, so it seemed likely enough. Caution was still needed, though. No sense in warning the bandits, after all.

Edwin approached the tower from the opposite side of where he had seen the sentry, clutching his stick tightly. Every step forward was nerve-racking, though he was able to still keep his footfalls essentially silent as he crept forward, as there wasn't much in the way of twigs to snap beneath the weight of his passage.

Yes, it was the middle of the day, and the grass's light-green coloration stood in sharp contrast to his own more forest-green cloak, but Edwin was still confident he could remain unseen.

Well, if he was seen, he'd just have to fight off whoever was inside again. It probably wouldn't be that hard, and it was what he'd come here for, anyway; still, he wanted to do this on *his* terms. In any case, his speculation was rendered mostly moot once he reached the base of the tower, where his cloak easily blended into the ivy around it, and as a result, he was able to breathe slightly easier knowing a single stray eye wouldn't immediately catch him out.

That was step two, done. Now, on to actually getting *in* the tower. Well, the prep for it, anyway. First, Edwin hid his backpack at the base of the tower, covering it with his cloak and a few loose vines. Unfortunately and fortunately, he wasn't able to pull any vines from the side of the tower, which meant he had to settle for slightly sub-optimal coverage of his bags, but also that using the vines to climb should be possible.

Second, Edwin made sure to check the tower's stones for magic, and while they were indeed magical, it was faint at best. Perhaps whatever sorts of enchantments were on the tower had long since faded. That, it was just a minor enhancement, maybe to keep pests away or help keep the stones clean or any number of stereotypical minor spells he could probably think of if he thought it was relevant. Or maybe it was an alarm spell. Hopefully not that last one; he wasn't ready to deal with everyone inside all at once.

Before he'd gotten too close to the tower to see, Edwin had managed to get a solid look at his goal, an empty window about halfway up the side of the tower, some twenty-five feet above the ground, that appeared to be large enough for him to easily climb through. With the aid of the vines and a much higher-level Athletics than the last time he had tried climbing up something, namely the waterfall cliff so long ago, climb-ing was a *breeze*. Edwin smirked into the foliage at the thought, pulling himself up one armlength and foothold at a time. He'd gotten so much stronger since he'd first fought that Stonehide, yet he still had so far to go if he wanted to actually feel strong enough to consider himself safe. This would help, though; he knew it would.

It didn't take too long to reach his destination, and peering through the window revealed a semicircular room on the other side of the wall, filled with slightly dusty crates and piles of sacks. There didn't seem to be anyone inside, so Edwin took a chance and pulled himself through the opening. It was a bit of a tight fit, but he was able to contort himself such that he could squeeze inside without too much difficulty.

Some sliver of broken glass sitting inside the long-broken window frame did manage to score a long gash along the length of his thumb, which hurt but didn't seem to be bleeding too bad— Oh wait, no, it was just a bit delayed. Okay, he knew he had a bit of clean cloth in one of these pouches; where was it? … Okay, grab that end of the cloth, wrap up the length of the cut, and tie it off. Eh, it wasn't the best, but it stopped the bleeding and still left him with enough mobility in his thumb to retain use of it if needed.

Now that that was taken care of, it was time for Edwin to take proper stock of his situation and the room he found himself in. The space was bigger than it should have been for how wide around the tower was, not that that was too surprising at this point (it had to have been some kind of Skill related to building. Spatial Efficiency, maybe? Or more direct, like Bigger Rooms?).

It was primarily a bit musty inside, but there was some sickly sweet scent permeating from somewhere else, though it was faint. Looking around, Edwin saw stacks of wooden crates, some pried open to reveal various dry foodstuffs. None of it was exactly what Edwin had been familiar with on Earth, but there were (some open, some closed) sacks filled with wheatlike grains, rice, various beans, and even some containing flour.

There was also a stunning variety of dried fruits and even berries, way more than he would have expected to find collecting dust in an old wizard's tower populated by bandits. Was all this food really grown locally? That seemed odd, but Edwin also vaguely recalled that because of its proximity to the Verdant and something called the … Rhothos— a giant river, he was pretty sure—Vinstead was *the* primary breadbasket for most of the Empire.

Foodstuffs of all sorts were able to be grown here thanks to the abundant life magic in the area, and it grew quickly and to unusual sizes, too. There was also a high rate of new varieties being created, which spoke of something *screwy* happening with genetics, and if he were a botanist, Edwin knew he'd be going crazy for the possibility of creating a greenhouse near Vinstead and figuring out what the "life mana" did on a molecular level.

But! That wasn't what he was doing, and he'd need to keep moving regardless to stay ahead of his dwarven pursuers. Though maybe Tara would be able to dissuade them? Eh, no. Probably not. The Enforcer was nice enough, but she was also just doing her job. She didn't really care about him on any sort of personal level, so there was no reason for her to intervene on his behalf, assuming she even found out about them.

More likely, his Adventurer's License would just create enough of a paper trail for the Blackstone dwarves to know they were on the right track, and they could just quietly bypass the Silver Blade as they continued after him. And that was before factoring in any supernatural tracking Skills they might have. Ugh, Skills made everything so much trouble. Still, Edwin could hold his own now, he felt. The confidence that had blossomed during his time with Lefi, that came with finding his feet and learning some fighting tips reassured him of that.

Edwin's attention returned to the sack he was holding. No, he wasn't about to stop and settle down, nor was he going to investigate how Mendelian genetics interacted with magic. He was an *Alchemist*, he should stay focused there. Honestly, why would he need anything beyond that? Alchemy was *fantastic*. Though he did admittedly need to figure out some stuff beyond just "pour mana into an object and mix together."

What he really could use was an encounter with some kind of Alchemist in the wild; then he could get a bit of a start on the less chemistry-like bits of Alchemy that his Skill was constantly telling him existed. Stuff like ... Essential Alchemy, or Potion-Making, or ... Alchemic Vitae? His Skill knowledge was *weird*; why couldn't it tell him what these things *were*, not just—

"An' just who in the hells are you?"

CHAPTER 38

An Unexpected Chat

Edwin nearly jumped as he spun to face the demanding voice, turning away from the random patch of wall he was staring at to instead come face-to-face with a figure clad in black robes.

Catabolic Alchemist

Oh hey! He had just been thinking about how he wanted to find another Alchemist. That was kind of convenient. Less so was the bloody knife the Alchemist was holding, but hey, you couldn't have everything. Hopefully this wouldn't devolve too quickly …

"Well?"

Edwin blanked, and he just sort of stared at the Alchemist hopelessly. "Uhhhhh."

"Wha' are you doing here; nah, wait, are you that Alchemist who Minthree tried to drag back here in a bag? Never mind that, the boy's an idiot. How did you get in, anyway? The window? Kind of impressive, I'll say. No' many people get Climbing. Was tha your Exile?"

Edwin was still struggling to process what was going on. Of all the outcomes to this scenario he'd been imagining, striking up a conversation with a guy holding a bloody knife was not one of them. "Say that again?"

"I've jus' been wanting a peer to talk to for so long! Come on! Lemme show you my work!" the black-robed figure, who, given the speckles of gray in his goatee, had to have been the oldest human Edwin had yet seen on Joriah, reached out to grab Edwin's arm before realizing that he was holding a sizable blade in that hand. After pausing for a moment, though, he made it vanish with a flick of his wrist and reached out again.

Edwin drew back from the attempted touch, letting his hand rest next to the dagger on his belt, and said, "Please don't."

"Oh, stop being such a baby. I won' hurt ya. Come on!" The Alchemist grabbed Edwin's forearm, but Edwin found that he was actually able to pull away fairly easily, much to his surprise. "Will you just come along? Lots ta see, lots ta see!" the old Alchemist insisted.

"Wait!"

The Alchemist spun around to look at Edwin. "Yeah?"

"I ... broke in here, you realize that, right?"

"Yeah?"

"And you're just ... okay with that?"

"Ahhh, well, you know, my guys started it, it's not that secure, and what's a little burglary between friends anyway? Do you know how *long* I've wanted someone to talk to about my work? Ages! Now let's go!"

It ... probably wouldn't hurt, right? At the very least, he might be able to use this to get a lay of the land once things went south. So, while Edwin made sure to keep his dagger close to hand, he still followed the Alchemist as he ventured into the next room over, which turned out to be some kind of kitchen. A few dried meats hung from the ceiling, and a pot boiled on the countertop, though Edwin couldn't see its contents.

The far wall held a doorway, opening out to the balcony Edwin had seen the sentry snoozing on, and off to the other side of the kitchen, a staircase ascended along the side of the curved wall, right next to another staircase descending through the floor. No handrails, which was ... iffy, and the stairs didn't look *quite* solid enough to support his weight, but the Alchemist bounded up them without hesitation, and when a bit of testing didn't snap the wooden plank off under Edwin's weight, he hesitantly followed the enthusiastic man up.

Seriously, am I just an extrovert magnet or something?

"You coming?"

"In a minute! These stairs are a bit …"

"Ah! Right, right. Here, I can give you a hand!" The stairs at the top began to creak under the weight of the man.

"That's … perfectly fine! I can handle myself all right! There's no need for you to come down."

"If you're sure! Oh man, this is such a mess, I need to …" The voice faded away as it was drowned out by clattering, rustling, and, in one instance, shattering. "Damn. I'll actually have to clean that up. Oh, you made it up! Sorry about the mess, I wasn't expecting anyone to ever see my lab."

The Alchemist was standing over a broken pottery jar, surrounded by its former contents, a yellowish salt. Edwin only spared a few glances for that particular mishap while the man moved to start sweeping up the powder, as his gaze was drawn more to the countless fascinating things everywhere *else* in the room. A glass jar held the slowly beating disembodied heart of some anima;, another jar held a ton of different eyeballs, some twitching of their own accord; a third a golden syrup sloshing around with no apparent driving force. The more Edwin looked, the more fascinating things he saw: a pile of color-changing glasslike beads, a frog with transparent skin hopping around under a bell jar, even an ant farm with ants glowing a bright blue. A half-dissected rat was on the lab table, looking freshly dead in a small puddle of blood.

"Well? What do you think? Pretty impressive, yeah?"

"Yeah … wow. I've never seen a lab like this before. Do you do … Biological Alchemy?"

"Alchymie Vitae! I'm hoping for the Class, myself, but it keeps just missing it every time I evolve. The *Grimoire* says I need the Vital Alchemist Path, but I just can' quite get it to work. Slimes don't count, an' I can't get anything more complex to actually formalize pas' the Vels'arrin stage. I always mess up with the Folthstar catalyst, though I'm not sure what I'm doing wrong."

"How do you have all this stuff, anyway? And why are you all the way out here? Not in a city or something?" Edwin felt like he was in a real-life hidden picture game; there were just so many cool things! Was that a circulatory system embedded in some kind of gel? It looked like it, given that pool of blood suspended in the center, which was beating like a heart ...

"... was done, I made most of the stuff myself! What do you think? Do you approve?" He looked at Edwin expectantly. Aww. He wanted validation. Edwin could relate; Impostor Syndrome was real.

"Yeah, yeah. Wow. I'm impressed at ..." Edwin tried to think of some platitude he could give. Compliment people. That way they wouldn't notice when you got distracted by something. He went on: "... your methods. I don't know if I could do it myself, I just don't know that I'd be capable of even half of what this stuff takes."

"Oh, I don' know; you certainly have the capabilities, I'm sure!"

"I mean, I have Alchemy, but I just don't have enough practice with this sort of thing to accomplish half of what you've done here."

"It's just a matter of mindset! Once you ..."

Edwin kept listening, but his attention was pulled away for just a few moments as he saw a distillery setup with two spouts and started wondering about how that might work; could you magically make one substance go down one side, and another the second way? That would be so cool! Unfortunately, by the time he realized that he was no longer processing what the Alchemist was saying, Edwin had missed the bulk of whatever he was going on about.

"... out of the way, and the fact that you don't *mind* what it takes, you're good to go!"

"Sorry, could you repeat that? I got distracted. There's so much cool stuff in here, and I didn't hear a thing."

"Ah, it's fine, I get what you're saying. You'll do *fine*. Stay here and work with me for a bit! I'm a touch low on fresh supplies, but my back-ups will do nicely before I can restock, you catch my meaning?" He winked, which was odd, but whatever.

Edwin just gave a noncommittal shrug in response. "Um, sure?"

"Excellent! You can help once it comes time. So what kind of Alchemy do you focus on?"

Well, fair's fair and all that. Edwin mildly felt like he was suffering from expectation whiplash, but if he was going to be getting some kind of instruction, maybe even a place to stay for a few days, the least he could do would be to help out when creating new ingredients. Heck, that would be its own reward in some ways!

Right, what kind of Alchemy he used. Well, fellow scientists and all, no harm in that bit of info. "I managed to get the Mana Infusion Skill, and so I've been using that. Charge up some chemicals and go from there. I've made some cool stuff, though I've never been able to work with already-magical materials. But I'm not sure that I want to stick around for more than a day or two. I am kind of on the run from some guys who wanted to steal my creations from me." It wasn't strictly true, but it was close enough.

"Empire?"

Edwin shook his head. "Blackstone dwarves."

"Huh. Never heard of 'em."

"So, what brought you out here, anyway? Also, I don't think we ever really introduced ourselves. I'm Edwin."

"Niall. Nice to meet ya, Edwin." Niall dropped down into a high-backed chair, looking at the ceiling. "Well, you know how i' is. I's the same story everyone in our line of work's got. As a kid, people were talking, worried about me when I started walking so late—took me until I was almost a year old, and by that point people were swearing that I must have something wrong with me. Still haven't managed to get the Skill, nor any other Physical." He kicked at a table leg in frustration. "You know the pain, righ'? Everyone knowin' your entire life tha yer different, solely because of something you got no say in?"

Edwin *could* relate, though it wasn't quite the same for him. Still, he nodded and let Niall carry on.

"Course, I couldn't keep up with any o' the kids, and it became obvious what my crippling was when I was ten and *still* hadn't gotten Walking as an option. I could walk just fine! It was just my stamina that was the problem. I didn't need the Skill, not really. But you know how it works; I don't need to tell you that. Well, because nobody wanted a boy with a broken Skill set, I ended up, well, ya know"—he mimed a kick from where he was sitting. "So, tossed ou' of my home, had to figure out wha' to do with my life, stripped of Citizenhood, an' with no hope of getting a license, had to avoid settlements, all that stuff. Least I didn't have to deal with the Management, so I could get other Skills."

There was anger there, Edwin was sure. However, it was buried under layers and layers of quiet resentment and even resignation, so it wasn't too obvious.

"Had to survive through a few bandit camps, and doing it without a Physical wasn' easy, but I managed. Being small and quiet helped. Got First Aid, Cooking, all the fun Skills." He shrugged. "Cooking went from potion-making to Alchemy once I found the *Grimoire*, then Life Alchemy. First Aid became Surgery then Anatomy, so I managed to make myself too useful to throw out for them at least.

"Never a single Physical or Weapon, though. Took me a few years, but I met Minone. He kept me alive for years after I saved his life, but he's … not around anymore. Not the brightest, you know? None of the lads downstairs are. Terrible conversation partners. Proud of 'em, though. They do their jobs and keep me alive. Then I get to do my work in peace. But now you're here! An' in this amazing tower! It's the perfect location, found it an' it was clearly abandoned for years, mostly Unobtrusive, and the location is phenomenal!"

"Wait, why weren't you able to get a license? Wouldn't that have helped in some way? Let you live closer to town or something?"

"Well, what do you think? Beyond the fact that it doesn't *matter* if you're licensed, nobody wants you anyway, the wait times are *atrocious*, you basically need to bribe the bureaucracy to get them to work, with far more money than anyone has at ten, the application process takes weeks, and don't even get me started on that Enforcer."

"Tara?"

"Who's Tara?"

"The … Enforcer?"

"Really? Must be new. In my day, it was a really cranky old Imperial Inquisitor, named … named … Ah, doesn't matter. He *hated* anyone that didn' have a spotless record, and his Wanted List musta been in the hundreds! Someone like me, not following the Basics? Oh man, first time he visited my village he about near threw me straight through the wall of my home. I was six! All 'cause I didn't bow quite deep enough to him behind his back, and I was missing Walking; I remember he said, 'worthless already, might as well deal with him before he's a problem.' I still remember that, all these years later. I hated that man. But you say he's gone? Good riddance to bad rubbish, I say." Niall took a deep breath. "My apologies. Thinking about him, even all this time later ... really boils my blood." He cracked a smile at that, grinning at some unseen joke. "Did that answer your question? I quite forgot what it was you had asked!"

"Yeah, I ... guess it does. Enough, at least?"

"So you up to stay around for a little while? I can teach you a ton o' stuff! Get you going on the right foot."

"For a ... few days, I guess. Could I see that *Grimoire* you've mentioned a couple of times?"

"Certainly! Where are my manners?" Niall sprang up from his chair and began rummaging around through a pile of books on one of the tables near the wall. After a few moments, he pulled out a black-covered tome and dropped it on a bit of empty space on the table nearest Edwin, where it thudded down. "Here you are! The informan' for everything I've ever accomplished! *The Zosiman Grimoire!*"

Edwin ran his fingers over the charred leather. It felt *ancient* yet new at the same time. It was well-worn and covered in small burns and discolorations on the patterned scales of the black leather. Bold, golden lettering glittered in the center, wrapped around a hole where it looked like a jewel once sat, declaring its name:

The Zosiman Grimoire—Fourth Edition
Complete Secrets of the Alchymic Arts

Finally. It was time to learn what his Class was supposed to do.

CHAPTER 39

The Career of a Lifetime

Alchemy, that most wondrous and sacred art, was allegedly pioneered by The First Brewer of Life, Death, Earth, and Sky, the legendary Old Goddess Salverria. It was her efforts that are widely regarded to have formalized the common practice of potion-brewing and unified it under the broader scope of "Alchymie," dividing it into four primary branches in accordance with the Three Attribute theory of the body. First and foremost among the disciplines, there was Alchymie Vitae, corresponding to Health and concerned with the creation and manipulation of True Life. Second was Alchymie Essentia, concerned with the matters of Mana, and in the extraction and manipulation of the true "essence" of an object. Thirdly was Alchymie Practicum, associated with fundamental Stamina and, accordingly, with enhancements upon other substances.

Salverria herself was legendarily an Alchymist Vital, and it is said that she was responsible for the creation of the Manticores, Chimeras, and even the noble Griffon, among others. More information, along with speculation for the required rituals and methods needed can be found in Section 5: Impact of Alchemy. According to Salverrian tradition, she was also responsible for the creation of vortithal, salverweed, talsanenris, shoriven, watergrass, and even wheat. However, as she has faded somewhat into the role of a creator deity for said peoples, the tales they tell of her prolific creations may be mythological. Still, these creations, if truly hers, would fall into the

purview of Vitae as well. It is the view of this author that Salverria most
likely was a real person, however with recent …

Though drier than even his history textbooks, Edwin found the *Gri-moire* endlessly fascinating. Sure, he was pretty liberally skimming it, but it was *fantasy science*! It was the coolest thing ever! He was learning so much! Also, he didn't have to memorize it for a reading quiz at 8 a.m.! Ah, tests. He was so glad to never have to deal with those ever again.

Vital Alchemy, or Alchymie Vitae, was the biology of Alchemy, as it dealt with everything pertaining to life. Herbology, animal crossbreeding, and some medicines (though overlap occurred there with Practical Alchemy), but above all the goal of creating life itself, which was allegedly *possible*, and not even hard for simpler forms of life. It required successfully bringing anything more complicated than a slime to life to unlock the Vital Alchemist Path, as apparently a slime wasn't hard enough to warrant it!

The Path itself was really cool, as there were all kinds of Skills that could result from it. When combined with Alchemy, it would give the rather uninventive Alchymie Vitae, but its effects, focused as they were on the creation of life, were nothing to argue with. Eat your heart out, Miller and Urey. Turns out all you need to do to make life is give a beakerful of organic chemicals a good shake with Alchymie Vitae.

Combining the Path with the Medicine Skill gave Vivificant, which let you … transfer life from one creature to another? Sheesh. If the description were even close to accurate, wait, how did that … A combination with an Eating evolution gave Vitachemical Infusion, which allowed you to directly absorb substances through your skin to take on their properties. Alchemist's Physique yielded Vital Alchemist's Mastery, which let you give yourself the traits of "absorbed creatures" at will—claws, scales, quills, feathers, muscles, and more besides.

All in all, it was an absolutely *bonkers* branch of Alchemy, and yet it was somehow the one that Edwin was least interested in or excited about.

Essential Alchemy enabled you to take the properties of one object and apply them to another. The book listed examples of making steel as transparent as water, or liquid water the solidity and structure of steel. Also, removing the melting point of ice to perpetually freeze it, or giving lead the weight of air, or the strength of mithril to cloth, or the temperature of fire to a rock, or … Well, there were a lot of possibilities, suffice to say. It seemed like *Zosiman* didn't have much experience in that field, though, as the chapter on it was disappointingly slim.

Practical Alchemy concerned itself about two types of creations, namely elixirs and concoctions, both "enhancements" to either organic or inorganic matter. Elixirs were proper fantasy potions, pretty much just magic in a bottle, encompassing everything from invisibility and flight to superstrength and magical healing, and those were just the examples from the introductory page! Concoctions were more like what Edwin had experimented with, explosions and objects with inherently abnormal properties, like liquids that ran uphill or metals that exploded on contact with water (Edwin was pretty sure the latter was just an alkali metal, but that just brought up the question of what a Mana-Infused version of *that* would look like. Terrifying.).

There was even a section on "Alchymie Ascendia" toward the end, which talked about solidifying abstract concepts, like spinning moonlight into thread (for invisibility cloaks and potions), bottling sunlight (for fighting vampires), or forging the tranquility of a forest glen into an actual shield. Edwin's brain just wasn't able to wrap around how that was supposed to work, but he supposed that's why it was magic, and not science … yet.

Any magic distinguishable from technology is insufficiently advanced. Edwin couldn't help but grin at the thought.

All of the Alchymie Ascendia was incredibly challenging, and the book even advised the Alchemist to wait until their Alchemy level was in the *hundreds* before attempting it because of how badly it could backfire if you didn't succeed on your first attempt. Scary. *Unfortu-*nately, while *Zosiman* was a fastidious historian and excellent chronicler (the herbology chapter was quite detailed and comprehensive, so far as Edwin could tell), his experience as an actual Alchemist was … limited. There were loads of details about Alchemy-related Paths and Skills, as well as tips on how to apply Skills to Alchemy in nonobvious ways. Some of the tips, like how Knives helped with chopping ingredients, were obvious. Others, like using Breathing as a filter for gases, were less so (and in that instance, kind of reckless).

That's not to say that the book had no tips on how to actually perform Alchemy, just that the "Formula for Salve of Aided Recovery" listed off a half-dozen ingredients with no indication how they were supposed to actually *combine*.

Niall had *experience*, though, which was why ...

"'Kay, 'kay. Carefully, jus' prick your finger with the silver needle an' let the drop fall into the bowl ..."

Proximity to the Verdant meant that most of the components needed for their experiments grew locally, as the life energy that made plants grow so well similarly meant that it was one of the places where the talsanenris—tal-san-en-ris, yep, he got it right—berry would grow in appreciable numbers. Storing them was tricky, as the white berries (about the size and shape of a really big blueberry) were so full of life magic that they had a tendency to spontaneously sprout into a new talsanenris bush if the white berries were ever simultaneously exposed to light and water.

But if they were crushed, the life mana would begin to seep out of their flesh. It was a tricky balance, but Niall had a handful of them, enough for one batch of salve, half a "cupful" (some terms were multiversal, it seemed), or about a hundred milliliters if Edwin's estimations were accurate and assuming a cup was *roughly* the same size as back on Earth, which seemed to be the case.

Once the berries were mashed in a mortar and pestle (granite mortar, but a pestle made of bone; that was important apparently), a few sprigs of something that smelled like mint but were shaped more like a cup and reminded Edwin of a miniature Venus flytrap were added. Next up were mustard seeds, some budding red flowers of something called wolf's tongue, and the spores from a forked stalk. One by one, they all were added in accordance to very vague yet apparently precise measurements (they were all in *pinches*! Or by *count*! What kind of Alchemist would let that stand?), boiled in a copper pot until the mixture turned clear. Then, using a recently cleaned, formerly tarnished silver needle (because that helped draw out impurities apparently), prick a finger and let a drop of blood fall into the mixture.

"An' that's good! See how it's all turning red? Now stir it that way five more times, then stir backward six times, before going forward seven more! Keep at that nice, steady pace; you'll know when it's done when it starts glowing! Oh, Infuse a bit more into the pot while you're doing that; it'll help keep the magic inside!" Niall was *thrilled* for Edwin to have managed what he had so far, and over the past two days had covered a *lot* of topics that Edwin was sure were really fascinating and cool, but that he couldn't understand for the life of him.

A lot about the body, for sure, though admittedly a fair amount of it didn't match up with Edwin's understanding of medicine, but he couldn't tell what was right or wrong at the moment thanks to how arcane the language was in which it was all phrased. The occasional appearance of Niall's accent did not help, either.

"So, what does the blood do again?"

"The blood triggers the Nystaril reaction, an' draws out the lasitan-saesrain from talsanenris, which activates the thorovillis inhibitors from the snaketongue spores an' *that*—"

Edwin cut off the Alchemist before his eyes could glaze over: "Please … I know you're excited, but just … keep it simple? Give me the overview."

Niall looked sheepishly off to the side. "Right, sorry. Anyway, the blood primes the solution so it knows essentially what it should be helping. If it's unprimed it'll jus' do whatever, and can be … chaotic. Sometimes it heals the cut, sometimes it does nothing, sometimes it *looks* like it does nothing and then makes the person drop dead of a fever two days later … Better to prime it, even if it does limit what you can use it on to humans, and focus the effects on yourself. More advanced potions want you to render down specific parts of the body for best results. Like a finger to regrow a hand, or … an eye to cure blindness, for a couple of examples. The more you render down, the more the potion can restore on its own without starving the drinker."

Huh. That was kind of sad. It made *sense* that magic potions would still have limitations and their own restrictions (some sort of attunement? That was … interesting), but it was still sad that his dream of a video-game magical potion that someone could just drink to instantly return from the brink of death, or hand off to someone else if they needed it, wasn't quite possible.

They fell into silence as Edwin stirred the elixir, the mixture staying equally liquid for quite some time. Then, all at once, it thickened into a glowing red paste, which brought Edwin to hastily cut the heat from the pot and remove it before it was overcooked. As he carefully scraped it out with a device more or less resembling a spatula, he reviewed the process in his mind. It was pretty simple, especially by material science standards, yet there were *so many* places for improvement. He'd need to track down more talsanenris berries and see if he couldn't make a better elixir. Selling them would probably give him some funds once his current money pouch ran low, and set him on on track to financial security.

Well, he could *theoretically* try to leverage his knowledge of mortar and concrete to make some money that way, but the required infra-structure to make enough to be commercially viable ... Hah. Nah, he'd let ... Aefra? Aerfa? Aeraf? ... Aerfa take care of making concrete a viable commodity. Edwin wanted no part in that whole process. He *should* try to make some more lime, though. He was perilously short on defensive options beyond his stick, and he missed having good old-fashioned explosions. Nothing beat blowing problems to smithereens.

Though healing potions were a close second, especially to help others with their problems. Which was his current task, actually. The bandit who attacked Edwin—Niall called him Minfour—had survived being set on fire, apparently, and had eventually crawled back to the tower at some point last night, covered in burns. It was really that as much as anything that prompted Niall and Edwin to make up a batch of healing salve for the Brute Minion. Edwin felt he deserved his injuries, yes, but that didn't mean he'd leave the guy to suffer when there was a simple, and viable alternative. Though actually ...

"Wait, if this is for Minfour, why did we prime it with my blood, and not his ... skin, or whatever?"

"Ah, I've got a potion for the bulk of his skin, this was more just to teach you! Don' you feel enlightened?"

"I mean I guess, but it seems like a lot to go through if you already had the potion. Also, doesn't that mean that the salve is optimized for me? And it's less useful for you in general?"

Niall waved a hand. "Don' worry about it! It's my thanks to you for being a good student, an' to start you on a Path of Medical Alchemy!"

"Well ... thanks, I guess." Edwin awkwardly accepted the tub of salve, putting it in his belt before digging it out a second later so he could actually test it. Fortunately, Niall was digging around a disorganized chest filled with all sorts of vials, so he didn't notice Edwin's actions.

It only took a minute for Niall to find what he was looking for, and red vial in hand, the Alchemist duo descended two floors, to where the dormitories were. While normally Niall had the nicest room claimed for himself and the other three were home to his five minions, Edwin had been given one of the nicer rooms for his own use.

It wasn't there that they were headed, though, instead visiting the former living room, now communal sleeping room that took up half the floor. Minfour (yes, the man had a real name, but Edwin didn't know what it was) was sprawled out on a pad off to the side, clutching more than a few nasty blisters and third-degree burns.

At Niall's prompting, Edwin tried rubbing a bit of salve onto the back of Minfour's hand, watching as the blister sank away and the redness slowly faded to reveal unburned, uninjured skin. It took a while and a few applications, but that was apparently just the inefficiency at work. On Edwin it would theoretically fix the same injury with a mere drop of salve, and in seconds no less. Magic! Gotta love it.

What was really impressive, though, was the potion that Niall had his minion drink. Over the course of mere seconds, starting from his throat and upper torso, a wave of pink flesh spread across the man's entire body, a faint trickle of blood being forced out as layer upon layer of skin was pushed up from below, replacing where it had been burned away and making blisters wither away in moments.

Now *that* was a proper magic potion! Instant skin graft for the entire body, with no rejection! It had to have been a dedicated skin potion for that level of speed on a nonprimed individual. Heck, that was practically at the level of a regeneration potion, which regrew the tissue wholesale.

... And regeneration potions needed a sample of the body part being targeted, the more the better. For a complete heal, he'd need just ... so much.

... Oh great.

Man, Edwin had such high hopes for Niall. They were getting along so well, too! He really hoped he wouldn't have to put pretty much the entire tower to the torch. Okay, well, maybe there was a completely reasonable answer to this dilemma. Maybe Niall was just harvesting his own skin and using regen potions to get it back, with large enough batch sizes to make it a net positive? No need for his "backup supplies" to be random people wandering down the road, right?

"So, ah, Niall, where did you get the ingredients for that potion? Seemed like you'd need a lot of human skin for that quick of a regrow," Edwin asked, with a fair bit of dread. *Please don't be a serial killer,* please *don't be a serial killer ...*

"Ah, some passing resupply." Niall waved his hand, studying the fresh layer of skin on Minfour. He got too close and sneezed suddenly, interrupting his statement. He recovered quickly enough, though, and continued his inspection. "Just a courier or whatnot. Nothing particularly noteworthy, just a good source of materials."

Edwin closed his eyes and breathed out slowly and carefully. *Great.*

CHAPTER 40

Pointed Questions

Edwin's first instinct was to immediately grab something heavy and start clubbing Niall over the head, while shouting about him and his bandit minions being murderers, but he restrained himself for the time being. This was not the time or place for that sort of action. Yes, he could be a little … reckless at times, and he should have probably figured out sooner that the black-robed bioalchemist in the ruined wizard's tower wasn't exactly sourcing his ingredients from ethically agreeable places, but he had just gotten too keen on the idea of *Science!* and hadn't really thought about it too deeply. Though, even if he had known from the start, would that have actually changed his actions any? Probably not, in all honesty. He'd learned so much from Niall that—

"You feeling all right?" Niall broke Edwin out of his musings with a concerned expression on his face.

"Hmm? Oh, yeah. I'll be fine, I just … don't deal with"—Edwin lamely gestured at the blood-covered minion in front of him—"all that well."

Niall looked back and forth for a moment in confusion, before coming to a realization: "Ah! Yeah, tha' makes sense. Vitae can ge' a bit messy at times. Go sit down; it'll help. Drink some water, maybe lie down? I'll wash up and get food ready."

Edwin nodded mutely as he retreated to his room. Good, he wouldn't have to deal with the bandits while he thought about how to, well, deal with them. Plenty of time to come up with a plan.

Edwin reclined on his bed, surprisingly clean for being in a bandit hideout, but it also made sense that a bioalchemist could keep his lair free of bugs. It was still dusty, but that was … tolerable. He retrieved his canteen from his belt and stared into the distance, thinking as he sipped his water. Actually, first he should check his progress. He hadn't checked his notifications for a couple days now, and he should probably make sure he was up to speed.

Level Up!
Alchemy Level 43→46
Athletics Level 25→27
Firestarting Level 36→37
First Aid Level 18→26
Flexibility Level 22→23
Identify Level 38→40
Memory Level 23→28
Nutrition Level 22→23
Outsider's Almanac Level 74→77
Packing Level 16→17
Polyglot Level 33→34
Visualization Level 41→42

Congratulations! For breaking into a habited building undetected, you have unlocked the Burglar Path!
Congratulations! For successfully brewing an elixir, you have unlocked the Potioneer Path!
Congratulations! For brewing and applying an alchemical healing potion, you have unlocked the Alchemical Medic Path!
You have unlocked the Potion Brewing Skill!
Accept Skill? Y/N

Ooh. Potion Brewing. That was tempting. *Really* tempting. Hmm. No. Well, maybe? No. He already had Alchemy at an honestly respectable level. But Potion Brewing wasn't … Well, it also was … Gah, he didn't know!

Hmm. He had a lot of Skills that were perfectly decent. Seeing, Breathing, First Aid, Survival, Nutrition … They were all useful in their own right, and all had strong potential for the near future, but he didn't want to clutter up his Skills list with all sorts of Skills that just reflected what he was capable of doing on his own.

Edwin wanted the sort of power he saw with Tara, summoning silver walls and suits of armor, snatching arrows from the air and no-selling powerful attacks. The sort of power that from what Rashin, Lefi, and Tara had all told him was the result of high-Tier Skills. And if he wanted to ever get to a halfway-high Tier, he couldn't just go around accepting whatever Skills were offered him.

Heck, half of the cooler effects Edwin wanted, like reflexes to snatch an arrow from midair or the ability to see the nigh-invisible, he could probably get with Attributes if he was lucky, and that meant he really shouldn't take many more Skills unless they were either *so* broadly applicable that he'd be able to level them constantly and easily while also benefiting all his other abilities or just so awesome he couldn't pass them up. Like pretty much anything with magic, actually.

But where did Potion Brewing fit into that? It was a really cool Skill, and synergized with Alchemy and possibly Nutrition, but would he be able to level it up easily enough? Would it help everything else he did enough to justify it?

Okay, fine. He'd decline it *for now*, because he didn't know how much Potion Brewing specifically he'd be doing in the future, and he could always re-unlock it later. Anyway, back to the problem at hand.

So, he'd need to take out five minions and one Alchemist with unknown capabilities. Edwin knew that Niall had no combat or physical Skills, unless he was lying, in which case … Hmm. Okay, Edwin would assume general supernatural physique, but also that Niall didn't have any hyperpowerful unknown combat attacks. Edwin couldn't plan for those anyway. He'd just assume that Niall was as unkillable as everyone else, and maybe he'd be pleasantly surprised. He was still confident that he could take the bandits, that feeling hadn't subsided any, and one more person wouldn't make a difference.

Regardless, his first priority should be neutralizing Niall. The Alchemist was just too much of a wildcard and was his biggest target besides.

The minions would most likely disperse, joining other bandit groups admittedly, but without their boss they wouldn't be kidnapping random people and turning them into potions.

He could kill the man, probably, but he wasn't sure if he wanted to. He still remembered watching Tara tear through bandits like they were paper, leaving them in bloody piles ... No. He didn't mind killing, but why bother when it could be avoided? He would just need to try and find some ropes; he could Infuse those with the help of Packing to make them almost unbreakable, possibly even resistant to fire in case Niall had something like Edwin's Firestarting that allowed him to burn through restraints. If worse came to worst, Edwin supposed, he would probably be able to slice Niall's throat without alerting the minions if he did it in the lab.

Ah, the lab. That was a set of complications of its own. There were some *insanely* useful things in the lab, but how would he know what was made out of murdered humans? Edwin shuddered. No. Just ... no. If he couldn't recognize something as being specifically *not* made out of humans, like dried herbs, it was going to be burned. That, sadly, included all the potions.

A part of him ached to put it to the flames, but his skin crawled at the idea at the same time. Maybe one day, Future-Edwin would scoff at his sentimentality, take whatever advantages he got, and not waste the sacrifices made by others, but Future-Edwin wasn't here. Present-Edwin was, and Present-Edwin was a sentimental ball of emotions (wait, how did they get here? Shoo.) whose mind and morality were still trying to cling to Earth, which he'd left behind. No, he wasn't going to use the potions that came from human experimentation. *Maybe* the notes, if there was anything useful there. But not the potions. Maybe not even the tower; for all he knew it was haunted by the ghosts of the bandit's murdered victims ...

Edwin had a thought and groaned. They weren't cannibals, too, were they? Ugh. He'd have to figure out some way to ask without raising suspicions over dinner. They probably were, weren't they? Ah, darn it all. This was probably above his pay grade, too. The smart thing to do would be to run and try to find Lefi or Tara; they handled this sort of thing all the time!

No. Edwin had decided that he was going to try and stand on his *own two feet*, and his confidence burst forward in response to the challenge. He wasn't going to go running for help the moment he found something hard—not that this would be. That wasn't how he'd gotten through college (for better or worse, he arguably *should* have gone to office hours more— Focus, Edwin). The same thing applied to taking down bands of murder-cannibals.

So … try and knock out Niall while he was in the lab, then tie him up with ropes, maybe chains if Edwin could find them.

Oh! If he got into a fight with Niall, Edwin needed to make sure that the Alchemist wouldn't be able to reach a healing potion. It wouldn't do for Edwin to fight through all the minions, only to be backstabbed by Niall, having healed himself of a mortal injury through quick potion application.

Then, with Niall out of the picture, Edwin could try to chain up the minions one by one. That wouldn't be too hard, but no need to take too many risks. He'd take them by surprise, maybe club them over their heads and chain them up while stunned. Not ideal, and more than a little traitorous (at least he already had the Path, so the System wouldn't rub it in his face), but he knew he would be able to manage it.

Edwin didn't really expect he'd be able to take them all *alive*; life-or-death combat would likely be just that, but he could at least try … and then he'd need to do something. He didn't know what, maybe lead them on a walk to the nearest town? Trying to remember where that was, relative to here, uh …

Level Up!
Memory Level 28→29
Visualization Level 42→43

Okay, there was one about a day's walk back the way he had come. It hadn't been that big, but Edwin remembered a building that looked like a small prison or something; they could probably handle the bandit group and let Tara, or whoever, deal with them.

On the other hand … *Should* he just let Tara take care of this whole mess right here? It was literally her job. Lefi, too, for that matter. Either one of them would be far more capable of taking down everyone. But ... no. Who knows how long it would take for Edwin to either find them or for a message to be passed along to them, let alone how long it would take them to get back here and find this place. That would put more people at risk, which he didn't want. Granted, if he failed, then they'd have no idea that this place was here at all. Did he want to take that risk?

Yes. I can manage it.

His confidence was scaring him slightly. He didn't feel *that* confident, surely? It was still six on one ... He could whip up something in the lab! That would make the fight even easier, if all he needed was some chloroform or whatever and a few seconds to take someone out of the fight.

Yeah, that would work well. With that plan, his protesting sense of self-preservation was satisfied. He could *do* this. Heck, he could do this *right now.* He didn't need any help!

... No, no. Calm down, Edwin. Make the potion first. Then you can go on your rampage.

Edwin's brain wandered slightly treacherously, wondering what he should take once he was done. He absolutely wanted the *Grimoire,* for one. It had way too much information on types of herbs and even creature body parts to leave behind. Before he left, he should also grab food supplies, as many nonhuman alchemical ingredients as he could manage, and oh! He should also check out the upper floors of the tower. He hadn't before, as there just hadn't been the opportunity to, and Niall hadn't offered to show him that far up, but Edwin should make sure there wasn't someone caged up there, waiting to be rendered into potion ingredients.

Hmm. What if Niall was able to kill and reanimate himself, Herbert West–like? It would be messy beyond belief, but if it came to that, Edwin should probably try to ... dismember him? Edwin shuddered.

No. *No.* He was *not* going there. He'd just make sure to tie up Niall even if he thought the Catabolic Alchemist was completely dead. Still, he should be absolutely certain that there hadn't just been some massive misunderstanding before he attacked Niall and his underlings. Probably hadn't, but he didn't really want to take that chance.

A knock on the door brought Edwin back from his thoughts. "Yeah?"

"Da boss sent me ta tell ya food is ready." Was that Minfive? The voice was gravelly enough. Edwin couldn't really tell them apart without Almanac, despite their all looking and sounding so different from one another.

"Okay, thanks," Edwin called in response. "I'll be up in a minute!" He smirked. It was like high school all over again, being summoned for food. He schooled his expression and made his way up the creaking stairs, to where three of the five bandits were waiting. Minsix was on the balcony, actually awake while on watch for once, and Minfour was, when Edwin asked, sleeping downstairs, recovering from the skin-regeneration potion.

"So ... I have to ask," Edwin said cautiously, as they served up the ladles of stew Niall had prepared, and he waited for Niall to indicate he should proceed. "These aren't ... from the resupplies, right?"

Niall immediately shuddered. "Good heavens, no! Tha' would be disgusting!" The Alchemist shook his head. Wait, had Edwin misjudged him? If this was the reaction for that sort of thing, were they actually *not* rendering humans into potion ingredients? "An' a complete waste, too! No, the meat comes from either hunting or the supplies they migh' be carrying. The suppliers themselves are much too precious to eat; they're saved for potions."

And there it was. Well, at least Edwin wasn't eating people, and now he knew for sure that the potions *did* have travelers ground up in them.

"I see ... Well, that's a relief," Edwin honestly replied.

"Could you imagine? Cannibals, ah! Truly disgusting. Potions, though, potions at least you're using them for good." Niall shook his head, apparently trying to get the image of eating people out of it. "An' now you've gone and ruined my appetite," he accused Edwin, who could only helplessly shrug in response.

"Sorry?"

"Ah, not your fault. I'll finish eating another time. I'll be on the top floor, Edwin, if you'd join me when you're done?"

Oh? That was interesting. Edwin watched as the Alchemist retreated upstairs, leaving him with the three hulking minions. He didn't stick around long, hastily gulping down his stew (it was *really* good, which he attributed to Niall's Cooking Skill) with a clear conscience before following his host.

Edwin paused as he prepared to venture to the floor above the lab. He wasn't sure what he was expecting, some torture chamber with blood and viscera everywhere, or maybe children in cages as they waited for dissection, and he needed to prepare himself. He took a deep breath and closed his eyes, stepping up to ... a perfectly normal room. Of all the things he was preparing for, that was not one of them. There weren't bloodstains on every surface, nor rusty dissection tables.

With a bit of quiet and brief poking around, Edwin found some bloodstained cloth off against the wall, a table with a rust-colored discoloration right in the center, and discarded restraints against another side of the wall, iron manacles with the key in the lock. They worked pretty well, actually. Edwin didn't take them out quite yet, but they would be useful once he needed to disable Niall.

Still, he was pretty sure this was a dissection room, just one that was kept pretty clean. That was a relief, that while his host may have been a serial killer, he was at least a neat one. Small mercies. Still, he should get moving. He'd waited long enough; no need to make the bandit leader suspicious.

Edwin made sure his knife was loosened in its sheath as he ventured up the final flight of stairs, so he could draw it at a moment's notice. It was hardly meant for combat, but it was still better than nothing, at the very least.

"Ah! Edwin. Glad you could make i'." Niall didn't turn as Edwin's weight caused the weather-worn wood of the top to squeak in protest. "Mind your step. The top can be a little rotten in places; it's why I don't come up here often."

"So then ... why are you up here now?"

"It's a good place to look out an' think, you know? Especially if you come out after dark."

"I can believe that." Edwin joined Niall as he watched the sun descend toward the horizon, washing the grassland in brilliant crimsons and golds. From up here, you could see for miles, all the way to the farmland in the distance, to the herds of ... either cattle, or horses, or something else, grazing in the grasslands here and there. Looking away from the farmland to try and see the end of the waving grasses was unsuccessful, the endless sea just fading into the distance beyond.

Level Up!
Seeing Level 26→27

"You mentioned wishing to leave?"

Edwin shrugged. "Yeah. It's been informative, working with you and reading the *Grimoire*, but I need to move on before my pursuers catch up."

"Have you considered the possibility they are no' attempting to pursue you, if you have yet to see them?"

Edwin shook his head. "I made the lord too mad, assuming he even survived, to let me go. He struck me as the sort of person to pursue a grudge to the ends of Joriah if he could. I have a head start, yes, but I need to try and keep it."

"I see. Pity. Well, if you find yourself coming back this way, you are always welcome here. When will you depar'?"

"Tomorrow morning, probably. It's a bit late to leave now. I don't want to travel at night again."

Niall chuckled. "Smart. I trust I don' need to tell you not to let anyone else know about us? We'll be found sooner or later, but I like this tower an' don't want to have to leave any sooner than I must."

"Nah, it's fine." Edwin sighed and shifted his position such that he was slightly behind Niall, who was still looking out over the grasslands. Edwin so desperately wanted to give some witty one-liner, but he settled for efficiency instead. No point in being *over*confident, after all. With a single continuous motion, he drew his knife and slammed its pommel into the side of Niall's skull.

CHAPTER 41

Not Quite the Answer to Life

You have unlocked the Sucker Punch Skill!
Accept Skill? Y/N

No, and … disable notifications for the moment.

As he watched Niall stumble backward, clutching a bleeding ear, Edwin winced slightly. His blow hadn't been great, missing the Alchemist's temple enough to blow an easy knockout. He had almost used the blade of his knife instead of the hilt for the strike, and he doubted that the man would have managed to survive a six-inch-long bar of steel shoved through his brain.

The only thing that had stopped Edwin was that he wasn't sure that he wanted to just outright *kill* the man that quickly. If it came down to it? He wouldn't hesitate, he told himself, but he wasn't going to just stab a guy through the head with no warning. That wasn't who he wanted to be.

Fortunately, the stumble wasn't so bad that Niall would be able to get away, but Edwin still quickly closed the distance between them so as not to take that chance. The Alchemist recovered slightly, trying to stabilize his footing. However, the weaker man was knocked fully off his feet by Edwin's shoulder colliding with the Alchemist's chest and tackling him to the ground.

Edwin moved quickly. If Niall managed to get off a shout to his minions, Edwin would find himself swiftly outnumbered and then he'd be in for a very annoying fight. No, he'd need to finish this fight quickly.

While he had managed to mostly avoid looking at Niall's expression so far, Edwin caught a glimpse of the man's face and saw it held equal parts surprise and pain. Niall drew breath to shout, but Edwin drove a knee into the man's gut to force all the air in his lungs out, and what would have been a cry became a wheeze. "Why?"

"Because"—Edwin shifted slightly as he kept the Alchemist pinned below his knees, leaving only a single hand free—"you ground people up and put them in *bottles*." He didn't raise his voice, but still did his best to infuse his declaration with as much disgust as possible.

That didn't seem to be the response Niall was anticipating, and his visage contorted into one of rage. "People?" He spat the word out, though Edwin's position on his torso meant there wasn't much volume or force behind it. "You call them *people*? Would *people* throw away anyone different with no thought for the person within? Would *people* willingly give their friend, their son, their entire lives up at the whims of a feather-brained bureaucrat who decided I wasn't worth living?"

Edwin struggled to keep the flailing Alchemist pinned. "How is what you're doing any different? Deciding that some people aren't worth their life and should be used for your experiments?" He maneuvered to keep one leg on an elbow, negating its leverage, and drove his other knee deeper into the man's gut. Meanwhile, his hands were occupied at Niall's left hand, keeping the flailing limb against the wood while he worked with a knife, carefully so as to not cut himself or the Alchemist.

Niall tried to get up, but a firm knee put a stop to that. In response, he gasped out his response. "Because they had a *choice!*" Edwin was quite content with Niall monologuing, as he mostly stopped struggling when he started ranting. "They could have seen the evils of those that surround them and acted against it, but did they? No! They let a child get thrown through a wall and went about their lives, muttering that he deserved it for the 'crime' of not being able to get a Skill! Are those the actions of a— Mmmphhh!"

Edwin finished his work, and a strip of cloth, cut at last from the flowing sleeves of Niall's robe by Edwin's knife, was shoved into the conveniently open mouth of the ranting villain, then held in place by a second strip of cloth. The Alchemist offered little resistance as Edwin rolled him over onto his front, though he did attempt a muffled protest.

Edwin was having none of it and pinned the man's hands behind his back. While he was absolutely stronger than the older bandit, it wasn't by much, and Niall was flailing like a madman to try and get loose, now that he wasn't talking. A surge of strength helped Edwin get a firmer hold, but a moment of distraction and a stray arm knocked Edwin's grip on his knife loose, and it was sent skittering across the room, where it fell into an open hole and clattered onto the wooden floor some ten feet below them.

Edwin, deprived of his weapon and having successfully gagged the Alchemist, changed tactics slightly, trying to get Niall into a choke hold, but he wasn't entirely sure *how* to do so. He tried to get an elbow around the Alchemist's neck and began to squeeze, but it didn't appear to actually be cutting off the wind flow down his throat. So, with what little leverage he could manage, Edwin lifted both of them up from the ground, twisted around, and slammed Niall's face into the wooden boards beneath them, over and over again.

It was a race to see which gave up faster: Edwin's grip or Niall's consciousness. It would be close, and even as the struggles of the old man grew more frantic yet weaker, Edwin's hands scrambled to try and maintain their grip as he forced Niall's arms and hands time and time again into the wooden floor they were upon.

Edwin struck blow after blow, desperately trying to maintain some semblance of control as their contest closed in on the finish line … As it turned out, neither beat out the other. Instead, with a creak and a groan, the board beneath them gave out under the abuse, sending them both cascading down to the floor below in a hail of splinters and dust.

The moments of weightlessness drove a spike into Edwin's thoughts, his throat closing up and his awareness beginning to dim. His breath grew ragged and the death grip he had on his foe weakened, the two of them separating from each other. The only thing keeping Edwin awake as the absolute *terror* of falling kicked into gear was a single-minded pursuit of trying desperately to get some semblance of support, and he made *darn well sure* he stayed above Niall as they went tumbling.

Then gravity reasserted itself as they both crashed into the floor below, pulling both figures into a limp pile.

At first, as Edwin tenderly extracted himself from above and around the broken body of Niall, he thought he might have killed the Alchemist, but for better or worse, broken bones began to set themselves and bloody cuts on the man's face slowly started to heal.

No fair, Edwin groaned to himself, *I want a healing factor.*

Still, while Niall's body may have been on the mend, it was still fairly helpless, which gave Edwin plenty of time to shackle the mad Alchemist in the same chains he likely had imprisoned many of his victims in over time. It was … appropriate, he supposed, and he grinned.

They'd made a fair bit of commotion, all told, and Edwin considered himself fortunate that apparently the minions were either too used to or too oblivious toward (or maybe both) loud crashes to come investigate. Or perhaps they were just instructed to never come upstairs no matter what? Ah, no matter. What was important was that Edwin had a chance to catch his breath as Niall slowly regenerated, stuck inside his manacles. A passing thought also got Edwin to modify his level-up template slightly, to help his sense of progress until he'd have enough for all his Paths to be completed. Was it the best timing? Eh, not really. But it wasn't hard, either.

Level Up!
Skill Points 399→404
Progress to Tier 2: 628/1590
Athletics Level 27→30
Flexibility Level 23→25

Perfect. He couldn't help but groan at seeing just how far he was away from his goal, though. At least, given how high level some of his Tier 2 Skills were, it should be a lot easier next time. Still, even with all his already-advanced Skills counted, he was only a third of the way to his goal, meaning he'd need to raise most of his current Skills to level 90 … He wasn't looking forward to it, but that was a worry for later.

A bit more digging around revealed three more sets of chains and shackles, which would be a slight problem. He wasn't sure what to do once all the minions were incapacitated, though maybe he'd be able to chain them together in some way? That was for Future-Edwin, once he had actually subdued the bandits.

Edwin tapped his fingers against his knee in thought. A modern chem lab would be a godsend right now, but he didn't have that, and likely never would. But he *did* have a plan. Make something to knock out the minions. He had half an hour at most before he ran the risk of Niall waking up, getting his gag out, and yelling for help.

Ha, it's just p-chem lab all over again. I can do this, he thought in triumph.

Thoughts and ideas flooded to him, and while he wasn't sure *where* the inspirations had come from, they paired wonderfully with the strange not-memories his Alchemy Skill was telling him that he wouldn't have to deal with, situations like a certain chemical having specific effects and a very similar chemical possibly having radically different effects.

No, Alchemy worked in broader categories. Something that worked on the body, if combined with something else, would still work on the body, just perhaps with a different effect. That meant his salve, tuned as it was to act on humans, meant he already had about a third of a knockout formula done. The next third would be something with the "sleep" association, and the final third would be figuring out how to combine them.

Edwin breathed out, trying to stay calm. Okay. His experience experimenting with mortar told him that physical laws still had some byplay in Alchemy, which meant he shouldn't have to figure out how to incorporate "the notes of a lullaby" into a potion. That was firmly in Alchymie Ascendia's wheelhouse, anyway, and effectiveness aside, he had no hope of pulling something like that off, something no amount of confidence or inspiration would change.

First Aid might help him here, actually. Memory vaguely told him it had something pertaining to … quick dealing with wounds? Anesthesia totally counted, or at least it should.

That would mean Edwin's creation wouldn't need to be perfect, and that his Skills could bridge the rest of the way. He flipped through the

Grimoire quickly, trying to get some idea of what he might be able to use for a second component to render into something that would create disorientation or unconsciousness. He didn't need to get the bandits fully under if he could disable them first; what could he …

Alcohol. Of course. Okay, now to try and find some.

A bit of digging around helped Edwin find several coils of rope (that would be useful later on), an iron ball with a hole through the middle, a few steel bars of varying lengths and thicknesses, and gloves! They didn't seem to be made of tanned human skin, so he could use them without guilt.

A couple extra sets of black robes, some tinder, flint, and steel, not to mention a huge variety of glassware, also turned up, though it all was of debatable usefulness to Edwin. There were tons of potions and … ingredients of arguable sourcing, but the mere thought of making something out of dismembered people sent shivers down Edwin's spine.

Even if he had time, there was no way he'd be making something with *this* lab setup. The notes might be worth saving, as a memorial to those who'd given their lives for research, but Edwin wouldn't touch them, and he wouldn't entrust them to anyone else. No, as much as it pained him in principle, the notes would burn as well … after he plundered their contents for Almanac, anyway.

He also found the second balcony! It was on the opposite side of the tower from the first one, and here on the dissection floor, but it was nice to put that mystery to rest. Looking out from it had no strange mental or optical effects insomuch as Edwin could tell, but it was a medium-sized outcropping, protruding about five feet from the outer wall, about ten feet from one end to the other.

The supports on the stone handrailing seemed vaguely … Ah, if Edwin had ever bothered to pay attention in his arts classes he might remember what style they reminded him of, but why would he? His grade in that class had gone *up* after he stopped paying attention, bless open-book tests and quizzes. But that was neither here nor there. It *did* however give him a further idea how to take care of Minsix, or whoever was on watch at the moment.

Okay, he was getting distracted. He'd found a bottle of something that smelled like wine on an end table out on the balcony, and that was good enough for him. He grabbed the bottle, consulted the *Grimoire* (there was an entire section detailing how to make alchemical alcohol, of course), and grabbed a clean-looking alembic, a fairly intricate piece in all honesty with some really cool (heh, puns) features. Edwin didn't have time to get too fancy at the moment, though, so he just emptied most of the bottle into the glassware and put it onto a stand, with the feed emptying into a small bowl.

It was basic, but it would work. To speed up the distillation, Edwin stopped his mad rush around to take the time to fill the glass bowl atop the condensation bulb with some ice water (how Niall got ice or kept it cold, Edwin couldn't tell, but the box he had found it in didn't seem to light up to his mana sense much at all).

Ten seconds later, Edwin had a decent flame going, but he had to be careful to not overheat the mixture, or else it would all evaporate instead of just the alcohol, and he'd need to do another round of distillation. While it was heating, he flipped through the *Grimoire* to see if there was anything that might help.

A certain herb caught his eye—it was a grass (seagrass, specifically) that, when dried in a very particular way, would absorb water, and *only* water. It also "tainted, like the Sea for whence it is named, the waters upon which it is added to" but Edwin didn't see that as too much of an issue at the moment. Even better, Niall *had* some of the stuff (it was very distinctive), though not much. It was brittle yet soft, and Edwin seriously wanted to study it, but it didn't stop him from lining his distillation bowl with the stuff, which already had a few drops of liquid in it.

Huh.

That was *really* fast. Were his Skills helping this in some invisible way? If so, awesome. Anyway, while his setup was running, Edwin continued his mad scramble to prepare everything.

He weighed the possibility of using one of the iron bars in place of his stick (and a more combat-ready dagger he uncovered in his search) as his weapon, but decided against it. No, that would be too lethal, and he wasn't there quite yet. Actually … he *did* have a use for one of the bars. Sure, his potion *should* disable the minions, but did he really want to count entirely on that? Ha. He grabbed one bar of medium length and thickness, tying a knot at a right angle to the bar around its center, then tied the other end to one shackle in a manacle.

You have unlocked the Knot-Work Skill!
Accept Skill? Y/N

Shush. Disable again.

A bit of testing showed the knot should hold. Okay, if that worked, that would take care of one minion and would use one shackle. Then, he'd have to subdue four more with two manacles. His primary advantages would be surprise and that he was armed, while the bandits tended to leave their weapons on the first floor when in the tower. Didn't seem that smart to him, but hey, what did he know? Maybe their brawls got out of hand when they were armed or something.

His bowl had accumulated a few ounces of distilled alcohol, as a quick whiff would confirm, and his seagrass seemed to be at capacity. This next part would be crucial, and all he had to rely on here was Alchemy itself. *Not ideal, but here we go.*

Edwin took a small scoop of his healing salve from its ceramic tub and placed it into a tiny mixing bowl, then poured in his alcohol. Stir, provide a bit of heat, release the heat, stir vigorously, apply a hint of flame directly to—wait, what? Please don't explode—the solution, let the puff of smoke dissipate. Oh man, that made him woozy.

A few deep breaths in the open air of the balcony (Niall hadn't woken up yet, fortunately, though his wounds seemed to have largely healed) cleared his head, and Edwin took a clean cloth and wiped up the solution into a rag, which he stuffed into his belt. If it worked as well on them as even a bare whiff of the stuff had done for him, he might be able to well push the minions over, one by one.

A peek downstairs showed that the minions had finished cleaning up from dinner and had returned downstairs to their quarters. With a bit of straining, Edwin heard some fairly loud discussion, perhaps as they quarreled over something. Still, it was quiet enough, and he crept down the stairs, trying to balance not being heard with not seeming like he was trying not to be heard.

As Edwin ventured to the balcony, he kept his not-chloroform in one hand, and his hastily assembled rope-and-chain contraption in the other. Minsix was leaning against the side of the outer wall, eyes closed and rhythmically breathing, and Edwin smiled a grim smile. It would make this next part a lot easier, though he'd still need to— Oh shoot, Minsix was waking up.

Okay, think fast. Edwin was crouched on the floor right next to the bandit's ankle, with a manacle in one hand and his rag in the other. His brain short-circuited, and following some muscle memory that wasn't his, his arm snapped out, hastily connecting the manacle to Minsix's ankle. That was ... strange. But not unwelcome.

Just as he finished connecting the minion to a literal anchor, the Bandit Club-Wielder finished waking up. "Huh? What'cha doin there?"

Edwin's panicked brain continued to be frozen over, a thousand clever quips instantly fleeing as soon as he had the chance for an amazing one-liner, alongside his actual *plan*. Instead, all thoughts of stealthily applying the knockout potion, or finessing the rag up to his opponent's face disappeared, and he just tried tackling the hulking minion (though in truth Edwin was about the same height, possibly even taller than the bandit, it didn't feel like it), his shoulder digging into the man's chest and ... doing nothing against the unyielding strength of the man's torso.

He narrowed his eyes. He could do this.

CHAPTER 42

Hitting the Bars

Edwin rapidly backed up, trying to get out of reach of Minsix.

"What was that for, huh?" he demanded. "If ya wanted ta fight ya coulda jus asked."

Edwin stayed quiet, not wanting to give the actual answer and potentially provoke the minion, but not able to come up with a clever lie, either. His brain may have been doing better, but it still wasn't great.

Lingering effects of inhaling the potion's smoke, perhaps? Well, he could still fight, at least. Edwin grabbed his iron bar and tried to quickly jab the man's chin with it, but the bandit blocked the attack, disarmed him, and grabbed his hand before he could properly react.

Edwin gritted his teeth in frustration. The outlaw started to say something, but Edwin wasn't listening. Instead, he twisted and dropped down, trying to leverage his miserable body weight to knock Minsix off his balance. Surprisingly, it *worked*, and Edwin felt his body respond easily to his commands, though the bandit was still in play.

Edwin landed within reach of his anchor bar and he snatched it back up again. Yes, it was perhaps more lethal than he would have normally liked, but better than nothing, especially given how close he would need to get in order to use his knockout potion, to say nothing of whether or not it would actually work.

With a quick yank on the rope attached to the bandit's ankle, Edwin was able to unbalance Minsix as he raised a foot to try and pin Edwin to the ground. Instead, the bandit nearly toppled over himself, grabbing on to part of the balcony railing to prevent falling on top of Edwin.

Edwin, for his part, scrambled to his feet and tried to swing his bar at Minsix's head, but the man raised his forearm to protect his vulnerable neck. Edwin recognized a Skill of some sort being activated as the arm snapped in place slightly. The iron rod struck ... and harmlessly rebounded off the activation. While it didn't quite leave a stinging vibration in the metal, it was close. As Edwin struggled to maintain his grip on the bar, he took a punch straight to the face, cracking his nose and sending blood cascading into his slightly open mouth.

Edwin's neck snapped back painfully, and he set his mouth into a tight line to prevent any more of his blood from running in. Taking a step back, he started blinking to try and clear his vision before a second blow could land. He partially succeeded, though another punch hit his upper chest, sending him reeling back directly into the doorframe, where his head cracked into the stone wall, with less pain than he had been anticipating.

Edwin raised his iron bar into a guard stance, holding it like a quarterstaff. His grip was hampered slightly by trying to keep a grip on his rag, but he was not about to let that fall. He may not have too much training with the stick, but he knew enough for his superior Alchemy Skills to come into play. He was so confident, and he knew he could *act* on that confidence.

Minsix was trying to break the rope connecting him to Edwin's bar, but a quick *thwack* with the iron stick put a stop to that before he could make much headway. That, in turn, prompted a retaliatory wild punch, but just poking the bandit in the chest with his iron bar, keeping him at bay, was enough to get him to switch to defense. Okay, now it was just a waiting game until Edwin got the right opening, and then he could strike.

Yeah, yeah. His confidence was back, he could *absolutely* do this.

Minsix took a couple of steps back, until he was up against the railing and could no longer retreat.

Perfect.

Edwin made sure Minsix wasn't able to regain his stance, keeping the bandit out of reach with the additional length provided by his iron club, and occupying him with the need to constantly fend off strikes with his Defensive Skill. When Minsix started trying to block the blows instead of evading them, Edwin knew he'd have to switch things up.

Edwin jabbed the center of Minsix's torso with the end of his bar, twisting it enough to actually connect. That attack bought him just enough time to slip the bar over the railing and between two of the supports. From there, it was just a matter of firmly yanking on the rope to break the minion's footing.

While less successful than the previous attempt, in part because the bandit was ready for it, it was still enough to get a bit of room to maneuver, and as Minsix cast his attention to trying to regain his footing with a sudden stomp—some Skill was being activated, according to Identify and Almanac—Edwin's off hand finally closed in enough to hold the rag open over the bandit's nose and mouth, exposing him full-force to alchemically potent alcohol vapors.

There was a moment when Edwin wasn't sure if his creation actually did anything, and he had the horrifying thought that he might have practically killed himself with his overconfidence. Then, as he watched the bandit stagger back, he grinned. Before Minsix could recover his bearings against the railing, Edwin pulled out his final weapon—the iron ball, strung around his shoulder by a length of rope—and threw it as hard as his Skill-assisted attack would allow. It struck the bandit at the dead center of his chest, overbalancing the somewhat drunk, partially conscious, and *very* loopy man, sending him slowly toppling over the railing.

Edwin stared at the sight through blurry vision, until a jolt ripped his melee weapon from his hand, the rope going taut in an instant as the manacle it was tied to, and the bandit *that* was attached to, fell down the side of the tower. The bar did its job perfectly as it clanged to the floor and raced to the edge of the railing, halting the fall of the bandit.

Looking over the edge (and a bit of effort clearing his vision) showed Minsix exactly where Edwin had wanted him, dangling from a single leg (ooh, that looked like it hurt) like a piñata. The rope didn't appear as though it was about to give way, and the bandit probably had enough of a supernatural physique that hanging upside down for a while wouldn't kill him. He was limp (and quiet) enough that Edwin probably wouldn't have to deal with him for the moment, at least.

Never mind that he had no clue how long the bandit would be out, how effective the knockout potion was, nor how hard it would be to do the same against the others. Not to mention whether or not Minsix would survive hanging upside down for however long he'd be there (people could survive like that for a few hours, right? Edwin vaguely recalled some roller coaster or something that got stuck on the top of a loop). Anyway, not thinking about that. He would deal with Minsix later.

Edwin didn't have *too* much time; the longer he took, the more likely it was that the other minions would come and investigate. Hmm, actually, if they weren't already here, he might have time. In any case, his first order of business was fixing himself up.

Digging out what was left of his tub of healing salve, Edwin applied a few dabs of the substance to his broken nose, flinching as the affected area heated suddenly and a few quiet cracks reverberated through his skull. Before he could properly process what had happened, however, the process was finished and more ginger touching of the base of his nose yielded no additional pain.

A couple additional dabs were applied to the back of his head and to his ribs, where a bruise was already starting to form. As he watched, the bruise quickly faded, not even going through its typical cycle of turning purple, just … vanishing.

Huh. So then, the salve wasn't just creating blood? He hadn't *really* thought about it when applying it to his broken nose, but Edwin had vaguely theorized that the salve functioned akin to a pluripotent stem cell, creating replicants of whatever it was exposed to. That would explain the rapid healing of cuts and to a lesser extent the healing of burns, as well as why a nonprimed salve might do nothing, or kill the patient—if it targeted bacteria, that could absolutely have no or few detrimental effects, but … making blood appear locally wouldn't make a bruise vanish like *that*.

"Further testing required." It had been a while since Edwin had found something he'd need to look into later, but he made a note with

Almanac on the salve to investigate its properties later on as he stashed it back in its pouch.

A quick peek over the side—Minsix was still hanging limply, though not without breathing—reassured Edwin his contraption was functioning as intended, and, after a brief trip upstairs to grab a few coils of rope and a new iron bar, as well as recovering his iron ball from where it had rolled off to, he strode down the stairs.

Mintwo and Minthree were in the living room, throwing dice on the table, playing some kind of betting game. Meanwhile, Minfour slept on a pad off in the corner. The two minions barely even glanced at Edwin as he entered the room, not noticing his iron bar, potion-soaked rag, iron ball, open manacles, or even the lengths of rope loosely coiled around his arms. They must have been *really* engrossed in their game to miss all the commotion upstairs. Surely they weren't *that* deaf, right? Ah, no matter. With a deep breath, Edwin finished descending the stairs and threw his iron ball as hard as he could.

Mintwo had no time to react as Edwin's thrown attack collided firmly with the bandit's shoulder, sending him sprawling and the ball rolling to some far corner of the room. Edwin felt like he had a decent grasp of the minions' combat capabilities at this point. They seemed to have a fair number of active powers—like Block or Knockback Blow, as he thought of them—but other than some kind of generic Toughness Skill (or was it the Health Attribute?), they didn't have much to help against surprise attacks.

Before Mintwo could recover, Edwin pounced on him, pushing the bandit toward his sleeping compatriot and pulling out a manacle. With his other hand, he tried holding his rag against the man's face, but found he couldn't hold it steady enough as the bandit started trying to shake Edwin off. He still managed to quickly snap one side of his manacles shut on Mintwo's wrist, fortunately, but before he could close the other end on Minfour, Minthree grabbed Edwin's ankle and yanked him off his compatriot, flinging Edwin across the room.

Edwin was exceedingly thankful he had taken the time to heal himself before engaging these bandits. It also felt like it might have strengthened him in some way, as his body responded *instantly*. He didn't even properly process what happened, but he landed on his feet next to the wall, just in time to fend off a swinging manacle still attached to the wrist of Mintwo. Edwin managed to block the swinging chain before it struck his head, but the other shackle clicked closed.

Great. That would be way more annoying to attach now.

Fortunately, positioned as he was beneath the stairs, Minthree wasn't able to effectively approach Edwin. *Un*fortunately, he ran down the stairs leading to the ground floor instead. Edwin didn't know *why* exactly, but the options basically amounted to him getting Minfive or retrieving his weapons. Maybe both. No time to worry about that, as Minfour was also rousing himself from his nap on the floor, meaning he'd soon have to deal with three, possibly four minions simultaneously.

Edwin's confidence waned even as his position firmed up. He was suddenly very doubtful that this was a good idea, but he couldn't back down now. Still, he felt so *alive*. Blood poured through his veins, filling him with adrenaline, strength, and clarity.

Granted, that clarity was primarily centered on the fact that he was an idiot. But he was also an idiot that could probably still manage this; he'd just … Hmm. He'd need to immobilize the minions for a second or two, that was all.

Edwin pulled a coil of rope from his forearm and held it in his off hand, trying to use it as something of a makeshift cloak or shield. Between that and his staff, Edwin felt decently confident facing the unarmed minion, though not too optimistic about his chances if Minfour finished blinking the sleep from his eyes, or if Minfive or Minthree showed up. Until then, though, he had range, which was *everything* in a brawl. Mintwo couldn't get too close without inviting a rod to the face. He chanced it, though, and Edwin retaliated with a wallop as hard as he could manage, the end of his bar solidly colliding with the bandit's jaw.

It barely did anything. A bit of blood trickled from the corner of the minion's mouth, perhaps a bit of broken skin on the chin where Edwin had struck, but nothing else. Shoot. So much for no passive enhancements; Edwin was convinced that blow would have at the minimum broken a normal human's jaw, if not worse.

As Mintwo tried to pull Edwin into a grapple, Edwin used his bar as a forced spacer, bracing it against the stairs to give him the leverage required, but as the bandit tried to lunge at Edwin, saying something

Edwin tuned out, he slipped off to the side altogether, removing all resistance.

The unexpected loss of resistance sent the minion stumbling forward, which in turn gave Edwin the chance to release the coil of rope from his grip and toss it over Mintwo's head. A yank on the cord drew the loops tight, pulling the bandit off his attack and holding him still, hopefully long enough.

While he had to contend with the flailing attacks of Mintwo, Edwin dropped his stick and pulled his rag open. In his position hanging solidly onto the man's back, keeping what was almost a noose tight across his throat, he was able to hold the rag in place … Come on, it was almost there … just a second now. …

He breathed a sigh of relief as Mintwo stopped struggling, slumping instead into unconsciousness.

He didn't have any time to celebrate, though, as Minfour was on Edwin, and he barely had time to kick his stick away before his new opponent could grab it himself. He ducked and rolled, getting away before the minion could grab him. He cast a wary gaze at his foe. He'd need to keep Minfour occupied, so he couldn't untie Mintwo, and hopefully even take out the bandit before Minthree could return with Minfive.

Edwin sighed as he recovered his bar, massaging his potion rag (was it getting drier?) to reassure himself that he could still manage this.

The easy part was over.

CHAPTER 43

Sticking Around

Edwin once again mentally berated himself for trying to fight, let alone in melee. He was *not* cut out for this in the slightest. He didn't have the Skills (or skills) for it, wasn't as strong as his opponents, and that opened him up to way too many retaliatory attacks. He wasn't sure why he had thought this was a good idea—though he felt a faint suspicion it was Skill-provoked somehow.

As it turned out, a few days of training from Lefi and about two weeks and a few weekends on Earth spent learning about fencing was no substitute for actual combat experience and System assistance.

Next iteration of the sleep potion would be a bomb. That way, he could benefit from Bomb Throwing, Throwing Weapons, *and* Alchemy all at the same time! Pity he didn't have anything that he could have … Okay, so he probably could have made the potion into a bomb by putting it into a glass bottle and sealing it.

But then he'd only get one shot—literally—and he needed to take down way more than one foe. Until he could prepare actual weapons (next time, he promised himself), Edwin would stick to doing what seemed to work best, throwing random stuff and hoping it worked out.

It was still annoying that throwing wooden dice at Minfour was more effective than smacking him with what basically amounted to a baseball bat, though.

Having snatched the tiny cubes off the table, Edwin sent them flying at the bandit, aiming at his eyes and face with what he felt was surprising accuracy. The assistance that Throwing Weapons provided still hadn't fully sunk in to his new "normal," it seemed. Each time, the minion was forced to raise a hand to block the attack, letting Edwin slip a bit farther away. Now that he had made it onto the stairs, Minfour kept trying to climb up after him, but Edwin was more or less successfully keeping him at bay.

A spark of inspiration struck Edwin as he threw his tenth die—only two left—and he uncoiled a length of rope from his forearm. The next time Minfour tried to climb the stairs, Edwin tossed the rope at him, easily ensnaring his head with the tangles of woven cord. From there, the next step was easy! Totally easy. He didn't need to hesitate. *Do it, Edwin!*

It's really cruel, though, he couldn't help but think. *Also really dangerous. What if—*

The delay meant that Minfour had enough time to untangle his head from the rope, and he started pulling on it, trying to get Edwin to release it or be pulled down the stairs. Edwin's eleventh die got Minfour to pause for a moment, but no longer. It was long enough for Edwin to get over his hesitation, at least, and he assessed the situation. Minfour had wrapped the coils of cord around his arms and was grasping it all firmly, insistently yanking on the whole thing. It wasn't ideal, but ... it would do. This time, Edwin didn't wait. With a deep breath, he let loose.

Firestarting.

Minfour swore profusely as the rope he had so firmly wrapped around his arms erupted into flames. No doubt traumatized by the last time Edwin had set him on fire, he tried to release the burning rope like it was a live snake, but that did little for the lengths he had already bound to himself.

Pieces fell to the stairs, and Edwin made sure to deactivate his Skill before the tower caught on fire. Wouldn't do to get that going too soon. It did nothing for the already-burning rope (and minion), but hopefully it would prevent the wooden interior from igniting.

Minfour, by the time he escaped from his fiery bindings, already had fairly severe burns on his palms and forearms. Edwin grimaced, but threw his final die at the bandit. On instinct—no, it was some sort of Skill that compelled the action, Edwin could finally tell; it was too sudden, too involuntary to have been anything else—the man raised a burned hand to intercept the projectile, but was unprepared for the explosion of pain that came from the tiny, wooden object bursting a fairly sizable blister and becoming lodged inside the wound.

He howled in agony, and it was enough for Edwin, who took the opportunity to jump, kneeing Minfour in the face as he hurtled past the man, landing with a stumble on the floor below. He didn't stop there, though, using the minion's momentary stumble as a chance to grab the man's face with his rag.

Before the bandit could properly orient himself, the potion did its job and Minfour toppled backward and slammed into the stairs with such force that Edwin half expected the boards to give way. The sickening sound—*crack!*—wasn't from the wood, though, and Edwin couldn't bring himself to look at first, though he couldn't avert his gaze forever. When he finally did chance a glance, he saw the bandit lying unconscious on the floor below where he had fallen off the steps, arm at an angle Edwin knew it wasn't supposed to be.

He had a moment to spare, so Edwin withdrew the key for the manacles from his belt pouch and chained the two fallen minions together. Minfour's broken arm should even help in keeping them disabled, as presumably Mintwo would be hesitant to cause too much pain to his friend to try to fight or move quickly.

Edwin didn't have time to admire his handiwork as he stomped out one patch of the floor still smoldering from where burning rope had fallen on it. No sooner had he managed to do so, however, than the descending stairs started to squeak and tremble as Minfive and Minthree barreled up them.

As he had more or less adequate warning, Edwin was able to prepare a bit of an ambush. He dove to the floor, and as Minthree's head poked above the floorboards, Edwin barely managed to wrap the rag around the bandit's face and hold tight before the man's momentum continued, carrying him forward regardless of Edwin's presence, and he was yanked from his position out into thin air. Edwin briefly fought back the panic that the free fall brought about and scrambled to try and recover his footing, unintentionally kicking Minfive in the face.

The kick didn't seem to bother the minion at all, but it did give Edwin enough of a foothold to finish knocking out Minthree, and as the bandit slumped against Edwin, he sidestepped to avoid having to take the whole weight of the man against him, shoving the bandit backward as he scrambled up the steps. It was just in time, too, as Minfive had recovered from Edwin's kick and was winding his club up to try and knock Edwin out. However, the way Minthree fell meant that Minfive had to quickly redirect his attack into the side of the tower, an insanely strong blow that Edwin could feel reverberate through the building.

In a display of speed that Edwin had trouble keeping up with, Minfive released his club as it rebounded against the wall, letting it fly into the air, as he reached Minthree, gently setting the Outlaw Laborer down on the stairs, and caught his club as it fell. Edwin had no *clue* what sort of Skill had to have been involved in that, but it must have been something impressive. Minfive barely even slowed as he stepped over his fallen ally, coming after Edwin with a murderous glare in his eyes.

The Elite Bandit Bodyguard bounded up the stairs and doubled back around to face Edwin in an instant. He said something, but Edwin tuned him out. That was apparently the wrong move, as when Edwin didn't respond, he bellowed in rage and brought his club around in a devastating swing.

Edwin raised his stick to try and block it, but the blow knocked it clear from his grip and across the room, then continued on its trajectory. Edwin felt a rib crack as the club connected with his side, sending pain lancing through his entire torso and knocking Edwin into the wall. He narrowly avoided falling into the stairwell, but revised that assessment as he saw Minfive winding up an attack aimed at bringing down his club onto Edwin's head.

A quick contortion had Edwin dropping onto the stairs below, the sudden stop as he landed hard on the steps renewing waves of agony from his injuries. He cut a hasty retreat downstairs as he fumbled to pull out his healing salve while simultaneously trying to keep his rag on hand. He failed and had to shove his potion cloth into his pocket before he was able to turn his attention toward tugging his shirt loose and applying the paste where the pain was most acute. He managed to get the lid back onto the tub before his fingers, slippery with sweat and salve, let the precious medicine slide from his grip, the ceramic container bouncing downstairs step by step.

He'd Infused the container through Packing, which was likely the only reason it didn't break, but it still was firmly out of his both literal and metaphorical grasp. He hastily tried to retrieve it, but he wasn't able to stow it again before Minfive was behind him. A haphazard toss of a small length of cord got Edwin mere seconds as the bandit hit it from the air like a baseball. Okay, it seemed he'd have to do some quick thinking.

The first floor of the tower was strewn with random rubble: broken lumber, piles of discarded cloth, a twisted tangle of lightly rusting but very pointy metal, and some rocks. Edwin wasn't sure where the rocks had come from—the tower walls, perhaps? There weren't any obvious holes, but that didn't matter too much at the moment.

He swept over to the pile and slipped his healing salve into a pocket before picking up a pair of rocks, throwing them as hard as he could at Minfive. Packing helped, he could tell; he wouldn't have been able to lift such heavy stones without it, but the real benefit came from his Throwing Weapons Skill, which helped guide each of the sizable rocks toward his target. One was swept aside by Minfive's club, but the other struck the bandit's shoulder ... and left no obvious injuries. His arm barely even moved. Great.

Edwin grabbed two more stones, each slightly smaller than a volleyball, and threw one underhanded, the other overhanded, as though he were playing dodgeball and was trying to sneak a hit in. Minfive's club blurred, and shattered the overhand throw, the bandit closing his eyes to endure the spray of stone fragments. His club moved on its own in an attempt to block the arcing underhand toss, but it missed, the stone colliding with his outstretched arm and forcing it to buckle. Okay, so Minfive wasn't invincible. That was good. If Edwin were to hazard a guess based on his Class, perhaps his Skills were more effective while trying to directly protect others? If so, that would explain his uncharacteristic display of speed when catching Minthree.

Minfive took a second to wipe the dust from his eyes, which Edwin did not waste. By the time he had finished, Edwin had scooped up two handfuls of small pebbles, throwing them like they were scattershot at the bandit. Minfive's club wasn't able to block all of the rocks—it tried snapping to one at a time instead of sweeping aside all of them—and a few connected with his face, blinding him once more.

What Edwin really needed to do was try to use his rag once more; he'd had luck with it so far, but getting close enough to manage that would be … problematic. Edwin grabbed another handful of the stones and started circling Minfive, trying to get back to the stairs. Going back up held a lot of potential, after all.

Shut up. No more jokes. I need to focus.

The next time Edwin tried to blind the minion, he had already grown wise to the tactic, closing his eyes the moment Edwin started his throw. Fortunately, Edwin was able to react quickly enough to delay his actual attack for a second, long enough for Minfive to suspect a feint and reopen his eyes just in time for Edwin's projectiles to connect, eliciting a new string of cursing from the bandit as he wiped his eyes once more.

With his last handful of pebbles, Edwin truly did feint his attack, and the bandit shielded his eyes with his hand, abandoning his two-handed grip on his club. That still obscured his vision, though, and was even better for making it hard to defend from Edwin's true attack, a high-speed rock hastily retrieved from a nearby rubble pile. The projectile smashed into Minfive's hand, actually leaving a visible mark as a pointed corner of the stone tore open some skin on the back of his hand. It wasn't much, but it was a start.

At this point, Edwin had finally managed to reposition himself such that he was at the bottom of the stairs, and after throwing his last blinding attack—Minfive blocked it by shielding his eyes with his hand—he darted up the steps. Minthree was starting to stir, but Edwin solidly stomped on his face as he passed, and the bandit slumped back into unconsciousness, blood trickling from his nose.

Edwin's thoughts raced as Minfive clomped up the stairs behind him. He'd only have a single chance to make any of this work, and as he reached the top, he realized he'd already missed his chance. Minfive had jumped over the body of Minthree and was just mere steps behind Edwin, eagerly reaching out to try and snag Edwin's jacket.

In response, Edwin drew his knife, rubbed it with what was left of his sleeping potion and threw it, the weapon traveling mere inches through the air before it pierced the bandit's outstretched hand, the steel tip embedding itself firmly into the soft skin on his palm.

To his credit, Minfive didn't immediately cry out in pain, though the sleeping potion may have numbed it. He did, however, unleash a dreadful tirade of cursing as he shook his hand in an attempt to dislodge the offending weapon. He didn't succeed, though *why* Edwin wasn't sure. Did the blood form a seal, or was there enough residual healing effect from his potion to heal the wound around the blade? Something else?

Minfive removed the source of his agony, pulling it free in a single strained motion, which prompted another stream of profanity. By necessity he had to release his club and let it clatter to the floor below, both hands occupied as they were. He swayed unsteadily as he seemed to fight against the effects of the sedative, which gave Edwin just enough of a window.

Edwin didn't waste his opportunity, and while his potion rag no longer functioned, he hefted the heaviest thing he was able to find on short notice—the iron ball he had used to such great effect thus far, looped around a leg of the table—and slammed the entire contraption as hard as he could into Minfive's head.

The bandit fell backward, his foot coming to rest on Minthree's body. The step he was on creaked ominously, but before it could settle or Minfive could recover, Edwin threw his entire makeshift weapon at the pair. It slammed into Minfive's body, and the sudden force proved too great for the precarious stairway, and the wood gave way, sending the two bandits plummeting to the floor below.

In most circumstances, Edwin wouldn't trust the mere ten-foot fall to take them out, but specifically where they were ... Peeking over the edge, he saw them both lying lifelessly on the pile of scrap metal and discarded weapons. What appeared to be the tines of a pitchfork had pierced Minfive's chest, while Minthree's neck had been split open by a rusted ... plow, perhaps? Besides, the man's skull was half crushed by the iron ball, even as the bandit himself was nearly decapitated by the metal blade.

Edwin looked away, fighting not to lose his dinner at the sight. He couldn't help but grimly think that at least his manacle situation was simpler now. He breathed out, trying to clear his head, and drank deeply from his canteen while the thrill of battle faded from his body.

The tower fell silent, the only noise the pained breathing and whimpering of his surviving victims.

CHAPTER 44

The Aftermath, Now Addition-Free!

Level Up!
Skill Points 404→417
Progress to Tier 2: 635/1590
Alchemy Level 46→51
Athletics Level 30→33
Firestarting Level 37→38
First Aid Level 26→28
Flexibility Level 27→30
Outsider's Almanac Level 77→78
Packing Level 17→18
Congratulations! For slaying a foe stronger than you, you have unlocked the Giant Slayer Path!
Congratulations! For successfully defeating the bandits led by the Catabolic Alchemist, you have unlocked the Superior Alchemist Path!
Congratulations! For ousting its previous inhabitants, you have unlocked the Master of the Ruined Tower Path!

Edwin unsteadily rose to his feet from his slumped position, his to-do list running through his mind across a backdrop of how much of an idiot he was for even starting all this. Seriously, what was he thinking? He must need more sleep. Anyway, he needed to cut down

Minsix, check up on Niall, and chain up all the bandits somewhere they couldn't get away from. Then, he needed to somehow get the si— four of them to … whatever that town was, about a day's walk from here. He doubted they'd go willingly, so he'd probably have to drag them along and it would be a whole hassle … He'd deal with that later.

For now, he'd just gather them all up and figure out how to keep them from running away while he slept.

Minsix was thoroughly unconscious, hanging limply from one leg, but he *was* alive, and Edwin, after a brief attempt to haul the man back up to the balcony, just cut the line and let him fall the last little bit onto the mounds of ivy coating the hill. Once on the ground, the man lay limp and unmoving, and it was only Edwin's supernatural Seeing Skill that allowed him to see the man's chest slowly rise and fall, reassuring him that the bandit hadn't been killed in the fall.

Getting down the tower was a challenge Edwin hadn't entirely anticipated. His … defeat of Minfive and Minthree had left some three steps missing from near the top of the final landing, and Edwin now trusted the strength of the surviving stairs even less.

Still, he was able to just drop down from the hole in the floor onto the steps to bypass the problem altogether, though he couldn't see how his prisoners would do it. Would he have to carry them down? Ugh. There were so many logistical problems involved with taking prisoners. They'd just be executed anyway, he was sure. But he didn't want to be the one who actually wielded the executioner's axe.

Was he being silly, and should he just grit his teeth and kill them anyway? Probably. But he resisted the part of himself that advocated for just killing them all now. He'd taken … most of them alive, after all, and he couldn't say he particularly *wanted* to kill helpless prisoners.

Outside the tower, Edwin knelt by Minsix's thoroughly unconscious body, looking at how flushed the bandit's face was after hanging upside down for … ten minutes? Not very long, at least, though he didn't know how long exactly. He removed the shackle from around the man's ankle, transferring the manacle to his wrists. With a heave, he picked up the *really heavy* minion, straining not quite as much as he had anticipated—

Level Up!
Skill Points 417→418
Progress to Tier 2: 636/1590
Packing Level 18→19

—Ah, that made sense. Still, hauling Minsix back inside wasn't easy, magical enhancements or no, but he accomplished it. Edwin dropped the limp body near the center of the first floor, fastening the chain so his prisoner was wrapped around a support post, then, as a last bit of extra precaution, bound the man's ankles in several coils of rope as well.

Before Edwin returned upstairs, a thought struck him, and he gathered up all the weapons from where they were stashed near the door, dumped them outside, and set them on fire. He couldn't use them, and it didn't make sense to leave the clubs (why did they all use clubs? Ah, wait, it probably had something to do with trying to not make their victims bleed too much, didn't it?) in a usable state.

Level Up!
Skill Points 418→420
Progress to Tier 2: 637/1590
Firestarting Level 38→39
Mana Infusion Level 62→63

Okay, the Skill Points had seemed like a good idea at first, but now it was just getting annoying. With a quick mental flex, Edwin changed it so they would only display if he had at least three different Skills leveling up. Anyway, with that taken care of, Edwin hopped up the steps to find Niall.

The bandit Alchemist was pretending to be unconscious as Edwin came up the stairs, but Edwin wasn't buying it, given he was in a completely different position compared to before. "I know you're awake."

Niall didn't respond, and Edwin belatedly remembered to pull the gag he had made for the Alchemist off, cutting the cloth that was holding it in place.

Niall spat out the fabric in his mouth. "Did you have to? Tha' tasted *foul.*"

Edwin shrugged. "I couldn't have you warning your men."

The bandit leader sighed in resignation. "Well, you got me, then. This day was always going to come, wasn' it?" Niall stopped for a moment, before quietly asking, "I suppose they're all dead now?"

Edwin shook his head. "Just ... Minfive and Minthree. Even they weren't entirely intentional. I'm not like you; I won't just kill whoever just because it's convenient," he insisted, trying to convince himself as much as Niall.

Niall turned away, his voice filled with sadness. "Minthree was with me for two months. The lad had barely broken free, an' now he's gone. Are you content with yourself?"

Edwin felt his emotions try to take over, but locked away his empathy for the serial killer before it could do anything. "Yeah, well, every last one of your victims had lives of their own." He rolled Niall onto his front and yanked on his chains, dragging him up by his manacles. "Now it's time for you to pay for that."

Niall's gaze hardened. "Then jus' kill us now. Get yourself a Path for the trouble; don't just deliver us like a bunch of helpless slimes to the Empire."

Edwin hesitated, then steeled his resolve. "No. That's a line I'm not crossing. I took you prisoner, and so you'll face justice, and that's not something I can provide. Not really. Now move it; I want to keep you all in one place."

"Ha! As though they'd give us any kind of 'justice.' They'll take one look at us an' send us to the noose."

Edwin shrugged. "Then that's what'll happen. Now, do I need to kick you down the stairs, or are you coming willingly?"

"I'm movin', I'm movin'," Niall grumbled.

It took some corralling, but Edwin eventually got all his prisoners more or less in one place. That said, he did leave Minsix on the first floor, chained as he was to a support post. Minthree and Minfive he dragged outside in the fading light, covering them with cloth behind the tower, doing his best to never look into their lifeless eyes, and mostly succeeding.

Niall, Mintwo, and Minfour he shoved into one of the rooms on the second floor, after giving it a quick search to make sure it didn't have anything weaponizable in it, then barricaded the door with as much random stuff as he could, turning it into a makeshift prison cell.

By the time he had their "cell" secured to his satisfaction, Edwin was exhausted. His wounds may have been taken care of by his healing salve, but it did nothing to offset the bone-deep weariness that came from pushing himself to his limits, and the emotional roller coaster that the day had been, to say nothing of the actual fight.

Still, he couldn't sleep yet. First, he needed to secure his room to ensure that if they broke out of their room, he'd have warning before the bandits were on *him*. Once that whole process was finished, Edwin was barely keeping himself on his feet. The sun had finished setting some time ago, and he swayed in the darkness, before hopping onto his bed.

Edwin wasn't sure if he actually fell asleep before his head hit its pillow, but it was a close race either way.

Edwin did not, thankfully, wake up to an Alchemist with murderous intent standing over him. Instead, he just … woke up. Completely on his own, for that matter, even the trills of birdsong that normally pulled him from slumber not capable of penetrating the stone walls of the tower. He stretched, almost completely rejuvenated, and after grabbing his weapons, he unbarricaded the door and cautiously peered out.

Content that his efforts to keep the bandits contained had been successful, Edwin ventured out of his room, double-checked the barricade to their room (it never hurt to be sure), and started claiming his loot from his vanquished bandit camp.

In the lab, he grabbed the *Grimoire*, some very basic lab equipment (tossing away anything that seemed to have so much as even a hint of biological remains upon it, which was a *lot*), including a nice variety of bottles and vials, and a good amount—probably five pounds—of dried herbs and other plants.

A good haul, even if he couldn't help but shudder every time he came across something that was very obviously from a murdered passerby. A birdlike skull that had to have been from an avior, a perfectly preserved human heart, even the jar of eyeballs he had noticed the first time he looked around no longer brought fascination, just nausea. There was just … so much, and the sickening feeling he got from handling any of the potions seemed to have almost seeped into the very tower itself.

Edwin decided the entire place would burn. He'd gotten anything of value out of it, and it would serve as a funeral pyre for Minfive, Minthree, and all their victims. It would also ensure he didn't miss *anything* that might leave this tower valuable to more people like Niall in the future. He didn't know if ghosts were a thing here—he should probably figure that out, actually—but if there were, destroying the lab would probably set a few to rest.

By the time Edwin had packed away all his haul (including a few small bags, maybe a pound or two, of the various dry foods from the kitchen storeroom), it was approximately noon, and even his Status seemed to agree that he'd done enough.

Level Up!
Packing Level 19→20

Overall, his pack weighed probably eighty pounds or so, but he was able to toss it around like it was just a moderately heavy backpack. Magic was *awesome*, letting him pack away half an Alchemy lab and have it feel lighter than his textbook-filled backpack from college.

Well, it was time to deal with his prisoners, he supposed.

The bandits had been … surprisingly docile. They all looked *very* cowed and hadn't offered much in the way of resistance as Edwin unblocked their room and "encouraged" them to go down the stairs (the minions were tall enough to just step over the gap, and Niall was able to as well, with much straining).

The gleaming knife Edwin held (turns out steel glowed slightly when you dumped enough magic into it—it took a *lot* of mana, though; it felt as though his mana had run a marathon by the time he was done) probably factored into it, all told. Minsix was slightly more hostile at first, but quieted down when Edwin started waving his glowing knife around, his expression whitening.

Huh. Magic weapons were apparently a very effective intimidation tactic. Good to know. Did it bypass their Skill defenses or something, maybe? Worth a test in the future. He wasn't sure how effectively he would be able to use Mana Infusion on his weapons, but if he could manage it …

Anyway, Edwin chained his prisoners together, putting Niall at the front, attaching him and his personal manacles to Minsix, who was in turn attached to Minfour, and finally to Mintwo. That way, if any of the minions tried something, they'd be wrenching on Minfour's broken arm. Cruel? Maybe a little bit. But it was effective, and that was what Edwin cared about.

Throughout the entire scenario, they had all been quiet (not counting Minsix, who started off shouting), giving little more than vague grunts even as Edwin got them to cooperate. He'd even had to decline the Intimidation Skill when it was offered up again. Niall, of all of them, was the first to break their silence, when Edwin carried Minfive's and Minthree's bodies into the tower.

"Wha' … Wha' are you doing?" he asked.

"I'm giving them, and all your other victims, a pyre," Edwin replied, straining under the weight of the body. "It's the least I can do."

"A … pyre?" Niall seemed confused for a moment before understanding flashed across his face. "No! You can't! This tower has stood for—"

Edwin cut him off. "I'm not letting it stay here for more bandits to move in and kill other people. If anyone cared about it, they would have driven you out."

Niall seemed quite distraught at the thought, even more than he had been regarding the death of his men. Odd, but okay. "No! If you burn it, then—" He cut himself off.

"Then what?"

"You'll set the grasslands on fire!" Niall hastily lied.

"Tell the truth." Edwin took a page out of Tara's book and held his shining dagger very, very close to the bandit's throat, watching as the man's Adam's apple bobbed nervously. "I'll know if you lie."

Niall cast his gaze down. "You'll … destroy all my findings. All my research, gone forever."

Edwin cocked an eyebrow at the Alchemist, but he didn't bother correcting him. "Really? You don't have that much longer to worry about it, by your reckoning."

"Well, yes, but ..." He shook his head. "Another might find i' one day."

"Not much of a concern for you, is it? You wouldn't know one way or the other."

"Well, the System—" Niall started, but Edwin walked inside, cutting the complaint short.

At the center of it all, he dropped the second corpse next to the first. Around them, he piled the last of the cast-off cloth.

Summoning the last bit of his magical strength, Edwin Infused his Skill as much as it would take, laid his hand against the wooden support in the middle of the building, and pushed.

Firestarting.

It was a lovely fire. The flames, visible only through the occasional gaps in the masonry, roared through the wooden supports. Edwin originally planned to stay around until he was sure that the entire building was gone, but a notification popped up informing him that wasn't required. So he corralled his prisoners and started leading them to the road. Behind him, the flames broke through to the roof, and looking in the right direction showed tongues of fire erupting from the top of the giant stone tower, like a massive, ivy-covered candle.

Level Up!
Firestarting Level 39→41
Mana Infusion Level 62→63
Congratulations! For destroying the Ruined Tower, you have unlocked the Razer of the Ruined Tower Path!
Congratulations! For willfully burning down a stable structure, you have unlocked the Arsonist Path!

CHAPTER 45

With a Nice Little Bow

Edwin had to admit that he was somewhat worried about what to do when they needed to stop for the night. He remembered that it would take about a day of walking to get from the Ruined Tower to the nearest town. At the same time, he *also* knew that was going at more or less full speed, traveling lightly and with just him and Lefi, both incentivized to walk at a decent pace. While his prisoners may have been fairly cooperative, all things considered, he couldn't exactly imagine them being *excited* about being led to their execution.

Between that and their chains binding them together, Edwin figured that it would take them some two to three days of dedicated travel before he'd be able to pass them along to the local authority figure and carry on his way, probably looking for more talsanenris berries.

It did leave him in a bit of a conundrum, though, which was how he was supposed to ensure that they didn't stab him or escape in the night. Maybe he'd be able to attach their chains to something? He'd need to keep an eye out for potential candidates.

The sooner he could be done with this whole mess, the better. He most certainly was looking forward to not needing to tune out Niall's endless complaints about how he'd destroyed "years of research" by burning down the tower.

Edwin could sympathize; he really could. Losing massive amounts of research because of a misplaced notebook or a computer issue? He could relate. Heck, had they been about anything else, Edwin would have probably stuffed all the notes into his pack alongside the *Grimoire*. But when paging through the notebooks, Edwin didn't see anything that was actually that *useful* to a normal, nonmurderous researcher. Sure, he'd kept some highlights and some of the more critical workings, but everything, every formula, every potion, had all been mere trial and error for each specific recipe. Niall hadn't done anything except perfect the sorts of potions that Edwin wanted no part in spreading to the wider world.

It would have been one thing if, through his experiments, the crazed Alchemist had discovered some underlying aspect of magical healing, which could be repurposed into creating potions that *didn't* require a steady stream of corpses.

Although a potion that required endless fresh bodies might be useful to an institutional power like the Empire, if they could use condemned criminals—Edwin glanced back at his line of prisoners—as ingredients, he didn't trust them enough. After all, since when had literally *any* Empire been on the moral high ground? Nah, if he gave such a potion to the Empire, it wouldn't turn out well. Where was he? Oh, right. Useful research.

What Niall had done was spend an ungodly amount of corpses perfecting the specific methodology needed for a single skin-regenerating, or bone-healing, or blindness-curing potion, each one at a time. And sure, he seemed to have pretty effective potions made that way, but Edwin couldn't apply that knowledge anywhere else.

It seemed like, not that he was surprised, Joriah hadn't undergone the scientific revolution yet. Pure trial and error on a specific task was what *alchemists* did, not scientists, which just made his heart ache. They were obsessed with results, rather than methods, so it never occurred to ask "why" something was the way it was, just "how" they could make something work. They might have a thousand different formulas to cure specific ailments, but there was no unifying theory explaining why the formulas worked, or why each of them worked differently.

Accordingly, they couldn't predict results with any more accuracy than mere guesswork. Unless they had tried it and marked down the results, they had no clue what switching out fireseed for sparkweed might do to a concoction, because they didn't investigate the underlying structure involving each ingredient.

Well, Edwin supposed, he would just have to fix that. All that combined with the vast majority of Niall's notes … not being that useful, all told. Not when page upon page was just about how many grains of muscle tissue produced the most effective results in an enhancement potion. The final result? He'd kept that, shoving the page inside the matching *Grimoire* one.

That was another thing, too! From what Edwin could tell, Niall hadn't done any original research, just the legwork for a handful of formulae in the *Grimoire* to include the sorts of measurements and timings that should have been a part of the original book.

He nearly told Niall, many times, just how useless all his work had been, and that that was why he had burned most of it, but Edwin decided each time that he was better off just staying silent. It wouldn't change anything, and Edwin just couldn't quite bring himself to face the man.

Far behind them, plumes of smoke billowed from the tower like it was a smokestack. Given how generally flat the terrain was around here, it was bound to be visible for miles. Thus, while he was surprised at how quickly he saw them, it wasn't all that surprising when, midafternoon, Edwin spotted a convoy of guards heading in that direction.

Even with his enhanced vision, Edwin's first vision of the newcomers was that of mere blurry silhouettes cresting over a distant hill, cutting a direct path to the tower. It took a few seconds of their race onward before those silhouettes resolved into a trio of mounted individuals. Shortly thereafter, presumably upon noticing Edwin and his followers, they swiftly banked, charging directly at Edwin's little band at a near gallop until they came to a nigh-instantaneous halt mere feet from Edwin's little group, mounted atop horses that towered above him.

"Halt in the name of the Liras Empire, and Magistrate Tokl'kori'cthail!" the first of the three armored individuals cried, unnecessarily, as Edwin and the others had already stopped, waiting for the cavalry to arrive. Running from someone on horseback seemed somewhat pointless, after all. Now that they were close enough, though, Edwin took the chance to Identify them.

Senior Lieutenant
Experienced Guardsman
Adult Satallan Horse

Wait, no. Aim a bit up.

Veteran Guardsman

"State your name and purpose, Outlaw!" Oh right, Edwin should be paying more attention to the avior lieutenant. Interestingly, the others were human. What was up with that?

Edwin stumbled over his words. "Oh … ah." He straightened his back to appear more official. "Adventurer Edwin, sir. I encountered a group of bandits kidnapping and murdering passersby. I took it upon myself to ensure they weren't able to continue. I'm currently taking them to town to face justice."

The lieutenant peered down from atop his steed, presenting a very intimidating figure as he loomed over them all. "Present me with material evidence establishing your claims! Produce your license forthwith."

"Oh, right!" Edwin fumbled around, trying to dig out the tiny stone medallion. By the time he had found it in one of his belt pouches, he looked up to see the end of some exchange between the guard and Niall, who looked as though he had just bit into an especially sour lemon.

He wanted to ask what he had missed, but figured he probably shouldn't trouble the man holding a giant spear on a steed that could probably crush Edwin without a second thought. "Here you are!" He lifted the trinket, and after a moment, the lieutenant nodded faintly.

"So be it." He sounded … annoyed, somehow? Figured. "I, Captain Laiare, do accept your story, Ou— Adventurer Edwin."

"Wait, just like that?" Also, shoot, was he about to say Outsider? He wanted that to be a secret! Did Tara tell someone? Oh, wait, Laiare probably cut off saying "Outlaw," didn't he? That would make more sense, if the lieutenant captain was mandated to be at least somewhat courteous to Adventurers.

"You have presented the requisite claims and produced your license when requested. Those whom you have apprehended are responsible for many crimes—"

Huh, how could they tell? Captain Laiare sounded absolutely certain.

"—and with the lack of protections, they are henceforth taken into custody to be judged for banditry, rejection of Citizen Status ..."— Niall made a choked noise, which seemed fair enough if what he had said about his childhood was true; there had been no rejection there, just being cast out for his differences—"as well as murder and assault. Do you wish to return to Valenasis to present your testimony as evidence?"

Edwin blinked blankly. "Wish? Do I not need to?"

"Not if you desire otherwise. There seems to be adequate evidence to convict these criminals in absence of your presence. I merely must confirm what the accused said; did you set the fire over yonder?" He raised a wing, indicating the plume of smoke that was once the tower.

Edwin nodded. "I couldn't stand to allow a place with such a foul history to remain standing. Also, it wasn't about to be used for any beneficial purpose, so I burned it, along with all of his"—he jerked his head back to indicate Niall—"notes. He's been complaining about it ever since."

Laiare scoffed, which sounded rather odd coming from a beak. "As do all those who betray their land for personal power when they find such things are worthless in the face of cooperation." He motioned to his men, who dismounted and moved to apprehend the bandits.

Upon seeing the manacles, one of them—the Veteran—turned to Edwin. "Key?" he asked in a low, gravelly voice.

"Right, right." Edwin fumbled for a moment before finding the key and handing it to the man, who accepted it with a nod.

They unlocked the manacles and just nonchalantly picked up each of the bandits, one by one, ignoring Minfour's cries of protest as his burns and broken arm were roughly manhandled with no regard for his comfort. Edwin couldn't help but wince sympathetically at the treatment, though he also didn't let himself feel *too* bad for the serial killer bandits.

It was interesting, watching the guardsmen at work. Their Classes had clearly been designed with this sort of interaction in mind. They easily took the bandits and fastened them to the flanks of their horses like they were just slightly heavy sacks, completely ignoring what little struggling the bandits put up and binding them in silver cords; Edwin couldn't quite tell where those had come from. It didn't seem to be a pure Skill construct, though Edwin couldn't exactly articulate why he thought that. Something to do with how his Almanac tags interacted with them, most likely.

"So ... what's going to happen to them?" Edwin asked the avior as the bandits' bindings were finished up; he intentionally avoided looking at Niall, not sure what he would see there, and not keen on finding out, either.

Laiare barely hesitated. "They shall most likely find themselves facing the noose come the morrow. Such is the penalty for banditry in this shire." Polyglot could choose some strange words, it seemed. Never often, just enough to remind Edwin that people didn't actually speak English.

"Good," Edwin agreed after a moment of consideration, trying somewhat to convince himself as much as actually respond.

He couldn't help but feel a bit guilty, no matter how much he told himself he shouldn't. It was all going so ... smoothly. He had expected more wrangling with the locals, trying to convince them of his story, getting them to actually carry out justice, and yet it was all so simple. Well, sometimes life just went smoothly. No looking in the mouths of gift horses and all. Honestly, being this close to a horse, he had to admit he wasn't particularly keen on looking *any* horse in the mouth, but the sentiment remained.

Then, they were gone. It was all so sudden, less than ten minutes from their showing up to riding off, and Edwin found himself completely alone once more. It was a sudden change, and he took a few minutes to adjust to his newfound freedom, seeing how it all just wrapped up so quickly and so cleanly.

Edwin took a deep breath as he watched the trio retreat into the distance, the thread of adrenaline-powered strength fading alongside them. He was alone, for the first time in a very long time. It was really nice, actually. There was a lot of stuff he wanted to do, that he couldn't do around Lefi or Tara or Niall.

He'd ... he'd head to the Verdant, he thought. A place overflowing with magic, life, and life magic?

Well, it was just *begging* for a scientist to take a look at it.

Name
Edwin Maxlin
Age
22 years
Race
Extraplanar Human
Class
Hedge Alchemist
Attributes
Mana 5
Skills
Magical
Basic Mana Sense: 32, Mana Infusion: 63 (Basic Mana Manipulation: 9)
Physical
Athletics: 33, Breathing: 26, Flexibility: 25, Nutrition: 23, Packing: 20, Seeing: 27, Sleeping: 27, Survival: 19, Walking: 39
Mental
Polyglot: 34 (Language: 36), Mathematics: 39, Memory: 28 (Research: 50), Visualization: 42
Combat
Bomb Throwing: 9 (Throwing Weapons: 48)
Utility
Firestarting: 41, Alchemy: 46 (Improvisation: 14), Outsider's Almanac: 78 (Status: 22), Identify: 40, First Aid: 28
Paths
Skill Points: 420
Progress to Tier 2: 640/1590
Current Plan
Adventurer 0/30, Warrior 0/60, Athlete 0/60, Scout 0/60, Researcher 0/60, Skilled Arcanist 0/60, Potioneer 0/60, Wanderer 0/60, Stonehide Vanquisher 0/60, Scientist 0/60, Outsider 0/60, Blackstone Conqueror 0/60, Mage 0/60, Novice Pyromancer 0/60, World Traveler 0/60,

Physical Arcanist 0/60, Field Medic 0/60, Unkillable 0/90, Path Less Traveled 0/90

Save for Tier 2

Micro-Biomancer 0/90, Realm Traveler 0/120, Alchemical Warrior 0/90, Pioneer 0/60, Alchemical Medic 0/60, Titan Slayer 0/90, Explorer 0/60, Giant Slayer 0/60, Superior Alchemist 0/60

Maybe

Novice 0/12, Trainee 0/60, Trapper 0/60, System Scholar 0/60, Survivor 0/60, Daredevil 0/60, Escapee 0/30, Lecturer 0/30, Steadfast Medic 0/60, Rebel 0/30, Arsonist 0/60

Probably Not

Lumberjack 0/60, Way of the Empty Hand 0/60, Pyromaniac 0/30, Exile 0/30, Master of the Ruined Tower 0/60, Razer of the Ruined Tower 0/60

No

Slave 0/12, Assassin 0/60, Killer 0/30, Traitor 0/60, Burglar 0/60

Completed Paths

CharLimitCanttalkmuchNocluewhathappenedDidmybesttohelpyouli, Mage, Skilled Arcanist, Physical Alchemist, Bomber, Linguist, Beginner

And Awoke a Star of Fire and Stone

Lord S'fashkchlil took a deep, raspy breath as he lay in his bed, stewing in his misery. It was all that depths-shunned Outsider's fault.

Soralash had found the human, half dead and collapsed on the side of the Highroad, and brought him in along with her normal suite of Surface goods and news. From there, the Outsider—a true Outsider, or so he had thought—had been brought before him, but spoke no tongue he knew, and so was passed along to Rashin, with the idea that they might be able to learn a bit about him and learn of the wonders he might provide.

A true Outsider … Some thought they were but a legend, but Rashin himself had interpreted the carvings pertaining to them, so S'fashkchlil knew this knowledge to be true. Thousands of years ago, true Outsiders had come to Joriah, bringing with them tales of mighty magics and advanced knowledge, sent as messengers by the gods themselves to aid those who had their favor. The mighty city of Vis'Daric and its inhabitants, the Gozau, were all that remained of their numerous creations, and yet what a legacy it was! It was S'fashkchlil's birthright to claim such a valuable asset, with his family legacy crumbling around him. Destined for greatness, bah. But that was before the human arrived, seemingly a gift from his ancestors. When he had heard Rashin report on the "concrete" from the Outsider's homeland, liquid stone that potentially could be used in place of Blackstone for walls and fortifications, that had settled the matter. His ancestors had clearly delivered a gift to him as an act of providence; who was he to shun such a turn of fortune?

He would not be as foolish as so many others he had seen, sharing their knowledge and fortune, cast aside the moment their usefulness was at an end. No, this Outsider would be a vein unto himself. However, for his Taskmaster, Break Spirit, and Inspire Greatness Skills to affect the boy, he would need to be a citizen of Clan Blackstone, a puzzle that Rashin, his most brilliant adviser, had solved for him. If S'fashkchlil were to make the Outsider a Free Shaper, by law, he would similarly be making him a Citizen, and thus the human would be focused, grow quickly, and become loyal to him and him alone, a thought that brought his fingers to twitch.

That alone was not sufficient, though, as it brought up an additional complication. By Dwarven law, any quenched Free Shaper must Tour in each of the Five Cities, sharing their knowledge and teaching, "such that their Skills may be spread and all the Highpeaks may benefit from their brilliance." That was something which must not come to pass. No, it would be preferable that none even know of the human's existence, yet such a secret would never stand. So he had to circumvent that law in a legal fashion.

Fortunately, the law was formulated in such a manner that the Tour was a tax, and as repayment of debts were exempt from tax, S'fashkchlil needed to establish the boy as a Free Shaper in repayment of a debt. It was the perfect plan, to entrap the Outsider in a Debt of Hospitality, bestowing him with luxuries he would not even recognize as such, and quench him as a Free Shaper, forever working off his debt until Break Spirit finished working upon the Outsider. Some of his court had grumbled at such treatment of a foreigner—they did not know of his true nature, which S'fashkchlil had ensured would not be shared—but he had silenced such murmuring by first assuring them that the hospitality of their kind was legendary, and surely if the Outsider truly protested such treatment, he need only lodge a protest directly to him, and he would be obligated to return him to the Empire. He had secondarily quashed such protest by jailing the protesters, which ought to buy him enough time for the Outsider to get a Broken Spirit, and once he had a demigod at his beck and call, S'fashkchlil would truly be unstoppable, as was only right.

For a demigod, it was so simple to fool the boy, and once he felt his Task sink in, he had breathed a sigh of relief. That the human thought his Task impossible did not lessen its effectiveness, and it might well feed into his Broken Spirit. His stubbornness was problematic, and while Break Spirit ought to have ensured his loyalty, the lord had never felt the Skill bite, curiously enough.

It should have happened the moment the boy had ceased trying to make weapons and escape, yet it didn't. Perhaps that was the power of an Outsider? That their minds were so difficult to bow? Good. When he finally fell before the might of the lord's Skills, then the Outsider would never waver. And he *knew* the boy would fall to Break Spirit; it was just a matter of time. Even S'fashkchlil's strongest-willed advisers had done little more than grumble about his treatment of a guest, as their loyalties were to him and him alone. The fact that Noble Communion had taught him this "English" he spoke in mere hours was proof enough that his mind was not unassailable, even if he had somehow fooled his Taskmaster sense.

For weeks, everything worked perfectly, and the lord saw *his* Legacy being built. One who was able to tame the untamable. But when King Shoroshal had demanded more men for the War Below after a devastating and completely unexpected loss, and he suddenly found his manpower gutted, nearly all his citizens sent off to the Dark Warfield, S'fashkchlil had, mistakenly and in a moment of weakness before his king, said he might have some form of alchemical Blackstone variant, and he had been ordered to supply it. He was furious. How dare that mere pretender to the throne demand the results of *his* work, of *his* efforts? Well, he'd show that depths-shunned so-called king what he had! Concrete would be a gamechanger; he could use it to seal up entire tunnels if the Outsider was to be believed, and he could cut off Shoroshal from the surface, leaving the lord as the undisputed king!

Lord S'fashkchlil attempted to swear under his breath, but the action just aggravated his injured and inflamed throat, sending him into another coughing fit, as it came up bloody. The damn boy had cheated somehow, yet he couldn't figure out how. He had killed Rashin with a blow to the head—*why* had the fool scholar never bothered to earn and complete the Path of the Warrior? Anyone with a modicum of Health should have survived such a blow, yet the scholar had always claimed that he never needed to worry about any more than a book falling on him. Yet the blow that had slain him had been so precise, so calculated to down a Healthless dwarf, it removed all doubts about the boy's true nature. That gods-forsaken, depths-shunned *human*, S'fashkchlil saw clearly now, was nothing but a devious spy planted in his ranks, meant to sabotage him. He was no mere lost Outsider, unsure of himself and ripe for the taking. No, he was clearly a trained assassin, meant to cripple him as soon as he saw weakness. Nobody else would be able to twist his Task of finishing his research into a Task that let him effortlessly fight through the lord's guards—who were an entirely additional problem, not even able to take out a single human armed with mere *rocks*—and escape, no doubt taking information back to his masters in the Empire.

Then there was whatever weapon the boy had used on him, which he had apparently smuggled in so thoroughly that it had gone undetected for *nearly two moons*. He'd never felt heat of its kind, and as it targeted his beard, he had lost enough hair, the strands detaching to prevent him from developing Forge Sickness, that whatever strange powder was used had gotten into his lungs, burning him from the inside out, to say nothing of falling in the Steel Rivers.

Though only two dwarves had died, many more were grievously injured, yet not a single one could tell what was used, cloaked deviously as it was as mere *rock*. And while the boy was no longer one of his Citizens, and thus his knowledge of the foreign tongue had faded alongside his ability to Task the human, Lord S'fashkchlil would sooner see his city burn than allow such an insult to go unavenged.

A presence appeared at the foot of his bed.

"Took ... took you"—he coughed, his voice hoarse; really, he should consider himself lucky to even be alive, but such thoughts were nigh-blasphemy to the self—"long enough. I have ... a Task for you."

The figure at the end of his bed stood and listened. As the human had been a nominal guest under hospitality, his debt had been expunged upon leaving, and even pursuing him as an assailant with clan assets would result in too many questions being asked, and the endeavor would likely be nullified. Worse, it might be usurped, and the alleged Outsider would slip out from between his fingers. But he still could not let such a slight go ... unavenged. Fortunately, S'fashkchlil knew the perfect person for the job.

Edwin would pay for what he had done.

Kaleb England, also known as NorskDaedalus, is an author who loves to integrate magic and science to tell interesting stories. England holds a bachelor's degree in physics.

Milton Keynes UK
Ingram Content Group UK Ltd.
UKHW030718041024
449263UK00004B/417